# *FEARLESS*

## KATIE GOLDING

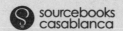
sourcebooks
casablanca

*For my father,*
*who always said I could be anything*
*and never added "except that."*
*I may be your princess, but you'll always be my hero.*

Copyright © 2020 by Katie Golding
Cover and internal design © 2020 by Sourcebooks
Cover art by Craig White

Sourcebooks and the colophon are registered trademarks of Sourcebooks.

Published by Sourcebooks Casablanca, an imprint of Sourcebooks
P.O. Box 4410, Naperville, Illinois 60567-4410
(630) 961-3900
sourcebooks.com

Printed and bound in the United States of America.
OPM 10 9 8 7 6 5 4 3 2 1

# Chapter 1

*Billy King—Present Day*

TURNS OUT THE WORLD'S A LOT BIGGER THAN MEMPHIS.

"Billy! Billy King!" My name is like cracks of thunder on the Spanish wind, and as I cruise past the press corps, I can't quite feel the relief yet that this is it. It's over. Flashes from the cameras are too busy sparkling through my helmet's face shield, shining off my motorcycle and nearly blinding me, there are so many of them. Valencia is already a massive festival, since it's the last race of the Moto Grand Prix circuit. But in all my years racing, I've never seen the press and the fans this excited before.

I pull off victory lane and stop in the designated winner's spot, already decorated with royal blue Yaalon Moto everything. The fans are barely held back by the chest-high gate rocking under their hands and their repeated chants of my name. "Billy! Billy King!"

"All right, y'all, just wait your turn," I call out to the crowd. My laugh rings with the pure, sweet adrenaline pumping thick through my veins, a testament to battling twenty guys on the racetrack for who'd come out on top. And then beating them all, one by one.

Life doesn't get much sweeter than this. Especially since tomorrow, I can finally go *home*.

Back to Memphis: the ranch and my saddle, my horse, and my ropes.

Home to Taryn: her whiskey hair and sapphire eyes.

I pull off my helmet, and after a quick wave to the fans, I start to find my breath again. I don't get to keep it long.

My manager's unmistakable twang cuts cleanly through the roar of the press corps. "I knew you could make it back, Billy!"

Frank yanks me off my bike and into a suffocating hug, slapping my back so hard I actually feel it through the armadillo spine of my leathers. At least he doesn't notice my wince from the pain in an ankle that's supposed to be long healed by now.

Telling him I'm hurt will only risk my future even *more* after what I did. Not that anyone seems to care about the reason *why* I did it.

Frank's too excited to pay attention to my stumble, setting my sponsor-coated Stetson on top of my head, then gripping my shoulders. "Not just first place, Billy! First in the *world*. Didn't I always say about putting bull riders—"

"Did Taryn call? She see it?" I wave toward the press and the fans again, beaming next to my blue motorcycle. They don't need to know there's sweat pooling in my leathers, and my feet desperately miss the buttery soles of my Ariat boots.

Mostly, though, I just miss *her*.

Frank clears his throat as I tip my cowboy hat toward the cameras, making sure they capture the names of all the people I'm paid to promote. "She hasn't called yet," he mumbles.

My pulse starts racing for a whole bunch of reasons I still can't make myself face, and I turn away from the Moto Grand Prix fans, praying no one caught the look I just felt flash across my face. My only hope is to keep clinging to Plan A: *act like it didn't happen, and maybe it didn't.*

"But she *will*," Frank adds in a rush. "You know Taryn. She's probably just—"

"Busy." I shift my helmet to my other hand, wiping sweat off my face. "Busy being mad at me."

Suppose she's right. I never was nothing special.

"Horseshit," Frank says. "That woman loves you. And need I remind you, you just won first place at Valencia, Billy. Twenty-five points, and that makes you a damned MotoPro Grand Prix World Champion. Now be happy, would ya? 'Cause you're starting to piss me off." He gives me a half grin and takes my helmet from me, slinging an arm around my shoulders. It does nothing to comfort the guilt swirling in my stomach. "Come on, cowboy. You about ready to show 'em what a champion looks like?" He nods toward the wall of reporters waiting to ask me the same questions they always ask.

*"How did it feel to win today?"*

*"Were you riding for anyone special back home?"*

*"Is it hard being an American in a European sport?"*

I clear my throat and tip up my hat so their lights won't cast shadows down my too-long nose. "Yeah. I'm ready."

Frank claps my back and heads off to organize the interview lineup, and I glance toward the press spot for third place, my twenty-five-year-old little brother already hamming it up for the cameras, probably giving sound clips about his smell-proof underwear again.

Frank is right. No matter what's been happening at home, I won here, and I should be celebrating. My knee surgery from two years ago has finally stopped causing me problems, and I've worked my ass off to get back to the top of the leaderboard. And like my father always says: I should try to be more like Mason.

He never lets love get in the way, and he's as good on a bike as he is at riding bulls. Everyone says so. It's probably why he's allowed to keep his hands in both cookie jars, and mine have been firmly tied.

No more wondering if that bull's gonna spin or blow when that gate opens. No more wondering if eight seconds are gonna be my last. Now, it's two red lights keeping me caged and my wrist on the throttle setting me free.

Mason finishes his interview, immediately turning to sign a lady's chest with a marker as red as her cheeks. Until someone walking by bumps his shoulder hard enough that he stumbles, nearly knocking her over.

"Hey!" Protective instincts blaze through me, and I'm three steps closer than I was a moment ago, my outstretched hand already steadying Mason by the shoulder. My eyes home in on the back of Santos Saucedo from Hotaru Racing, strutting away with a chuckle.

Mason looks at me, and neither of us has to glance at the surrounding press to know they saw that shit go down. And I'm not about to let our family name get tarnished.

"What was that, friend?" I call out to Santos, cupping my ear. "We didn't catch whatcha said."

Santos turns and rattles off something in Spanish that makes the press collectively gasp. *The nerve of that guy.*

"Oh, I'm sorry, man," I drawl, acting all guilty. Mason crosses his arms. He's three inches and a good fifteen pounds littler than me but with twice the ego and ten times the temper. "We don't speak fifth place." I flash a grin that is sure to ramp Santos's annoyance through the damn stratosphere, but he can kiss my ass. Nobody messes with my brother but me.

A thick hand settles heavy on my far shoulder. "Thanks,

y'all," Frank says behind us toward the press, "but we gotta get Billy and Mason upstairs to get their medals. The Kings'll have more time to answer questions later, I promise."

I salute a scowling Santos, letting our manager sweep us out of the parc fermé and toward the stairs to the podium. The last thing I need is for Mason to back me into another damn corner. Thanks to him, racing's about all I have left.

A familiar throb that has nothing to do with leaning my bike through pin-tight turns twists through my insides, my ankle hurting more with every step as I climb the last of the stairs. And three feet from the door that gives me back to the crowd I've spent years trying to convince to love me, I find myself desperately wishing they'd just mail me the medal they want to hang around my neck.

"Showtime, boys." Frank opens the door to a blast of sound that's my name on repeat, and since I don't get a choice, I'm first outside onto the podium.

The sun is in the wrong spot and the wind doesn't smell right, but I wave and smile a little harder at the cameras taking my picture. Even though the one person who matters probably won't ever see them.

She still isn't answering my calls.

No matter what I do, she hasn't forgiven me, and it's why I need to get my sorry ass back to Memphis. Running home's the only way I'm ever gonna get her back.

―――

I'm already sweating in my best pearl-snap shirt despite the cool November air, hinting at the icy December we're gonna have. I pluck once more at my starched collar, pointing my battered old boots toward the barn, trying to gain some kind of confidence from being in Memphis, even if my body still thinks I'm in Spain.

My ears haven't stopped ringing from the end-of-season awards ceremony, my tux a wrinkled mess since I went straight from the televised stage to the Valencia airport. But I'm back under the same Osage orange trees I grew up climbing while my horse munched on the bumpy hedge apples. And when I head inside, the chatter from farmhands is gonna be in English and not the liquid Italian of my pit crew.

None of it's making me feel better when I'm about to see her, and I know damn well all she's gonna do is yell at me, and all I want to do is kiss her and get back to how we used to be. I've only been gone a week this last time. But it was a week too long after the way she sent me off.

I touch my hat in Hargrove tradition as I cross under the homemade "Bless Your Boots" sign hanging above the barn entrance, instantly welcomed by a chorus of sniffs and snorts from the horse stalls I pass. It eases something in my chest that's been wrong since I last left home for the circuit.

Since I could kind of use it, I go ahead and stop by Gidget's stall, hooking my arms over the latched gate. "Hey, buddy." He stops fluffing his bed of straw, his ears already turned my direction before he lifts his head and stares me dead in the eye. A broad grin stretches across my face when he huffs and starts walking over, his pace extra slow and stompy, clearly irritated with how long I've been gone. At least he's willing to forgive me for it. "I know, bud. I missed you, too."

I reach out and stroke the side of his neck, wishing

everything was as simple as blazing-fast blue motorcycles and golden horses who only ask that you bring treats before you ride. But like everything else I wasn't supposed to fall in love with, Gidget isn't really mine. He's Lorelai Hargrove's, the future heiress to the Hargrove Horse Ranch.

No one except a rancher's daughter could afford an Akhal-Teke of their own. But no one really cares that I ride Gidget all the time, either. Lorelai is usually too busy training for our next race. She's Frank's original rodeo-racing experiment, and she's fast, feisty, and stubborn. Once the sponsors let her move up from MotoA and into MotoPro with me and Mason, we're all gonna be screwed.

"No, I didn't bring any apples," I tell Gidget when he starts nipping at my shirt and sniffing toward my jeans. "I'll bring you some later, though. Promise."

"Hey, Gidget. I didn't know your cowboy was back." James smiles on his way behind me, leading a silky chestnut mare out the other entrance to the barn. "Glad to have you home, Billy."

I return his smile on instinct, tipping my hat in the direction of his silver mustache. "Thank you, sir. Good to be back."

"Girls are working Bopper, if you're wondering. Though you might wanna take a bodyguard with you," he adds with a rumbly chuckle. "They're out for blood, those two."

I chew on my tongue, knowing better than to bite the hand that feeds my horse. James is married to Lynn, who owns Hargrove Ranch. And I've spent the last year very unsuccessfully trying to convince Lynn to sell me Gidget. She won't budge, though. Because I don't have the land to keep him on. "Yes, sir."

James is still happily making his way out of the barn and looking like he's whispering to the mare about me. I doubt it has anything to do with my record-breaking win, because whatever it is he says to the horse, he cracks himself up.

I make a face at Gidget, who's still sniffing for food in my shirt pocket before I press a kiss to his nose. "Well, buddy, wish me luck."

Gidget snorts because we both know I'm fresh out of it. Any last bit of luck I had, I just used up in Valencia salvaging my career. But taking a risk has never stopped me before. Hell, the first time I rode a bull, I was convinced I was gonna die.

One second was all I got. It was enough, though. I woke up on a stretcher begging my father to let me have another go despite my mama's tears still running down her cheeks. That next time, I lasted for three seconds before Nova Bomb spun and sent me flying, cracking two ribs and fracturing my collarbone.

I'm always better on my second attempt—*always*. Still, Taryn says that's the worst thing about bull riders: we don't expect to stay on. It's just a game of how long we can last until the bull beats us, and it always beats us. But no bull bucking me ever hurt as much as when Taryn did it.

It's a long walk toward the training pen, set far enough in the pasture that the colts don't get distracted by the noise of the barn and the commands of the trainers. But with the wide-open sky and no trees between us, Taryn sees me coming every step of the way.

I know it, though she pretends she doesn't—she refuses to look my direction. But she's sitting a little stiffer in the saddle, the clenched muscles in her long legs stretching her jeans, and accusing me of the crimes she screamed at me from across her kitchen table.

I cast them out of my mind. I don't want to be mad, and seeing her sit a horse like that has always sent a freight train barreling straight into my chest. It's almost as good as when she wakes up slowly next to me, her silky spine long and bare as she reaches for the coffee I've already made and set on her nightstand. When I'm lucky enough to be home.

"Afternoon, ladies," I drawl to Taryn and Lorelai, taking the last few feet up to the fence of the training pen. My heart's beating straight out of my chest, a fresh brew of sweat tickling my hairline, and I can't stop thinking I should've shaved. But I couldn't get my truck here fast enough.

Lorelai tosses her wildly curly brown hair. "Taryn, I'm heading to the house. Call me later." She throws me a murderous look before leaving the way I came.

Taryn still hasn't said anything, except small corrections to the colt she's working. Round and round she goes, her hands light on the reins and the sun on her hat but not on her face. Pride laps at my heart from the dirt smeared on her shirt and mud caked up her jeans, everything about her more beautiful than I remember, and so damn *hard*. A woman who works, every day of her life. A woman who *rides*.

I can't keep the adoration out of my voice. "Hi, honey."

She gives two clicks to her colt and turns him the other way, bumping his trot to a canter and testing his different gears. It prods my smile even more, because she knows them all—on a horse, on a motorcycle. She's even taught me a few tricks that have helped me keep an edge on the racetrack, because she doesn't only train colts. She also races Superbike eight months a year, and then she comes home to Memphis and barrel races in rodeos.

I never stood a chance over whether I was gonna fall in love with her. It was always just a matter of how long she was gonna let me hang around.

"I brought you something." I pull my medal out of my back pocket and hang it on the fence post. If anyone knows what it takes to earn this, it's Taryn. And she should have this, more than me. "Hope you like it."

On her next pass, she reaches out and knocks my medal off the post, letting it fall in the dirt. "Fuck off, Billy."

Frustration simmers in my chest, and I keep watching her, remembering how sweet she was before I ruined it. When once upon a time, she loved me back.

At least she cussed at me.

She never yells at her horse when Aston Magic starts being moody, and she lives her life by the motto "Kill 'em with kindness." I've seen her bite her tongue so many times, she shouldn't have one left. But none of that restraint ever seems to apply to me, and the moment I get downgraded to the sweet-pea public persona, I'm calling in the big guns.

Two more circles, and her colt's hooves have firmly buried my medal beyond sight.

*Stick to Plan A*, I tell myself. *Act like it didn't happen, and maybe it didn't.*

"He's looking good," I muse mostly to myself. "He from Buddy Holly's line?"

"Goddamn it," she mutters, pulling her horse to a stop and dismounting. "You just can't leave me alone, can you?"

I risk a smile; it's been a hell of a long time since I've had the pleasure of her riding my ass about something, and I missed it more than she'll ever know. "No, ma'am. Apparently not."

She feeds her colt a treat before leading him toward the gate. I hurry to open it for her and wait while she leads him through, my eyes stealing a quick peek at her curves in her jeans and her long blond braid swishing from under her cowgirl hat. Damn, I missed her.

I remember to latch the gate once I get my blood flowing back above my belt line, turning to find her already walking away. "Aw, come on, Taryn. I know you're mad, but—"

She whips around, and I'm struck dumb at the pain sparkling in her blue eyes like she's moments away from crying. And Taryn isn't a crier. "I'm not just mad, Billy. I'm done. And I told you that. So stop torturing me by showing up here and calling me all the time, and find a way to get it through that thick head of yours. It's *over*."

Her voice wobbles on the last word, and it's left me no kind of man. My head hangs, every endless prick of pain she's feeling cutting me a thousand times over because I caused it, and she's the only one who can make me feel better about it.

Her boots shift in the fresh dirt beneath her, but she's not walking away yet, and I risk a small step closer while she's giving me the chance. I'd bet my bike she doesn't want to be broken up any more than I do. But lines in the sand have a bad habit of shifting, and it isn't always easy to see where they land.

When Taryn shifts again, my gaze lifts to her hand fisting by her side, her other grasping desperately to the reins. One more step, and I breathe deep the call of leather and sunflowers, peach shampoo and lavender bug spray.

My eyes finally dare to meet hers, simmering sapphire and begging me for a thousand things I don't know how to give her when I can only think about the one thing I want. The one thing I shouldn't have done and all the soul-twisting reasons I'd have to do it again if faced with the same decision.

"I'm sorry," I croak out, her eyelashes fluttering closed as I run a knuckle down her cotton-soft cheek, only a breath away from kissing her. I've done it so many times, and it's not fair that the last time, I barely brushed my mouth against hers before I'd sprinted out the door. I can't let it end that way. "I'm so sorry, honey."

She shivers, a small noise that threatens to crack my heart right down the middle escaping her parted lips. Then she reaches up, barely covering my mouth with her fingertips, stopping me. "No, Billy," she whispers. "I can't do this anymore. You've already broken my heart once. I won't let you do it again."

Two tons of guilt and a sharp buck of fear lock my words in my throat, and she spins to her colt and leads him away. Back to the barn and her truck and her family's farmhouse ten miles down the road. And I know it's supposed to be hopeless, because she told me it was, but I can't help it.

Nothing in me knows how to hang it up and walk away. Not even when I've only got three months before the winter break melts into next season's testing, pulling us to the opposite ends of the earth along with it.

I *love* that woman, and I'm not giving up on day one.

"I missed you!" I call after her.

"Missed you, too." Hope sparks in my chest as she peeks over her shoulder with a look that takes everything funny out of her words but, for some reason, still gets me going. "Had you right in my sights, and the damn wind shifted."

*Jesus.* Maybe day two will go better.

# Chapter 2

*Taryn Ledell—Back Then*

THERE WASN'T ANYTHING SPECIAL ABOUT BILLY KING. He was just another cowboy.

At first, anyway.

"Admit it," Holly was saying, nuzzling kisses onto my horse's nose while I relaxed in Aston Magic's saddle. "After winning this morning, you've completely run out of room on your trophy shelf and have taken to stuffing your barrel racing medals into your underwear drawer."

"Come on! Just a couple in my nightstand." I winked off the compliment, patting my mare's neck. We were smack-dab in the middle of traffic between the warm-up pen and outdoor arena, people coming and going from one rodeo event after the other. But I hadn't seen Holly since Fort Worth, and I'd really missed her.

It didn't help that the annual Starry Nights rodeo—where, in true Kentucky tradition, they scheduled everything backward—was the last rodeo I was able to attend before starting the long back-and-forth of the international Superbike circuit.

Holly shook her head, widening her eyes at Aston. "I know, girl. I hate her, too."

A genuine laugh from too many years of friendly competitive banter rang through my heart, Holly leaving another kiss on Aston's nose before she stepped toward me, stretching up as far as she could to hug me as I carefully leaned down from the saddle, breathing in her curly hair tickling my nose. "I love you. Been way too long."

"I know, and we all miss you so much. But we're so proud of you."

"Thanks," I mumbled, wondering if she'd still say that if she actually googled me.

It hadn't always been this bad. In the beginning, racing was a dream after the nightmare of leaving sports medicine. But under my new publicist's slimy hands, my racing image had become less about my placements and more about my photo shoots. Now, every fan in the sport knew my face, my bra size, and not a damn thing about where I stood, on or off the podium.

"Hon, I mean it," Holly said. "You may be famous over there, but to me, you'll always be the same lanky beauty queen who couldn't rope if her life depended on it."

Everything in my heart squeezed as I held Holly tighter, and I wished so much that what she said was true, that the people who knew me really were proud of me. At the very least, I was back home where the world smelled familiar: like fresh dirt, stiff hay, old ropes, and Old Spice.

*Old Spice?*

"Pardon me, ma'am."

I lifted my head, finding a jean-clad knee next to my face and a cowboy smiling down from a golden horse like he was waiting his turn for a hug, tall and lean in a black competition shirt, a Stetson to match, and his voice just as dark and deep as both. He was also paying no mind to the fact that traffic was now even more blocked with two horses standing side by side, and people were starting to grumble as they passed by. *Jackass.*

I looked at Holly questioningly, but her bunched-up

eyebrows said she had no clue who the guy was. He couldn't possibly have recognized me from my racing photos. No one in America gave a flip about Superbike, seemed like.

I looked back to the cowboy, telling myself to be brave. Assertive. Fearless. "Can I help you?" I asked, bleeding Southern politeness through my tone.

"Oh, Gidget wanted to come say hi. He saw your mare when you were barrel racing and thought she was real agile. Pay me no mind." He sat back in his saddle, his hands crossed on the saddle horn as he started whistling a tune that was far too relaxed to be believed while his stallion tried—and failed—to get the attention of Aston Magic, swishing his tail into hers and bumping her nose.

*Okay, so definitely not a racing stalker or an immediate threat.*

The knot in my stomach slowly unwound as Aston snickered, then nipped at his stallion. Served his horse right. I arched my eyebrow in the cowboy's direction, a sugary smile curling around my double entendre. "Doesn't seem like she's interested."

He kept grinning away under his black hat, the rim so wide it was almost as broad as his shoulders. "Well, Gidget's real nice, but he gets excited when he finds something he likes, and that can take some getting used to."

Holly let out a sharp laugh. "You sure we're still talking about your horse?"

I looked away to hide my snicker. *Damn, Holly.*

"Yes, ma'am, certainly." He sounded a little offended, but the slight touch of ire faded instantly from his voice. "And since I already interrupted y'all's conversation, if you don't mind me saying…"

"Go right on ahead, honey," Holly told him. "I can't wait to hear this."

I looked back to Holly, but this guy apparently had guts of steel. He was staring straight at me. "Congratulations on winning, miss. Even though I think that other girl ran it a little cleaner."

My eyes popped in disbelief, darting to Holly and back to him. "I'm sorry, *what*?"

He scratched at his jaw, rusty with dirty-blond stubble. "Tonya Ladle, I think her name was? You're real fast and all, and your quarter horse sure seems to know what she's doing. But I just thought that other girl's turns were tighter."

Holly's face flushed and deepened in color, and I sat up straighter in my saddle, my feigned indifference churning into fast-growing irritation. "*I'm* Taryn Ledell. Not Tonya Ladle. *Leh-dell*."

His hand shot out toward me across the space between our horses, his grin bigger than ever. "And I'm Billy King. Nice to meet you."

"Oh *wow*." Holly burst out in laughter. "Taryn, honey, since you're fine"—she tried to contain her chuckle but couldn't, making eyes at the cowboy and then at me—"I'll, uh, head on out. It was good seeing you."

She couldn't be serious. "Holly, really—"

"Really." She winked, already backing up into the crowd and disappearing within the camouflage of Wrangler jeans and pressed shirts, waving over her shoulder. "Congratulations again!"

I looked at the reason my friend just bailed on me, and Mr. Wearing Too Much Old Spice was still grinning from his saddle and reaching toward me over the lariat he had strapped to it. Heat flooded a bunch of parts of me that shouldn't have been affected by just a damn smile, and I mentally refused to shake his hand.

Why in the hell were the most annoying cowboys always the cutest? Especially with lopsided smiles and teeth that were pearly white but just a little bit crooked because he hadn't been forced to suffer corrective braces like I had.

My gaze drifted as far from his easy country grin as I could stand, landing on his horse's golden mane. There was hardly anything there. And his muscles were all uphill and forward built. Not the level or even downward build of a quarter horse.

*But a lariat was strapped to his saddle horn...*

A whole lot of something wasn't right.

"Where'd you get this horse?" I asked, inspecting his stallion more closely while my mind raced to put the pieces together.

His arm pulled back. "Huh?"

Aston Magic was beautiful, but this guy's horse had no equal at the rodeo. And if I wasn't mistaken, not only was it the precious gold of an Akhal-Teke, but with the guy's telltale Memphis twang, it should have a brand in the shape of—

"Oh my God!" A couple walking by jumped and stared at me, but I couldn't do more than gawk in utter astonishment. It was right there, and I couldn't believe what I was seeing. "This is a Hargrove horse!"

A funny smile crept across Billy's lips. Like he was impressed and still not the slightest bit guilty. "You from Memphis? What a small, funny world it is."

"No, it's not," I snapped, way past seeing him as a

potential distraction and closer to imagining what he looked like in handcuffs. The police kind. "And he's for dressage, not for roping. Where'd you get him?"

Billy's nose scrunched up like he couldn't believe I was accusing him of doing anything wrong. Wonder how long that had been working for him? "I borrowed him."

My eyes nearly flew out of my skull. "You *borrowed* him?"

There was no way Lynn Hargrove knew about this. I didn't exactly know her, but I knew about her, and she didn't just let farmhands take her prize stallions to rodeos in Kentucky because they wanted to have some fun on the weekends. He'd probably stolen a fifty-thousand-dollar horse.

"Yes, ma'am, I borrowed him," he drawled, starting to sound a little indignant about the accusation. "And it's been real nice talking to you, but Gidget and I gotta—"

"Oh, *hell* no. You're not going anywhere. Give me that horse." I went for his reins, but he'd already sidled them out of my reach, allowing a new flow of traffic to fill up between us.

"Now, hold on just a minute—"

"Come back here!"

More people turned to stare, and I would've too if our situations were reversed. But they didn't realize the magnitude of what he had done. Especially when he was laughing at me about it. "Wish I could, honey, but I gotta go rope. I'd love if you'd come watch me, though. And it was nice meeting you."

With one touch of his finger to his hat, he was gone, trotting his "borrowed" horse toward the arena, his lasso ropes thwacking against his jeans with the motion.

No sight had ever pissed me off more.

I gave two clicks to Aston Magic, urging her to go after them. But we never caught up.

Apparently, that was the moment when the whole freaking world needed to talk to me, and there were too many people crowding and blocking us, stopping me to say congratulations, welcome back, and asking where I was riding next.

By the time I got to the outdoor arena, I couldn't find him. All I could hear was his damn name blaring through the speakers and echoing on the wind.

"All right, folks," the announcer boomed. "Next up for calf roping, we have Billy King. If that last name sounds familiar to you, it's 'cause his baby brother, Mason, took first in the bull riding showdown this morning. Them King boys are ones to watch, I tell you. Let's hear it for Billy!"

The crowd cheered like they knew him, and despite my temper sparking, I couldn't help sitting up a little higher in my saddle. Peering through teased high hair and black and tan Stetsons, I finally saw him: sitting atop that golden horse with his heels sunk in his stirrups, the sun shining off his belt buckle, and a fearless grin beaming from behind the rope he had clenched in his teeth.

I narrowed my eyes. He probably wasn't any good. And the second he was done, I was reporting him. To... somebody.

*God*, what was it about this guy that had pushed all my freaking buttons?

At the harsh sound of the buzzer, a calf was loose and running. But Billy's horse bolted faster and he was already there, his outstretched arm casting a lasso that found its target with ease, his stallion instantly pulling to a stop and backing up while Billy swung off his saddle.

*Fine, so maybe he trained the horse for roping, too.*

Faster than a wink, Billy ran up to the calf and grabbed it and flipped it—and those calves are freaking *heavy*. But it was already done, Billy whipping the rope from his mouth and twisting it around the calf's ankles, then leaping up from the ground with his hands in the air.

*Damn...*

The fans shot to their feet, their cheers a blast of sound that reminded me again of the Superbike circuit. I took a steadying breath and promised myself I wasn't going to worry about it. Not the coming press shoots, the pressure, or the insinuations about my greasy-handed teammate, Colton.

None of it.

"And that's how it's done, folks!" the announcer hollered. "That man is slicker than snot on a doorknob. Whoo!"

Billy flipped his hat into the air, and I slowly clapped along with everyone else. Under protest. And maybe I whistled a little, too. But only because he was...he was really something.

I should've known better than to draw attention to myself. The jackass saw me, smiling even wider as he pointed in my direction, then did one final wave, his hands blinking at the crowd instead of hitching at the wrist like he was Lane Frost reincarnate before he collected his hat and his horse.

The crowd got ready for the next calf roper, and I turned away from the arena, swearing to myself ten times over that temptation could fuck right off. I had a job, and

FEARLESS 21

it wasn't at rodeos anymore. After tomorrow, I'd be leaving for Australia. For the Phillip Island Grand Prix Circuit and testing ahead of our first race of the season. I had things to focus on, and I'd never see this cowboy again.

Which is exactly why I never should've walked Aston over to the arena exit, where I knew Billy would be waiting. Right then, he was still no one. Just another stranger, a name I'd be able to forget if I tried. And I needed to get Aston brushed and back in her trailer.

But temptation also knows there's a devilish part of me I can't deny—the part that did it right and got her degree, then flipped it all off to race motorcycles for a living—and she *loves* breaking the rules.

Billy started scrambling the second he saw me coming, dusting off his shirt and tucking in the back, then showing his teeth to his horse like he was asking if something was stuck in them. His horse pulled back his lips and did the same, and I couldn't help smirking a bit, they were so cute. It was also a relief: they clearly knew each other, borrowed or not.

Maybe reporting him wasn't necessary. Lynn Hargrove must have known he was here with her horse. No one from Memphis would ever risk crossing her.

"Don't embarrass me now," Billy was whispering to Gidget when Aston and I walked up to the arena exit, my temper and tongue firmly in check. When he turned toward me, he took a long time tilting his eyes up to mine, like I was miles above him. But he skipped over the parts where other men usually lingered. "Well, hi there," he drawled. His horse snorted and nosed him in the back, making Billy stumble, and it took all my experience training colts not to laugh and encourage the stallion's bad behavior. "Damn it, Gidget," Billy muttered before looking at me and resuming his smile. "Thanks for bringing me all that good luck."

Okay, so he could keep his cool. Didn't mean he was special. He was probably like the rest of the calf ropers—cocky and twitchy and only interested in listening to a woman for as long as it took to get her zipper down. "Didn't seem like you needed much. Definitely not your first rodeo."

Billy grinned, shaking his head. "No, ma'am. It's my second." He was doing just fine...until Gidget bit the back of his shirt and pulled it out from where it'd been tucked in, jerking it around before Billy got free. "Really?" he grumbled, but he never raised a hand to his stallion. He just started tucking his shirt back in. "I'm trying to talk to this lady. You can wait." He turned to me, calm as anything. "Sorry. He may look like a horse, but he's really a heifer when he's hungry."

Aston shifted beneath me like she wasn't impressed, though I was having a harder time than ever keeping a straight face. "It's all right."

But it apparently wasn't, because Gidget's nose was right back in Billy's face, blowing raspberries. I couldn't help it anymore, clasping my hand over my mouth.

Billy took a deep breath, holding up a single finger. "If you'll excuse us."

I nodded, pulling my hand away and chewing the hell out of the inside of my cheek to keep from laughing. Which was so *weird*: cocky guys in my experience were typically grabby and pushy but hardly ever funny. At least, not as funny as they thought they were. "By all means."

He took Gidget's lead and walked them a few feet away.

He kept his head close to his horse's, talking and gesturing and looking like he was cutting a deal to get him to behave. It ended with Billy pulling a treat from his back pocket and pressing a kiss to Gidget's nose while he ate it. *Aww.*

Aston huffed and shifted again as Billy led Gidget toward us, my quarter horse clearly over the advances of the Akhal-Teke and ready to be pampered after working her ass off in the arena. And as much as Billy was...intriguing, to say the least, Aston Magic came first.

"Sorry about that." Billy made a supposed-to-be-stern face at his horse. "Gonna have a long talk about our manners when we get home."

*Oh, damn it, that was cute.*

"It's fine." I kept my spine straight and chin high, voice kind but firm. "But I can't stay, so you may as well get to telling me what your deal is."

"Ma'am?"

I sighed—so much for sugarcoating it. I leaned down from the saddle, closer to where he was standing next to his horse. There were still plenty of people around, and I didn't want to embarrass him any more than I was about to. "Drop the Mr. Innocent act, and be straight with me. What is your goal here? Because I'm telling you right now, I'm not sleeping with you. No matter what war you're about to head off to."

Not entirely true. I hadn't decided yet whether to sleep with him. He was hot and seemed nice, and it'd been a long time since I'd had a man in my bed. And heading off to the circuit meant my chances were narrowing quickly.

Billy ducked his head so I could only see his hat as he looked away and shifted his feet. When he looked up, there was some pink in his cheeks, his hand fidgeting with his reins, and his thumb stroking the leather like a lover's lips. "Don't have an act or a goal. I was just wondering if you'd let me hang around you a bit, see if I can get you to like me some."

I took another look at everything about his size, his build, the way he held a rope, and the adrenaline still clearly drugging his veins and shining in his blue eyes. "Are you a bull rider?"

A new kind of smile tugged at the edge of his lips—the guilty kind. "Maybe?"

*Damn it.*

Of course, there had to be a catch. I had sworn off his kind long ago, knowing too well the faces of bull riders' wives, their girlfriends. The pain and worry the women go through. Because I used to *be* one of them.

Kind of hard not to date bull riders when you're working the medic tents at rodeos. They're the only men you meet, because they're the ones always getting hurt. I should've known better, because before I knew it, I was setting bones for men I loved. Watching them get bucked and broken and praying they would wake up. In the ambulance, in the hospital. At *all*.

Bonnie Landry had been the last straw for me and that way of life. She'd *loved* Beau Blackwell and supported his bull riding career every step of the way. But Beau wasn't as lucky as Eric, who broke his arm in two places. He wasn't as lucky as Austin, with his busted ribs and concussion. He wasn't even as lucky as Cash, who'd never walk again.

Beau Blackwell got bucked at twenty-six years old, two days before his wedding, snapped his neck and died, and Bonnie Landry wore a black dress that Sunday instead of a white one.

I stopped working rodeos after that. I broke up with Levi after that. And I promised myself that I would never forget how it felt to be so helpless over your future. Because those bull rider wives, those poor girlfriends, they watch their men volunteer for their deaths. And all so they could have eight seconds of glory when they could've had a lifetime with her.

I wasn't doing it. I'm worth more than eight seconds.

*What a waste.*

"Bye, Billy. Congratulations on your win." I gave two clicks to Aston Magic and turned her away, struggling to swallow my disappointment as I headed back the way I came—to the pens and my family's travel trailer and my laptop with the turn sequence for Phillip Island I was supposed to be learning.

I'd be able to forget him. If I tried.

Maybe tried *hard.*

"Hey, Taryn, hold on!"

I never should've looked back.

Billy was already up in his saddle and trotting Gidget toward me, catching up. "I don't ride bulls no more. I swear it."

I scoffed, still walking Aston toward the pens. I didn't even care to act gracious or charming or any of that fake stuff anymore. All I could think about was the scent of his cologne mixing with my fabric softener. I hadn't been laid in *months.* "Bullshit. Bull riders don't stop until they're too old or too broken to keep going." I gave him a quick once-over. "You're neither of those things."

"Well, that's kind of you to say," he said. "And I'll grant you, that's usually true. But in my case, I got a new job, and I can't do both. I'm not allowed."

I stopped Aston and looked over, my curiosity regrettably piqued. "You an elementary school teacher or something?"

He laughed, the sound pure and crystalline. No man should be allowed to laugh like that. Especially when he could throw calves like they were feather pillows. "No, ma'am. I'm a motorcycle racer."

*Oh shit.*

I didn't know what that meant. He wasn't on the Superbike circuit with me, but the fact that he even *mentioned* a motorcycle...

The devil was whispering all my favorite words.

I urged Aston on, resolute to keep my cool. Just because he was also from Memphis, roped like a god, was sweet to his horse, and apparently rode a motorcycle for a living didn't mean meeting him was destiny. Chances were I'd never see him again. "That right?"

"Yes, ma'am. MotoPro."

Really? *Damn*—those bikes were *fast*.

He guided his horse around a group of people stopped in the middle of the aisle. When he came up beside me, he tipped his hat a little farther back so his face wasn't as shadowed. *God*, he was cute, with one of those iron-sharp jaws that always felt really, really good in your hands.

"It's kinda like Formula 1," he said, "but with motorcycles instead of cars. And my contract with Yaalon, well, it says I can't ride bulls anymore. My brother Mason can, but he's with Blue Gator on a satellite team."

My brow furrowed. As a Superbike racer, I knew plenty about the Moto Grand Prix circuit. But the last thing he said didn't seem right to me. My contract with Munich Motor Works had all sorts of provisions, but MMW never said anything about me barrel racing when I was home. "How come?"

"How come Mason can ride bulls and I can't?"

"Yeah."

He shrugged, no stress in the movement or twitchiness to be found. "Don't know. Probably because he's better at it than I was."

Another thing that didn't sound right. Bull riders were famous for their egos. "You ever miss it?" I tested.

"Hmm, sometimes, I guess. It's a hell of a rush. But I get that from racing now, so I don't mind giving it up." He sounded totally sincere as he smiled at me and said, "Besides, I got too much to lose."

I cocked an eyebrow at him. "In all my life, I've never heard a bull rider say that."

"Well, I told you: I'm not a bull rider no more." He winked at me, and Lord, if he was telling the truth? I was in so much trouble. "And hey, since I'm not, you wanna be my date to the Mutton Bustin' tonight?"

I burst into laughter, no idea why my heart was jumping to agree and even my overly critical brain was struggling to refuse. "No?"

"Why not?" He'd still never lost his grin, drifting his horse closer until his leg bumped mine, sending a *zing* through my veins that hit me straight between my thighs. "It'll be fun, cheering on all those little kids climbing up there to ride their first sheep. And I hear after, they're gonna have a dance for the big kids. And I'm a great dancer."

"Oh, are you now?"

"Yes, ma'am."

I couldn't make myself stop smiling as I walked Aston up to her designated pen, then got down from the saddle, tying her lead and endlessly debating.

I had hard and fast rules about dating bull riders. But Billy said he wasn't a bull rider anymore. Plus, it was so sweet that instead of asking to take me out to a bar, he wanted to watch toddlers try to ride sheep. Where the families were.

I turned around, finding him down from his saddle and standing a comfortable distance back from me, absently petting the underside of his horse's jaw. "I promise to get you home at a decent time. And I won't try nothing. I just...want to dance with you. If that's okay."

His drawl was slaying all my defenses, husky and deep and rumbling beneath black cotton fabric doing its absolute *very* best to stretch across the broad expanse of his upper muscles. His arms were bigger than I'd realized, too. I bet with one solid flex of his biceps, the seams would be forced to rip apart.

How awful for that poor, innocent shirt.

*Get a grip, Taryn.*

"I don't...know you," I said, because I honestly couldn't think of anything else to say.

The dancing part didn't sound too bad, and it had been forever since I'd been on a real date with a guy and not just hooked up. Even longer since I'd been on a date with a *nice* guy. I wasn't sure they existed anymore, truthfully. And I was tired of being disappointed when they all turned out to be after the same thing, which *definitely* wasn't my brain. It wasn't even my damn bike.

But Billy...

He was so disarmingly kind but still confident enough to ask for what he wanted—and in that Stetson blacker than any lingerie I'd ever dared to buy.

He nodded to himself, taking a small step closer and

slipping his hat off his head. My eyes widened a bit at the shock of sunny blond hair, seeming to match so much better with the gentleness in his baby-blue eyes. "Well, I'm trying to fix that, Taryn. If you'll let me."

I don't know why I said what I did. I don't know what was wrong with me.

I knew better, and I never should've looked back.

*Never.*

"Pick me up at seven."

# Chapter 3

*Billy King—Present Day*

I WAS FINE AFTER SHE LEFT THE TRAINING PEN AT Hargrove Ranch. I smiled at Gidget on my way past him in the barn even though I didn't stop by his stall, heading straight to my own truck parked out front. I got in and shut the door, and I was okay. But then I noticed the dust on the caliche driveway. It still wasn't settled from Taryn driving down it faster than even Lorelai dares to, and when I put my key in the ignition and tried to turn it, I...I *couldn't*.

Still haven't.

Everything Taryn said about putting her first keeps playing in my head, and I think...I think she may be serious. She may really be done with me this time.

The idea of never being able to call her or dance with her again... I grip the steering wheel hard with one hand, throwing my hat onto the seat next to me and wiping sweat from my brow. I keep telling myself I made the right decision that night in North Carolina, that the consequences would've been so much worse the other way. But it's getting harder to remember why I felt like that in the moment.

I stare at myself in the rearview, my father's stormy blue eyes staring back. "It's gonna be fine. You haven't lost her yet. So stop fucking crying about it."

I reach for the ignition, and my wrist turns all the way this time. My truck's old engine sputters to a start like she's gonna stall, so I give her some gas until she's definitely gonna be fine. The sound isn't nearly as sweet as opening up the throttle on my bike, but I find a good quarter of my smile and pull out of Hargrove Ranch, heading for home.

Well, heading for Gary "Cannonball" Willis's house that my parents have been renting from him for nearly thirty years now. And I should've moved out long ago, but it's hard to justify paying for an apartment when I'm gone all the time. Besides, my parents can use the rent money I give them for my childhood bedroom. Although I think my father charges me more than he makes Mason pay for still living there.

My arm makes the familiar pull on the wheel to swing my tires into our gravel drive, leading up to the front of the house. The yellow paint is faded and cracked, but you can only tell once you look past the blooming flower beds, currently covered with a bedsheet against the dropping winter temperatures.

The two front windows with their curtains pulled closed tell me that my father's watching TV in his study, and my brother is probably up to no good in his bedroom. A couple of chickens shuffle and scurry at the sound of my diesel, and my brow furrows at the red GMC Sierra parked next to my mama's Dakota, my father's old Ranger nowhere to be found.

I pull off the driveway and park under the oak tree next to Mason's latest and greatest white truck: a brand new Dodge Ram Rebel with off-road tires and a lift kit. I scoff as I grab my hat and get out, wondering where he's hiding his step stool to reach the running boards just to climb in that damn thing. Ostentatious as hell.

"Hey, Mama," I call out when I stride through the front

door, reaching back to catch the screen at the last minute before it slams. The layered scent of Lemon Fresh Pine-Sol competing with vanilla candles and something that smells like dinner slams full force into me. A little more of my smile finds my face.

"Hey there, Billy Bear," she calls back.

Like I've done since I was little, I tap my fingers down the long antique entry table, hopping over lace doilies and flicking the crystal candy bowl that's always empty because of Mason's sweet tooth. Family portraits fill our tiny living room, along with a tall grandfather clock that only I can get to keep time, it seems. Standard lumpy old sofa next to an oversized recliner, but ours is currently sporting a pink throw blanket. No one but Mama spends any time in there anymore.

It's been a kind of hard I didn't expect: when the thing you love to do most in the world takes place on the other side of it, getting you gone way more than is good for anyone you care about. Yourself included.

I round into the kitchen, sliding off my hat and hooking it onto my designated chair at the dinner table. Mama smiles up at me from in front of her gas stove. "Taryn wasn't home?"

I shake my head. "Nope. And what's Cannonball's truck doing out front?"

"Oh." She waves me off, going back to what she's stirring in her trusty orange saucepans and iron skillet: Hamburger Helper, mashed potatoes, mixed corn and peas and carrots and lima beans, and I think she's even got biscuits in the oven. Smells damn good, too. "Your daddy's truck hasn't been running right, so Cannonball's letting him borrow his extra so he can get to work."

Frustration sours every part of me, and I can still hear the snickers at the VFW, talking about "Borrower Bill King" and who they assumed he was *sharing* with Cannonball in return for use of his friend's stuff. Nearly got myself arrested that night. Also scored a couple of stitches from the wrong end of a broken whiskey bottle, but I never did find the guts to explain to my father what started the fight.

I reach over to pick out a piece of hamburger from the skillet, mentally ignoring Frank's voice in my head yammering on about my protein intake and shaving hundredths off my lap time. "Please let me help. What if I get him a new truck for Christmas? Maybe that Raptor he's always sighing at on the Waylon Gimley Ford commercials, or even—"

She smacks my hand but still lets me eat the meat, then hands me a stack of silverware cradled in clean cotton dinner napkins. "You do help, Billy. All the time."

I take my dismissal and head to the table, setting it for her. Mason should be getting the glasses and pouring the sweet tea, but he's probably jerking off or something in his room, like always.

"What's that?" Mama asks.

I lift my head, praying I didn't say that out loud. "Ma'am?"

She's pointing directly at me, but I still look over my shoulder through the bay window, out into the backyard. Nothing out there but a half-rotted tree swing, some wood that needs chopping, a few goofy goats, and some trash-burning barrels that them damn goats keep knocking over. I look back to Mama, who's still pointing at my leg. "You got a hitch in your giddyup."

*Shit.* I didn't realize, but now that I think about it, I've been kind of favoring my leg since I walked in the door. I half shrug, getting back to setting the table. "I'm all right. Just stepped down wrong is all."

The layered smells steeped in the kitchen start to turn against me, flipping my stomach, and I hate so much that I'm now lying to her about all this.

"Billy," Mama says, her voice low and serious. "Are you and Taryn fighting?"

My hand freezes in place, a fork suspended over the faded wooden tabletop. My pulse just went from two digits to three, and I notice a tremble in my fingers before I get control and gently set the fork down. Somehow, I can battle the fastest men on any racetrack the world throws at me, but I can't bring myself to look at her. Like that's ever made a difference.

"Is it your fault?" she asks, and because I can't take telling her three white lies before I eat the supper she made for us after working a retail counter all day, I come clean, and I nod. Still not looking up, though.

She loves Taryn. Not more than me but *a lot.* And not only is she probably gonna be on her side in all this, but she's gonna be so disappointed when she realizes I probably cost her "her one good chance at having a daughter." Mason's sworn he's never getting married unless it's to a female Klingon cosplayer at a Comic-Con in Las Vegas.

"Well, as long as you know it," Mama says, and I peek up to find her stirring dinner. She glances over and winks at me, then looks to the simmering meat and noodles. "It's the first step to fixing it, and admitting your mistakes isn't something your daddy has ever figured out how to do."

I smirk to myself and finish setting the table. Like I

don't know that after years of listening to her ride his ass about it with no end in sight.

"Speaking of," she says the very moment I'm done with the last of the plates and silverware, and I groan, wishing I'd gone to take a shower instead of coming in here when I got home. "He's waiting for you in his study."

"Seriously? We just got home today. He can't wait?"

She gives me a look that's filled with motherly patience, but still like I should know better by now. "Nope."

I roll my eyes and head out of the kitchen, directly toward my father's study. I knock but don't hesitate to enter since he's already waiting, shutting the door behind me. I breathe in leather upon leather, with a hint of older leather on top.

"You're late." He points at me with a red marker, standing in front of an old Magnavox TV with circles drawn on the screen. He's got it set up on his desk, crowding up the little space not spilling out books, belt buckles, mounted animals we've hunted, and the giant family trophy box starting to overflow, too.

*Where'd he get that Magnavox?* There's a flat-screen on the wall I gave him for his birthday. Must've borrowed it from Cannonball. Like everything else we "own."

"Sorry."

"Ah, it's all right." He waves me off and goes back to circling motorcycles on the paused screen. "I've been showing Mason here how y'all are gonna take Qatar next season."

Mason makes an inappropriate hand gesture behind his back. I flop into the second barrel chair next to him, then lean over and smack the back of his dark-haired head for being disrespectful, even though I don't wanna do this, either.

I know our father is proud and wants to help. But even though he can fix anything with wheels and ride anything with legs, he doesn't know shit about racing MotoPro. Especially against the Spanish and the Italians and the French and the Germans who've been doing this a hell of a lot longer than any Americans have.

Mason snickers and holds up a finger to his lips in a "Shh!" motion, then reaches into his seat and pulls out a kid-size bag of potato chips, shoveling a handful in his mouth.

"Mama's cooking dinner," I whisper-hiss at him.

"So?" he garbles, his mouth full. "Hungry."

"All right, boys, y'all listen up now." Our father straightens, turning toward us. "So, Billy, you did real good in Valencia, but see how Mason is coming up behind Franco here?"

Mason cracks up laughing, spraying chips everywhere. "Franco!"

I glare at my brother, full of loyalty to my soon-to-be-retiring teammate. "Don't call Francesco that in interviews."

"And why not?" He gestures his bag of chips loosely toward the TV. *Too loosely.* I don't smell any whiskey on his breath, though. I don't think. "It's got a nice ring to it."

"You don't want to start picking fights with him, Mason," I snap, empty of patience for his cocky attitude. "He's been winning races since before you were finished with your training wheels, and you need to learn a little respect for your elders in this sport."

"Almost had your slow ass in Valencia!" Mason squawks at me.

"Billy, hush up. Pay attention now." Our father snaps his

fingers, clapping at me and not even bothering to address Mason. Scolding his favorite usually isn't high on his priority list. "You see what I'm saying here? If you come up— wait a minute." He stops and stares at me, his hands spread out. "Where's your medal?"

"Um…" I smooth my hand down the back of my hair, wondering what the hell I'm gonna do.

"Got mine," Mason announces, holding up his third-place medal from Valencia. Must've pulled it straight out of his ass.

"Well, would you look at that." Our father takes the medal, holding it up to the light. "Isn't that something… Billy, where's yours, Son?"

Mason's grinning like he knows it's buried under dirt and horse shit in the training pen at Hargrove Ranch, although he can't actually know anything about it. There's no way. Unless Lorelai was spying and told him. She always did like him better.

"I lost it?"

My father sets down Mason's medal on his desk, then crosses his arms my way, his jaw setting firm and the black prickle of a five-o'clock shadow getting darker with each word. "Your MotoPro Grand Prix World Champion medal. It's just gone."

Mason crunches loudly on his chips next to me, then smacks salt off his fingertips, his voice thick with sarcasm that hits way too close to home. "God, Billy, why can't you be more like me?"

I wait, but our father doesn't contradict him. He just turns and picks up Mason's third-place medal, putting it in the first-place spot in the trophy box. Then he goes back to the TV screen. "So, Billy. Like I was saying. When you're in

Qatar next season, and you come up on someone this way, what you need to do is what Mason does right here…"

———~~~———

Mason reaches over and knocks my chest, his other hand on the steering wheel of his truck and the radio playing too loud to talk. "You about ready to get that stick out of your ass?"

I don't respond other than to look out the window, watching the passing couples strolling down the dark sidewalks and neon beer lights filling up the bar fronts. I didn't even want to go out tonight. I was perfectly happy staying in my room with the door locked, pining over my stored racing Yaalon motorcycle, and *quietly* rewatching one of Taryn's favorite movies, *Seven Brides for Seven Brothers*. I was trying to see things from Milly's point of view instead of Adam Pontipee's for once. But I didn't even make it to the damn barn-raising scene. Again.

Doesn't help that my dinner's been sitting like a rock in my stomach since I left the table—not that I ended up eating much. And I hate the way Mason's truck stinks like new plastic. If anything, I could've used some fresh air, maybe some dirt bikes or four wheelers. Instead, I'm choking on that cologne he sprays too much of and can't even pronounce.

"How about we go to Joe's?" Mason says far too innocently.

I peek over to where he's tapping his thumb and bobbing his head to the music, practically busting out of his pants to get into something. Most likely a brawl. "Nah."

He groans, slowing for a stoplight. "The Round-Up, then."

"Nope. Too risky."

He rolls his eyes at me, but I don't want to go to the bars Taryn and I always went to together. Too many people know us and would ask where she is. Too many memories of showing her off on the dance floor until she was pulling me out the front door. Taking her home and kissing her good night on her front porch, then climbing through her window for another longer, better one.

I pull my phone from my pocket, open my messages, and type out a new one. Before I hit Send, I read over all the texts I've sent her this past week. Ones when I was racing with everything I had in Valencia just to prove I still had a professional future and missing her more with every mile between us. Texts she hasn't responded to. Even though there's a little check mark next to every single one.

*Backspace, backspace, backspace...*

"Well, where do you want to go then?" Mason asks.

"I don't know. Home?"

He scoffs, batting my words away. But as the light turns green, the ballsy little racer in him perks up. "I know where we're going." He checks his mirror and crosses two lanes, much like he does before he attempts to cut me off in a turn. Then he takes a right, heading farther into the bar district but off the beaten path.

I put my phone away, taking more of an interest in whatever he's gonna get us into. "Where?"

"You'll see."

My trust in him is plummeting by the second, Mason's Rebel riding smooth down the potholed roads until he takes another right turn, then a left one, and I figure out exactly where my brother is taking me to "relax."

"Can't believe we're doing this," I grumble when he

parks down the street from Up-Chuck Buck's, where the music's a little bitter and the whiskey flows like Sunday prayers, fights aren't unheard of, and puke stains the floor.

"Come on, man." He claps me on the shoulder. "No way she's gonna be in there."

I grumble and huff, but I get out of his truck. Mason whistles to himself and tips his hat at a few ladies on our way down the sidewalk, the night getting colder and seizing up my ankle. The music is getting louder the closer we get, accompanied by a thick wind of smoke from a small group of people hanging around outside. So much for my fresh air.

"Hey, Brother, hold up. I got it," Mason says when we get to the door, pulling out his wallet and paying for my cover charge.

I check behind me, then look again at my brother, my suspicions skyrocketing. "Who are you and what've you done with Mason?"

"Told ya, I'm captain of your cheer-up brigade." He grins and shoves me into the bar, and not two painful steps in, my eyes flag on something all kinds of wrong.

*Damn it.* She wasn't supposed to be here.

But there she is: tall in her best jeans and going-out Ariats, a long-sleeved white shirt sucked to her chest and covering her tan arms, one hand hooked in her back pocket as the other tosses her hair. She's so damn pretty, it's like she comes with a spotlight.

My head whips toward Mason, my eyes narrowing into slits.

"Oh fuck me," he says, the color melting from his face like he's seen a ghost. "That just ain't fair!"

I lean over his shrinking body with the three extra

inches and fifteen pounds I got on him, keeping my voice low even though the music is already making my temples throb. "You knew about this?"

His eyes fling up to me, shaking his head. He may have the guts to challenge me on the track, but he damn well knows who the big brother is when we're home. "Uh-uh. I swear it."

I look toward Taryn again, and she's still talking to some people she rodeos with. But I can't remember their names, even though I know I've met them before. She always took care to introduce me.

"You wanna go?" Mason whispers. "I don't think she saw us yet."

I grit my teeth. "I don't..." Have the first fucking clue what to do. I'm not prepared for another round with her tonight. But I can't waste an opportunity this perfect, either. "Just...*shit*."

There's too high of a risk that if I go over there, she's gonna knee-jerk into being mad and send me off quicker than she can snap her fingers. But maybe if I wait... just *maybe*, she won't be able to resist. To double-check whether I'm here to see her or if I'm already trying to get *over* her. She should know better, but she gets jealous. Quick.

I duck off to the bar, wobbling up onto a stool where I can take the pressure off my ankle. Mason knows better than to follow. Smartest thing he's done in a while.

"Water."

The bartender snarls his lip at me but gets my water, taking my money. It doesn't take long for the seat next to me to get taken—pretty women come and go, ordering their drinks and barely glancing my way. Probably because

I never say nothing, pulling my hat a little lower as I try to bob my head to the music, but it doesn't feel right, and this whole idea was so stupid.

Nothing's gonna be fine until I get her back, and I'm too chicken to even walk over there right now. I probably couldn't even if I wanted. This pain in my ankle isn't just an annoyance now. It's all the time, definitely getting worse, and actually starting to worry me a bit. But I can't risk going to a doctor without Frank finding out what landed me there. And once Frank knows, my Yaalon rep knows, and they can't find out *shit*.

I need my damn bike. The freedom and the speed and all the opportunities it keeps affording my bleak little life. I haven't been racing that long, but people are already muttering about me retiring and making room for others, about old injuries and how long I can keep going with my knee the way it is.

But I'm not ready to retire, and I can't get hurt again and speed up the damn process. I *need* my ride. More than I've ever needed anything, except maybe Taryn's forgiveness.

Another statuesque profile appears in my peripheral, but this one smells different. More right. I tug my hat down more, sipping my water. Looks like jealousy won and Taryn lost.

"I thought all crying cowboys drank whiskey?"

She's using her press interview voice—totally controlled and utterly fake. It's like the red lights going out in my mind, and the words pop from my lips before I can make them stop. "I'm not crying. And don't act like you don't know I don't drink."

Taryn leans onto the bar next to me, her weight braced on her forearms. She flares her eyes in my direction: smoky and dark with more makeup than she usually wears, but she still smells like sweet Georgia peaches. "*Well* then. I expect you'll have no problem finding a new dance partner with that kind of attitude."

Yep, she definitely lost. Big time.

"And that's another thing," I tell her, since I'm apparently just gonna do this now. "I've been thinking—"

"Always dangerous."

"And we're not over."

She scoffs, her gaze drifting to the stacks of bottles behind the bartender. "Yeah, okay," she mutters, but this time, it's the *real* her. Something loosens in my chest until she smiles at the bartender with everything she's got. I've seen that look on top of plenty of podiums and magazine covers, and it lit up my entire living room the first time I told her I loved her. It's knocking the bartender on his ass, but the jealousy bait isn't working on me. Never has. "Shot of Fireball, gorgeous?"

He eyes her chest, sticking a crooked smile on his gruff, ugly face. "Sure thing, darling."

Still isn't working.

"You're mad at me, fine." I take out my wallet, throwing down a ten for her shot. "So we take a break, you cool off, and I'll give you the space you need. I swear it."

She swivels all her disbelief at me as the bartender sets the shot in front of her, Taryn forgetting her facade along with it. "If that's true, then what are you doing here? And tell the truth for once in your life."

I stare her right in the eyes, and I don't blink. "I wanted to stay home and watch a movie, but Mason wanted to go out, and you don't come here."

She gets that crinkle above her nose she always gets

when I'm finally right, and if history means anything, now she's gonna get mad at me for it, too. "Well, you never come here, either."

I turn on my seat to face her a little more, waiting as she throws back her shot of Fireball and never sputters the slightest bit. "See? We're both avoiding each other, and we both end up in the same place. We're supposed to be together, damn it, and you don't walk away from that."

She plants a hand on her hip and arches her perfectly shaped eyebrow down at me. "Walk away, huh?"

Okay, so maybe I sent her running more than she's walking anywhere, but I'm not correcting myself. "Look, you told me not to do something, and I did it. Except we both know the reason why I did it wasn't as simple as I just *wanted* to. I've never purposefully tried to hurt you, and I didn't do it now. This line in the sand stuff…it isn't worth it, Taryn. And in case you haven't realized, I've never drawn a line in the sand for you."

Her eyes narrow, and I'm sure I'm doomed. But then she shakes back her blond hair, everything about her inexplicably resetting a good six months—back to *before*. "You wanna dance?"

I blink twice, and I think I just had an aneurysm. Why is she asking me to dance when she's been telling me we're through for over a week now? She can't be drunk. She only had the one shot of Fireball—so far, that I know of. And I don't want to walk into a trap, but it's *Taryn*.

All I've ever really wanted was to dance with her.

"Yeah," I say, sealing my fate. "I do."

# Chapter 4

*Taryn Ledell—Back Then*

"YOU REALLY RACE SUPERBIKE?" BILLY SAID AGAIN.

He was blinking at the ground like he was having trouble seeing straight, walking next to me toward the barn they'd designated for the riders' dance. And I understood exactly how he felt. I was having a hell of a time equating the legendary farmhand-turned-motorcycle racer with the man who'd been so great with all the kids through the Mutton Bustin': cheering them on beside me until he hopped the fence, helping to dust them off after they ate dirt.

He never took credit for making sure they all walked away smiling or sought any praise himself. He'd even changed out of his black competition shirt and into a pale-green pearl-snap one sometime before he picked me up. No one would ever know he was the guy the rest of the rodeo couldn't stop talking about.

Still, history dictated that once I told him my real job was racing Superbike, all I would hear for the rest of the night were his best track times on the Moto Grand Prix circuit. Possibly a long list of the ways his motorcycle is technically faster than mine.

*Moment of truth.*

I squinted into the setting Kentucky sun, soaking up the last bit of heat after the brisk day, and prepared myself for the inevitable undoing of Prince Charming. "Yep, I really race Superbike."

He fidgeted with his hat and smiled at me again like I was something he'd dreamed and somehow had been brought to life. "I, um, I always like how fast the tracks feel in Spain. Do you have a fav—"

"Jerez, Catalunya, Aragón, or Valencia?"

He slowed and blinked at me some more, then finally unstuck his words from his throat and got out, "Jerez."

"Always loved racing there," I admitted. "And Aragón."

Billy cracked half a smile, kicking at an errant rock in our path. "Yeah, Aragón is fun. But it isn't exactly Laguna Seca, and we don't get to go anymore."

I stopped dead still, my hand on his arm. A very hard, muscular arm. "Seriously?"

He shrugged. "Yeah. We go to COTA in Austin, but that's it for the United States now. And I'm not gonna lie, I kinda miss that corkscrew."

I totally got flustered just from him saying that, my mind already imagining him flying over the blind crest that melts into a sand-bordered *downhill* switchback that is the most fun, most terrifying thing you could ever do on a motorcycle. Other than racing Isle of Man, of course. But that's practically a death wish.

"I am so sorry," I told him with full sincerity. "Because yeah, I have a favorite racetrack, and Laguna Seca is definitely it. Specifically because of that evil bitch of a corkscrew."

*Shit, I shouldn't have said that.* But it was too late to pretend I didn't exactly have the beauty queen lexicon I was supposed to. At least Billy didn't balk at my colorful answer. His smile went from half-lit to full wattage, the rich depth in his voice swearing he meant every word. "Well, I'm glad y'all still get to ride it then. Since it's your favorite. And I...well, I really appreciate you coming out with me tonight, Taryn. It's a real honor."

A deep blush took my cheeks, not unlike the one he'd sparked when he'd picked me up.

His truck wasn't fancy, jacked up, or tricked out. It was a few years past needing full coverage and had the dents of a working man. But the floor mats were freshly vacuumed, and an air freshener was hanging from the rearview.

Still smelled like the dirty parts of a farm and some freshly spritzed Old Spice, but I appreciated the effort. And he'd never said anything about cleaning it for me or wanting to make a good impression on our date. No "Sorry about the mess" that wasn't there, so I'd say "What mess?" and we'd both act like we didn't know what was really going on. But in so many ways, Billy wasn't like anyone I'd ever met.

He wasn't trying to run circles around me like the cowboys at home or even flatter me into oblivion like the guys on the Superbike circuit. He didn't stare at me in the *hungry* way men usually watched me, either. Like they wanted to devour me—body, mind, and soul. It was more like how I felt when I saw him rope, like you were witnessing a miracle. And it was making me into something I didn't know I could still be. Hopeful, trusting, *romantic*.

I focused on the dirt beneath our feet, walking next to him and fidgeting with the long ends of my hair more than I could help. "You said that already."

"Well," he drawled, "I meant it."

I snorted and took his elbow when he extended it to me, mentally side-eyeing myself for falling for such a sappy maneuver. But there were worse things than sappy. And Billy made me feel like I was experiencing this for the first time all over again. No monsters behind me or in any of my closets, because he'd beaten them to the punch.

It wasn't true, but it felt like it.

Reality came crashing back when a guy ran up from out of freaking nowhere, planting himself in front of me and holding out his hands. "Miss! Miss, I gotta stop you! You're making a huge mistake!"

I jerked back, panic climbing up my throat as I clamped the hell out of Billy's bicep. Fight-or-flight responses waged war inside me, my mind quickly going down the list of things my self-defense coach said to watch for.

But this stalker stuff wasn't supposed to happen here. I was home, away from the circuit, where no one knew me!

"Mason, what are you doing?" Billy said, lightly tugging on my arm and winking at me.

I locked my jaw shut and sucked in air through my nose, forcing myself to breathe and think. It was possible my paranoia was getting out of control. But there were still the piles of letters at my parents' house. The threatening emails from strangers and random phone calls clogging up my cell phone. The endless barrage on social media. And there will always, *always* have been that guy outside my hotel room in London, standing there smiling with a length of rope coiled under his jacket and a bunch of chocolates the police said were laced with GHB.

If my manager, Mike, hadn't stepped out of the elevator behind me a second later, I don't know what would've happened. Well, I *know*, but I don't like to think about it. Too fucking scary.

This guy was a little smaller than Billy, and when I squinted against the setting sun to better see his face, he had the same blue eyes, same high cheekbones, same long nose, and same black hat. Name rang a bell, too. *Gotta be the brother.*

"Miss, you don't want to date this guy," Mason said, the sour stench of whiskey rolling off his breath. "His truck is older than Methuselah, he thinks deodorant and cologne are the same damn thing, I once saw him try to put lipstick on a duck, and he's banned from going to Applebee's in all fifty states. Not that it matters, because he'd rather eat chicken nuggets with *ranch* for every meal if he could. Now, by comparison, my truck actually has power steering *and* heated seats, I respect the choices of farm animals, I'm only banned from Walmart and Long John Silver's, and I'm a way better bull rider, dancer, *and* lover—"

"All right, that's enough," Billy growled.

He let go of me and took Mason by the shoulders, marching him off a step as Mason called back, "And the doctors still haven't figured out what the fungus is on his foot!"

A snicker burst from me, and I clapped my hands over my mouth to cover the sound, praying Billy didn't hear.

"*Git*, Mason!" He flung his brother's hat farther ahead, Mason scrambling after it.

"Dick!"

"Don't let me catch you drinking tonight," Billy warned, pointing at his brother's back.

*Too late*, I thought. Though Mason was clearly of age… Billy had to be in his late twenties at least, and Mason wasn't that much younger than him.

Whatever. It was their business.

Mason hooked his hat on his head, then started creeping backward toward the barn, pulling out a flask from somewhere behind him and grinning as he took a swig.

"Whatcha gonna do? Tell on me like when we got busted with Duke Bricker's Arabian?"

Billy's spine went rigid. "You were the one who stole it! I was trying to put him back!"

Mason cackled and took another swig like Billy's words were the furthest thing from the truth. "Sure, Brother. Whatever you say." Then he turned and disappeared into the barn.

Billy deflated, shifting his weight and clearing his throat when I slowly walked up next to him, doing my best to take in everything said between the two men—and all that wasn't.

"That's my little brother." Billy was looking down, a hand hooked on his belt as his other thumb flicked once at his nose. His eyes were hidden by the wide brim of his hat, and I wondered for a minute if that was why he wore it that way—not overly big so everyone could see him coming but big enough that he could disappear beneath it when he sometimes needed.

It killed me, standing there unable to do anything while his voice replayed in my memory, saying Mason was a better bull rider than him. But especially after meeting the brother in question, Billy's words sounded more wrong than ever. There wasn't anything about the junior King that seemed better than Billy to me in any way. Though I had some pretty strong suspicions Billy didn't know that in the slightest.

I nudged his arm, waiting until he looked at me. "He kinda sucks."

Surprise lit up Billy's eyes, but it was more thankful than anything else and just a touch mischievous. I spotted a faint flicker of the gleam I'd caught earlier, right before he'd roped. Because hidden somewhere inside this man, beneath the gentle manners and the country drawl, lived the heart of a racer. A competitor with the singular, driving need to win.

A need I knew so well—*too* well.

My eyes fell to his lips, thin and modest as they were, and my heart started aching for him to lean over and kiss me, even if just to make himself feel better. *Especially* to make himself feel better. I didn't mind, and then we could blow off the dance, and I could make us *both* feel a hell of a lot better.

But Billy just laughed it off, and he never said a bad word about his brother. "He's all right. Come on."

He took my hand and nodded toward the barn, and despite desire cussing at me for not suggesting we sneak off to somewhere more private, I let him playfully tug me along.

"So when did you start rac—" My voice cut off as we ducked under the crepe paper swags at the barn entrance, my breath entirely lost. Not that I wanted to breathe in that moment.

Thankfully, Billy said it for both of us. "*Dang*, you almost don't even notice the smell."

I stifled a laugh, entranced by the decorations that, as Billy so eloquently said, almost covered the dormant stench of moldy straw and horse manure. But strings upon strings of lights were draped across the rafters, mason jars set everywhere else and filled with flickering white candles. A band was playing on a makeshift stage, but most people were busy dancing, with a few couples showing off in the middle.

Billy smiled at me, wiggling his eyebrows for extra

measure—*dork*. "You ready to show these yokels how we do it back in Memphis?"

"Hell yeah." I held up my hand for a high five. "They have no idea what's coming for them."

Billy chuckled, his calloused palm meeting mine. It only took him a second to slip us onto the dance floor, melting us seamlessly into the crowd of folks spinning and twisting, some much faster than others. But Billy was slow, simple, and steady to the country love songs of my youth, his palm lightly cupping my neck under my hair, our other hands tangled together and held over his lower back. Two steps to the right, two to the left, Billy gently shuffling backward and asking me to come along.

"See?" He nodded at himself, satisfied. "Told you I was a great dancer."

A bright smile lit up my face, taking root somewhere a little lower and spreading out steadily through my chest. My cheeks were almost starting to hurt from him making me smile so much. "Mind-blowing."

He nodded again, more satisfied, and I couldn't figure it out. How he was doing everything wrong and backward, and I was totally falling for it. I'd never liked it before—when men would dance with their arm over my shoulder instead of putting their hand on my lower back. It felt funny and exposed and like they were trying to wrestle me or something. But with Billy, it was like he was opening a door for me.

He wasn't trying to touch me anywhere he shouldn't. He was barely touching me at all, the slight pressure of his fingertips on my neck telling me which way he wanted to go and teasing me every so often with acting like he was gonna massage his way up into my scalp but never freaking delivering.

The risk was all on him, too. My arms around his body instead of his around mine. Letting me choose whether I wanted to rest my hand on his concrete bicep and keep space between us or hook onto the sturdy swell of his shoulder and bring him all the way in.

He was so...*different*. And so damn *hot*.

"You don't really talk that much, do you?" I asked, already a little lost in the way his blue eyes looked silver under the lights and had never looked away from mine once.

"Well, the way I see it, everything I wanna say, George always says it better."

My brow furrowed for a minute until I paid closer attention to the song the band was playing: George Strait's "I Just Want to Dance With You."

It was so hard not to laugh at the cheesiness of it all, but it was so sweet nonetheless. He paid attention to everything. He listened.

With a firm promise to myself that I wouldn't get carried away, I slid my hand to his shoulder, bringing him in closer. Billy's grin grew deeper, our hands tangling a little tighter behind his back. But his eyes were soft and hopeful and still a little like he was waiting for me to vanish into a puff of smoke.

I practically needed a friggin' cigarette from what he was doing to my body.

Every graze of his fingers under my hair made lightning crackle down my spine, and I desperately craved the width of his whole hand, everywhere. My mind raced with images, my skin happy to imagine the scrape of callouses as he'd grasp my shirt and tear it off me. The strength in his hands as he'd palm my flesh and pull me close, crushing me against hard muscles worn by harder men.

His lips could've been my world, his stubble, my galaxy. And in the hot air of the barn, sticky with sweat and sweet with his cologne, I was shivering from each innocuous scrape of his jeans against mine until I couldn't take it anymore.

I looked away, my heart racing and too much heat in my cheeks, sure he would see. I didn't act like this: falling for random cowboys just because they smiled pretty on their golden horses, borrowed or not.

I may bed them, but I didn't fall for them. Not anymore.

Billy shifted a little closer, standing a little taller and touching his jaw to my temple. Need and want burned so hot through my body, I didn't remember deciding to fist my hand in his shirt or to lean my head deeper against his. But something in me must have known he was exactly what I had given up searching for.

Billy squeezed my hand behind his back, slowly settling my fingers on his belt before he let go. And when his arm wrapped around me until we were still dancing but mostly just holding each other, my battle was lost right then. Because nothing felt like it was supposed to.

I felt so *safe*, hugging his steel-hard body under clean, pressed cotton. My cheek on his shoulder and my face hidden by the wide brim of his hat, not knowing how we weren't bumping into everyone around us but trusting Billy to protect me nonetheless.

We could've danced forever, and it would've been fine with me.

---

"I had a real nice time…"

I chuckled at Billy's words and leaned against my

family's RV, dark as the rest of them and sleepily quiet. "You said that already."

"Well," Billy drawled, "I meant it."

I laughed again, kinda loving watching him squirm under the Kentucky moonlight and wondering how much he was regretting his earlier promise of "I won't try nothing."

I definitely was. He hadn't tried a thing all night.

We'd danced a lot and talked even more about racing, our horses, traveling, rodeos, and me graduating from Baylor. And he'd bought us some waters, but he never so much as looked at a beer. He'd been a perfect gentleman.

*Too* perfect.

"Billy?"

His head snapped up from where he'd been fidgeting with his hand, picking at the cuticle on his thumb. The wind was all but dead, the season too young for crickets, and my voice was so loud in the dark air lingering between us. But I wasn't interested in pretending with Billy anymore; my truth seemed safe with him, and I was ready to hear his.

"What is it you want?"

"Sorry, I don't follow your meaning."

"With me."

He half smiled, half shrugged, looking down and muttering, "Nothing. Told you: just wanted a dance."

Since we were apparently showing off our *terrible* acting skills, I let out a dramatic sigh. "That's too bad. 'Cause I was kinda hoping you were gonna ask for more."

His eyes lifted to mine, sparkling with adrenaline and a drop of danger that I was impatient to ignite. "Phone number?"

"Sure."

His smile lit up another notch, a little more crooked and a lot more sexy, and I waited as he pulled a cell phone from his back pocket, unlocking it and handing it over. Not the super latest version of anything and with a well-tested camo OtterBox case around it.

*Holy crap, his wallpaper is a selfie of him with his freaking horse? Ha!*

"Wait." I stopped, serious. "You're not gonna send me dick pics, are you?"

He snorted and looked away, shaking his head and seeming more embarrassed than I knew was possible for a bull rider-turned MotoPro racer. "*Damn*, girl. I can't believe you just said that."

I couldn't help laughing. "Well? I have to ask now, because unfortunately, it wouldn't be the—"

"No, ma'am," he interrupted, his voice stern enough that I knew he wasn't screwing with me. "I wouldn't do that. I just figured maybe I'd call you once in a while."

I arched an eyebrow at the last part, putting my real number in his phone. He totally said call, not text. Hope he meant it. Phone sex was *fun* and a necessary evil when I traveled so much for the circuit. Plus, I bet his accent sounded even better when he was talking dirty. "Once in a while, huh?"

"Well, I didn't wanna presume anything."

"Sounds to me like you've got a bad habit of cutting your legs out from under you." I held out his phone at arm's length and took a quick selfie, saving it to the new contact. It wasn't great, thanks to the lack of light, but it was clearly me—not photoshopped or airbrushed, padded or provocatively posed with Colton's hands smeared all over me. "Here you are."

Billy took his phone, smiling at the photo before he locked the screen, and put it back in his pocket. "Thank you. That was real kind."

I snorted and leaned against the RV once more, indefensibly full of butterflies for being an adult on an elementary date and allowing myself to get completely swept up in it regardless. "You're too much, Billy King."

"I promise you, I'm not."

"No, you are." I meant what I was about to say, but I threw him a wink to ease the blow. "You're almost too kind to believe, and I'm starting to wonder if all I'm hearing are sugar-sweet lies."

Billy laughed, giving me half an eye roll. "Oh, so I'm too nice?"

"Yup."

He shifted his weight, his eyes darting low and to the left again. "I haven't heard that one before."

*And the bullshit radar goes ping!* I tilted my head, grinning as I made a mental note of his most obvious tell. "You dirty rotten liar."

Billy cracked up, holding up his hands. "Okay, so maybe I've heard it, but it doesn't mean I agree."

I chuckled along with him, amazed how the white lies tumbled from his lips like prayers from a preacher. "Uh-huh."

Billy laughed harder, his eyes catching mine while an unnamable force looped around us and tied a bow until we weren't really laughing anymore, but we couldn't seem to stop smiling at each other, either.

My whole heart was thumping strong in my chest while everything in me begged to kiss him. But I couldn't bring myself to make the first move—I wanted Billy to *go for it.* To step up and take the risk and feel all the elation of me rewarding it with full-on acceptance because for once, what a guy wanted was exactly what I wanted, too.

He let out a deep sigh that was almost more of a groan, sinking my hopes. "You're not making this easy on me at all, are you?"

"Making what easy?"

He looked away, unable to hide his smile. "Nothing."

It was too much fun; I couldn't resist. The way he was, the way he made me feel. "You want to kiss me, Billy?"

He grinned at the ground. Probably, I was pushing too hard, too fast, but I didn't really know any other way to go. Not when I wanted him to kiss me that damn bad.

When he lifted his head, there was no fear in his blue eyes. Just a pure kind of acceptance that he wasn't going to be happy until he got what he wanted. "Yes, ma'am. I do."

My heartbeat took off as Billy stepped closer, his hat hiding both of us from the February moon. The rich scent of him was too tempting: I pulled it deep into my lungs, drowning in the masculinity rippling off him. But he still wasn't touching me, no matter how much I wanted him to.

"Would that be all right?" he whispered.

I don't remember nodding or breathing, just beaming at him and praying my self-restraint could hold on a little bit longer. "I'll answer that in a minute."

Billy smiled, and then I finally got everything I'd been craving. He brushed his fingertips over my cheek with a touch softer than the wishing petals of a dandelion, hooking a knuckle under my chin and tilting my lips up to his. My eyelashes fluttered closed, my pulse thundering through my veins as I waited and waited, desperate for the first crash of his mouth against mine.

All I felt was space between us, growing longer and wider until it just wasn't anymore—the first brush of his lips so soft, I wasn't even sure that I'd felt him. But Billy was there, his kiss as slow as his drawl, careful and gentle, and little more than a sip of an ocean I was eager to disappear into.

I took his jaw between my palms, prickly with stubble but sculptured and strong. Drawing him down to me, I quickly melted into the shocking plumpness of what I'd considered to be thin lips but now felt rich and deep, and a whole new shade of delicious. Then he *moaned*, his hands squeezing my waist and pressing me up into him. It was like embracing iron, rippled and smooth, the bite of his buckle scraping my belly, and my hips pressing hungrily toward the long, thick swell growing behind his zipper.

He took a needy gasp for air, and I hugged him closer, slipping my tongue into his mouth. A growl churned from low in his throat as the kiss turned dirtier, the strike of his tongue and bite of his lips getting wonderfully sharp. But not sharp enough for what I wanted when my body was catching fire everywhere he touched me: his wide palm secure on my lower back, his other hand buried in my hair and massaging my scalp.

He felt so good, *too* good. And he hadn't grabbed my ass *once*.

"You know"—I leaned back, my hand on his chest and Billy breathing hard, blinking at me with his hands suspended in place—"you don't kiss like a bull rider."

His brow furrowed, the slightest spark of suspicion in his eyes. "How many bull riders you kissing?"

*Nice.*

"Hopefully none."

He half rolled his eyes, but he was smiling again as he settled his hands on my waist, his thumbs petting the space leading to my hips. All trace of jealousy totally and completely gone, thank God. "All right, what do you got against bull riders?"

I did my best to calm my libido—which wasn't helped by tapping his rock-solid chest with a single finger. But I wanted to set the record straight before we stumbled into a problem. I was never going back to that life, not when I had waited nine hours for Travis to wake up and not when I had been more terrified than I knew a person could be when Jace was airlifted. "You put your bull above everything else. And I'm telling you right now, Billy King, no eight-second bull ride is ever going to come before me."

Billy didn't groan, didn't flinch, didn't blink. He just nodded. "Okay."

"I'm serious."

Serious as Bonnie Landry's black funeral dress and the poem she brokenly read over Beau's glistening coffin.

"Yeah?" Billy drawled, but his smile was clearly teasing as his hands slid from my waist to lock somewhere over my lower back. He pulled me closer until I was nearly gasping from the tease of his erection against my hip, straining his zipper and parching my mouth. His eyebrow arched in the picture of confidence, then he leaned down close enough to kiss me again, whispering against my lips, "Good thing I'm not a bull rider no more…"

*Good thing indeed.*

I dissolved fully into Billy's lips, lost in the gentle press of his palm coming up to cradle my cheek. The sweet scrape of cowboy callouses had me shivering and reckless,

Billy slowly starting to kiss me more desperately until he had me tucked hard against him, and I was ready to let him have me right there in the freaking open.

Why hadn't I stopped us from going into the dance or left it early in favor of a dark tack room nearby? And now I had to leave—Australia was calling, along with the curves of the Phillip Island track.

When I pulled back from him, I was filled with regret, riddled with longing, and already hating so much that I didn't know when I'd get to see him again. "I gotta go," I whispered.

Billy nodded, his voice thick and more than a little breathless. "Me too. To Malaysia."

I cracked up laughing—the randomness of his response way beyond anything I'd had a guy try to pull on me before. "Right. To Malaysia."

"I'm serious," he said with a chuckle. "I gotta go do my testing in Sepang before we race in Qatar."

*Okay, that actually made sense.*

"And I know it isn't right to ask a woman to wait on a man, but since you're a busy woman, I figured maybe it'd be okay, just this once."

My stomach tightened as Billy bit his lip, already nervous over whatever he was nervous to ask. He had to have a catch somewhere, and it was getting harder to remember that when his hands petting my waist felt like pure heaven.

"I'm about to be gone for a while," he said, "but I'd really, *really* like to see you once I get back to Memphis. If you're back, too."

A devilish thought hit my mind, images of midnight surf and my white bikini in a pile on a bungalow floor already tantalizing me, and I couldn't keep it from slipping out of my lips. "Well, I happen to be heading to Phillip Island for my own testing and race in Australia. Wanna meet me in Jakarta when you're done in Qatar? I know a great little beach resort, super private."

Billy laughed. "No, ma'am. That I'm gonna have to pass on."

"*What?* How come? Indonesia is, like, an entire world better than anywhere else on this planet."

He squinted up from under thick brown eyelashes. "Because I don't know where the good places to take you are? At home, I know which creeks don't get overrun with tourists and what walking paths are okay for your horse's feet without fouling up their shoes. And I don't have my horse in Jakarta, so I can't take you riding at sunset to a cicada choir."

Everything in me melted even more, and I didn't even care that he was making me wait for our next date just for his pride. The look in his eyes swore he'd make it worth it.

I slid my hands up his ruggedly solid chest, loving every thump of his heart under my palms and the smile in his eyes growing bright when I stretched up on my toes, eager to kiss him again. "All right, then."

"Thank you," he breathed.

"Billy, shut up and just kiss me."

He chuckled, bumping my nose with his and holding me a little tighter. "Yes, ma'am."

*Goddamn*, could that man use his tongue in incredible ways: never rushing or bullying, just going so slow, so deliberate and soft and thick, it was almost *too* intense.

Couldn't wait to see what else he could do with it...

*Oh God, I'm never going to be able to stop.*

I stole a last kiss from Billy's addictive lips before I

slipped out from under his arm, turning for the door while I still had the ability. "Bye."

"Oh, now, see, I don't like that word," he said playfully.

I pivoted back, tilting my head and unable to wipe the grin off my face. Whenever I was gonna see him again, it wouldn't come quick enough. "Talk to you soon?"

He grinned, already walking backward toward his truck and touching a finger to his hat. "Thanks for the dance."

There wasn't a word big enough for how much trouble my heart was in.

My poor vibrator, too.

# Chapter 5

"YOU WANNA DANCE?"

"Yeah, I do."

Taryn waits as I get down from the bar stool, the shadow of a smirk curling her lips when I lead her to the dance floor. I'm not sure what that look's about, but I'm sure she'll let me know when she's good and ready. In the meantime, I'm not looking a gift horse in the mouth.

I'm only gonna get so many chances to convince her that leaving me is even worse than what I did in the first place, and I'm not about to waste this one. Even if we are at Up-Chuck Buck's, choking on smoke and the stench of sour whiskey.

She turns toward me once we're in the middle of all the couples, like we've done so many times—my palm slipping under her hair as she hooks onto my shoulder, our clasped hands held low over my back instead of hers, because she's always been more comfortable that way.

I lace my fingers through Taryn's, and something in me softens at the cool band of her Aunt Sylvie's ruby ring. Taryn never takes it off, and it's almost cruel how much I've missed the little stuff like that. But it also makes me wonder what she's told her cousin April about us. The same cousin whose wedding I missed because of the damn "incident."

"I, um..." I start. But with one sharp look from Taryn,

my apologies die flat on my tongue, swelling thick in my mouth with the weight of all of them.

Everything is just so *wrong*. The lights are too low, neon signs tinting her hair unnatural colors. And there are so many people, the temperature's a good ten degrees hotter than it should be. I also can't seem to move us without some stranger brushing up against her in some way. I hate that. She's not exactly a fan of it, either.

I keep my steps small, my ankle already protesting and my eyes on the people around us instead of Taryn. But no one's looked at her like they know her, except for Mason—twirling around some girl I've never seen before and giving me a thumbs-up like I'm not dancing on death row. The music's also some new singer I don't recognize, like a Clint Black wannabe mixed with Imagine Dragons, but it's still country, so I guess that's fine. Doesn't really change the fact that I can't even enjoy holding her again, I'm so on edge from everything.

"This all we gonna do?" Taryn asks after a minute. "Shuffle around? I thought we were gonna *dance*."

Nothing about her words or her voice is as sweet as she tried to make it sound, and just like at the bar, she doesn't even sound like *her*. I nearly sigh out loud, wishing there was an easier way for us to get through this.

She wants to march me out front and yell at me? Fine. I've got a couple of things I want to say, too. Like she's gotta know that in some way, she's taking all this too damn far. But she also knows I never turn down an opportunity to dance with her, and I'm not steering off course when she's clearly directing my every move. "All right."

I check around and shift us over to make sure we've got plenty of space, and Taryn's grinning like she's going in for her kill. Scares the shit out of me and has always made me glad we don't race against each other.

It's two beats for the chorus to start, and then we're off, Taryn spinning out under my arm, twirling back and ducking as I twist around her. It's killing my ankle to do this and giving me way too many flashbacks of how I was feeling before my knee surgery—the one I put off for almost too long, causing it to take even longer to recover from. But this is worth it for a catch of her hand here, a tug on her hip there, and all while she's flying around me as others whoop and holler at her golden hair crackling the air like summertime heat lightning.

Every move with her is so easy, but I...I can't seem to remember when we learned all the steps. I know it wasn't like this in the beginning. Everything about the way we dance now, it's all so damn *complicated*.

Taryn twirls into me, her back to my chest and my arm across her hips, and thank God for that, because my ankle is *killing* me, and I'm wincing with every step. But I can't quit, not when I'm this close to winning her back.

She takes my hand and tries to twirl out under it, but I catch her and hold her instead of letting her go. "What's wrong, Billy?" she asks, a little out of breath as she drapes an arm around my neck and goes back to our starting speed.

I shove the truth as far from my brain as I can muster, looking deep into her eyes and thinking over all our greatest hits: our first dance, first kiss, the first time I told her I loved her. Not my ankle, grinding and sore, crumbling apart under me. Right now, that truth would end everything. "Nothing. Just wanted to slow down for a second. See your face. I missed you."

"Uh-huh. And nothing's wrong with your foot, either."
She smiles like she does when she finally breaks a tough
colt, and instantly, I know I'm busted.

Her voice echoes in my head from not ten minutes ago:
*"Walk away, huh?"*

No doubt about it, she brought me out here just to
prove she knows I'm hurting. And apparently doing a
crappy job of hiding it from her. She's always doing this
shit to me. Like she's never stretched the truth once in her
whole life.

I go to spin her out, but she plants her feet and stays
locked into me, and she's not going anywhere. "Nice try.
But I saw you limping when you were coming up to the
training pen, and you were hobbling your way over to the
bar when you got here and thought I wasn't looking. But it
isn't the same side as your surgery, so why the hell are you
acting like you need a pair of crutches?"

I let a breath out through my nose, adjusting my grip on
her, since she seems to be settled in for the long haul. Then
I say the first excuse that comes to mind. "I got a blister."

"Liar."

I peer down at her, my patience all but gone when I'm
already jet-lagged from racing home from freaking Spain.
"*Damn*, woman. Let me alone, will you?"

She yanks me closer, her tone sharp and eyes blazing.
"You want to rethink that question before I take you up
on it?"

I grit my jaw and look away, Taryn all but leading us
as we dance now. The people she was talking to when I
first got here are staring—Maggie and…John? Maggie
and Jake? Could be Jingle Bell for all I care. I fake a smile
their way.

"What's wrong with your foot, Billy?"

"It isn't my foot, all right?" I grit out. "It's my ankle. And it's fine."

"Oh, it's *fine*—"

"Yeah, it's fine!"

Taryn stops us dead in the middle of the busy dance floor, glaring me into the ground. Then she hooks her arm through mine, marching me off toward the exit.

*Fuck.* I'm ready to pass out with every step, and I tug my hat lower as she waves off the bouncer, pulling me out into the parking lot.

My lungs hurry to swallow the crisp night air, and I blink a little faster to calm my eyes in the wind. The rest of me is mostly worried about Taryn getting cold when she's only wearing a long-sleeved shirt and no jacket. But she always gets pissed when I say stuff like that, so I stay quiet as she unhooks her arm from mine and nudges me toward the back of her truck.

"Get your sorry ass up here," she says, laying down the tailgate. "And let me see."

I hop up and scowl at her like I don't wanna, even though I've wanted her to check it for a while. I just didn't want to do it outside Up-Chuck Buck's with a bunch of drunk cowboys snickering over their bottlenecks while they stand outside smoking.

"Take that crappy old boot off."

"I'm going," I tell her, not even bothering to hide my grimace as I slide it off.

Taryn jerks back like she's seen a snake. "The fuck is that?"

Except she's not staring at my battered old Ariats. She's staring at the wooden paint stick duct-taped to my foot and up around my leg. For support.

"You like it?" I'm nearly out of breath from the agony of just getting my boot off. *Screw it.* I collapse on her tailgate, exhausted from limping all damn day and acting like it's fine when it's not. Nothing is. "I'm thinking of making it into a patent."

"That's the most irresponsible damn thing I have ever seen. Get it off your leg."

I roll my eyes at the stars above me but unhook my knife from my pocket, handing it over. I wait as Taryn carefully slices the tape up the edge of the paint stick until it peels back, unsticking from my sock. Wish they were cleaner. At least she won't know they don't match.

Taryn throws my cobbled-together splint farther into the bed of her truck, the paint stick clanging off the tool-box and rattling to a stop by her spare tire. She snaps my knife closed, then holds it out to me. Still kinda threaten-ing, though. "Don't ever do that again. You hear me?"

I nod, taking it from her and hooking it back where it goes, then pillowing my head with my hand so I can see her. "Yes, ma'am."

She sighs and swishes her long sheet of shiny blond hair over her shoulder, her hands impatiently planted backward on her waist. "Take off your sock."

"No way!"

"Billy, I've seen you naked as the day you were born. Lose the sock."

I peek toward the bar, the bouncer still watching us from the door and probably seconds away from calling the cops on me "for harassing her." Wouldn't be the first time, since she loves yelling at me outside honky-tonks.

"I promise I'll be gentle," she adds.

I take one more glance around, but most people have

started to ignore us since we're not cussing or kissing. No sign of Mason and his big ol' loves-to-gossip-to-the-press mouth, thank Christ. "Fine."

I groan and sit up, taking off my sock and stuffing it into my boot. Glad I can't see the disappointment sure to be all over Taryn's face when she sucks in a staggered breath, then quietly says, "Oh, Billy. What have you done?"

I swallow thickly, my voice low with the shame rotting my gut. "You know what I done."

She doesn't say anything else, and it takes all my courage to make myself look at her. But she's not giving me the I-told-you-so I was sure was coming. She's too busy frowning at my foot, her hands gently reaching out to my ankle—purple and bruised and swollen and hurting even worse thanks to what *she's* done.

"You insisting on a dance marathon in there probably didn't help it," I remind her, just because she's always right, and sometimes, she needs to remember she can be wrong, too.

This apparently was not the smartest moment to attempt that risky maneuver. Taryn straightens and glares at me, then pushes me square in the chest. Not hard, but still. "Jackass. How the hell was I supposed to know you're walking around with a broken ankle? It is not my fault you're always lying to me."

*Broken…? Shit.*

"I don't lie to you," I counter. "I protect you. There's a difference."

She huffs out a breath. "Lying about lying aside, do I look like I need protecting?"

I know what she wants me to say. But I'm not saying it. Not tonight. "Sometimes."

Her temper flares in her eyes, and she turns away, growling curse words. I hold my breath. She's fuming real good now, in the way only I seem to be able to get her to do. But I swore I'd never take for granted that she shows me the real her, imperfect and demanding and flawed, and I won't disrespect that trust by using it against her.

When she comes back, she sticks her finger in my face, her voice strained with trying to keep from yelling. "That is an argument for another night. And we're gonna have it. So you remember you've got that coming."

Future *anything*? I'm there. "Fine," I snap like I'm upset.

She blows out a breath and goes back to looking at my ankle, her touch still careful as she inspects every part of it: following from my leg where the color is fine, then fades and deepens to purples and reds like the worst parts of a storm blowing in, clouding up the Doppler.

But it's not her hands that have me so mesmerized; I barely feel what she's doing. It's the focus in her eyes, her mind asking a thousand questions about what's wrong with me and looking through all the files in all her memories of all the endless stuff she knows for some kind of answer.

I've never known anyone as smart as Taryn, and it's saved our asses more times than I want to admit. Usually because I was doing something that she told me not to do in the first place. But she's always forgiven me for it afterward, especially if I had a good reason. *Always.*

The wind picks up a little, swirling peaches and lavender around us, and I can't keep the question inside me anymore. "Why are you leaving me, Taryn?" The words hang between us like we're the only two people in the parking lot. In the country. In the whole world. "How are you just gonna... go?"

She doesn't answer. Not right away at least.

Her eyes flash up to mine, then down to her hands, hovering over the darkest spot. "Does this hurt?"

Pain rips through my ankle, and I hiss through my teeth.

"Okay, okay, I'm sorry!"

She quickly moves her hands higher up my leg where it's safe, giving me a second to blow out a breath and stare at the stars to get the nausea under control. Then she softly sniffles.

Must be allergies. She's got a problem with mold, and sometimes cedar. Got a problem with gluten, too, but that makes her yack, not sniffle.

"Stay here."

I nod, watching her over my shoulder as she walks around to the passenger side of her truck and opens the back door. Where she keeps her first aid kit. It doesn't take her but a second to grab it, slamming the door once she's got it, and I wince and keep my mouth shut when she comes around to my side.

Back to Plan A: *act like it didn't happen, and maybe it didn't.*

She sets the kit next to me on the tailgate, popping it open and taking out a whole bunch of stuff that doesn't seem necessary. But I still let her press a big cotton pad the size of a diaper over my ankle. It also covers most of my foot and the bottom part of my leg. "Hold that there. Don't move."

I do as she says, Taryn switching to wrapping an ACE bandage over the top of the pad. Which isn't so bad and starts to make my ankle feel a little better, until I realize just how damn bulky it is. "How am I supposed to get my boot on?"

"You're not." She taps the top of my hand, and I sigh

and let go of the pad, getting out of her way. "When you get home tonight, I want you to ice it for twenty minutes and keep it elevated."

I bite the inside of my lip, kinda wanting to ask about the chances of us going home together and her icing it for me while I list off all the ways I'm sorry. But I'm not pushing it. At least I got to dance with her.

When she finishes, she tilts her head at it, then *hmpfs* like she guesses it's okay. "Any better?"

"Yeah." She's not yelling at me. Things are *a lot* better.

"All right." She crosses her arms and stares me down. "This isn't good, Billy. You need to see a doctor."

I grin from ear to ear, firmly on Plan A. "Just saw my favorite one."

She doesn't crack a bit. "I've told you: I'm not a doctor, and it's not the same. You need X-rays. Maybe surgery. Yesterday."

I swallow at the fateful words I've heard before, looking down and loathing how I can't even get her to smile now. "It'll be fine. Just needs some rest. And I'll ice it and prop it up like you said, I swear."

"Billy, what is wrong with you? It's not just gonna get better. You have to deal with this. I'm telling you—you get down off a horse the wrong way or your bike slips out from under you, and your ankle? It could shatter."

I look up on instinct, because that's just freaking scary, and it doesn't help that she's always right and probably is this time, too.

"What's Frank say?"

I clear my throat, tugging on the brim of my hat and trying to think of something. Anything. But my arsenal of ready-to-go excuses is bone dry. "Hi?"

Her eyes flare, that temper of hers right back to blazing. "Billy!"

I scowl at the parking lot. "I hate when you say my name like it's a damn curse word."

"I cannot believe that after everything you've gone through these past two years, with the surgeries and the specialists and the physical therapists and the second surgery because you didn't listen to anyone after the first, that *once again*, you haven't told him you're hurt. Did you tell him that you—"

"No, I did not," I snap at her, Taryn's spine going ramrod straight because I hardly raise my voice at her, ever. I may egg her on, but I really try not to yell. "You know I can't do that."

"But—"

"I'm not gonna live my life as another damn borrower, Taryn! They've taken my ropes, and they're already trying to take my bike, too. But I'll be damned if I have to crawl on my belly when I should be man enough to help myself. I want my things to be mine, for Gidget to be *mine*. And I can't bring home a horse with no land to put him on, and I can't buy us our dream ranch if I lose my damn job. *No*."

She drops her face into her hands, shaking her head slowly before she tosses her hair, looking up at me. "When push comes to shove, it's not gonna matter what your job is, what people think of you—your father included—or how much money you got in your wallet. You're never gonna get anywhere unless you can figure how to start standing up for yourself, start telling the truth, and start making some apologies. And…buy some new damn boots!"

"All I've done is apologize, but you won't forgive me!"

"Because you're still not—you know what? No. Get off

my truck." She grabs the first aid kit and my abominable boot, shoving both at my chest and shoving me until I'm toppling off her tailgate, wobbling to catch my balance on my one good foot.

"Okay, I'm down!"

She slams her tailgate shut, snatching the first aid kit from my hands and hurling it into the bed. "Go home, Billy. You're not my problem anymore."

I rock backward in everything I thought I knew, something in my chest splitting wide apart and leaving me scraped raw as she stomps toward her driver's door, yanking it open.

We've had our fights, and I know we're going through something right now, but...

"Is that what I was? Your *problem*?"

She stops with her hand on the door, her hair shimmering down her back.

The winter wind is raging like a storm's coming in, music pouring from the bar and a jacked-up diesel rolling by with high school kids hollering out the back. But all I can hear is those words.

*Not my problem anymore.*

They're louder than the pack of Harley cruisers creeping by on the road, their engines throaty and crackling. And the longer Taryn keeps her back to me, the more something starts to change in the space between where we're standing. Memories of all the times I spent racing home to her flash through my mind, flying far away from my fans and my career and my future.

I look away from her, the bikers pulling in and parking one by one in a long row. And under the call of their horsepower, it builds and builds—the pain, the betrayal, the embarrassment and the shame—until it comes blasting out of me.

"That's a damn fine thing to say to someone you said you loved! *Christ*, Taryn. I don't care how mad you are. That isn't right!"

Her head hangs, but she still doesn't turn to tell me she's sorry, and I can barely stand to look at her, I'm so hurt by what she said.

She knows damn well how it's been for me in my life. That it never seems to matter to anyone that I do my best not to complain, not wanting to cause stress for people who already have plenty to stress about. She used to say it wasn't being honest, keeping that stuff to myself, that it was important to share it with her because it was part of being together. But here we are now, and the truth comes out.

Nine months, and I was nothing but a problem.

That ends today.

"You know what?" I say. "You win. It's over!"

Nausea swarms my throat, shock hitting me when I realize what just came out of my mouth, and I already know: I can't take it back.

It's the same bottomless feeling I had in North Carolina when I knew I'd crossed the line, the same emptiness that plagued me the whole ride home because I knew what I would be coming home *to*.

The entire trip, I prayed she'd listen, that she'd understand how after getting so twisted up in the pressure of the moment that you do the worst possible option out of all of them. But Taryn never makes the wrong decision. Especially when she has to choose between what's right and saving something really, really important. Even if it means possibly losing everything.

Her shoulders slump even further toward the pavement, and I grit my teeth through tugging on my boot as best I can, limping toward Mason's truck.

"Billy, wait!"

I don't get far before Taryn comes running up and plants herself in front of me, looking so ashamed that I'm having a hard time reminding myself why I've never been so mad at her.

"You were never my problem," she says. And then the world turns upside down, or maybe it's time that turns back, because she *kisses* me—her hands on my jaw tugging me down until she gets tired of waiting and takes what she wants, wrapping her arms around my neck and pulling herself up, a sharp strike of her tongue stinging me to life.

I find my arms and circle them around her waist, hugging her up into me and kissing her with all the longing that's been plaguing my soul since the first time she said I'd never touch her again, filled to the brim with gratitude as she melts a little more, fully mine.

*God*, I've been so scared, more scared than I've been letting on to anyone, especially her. For a moment there, I really thought I'd lost her. That we were over.

I'm not ready for it when she slows me down, her breaths shaky when she pulls back. I press a kiss to her forehead, desperate to take her home and spend the rest of the night, the next three months—hell, my whole life— making all this up to her.

"Billy, you were my *everything*." Her voice cracks over the last word, her blue eyes lifting up to mine.

I've still never gotten used to hearing her say that, and I brush a stray hair from her face, unable to ignore the goose bumps on her neck. I need to get her home, get her warm.

"But I wasn't yours."

The words hit like thunder, cracking apart the sky and the shaking the ground beneath my feet. "Honey, *no*! That's not—"

"Your ankle says it all, Billy. I wasn't enough."

Something, everything, in me just broke.

My heart is leaping terrified in my chest, and I drop my hands from her shoulders to her belt loops, frantically tightening my grip on her because I can already tell, I'm losing her.

It's happening, *again*.

"Taryn, I didn't have a—"

"You had a choice, Billy. It wasn't easy, I'm sure. But you had a choice. And you knew what would happen, and you didn't choose *me*." Her voice is so calm at the end, so accepting, it sounds like death.

I know it for sure when she pulls her hands from my chest and starts pulling mine from her. "Honey, *please*..."

"Please don't call me anymore," she whispers. "I just...I can't. And I wish it could be that simple, Billy. I really do—that I could just forgive you and we could go back to how it was. But it's not...it's just *not*."

I hate how much she looks like she means that. How much it's killing her to say it. "What do you need? Tell me, and I'll do it."

She shakes her head. "I need more time, I need...I need to feel *safe*." She takes a broken breath, and I hate how much truth is in that, too. But she still reaches up and cups my cheek in her palm, and I cover her hand with mine, soaking her up while I still can. "Please always be careful, no matter what you're doing." I nod, not trusting my voice as Taryn stretches up and brushes a last kiss across my lips, trembling through her tears. It doesn't last nearly long enough before she takes a step back, slipping all the way out of my touch. "Bye, Billy."

The words are barely more than a gasp before she turns and runs, and it's like a fire burning up my chest and turning all of me to ash when she gets in her truck and drives away. I still see it, even though my eyes are prickling and my throat's burning, my stomach rolling like I could puke at any second.

A bunch of drunk cowboys laugh from the door of the bar as I stare after her exhaust and all the shining stars that just witnessed that, wondering how the fuck I'm supposed to fix things now.

Everything, just *everything*—my ankle, my relationship, my whole life—it's all so goddamn broken, and I don't…

I don't even know where to start. I don't know how to do anything without her anymore.

# Chapter 6

*Taryn Ledell—Back Then*

KENTUCKY WAS LIGHT-YEARS AWAY.

"*Magnifique*, Colton," the photographer praised my teammate again. The press room was pitch-black, neon streaks running down the dark walls with our six-foot-high numbers propped against them. Sweltering lights blasted from the ceiling, our bikes docked beside us, and a giant fan blew the potent scent of som tam and gai yang and, like, four different curries and a shit ton of rice that were set up on the craft services table.

Everything we'd done a hundred times before, but I was having a harder time than ever swallowing the price of it all. Especially with Colton's hand glued to my hip.

*One night.* How could one night with one guy, two years before, be such a damn mistake?

He kept towering over me as my gaze burned a hole into the wall behind his shoulder, Colton wearing the exact same leathers I did, apart from the different patches of his individual sponsors. His muddy hair was waxed, flat-ironed, and expertly tousled, and his whole soul reeked of some cologne I couldn't name but was sure he'd probably paid too much for at the outlet mall in his New Jersey hometown.

"Taryn, arch your back, head up, up, up!"

*Ugh.* I wondered what Billy's press shoots were like. Probably forward facing and not a single close-up of the swell of his dick in his leathers. Opposed to my infinite portfolio of side-boob shots.

"What is wrong with you today?" Colton lugged me closer, my stomach complaining and the gluten wrecking my system threatening to rear its ugly head once more. Hopefully all over my so-called teammate. "Is this about that guy you met?"

*Dolly Parton, give me strength.*

I hadn't wanted to tell Colton about Billy—it was so completely none of his goddamn business—but it was a convenient way to get him to back off once we landed in Australia and started our press circuit for the season. Or I thought it would be.

All it had actually done was spur on his advances *more*; he hadn't been able to shut up about me and Billy since leaving Phillip Island and heading to Thailand for the Chang International Circuit. I probably should've expected it when Colton lived to win, and I had accidentally served up a new rival to overtake. But as far as I was concerned, there was never a competition in the first place.

If there *was*, Colton had totally lost two years before. Right around the time he stopped going down on me, moments before I was gonna climax, only to say, "You cool with butt stuff?"

No, I was not cool with "butt stuff."

"Yo, hold up!" Sheldon called. I peeked over to find my publicist jogging my way. "Just a minute there, baby girl." He smacked his gum in my face in a way that dripped of his New York advertising roots, fidgeting with my helmet and messing with my hair-sprayed ponytail. "See you been hitting the gym, eh?"

I closed my eyes, praying again for strength, or maybe

peace, or anything to keep my tongue and fists still as he pinched at my leathers over my hips and *tugged up*, making my wedgie even worse. And no, I hadn't been hitting the gym. I'd been hitting the toilet with nonstop diarrhea and puking since someone had *lied* to me at some point the day before, and I had been glutened.

Totally and completely glutened.

"All right, baby girl, ass is looking tight now," Sheldon said.

My temper roared in my veins, and I bit my tongue to keep it still.

"There we go, that's the money shot…"

I didn't have to look to see it: Sheldon backing up, smacking his gum and his hands out in front of him like he was a movie director framing a scene. One that showed only my ass.

Colton tightened his grip on me. "So tell me more about this new guy."

I blocked the spice of his cologne and remembered in detail the pine of an air freshener, dangling from a rearview.

"Did you tell him about me?" Colton asked.

I glanced up, disgusted by the smugness in his grin. Five more minutes. Then I was free. "No."

"Hey, Taryn! Actually, yeah, look at each other," Sheldon called out. "This is gonna be great—their chemistry is *fantastic*!"

"Now, that doesn't seem right," Colton breathed. His hand on my hip spread a little wider, his thumb hidden from the camera dipping a little lower. Toward my parted thighs. "If I was him, I'd want to know that you fucked your teammate."

My heart screamed in my chest, and all I wanted was to

shove at his. I'd been new to the sport—young, vulnerable, reeling with culture shock—and he totally took advantage of me. I found out pretty damn quick who he really was.

But it didn't matter how much I hated him. It didn't matter how much I wanted to punch that smirk off his face. I wasn't in a position to throw fits. Not if I wanted to keep my job.

"Taryn, if you could now turn around, s'il vous plaît." The photographer twirled his finger at me.

*Finally.* I knocked Colton's hand from my hip and turned all the way forward, moving my helmet between us, determined not to listen to another word out of his wretched mouth. I was a professional, and I could get through the photo shoot. Then his ass was mine on the track: three practice sessions, two superpoles, two races, and there was only going to be one winner as far as I was concerned. Anyone but him.

"Hands on hips, perfect!" the photographer hailed. Sheldon whispered his way, then threw me another thumbs-up. "Lean to me, yes! Fierce eyes, Colton, *fierce*. So perfect. You're gorgeous, Taryn, *gorgeous*! Now, open your mouth for me, *chérie*."

*The fuck?* Who stands around with their mouth open like they were a frog catching flies? But I knew exactly what this was about and what Sheldon hoped men would imagine *putting* in my mouth and why they would buy countless magazines to do so.

My eyes searched for my manager as Colton snickered, everything in me so far past exhausted and with so much more in the day still left to do. But between the Thai makeup girls, the hair stylist, and the modelesque assistant hired to guard the cappuccino machine no one had even looked at, Mike was nowhere to be found. The jagged line in my heart cracked a little further.

A room full of people, and no one to save me.

There wasn't anything else to do. I told myself, like I'd done too many times before, that I was fully dressed in my bulky racing leathers: angelic white and liquid-fast blue. I reminded myself how I'd fought through hell for the chance to even wear them, and I wasn't going to give up hitting heavenly speeds while an engine roared between my legs just because I was flashing my bottom row of teeth. I knew my worth.

*Fuck it.*

"Su-*per*, Taryn," the photographer schmoozed, creeping ever closer. "Little more, *beauté.*"

I dropped my jaw another click, tilting forward and desperately wishing the acid sloshing in my stomach would choose another time to make an appearance. I didn't have the time or the energy to keep throwing up anymore.

"I know you, Taryn," Colton whispered beside me. "And this guy may like you now, but he's gonna bail when he figures it out."

His voice swept over me like a plague. I wouldn't take the bait. I focused on every other person in the room, every other sound. A side door opened, my manager, Mike, finally coming inside. One look at me and his big brown eyes drooped like a bloodhound's, his hand covering his face.

"More," the photographer begged between every snap of the camera, the guy squatting down and crawling toward us. "Chin up, up!" Lights blared in my eyes, blinding me, nausea rippling out as a cold sweat under my leathers. None of it saved me from hearing Colton's words between the clicks of the camera as the photographer kept begging, "*More.*"

"I know what you look like, sound like, taste like…" The words dripped thick and slow from Colton's polluted tongue. "I'll always have been inside you before he was."

The acid erupted like a volcano up my throat, gagging me and spewing out toward the photographer. He toppled backward in his crouch, vomit painting his front. "*Merde!*"

Mike ran toward me as I stumbled forward, clasping my hand over my mouth. "*Taryn!*"

Tears bit at my eyes, shame and disgust roiling through me and calling up another wave when I heard Colton's voice again.

"Oh, fucking *sick!*"

"My camera!"

Mike caught and steadied me, tucking me against his burly chest. The long hairs of his beard tickled the back of my neck, the smell of peppermint Life Savers flooding my senses. I couldn't find the strength to stand all the way up, but it didn't matter.

"I gotcha, T," Mike breathed on repeat, fixing his grip on me and turning us so I was thankfully shielded from everyone's prying eyes.

More peppermint floated down to me on his breath, my teased and sculpted ponytail like sandpaper against my cheek. Sour axes bit at my throat, my heart hamming out of control as goose bumps raked over my skin.

"What happened?" Sheldon yelled. "Is she pregnant? What the hell is this?"

Pissed-off French followed, and I squeezed my eyes shut, telling myself to suck it up.

"She just needs some water and a minute. She'll be

fine." Mike patted my back, breathing down to me, "Come on, T. I know you're hurting, but we gotta get this done."

I nodded and somehow, *somehow*, pulled myself upright. I kept my hand over my mouth, taking a sorry kiss on my temple from Mike, then shuffled off toward the bathroom.

With the door firmly shut, I was able to block the bickering in three different accents. I didn't look at myself in the mirror, keeping my eyes down as I scooped water into my mouth, gargled and spit, then repeated until I couldn't spare any more time. But I'd almost gotten the taste all the way out. Almost.

*What a fucking disaster.* And only the second track of the season. At least the racing, the actual *racing*, made it all worth it.

Still, I bet Billy didn't have to put up with this shit.

---

Three turns to go. Two hundred and ninety kilometers an hour. And I was right on Colton's ass.

*Taste this, motherfucker.*

The world blurred by as my tires clung to the track with everything they had left, the earth flat and hot and chewing up my rubber faster than I could burn it down. But the sky was blue and the stands were full, the Thai fans on their feet and bellowing out their cheers and chants every time we soared past.

My pulse thundered in my ears, sweat soaking through my leathers and pooling in my sports bra. Nineteen grueling laps, giving it everything I had. But my bike was liquid speed, strong and vibrating and *mine*. And as my eyes zeroed in on the coming turn, fury and determination blazed hot through every single one of my bones.

They may have published those pictures of my ass all over the world, but I swore to myself that it was fine. Good, even. Because when it mattered, all Colton—or anyone else on this racetrack—would ever see was the back of me. They may as well get used to it.

Colton hung his leg in preparation for the turn, both of us downshifting once, then twice. The growl of his transmission was a perfect match to mine, but Colton's Jersey style was always sloppy. In *everything* he did.

Hundredths of a second ahead of us, Sophie Bennett—my best friend on the circuit and a devilishly fast Brit—leaned perfectly into turn ten. Half a heartbeat later, Colton moseyed into the apex like he was cruising the boardwalk. I kept my knee tucked. Waited to brake until the last moment. Then I cut past him sharply on the inside, my body laid flat and the track whizzing past my helmet.

G-forces clenched my muscles as gravity called to me like the toxic lover she is. But my lean angle was perfect, and a grin took my lips as Colton's bike seemingly streaked backward beside me.

"Shit!" I heard him yell as I popped the clutch and accelerated through the rest of the turn, yanking my bike vertical and riding the torque into a wheelie more than I should've. But *fuck it*. A satisfied roar barreled out of my lungs, tingling from my hair to my boots as I let myself feel every delicious lick of the victory, securing second place.

*Two turns to go...*

Sophie was dead ahead, her black and neon-green Kentaro bike clearly holding first place. She barely touched the soft right of turn eleven before ducking down in the straight to turn twelve. *Damn*, that woman could find a line. Pride knocked at my heart for her, but she and I would celebrate later. We always did, no matter who finished where.

The fans started calling her home, the checkered flag out and dangling above the finish line. I glanced over my shoulder to check the gap between me and my dick of a teammate. But Miette Serieux and her Dabria Atrani were cutting around Colton with the precision of a deadly red shark on the hunt.

*Ha ha, fucker!*

Then Miette ducked low, coming for me.

*Oh shit!*

I bent low over my MMW, my adrenaline climbing as I pushed my engine faster, *faster*, my biggest threats closing in from behind while my best friend stayed the course ahead, the last turn of the race upon all three of us.

Sixth gear, fifth, fourth, third gear, and lean…

---

"I don't think tha' was a fair question," Sophie slurred into her lotion bottle in her best/worst Colton impression. "Clearly, I was having mechanical problems today. But my team will have it sorted before Aragón, you can bet my spermy hair gel on it."

I burst out into laughter at her subsequent finger guns, accidentally spitting champagne all over her rose-gold bedspread and silk pillow.

"Girl!" Sophie swiped her bottle of celebratory champagne from my hands, chuckling as she took another deep swig.

"Sorry! Stop making me laugh."

"Like it's hard when he's such a wanker," she said, passing the bottle back to me. Not that I needed to drink more when we'd been celebrating in her RV since escaping the rager on the paddock. All in her most well-deserved honor.

Predictably, Colton had pouted and grumbled through all our postrace interviews, refusing to congratulate me or Sophie. I'd never felt prouder.

"Okay, moment of truth." Sophie clasped me by the shoulders, fierce determination in her eyes. "Are you too drunk for this? Because honestly? I'm too drunk to do it myself."

I trilled a low kitty growl through my teeth.

"Stop flirting with me, you American milkmaid."

I cracked up laughing again, nearly doubled over sideways.

"Can you do this? Or am I better off shaving it again and going full Lupita?"

"Yeah." I chuckled, setting down the champagne bottle and holding out my arms. "I got this." What I got was Sophie collapsing backward into my lap with a happy sigh.

I shook my head with a smile, dropping a kiss to her forehead before I started smoothing down her edges. It honestly kinda sucked that I hadn't met her until I was in my twenties. Sophie just *got* me, never expected me to be perfect, just real. And she didn't judge me, no matter what.

"Are your hands clean?" she suddenly snapped.

I rolled my eyes. "Clean enough. Now sit up." I hoisted her forward, then very carefully, I started to part and twist her hair into a tuck and roll. Not that I was probably doing the best job of it in our wobbly condition. "Moment of truth," I said once I'd finished, Sophie groaning as she got up and stumbled her way to her bag. She took out two mirrors, holding them up to check my work.

I only got half a lip snarl. I must've been improving.

"Good enough," she said, tossing down the mirrors and grabbing up a silk scarf. I got up and turned down her bedcovers as she tied it around her hair with expert speed. But I only barely had the sheets turned down when she hip-checked me out of the way, then crawled into bed, hugging her pillow with a warm moan.

"Congratulations," I whispered with a smile, covering her up.

"Mmm, you too," she moaned again, patting my hand once she found it on her shoulder. "Say hi to Cowboy Billy for me."

I snorted, carefully adjusting her head wrap so it covered a section she missed. Then I backed up and turned off the lights, shutting her door behind me. "She's out," I whispered to her manager, taking a sleepy high five from Derrick, dozing on the RV's sofa.

"Have a good night. And hey—congrats again. Hell of a race today."

I smiled my way out of Sophie's RV, then headed to my own, rushing through my shower and barely even getting all the soap off my body after scrubbing myself clean of racing exhaust and sticky champagne. Heading to my room, I traded my towel for my favorite Baylor sweatshirt, not even bothering to hang up my leathers before I practically dove into my bed.

The world outside might've been bustling with people, food, music, languages, and the pure *beauty* that was Buriram. But inside my cell phone was a whole other world: one with Osage orange trees and sunny fields and a slow-drawled cowboy who smiled sweetly next to his golden horse.

I stretched out and covered up, my legs sore from racing and my abs sore from puking over the past couple of days. But a smile was already spreading across my face, flutters all a-fluttering when a quick swipe of my thumb opened my phone straight to my messages.

> I don't know what these are called.
> But I saw them this morning and thought they
>     were pretty.
> m.y.

A bouquet of wildflowers was propped up against his crossed boots, sunlight raining down and blue skies in the background like he was stretching out in a field somewhere. The ends were still fresh with dirt and roots like he took care when he picked them, not just grabbing and ripping, and a red ribbon was tied around the stems, the petals a delicate mix of soft blues and pastel purples. The image was also focused purely on the bouquet, but when I looked at the blurred background, I could clearly see his horse running around in the pasture.

Warmth and grace spread through me, and I closed my eyes, imagining the smell of worn leather saddles, raw fields swaying in the breeze, and fresh-churned dirt muddying up your horse's legs. I was almost home.

When I'd had my fill of the fantasy, I scrolled through our last few exchanges, just for fun. Billy loved to send me flowers. He'd texted me a hand-picked image every day since I'd given him my number. Some of them, like the wildflowers, were real ones he'd gather and wrap like he could actually give them to me, despite the oceans constantly between us. Some were professional photos of roses, sunflowers, an orchard with a couple riding horses through it during sunset. I even got a GIF of a dancing gerber daisy one morning that had me giggling every time I thought of it.

For a hot minute, I'd started to wonder if Billy King might actually be perfect. But no. The chip in his perfection was that dating Billy was like trying to catch a firefly: really hard to catch twice and constantly teasing you with the possibility as it sparkled just out of reach.

For starters, he'd been heading home from Qatar right when I was hopping a plane to Thailand, and we missed each other by mere hours. Worse, once I was scheduled to get home to Memphis, I'd arrive about three seconds after he'd be heading to Argentina.

The leapfrogging in our schedules was already making my head spin, and I'd only been on one actual date with the guy. Six weeks prior.

Still, it was one hell of a date and a hell of a kiss, and as I scrolled past the flowers he'd sent me, the good luck texts before my races and the congratulations after, the waiting to see him again *still* felt worth it.

Nary a dick pic in sight.

I opened a new message, that fun little sparkle that lit up my veins whenever I thought of him fully shimmering as I sank deeper into my mattress.

What are you doing, cowboy?

It only took a few seconds for the blue checkmark to appear next to my words, then his picture to pop up with a small ellipsis, brewing his response. The last bit of anxiety from dealing with Colton eased from my stomach, my pulse almost giddy at the prospect of everything Billy.

Wishing I was better at playing this guitar. m.y.

I pouted at my screen, torn between admiring his humility and equally disapproving of how he always sold himself short. I'd googled him after our date—what woman wouldn't?—and I'm ashamed that I was surprised by what I found. Because Billy "my brother is better than me" King is very aptly named. Except for the middle part.

It had been almost strange at first, seeing a picture of him in his Yaalon Moto racing leathers. But he was wearing the same friendly smile, the same sweet baby-blue eyes and sunny blond hair, and something clicked. Like it was exactly what he was supposed to be wearing. And watching him flip down his face shield on the starting grid, taking hole-shot in the first turn and leaning so deep, he could've as easily been lying in my bed...I was *sunk*.

He always started off so quietly, sneaking up through the pack until he'd blare past them without warning. He never looked over his shoulder, never showed a shred of hesitation. He'd launched his whole career by topping podiums before people even knew what to do with him. Until a bad wreck nearly ended it all.

The articles I read talked about some knee surgeries and how it might be kinder to him and the sport to just retire now and let someone younger move up. But that was preposterous to me: he was too *good* to retire. And moto seemed to be so much of what made him who he was—like when he roped that calf and rode those bulls.

Racing was the other side of the Billy coin, the balance to his sweet and gentle nature. His kindness flipped to ruthlessness, the brand nickname scrawled on the back of his leathers making all too much sense:

*FEARLESS*

I couldn't wait to get home to him.

I snuggled up on my pillow and flipping to my calendar, checking the date for our next "real date" for the thousandth time, but it was still so far away.

You didn't tell me you played guitar

I didn't get a text back. Billy's grin lit up my screen, steadily vibrating and the little camera wiggling at me to accept the video call. I held it up, answering with a bright smile that barely matched the light sparkling in my veins. "Hey, you."

"Hey there." He was sitting against a wooden headboard in front of a soft green wall covered with baseball and bull riding posters, hatless, shirtless, and with an acoustic guitar propped across his jeans. I took a quick screenshot. For later. "How you feeling? Any better? Still can't believe someone glutened you. I have half a mind to suspect sabotage."

He was so freaking sweet. I nodded, still a little tipsy. "Feeling much better."

Billy's smile smoothed out, right back to normal. He couldn't stay mad at anyone for any length of time, I was convinced. "Well, good. I'd hoped so. You raced real pretty today." *Aww.* "Look even prettier." *Ugh.*

I rolled my eyes, wishing as a rule he wouldn't draw attention to my looks when it was such a sore subject for me. And I'd told him that, twice already. But I was still powerless to stop the heat flooding my cheeks under the gargantuan weight of my crush on this guy. "Whatever. Wanna know what would make me feel even better?"

"What's that?"

I widened my eyes seductively. "Lose the jeans, cowboy."

Billy snorted, his hands fidgeting with his guitar. "You specifically said no dick pics."

"This is video," I countered. "It's different. And I'm asking for it. It's not unsolic—un*solac*—unsolicissed?" What was wrong with my brain? "Unwanted."

Billy laughed, shaking his head at me. "Ya know, I'm flattered, honey. Truly I am. But, uh…are you drunk?"

"No," I sneered. Then I gave him my best sweet-yet-sultry smile I'd had down since junior miss pageants. "Now, come on. Don't be shy. Drop the zipper."

"Taryn…"

"Just a little bit?"

Billy nodded to himself but made no movement toward removing his Wranglers. "Maybe another time. When you're a little more…awake."

"Fine," I mumbled. But it was not fine. He was so *gorgeous*, and I was in so much pain. Like physical fucking pain from wanting him. "Play me something, then. Let's see how bad you really are."

Billy chuckled, his cheeks darkening as he scrubbed at his forehead. "Seriously? You're gonna make me do this? I told you I wasn't any good."

I didn't respond other than trying to give him a look that promised I wouldn't laugh or judge him but that I also wasn't taking no for an answer. If he wouldn't have phone sex with me, I wanted to hear him play the guitar. And if Billy said he sucked at something, he was probably brilliant at it.

He sighed. "All right." He shifted a bit on his bed, tilting up his guitar and placing his hands over the strings. "*Shit,*" he hissed to himself, moving his left hand a little farther down and double-checking his right hand.

He let out a long breath, faintly bobbing his head to a beat only he heard, and then he began: the slow rhythm of strings being strummed, one after another but in a pattern so smooth, they all sounded like one thing. One easy scoop, low to high, the last note dancing a little here and there to create a melody that never strayed too far or too fast, before he'd go back to the basics and start building all over again.

It was so beautiful, like something you'd hear in a movie when the characters would walk along the beach at midnight. Almost a little Spanish-inspired, and a little heartbreaking. But mostly just the complicated, gentle layers that made up Billy's heart.

He nearly played me to sleep, stopping even slower than he'd started before his hands stilled, and he looked up. His voice was unbelievably warm, like a weighted blanket on a cold October night. "Taryn, you still awake, honey?"

I nodded on my pillow, my limbs lost in the mush of my sheets and down comforter, my phone propped up next to me. "Barely. Thanks for the flowers, by the way."

"Oh. Yeah," he rumbled. "They're really from Gidget. He picked out all the best ones. Well, the ones he didn't eat first."

My chuckle melted into a yawn, and I covered my mouth to hide it, pulling my covers higher up my shoulder. The corner of Billy's lips turned up, then he set down his guitar, reaching toward his phone. I had to bite my lip at the dazzling view of his bare chest coming closer and closer, almost close enough to lean my head on. Then it all kinda tilted and righted, a tender feeling spreading hot from my chest and all the way to my toes when I realized he was lying down. *With* me. The only way he could, nearly nine thousand miles away.

"Can I ask you something?" I whispered.

Billy pillowed his head with his hand, his eyes searching mine through the screen. I could almost feel his hand brushing my cheek before settling on my waist. "Shoot."

"All your texts, you put m.y. at the end." I shrugged, feeling kinda silly about even having to ask. I'd researched the acronym, but it wasn't known in Urban Dictionary or anything. "What's that about?"

Billy chuckled. Then his eyes darted low and to the left. "Typo?"

I shook my head, too sleepy to play another round of twenty white lies but still smiling anyway. "Uh-uh."

He groaned, turning more onto his side and mumbling into his pillow, "It's stupid."

"I highly doubt that, considering it's *you*. Tell me…"

He rolled back so I could see his eyes, then scrubbed a hand over his face. He hadn't shaved in so long, his stubble had darkened into the start of a beard, and I bet it would feel like heaven in my hands. "All right." He halfway shrugged, but he never blinked. "Missing you?"

It took all my inner strength not to react other than to very calmly arch an eyebrow. My mind, however, was busy speeding over all the little *m.y.*s that had been punctuating his text messages. And for quite a while now.

"That so?" I didn't last long before my heart got the

best of me, and I laughed, Billy looking so reassured I actually felt a little bad about teasing him. But that just made me melt all over again. "I miss you, too."

But even that wasn't the right word for it, not when he'd invaded my world like someone turning on the lights after searching all your life in the dark for the switch. I couldn't get enough of him, my heart aching at just the *idea* of the vast expanse of the Pacific Ocean between us. But there was still a big part of me warning that it was too soon to feel how I did.

I barely knew him, and it's not like we had slept together—though *God*, did I want to. But we didn't have that option with our racing schedules.

So we just talked and texted. Every single day.

Billy seemed to consider my answer for a minute, then kinda squinted at me. "For real?"

I laughed again, wishing I could feel like this all the time. "Come here," I whispered, waving at him through the phone. "Wanna tell you something." He leaned his ear closer to his screen, and I pulled my phone closer to my lips, breathing my secret. "I like you, Billy King. Kinda a lot."

He pulled back, acting scandalized. "Nah!" But him playing around didn't keep me from noticing his eyes were sparkling with mirth as he propped himself up on his elbow. "Well, isn't that the best thing I've heard all day."

"It's ten in the morning," I reminded him.

"Not where you are. And that's where I am. So my day is done." He collapsed on his bed, his eyes to the ceiling and a huge grin stretched across his face. "Wow. Imagine that."

I laughed to my heart's content, letting the feeling fill

me up until I was sloshy with happiness and even more desperate to see him again. Then a huge crash echoed from somewhere on his end.

Billy never flinched. Not even when a familiar voice started barking at him, "Hey, dumbass, you about done stringing up cats? 'Cause I think you're getting worse. Come check out this boat dock with me, I got an id— Billy? Hey, Billy, you give yourself a stroke or something? *Billy!*"

Billy blinked. Still grinning like he'd won the lottery, tax-free. "She likes me."

I laughed harder, my cheeks starting to ache from the sheer force it.

Mason groaned in the background. "Well, congratu-fuckin-lations. Now, you gonna help me build this jump ramp or what?"

*Build what?*

Billy looked my way, mischief and adrenaline drugging his eyes and his wink even quicker than his words. "Gotta go, honey. Sweet dreams. Call me when you wake up."

And just like that, he was gone.

# Chapter 7

*Billy King—Present Day*

MASON'S BEEN CHEWING ON HIS THUMBNAIL IN THE passenger seat of my truck the whole ride over, his boots kicking restlessly at the floor mat. I pull in and park a couple of spaces away from a rusty Ford Taurus sitting on two donuts and with a zebra-print steering wheel cover. Evidence of the first line of defense and Mason's whole reason for existence over the next twenty minutes, as far as I'm concerned.

It's going to take a miracle to get us past June Harper. The last time she caught Adam stitching me up, she swore the next time, she'd report him to the proper authorities, and she threatened to ban me from the clinic. Talk about an overreaction. It isn't technically illegal for a vet to treat people, just frowned upon. But Juniper's got her "standards." And a *huge* crush on Mason, if I recall. Which is why he is the perfect decoy for today's mission.

Problem is, his big mouth has a tendency to get wider the more his nerves get to him, and I can't risk him telling anyone back at the circuit, *anyone*, what we're doing today. But I also can't do this without him, so having a loose-lipped wingman is a risk I'll have to take.

"We're gonna get busted, man!" Mason whips around to check through the back glass like the cops are gonna pull in behind us any second.

"Hey!" I reach over to place a steadying hand on his shoulder. "Calm down. It's fine."

He shakes his head, looking at his lap. "It's not, though." He chews on his bottom lip a second, then hurls some pocket lint at the floorboard. "This is all my fault, isn't it?"

If he'd asked me that two weeks ago, I'd probably be giving a different answer. "Yeah, it is."

Mason's eyes grow huge with shame he doesn't know the first thing about dealing with.

*Aw, hell.* I crack an easy grin and clap him on the back. "Nah, it isn't your fault, man. It's mine." I blow out a breath, looking out the windshield. "My head's just…messed up right now."

Even worse, I don't have my bike to help me clear it. I have my home one, but it isn't as fast, and it isn't the same. I haven't even ridden it since I've been back, because it's just gonna make me miss my Yaalon even *more*.

Mason sinks a little lower in his seat. "But I—"

"Look, you trust me or not?"

He makes a face like he's considering it.

"Fine. Um…" I rack my brain for evidence. Got plenty, so it's just about choosing the right payoff. "Okay. Remember that Labor Day weekend when we snuck the Winkley twins out to the swimming hole after the VFW picnic?"

Mason cracks a hint of a smile. "Yeah."

"And wasn't it worth it, seeing Tammy Fae in that pink bikini?"

"Purple," Mason corrects. "Mari Lynn was in the pink one."

"That's right," I remember, chuckling.

He had the biggest crush *ever* on Tammy Fae Winkley, and if I'm not mistaken, she rocked his world that night behind the water tower. He was smiling way too bright the whole time my mama was reading us the riot act the next morning.

I reach over and knock his chest. "And still, you were sweating bullets the whole time we were out there."

"And for good reason. Their daddy called the sheriff on us!"

Yeah, he did. "Okay, but did you get arrested?"

Mason slumps in his seat, his elbow on the door and pressing his fist to his mouth. "No."

*Damn right, because I'm a smooth-talking sombitch.*

I'd pulled the cop aside and made a plea on behalf of Mason's future football scholarships—he was our star running back, and we were destined for the state finals—*and* I promised to mow the yard in front of the police station every weekend for the rest of the year. And the whole damn next spring.

"So you gonna help me out here or not?" I cock my head at my kid brother. "Or can you not do it?"

He glares at me. "Please. Just remember you're paying me back for whatever this ends up costing."

*Sure I am.*

Mason gets out first, slamming the passenger door on my truck. "Sorry," he says before I can even start scowling at him, holding up his hands before he starts tucking in his shirt, fixing his hat, and checking his breath. He grimaces. "You got something? I haven't been drinking nothing but Dr Pepper all day."

"Check the glove compartment." I jerk my chin that way and keep an eye on the highway behind us while he goes back for the mint. I wasn't really worried about it, but Mason's got me kinda twitchy. "Hurry up!"

"All right, all right." He shuts the passenger door softly, then screws up his face at me through the windows.

*Showtime.*

It's only a few steps to the entrance, but every single one is agony the more I try to act like it isn't. I pull open the door to the blast of a heater, the odd relief of antiseptic, and a whole bunch of empty waiting room chairs. Something about it feels like the dark hospital from the morning of my knee surgery all over again.

I paste on a smile as I tip up my hat. "Hey, June."

"Well, well, if it isn't Billy King." She purses her lips in the sunny office just like she did in Algebra II before she'd formally protest homework as a violation of her rights. "I see you're not bleeding at least. Maybe you do learn."

Mason sneaks up behind me, flicking my hat and slipping around my side, wiggling his fingers up by his grin on his way to her desk. "Hey, June Bug."

She perks up, eyeing Mason like a fancy purse on sale. "Make that the King *brothers.*"

He leans his forearms onto her desk, swooping off his hat and plopping it onto her head, June giggling as she adjusts it. Mason winks, plucking a sucker from the jar between her phone and desktop computer.

"Adam in the back?" I hook a thumb over my shoulder, taking a small step past her desk and trying to keep all evidence of any physical discomfort off my face.

Maybe Mason was right and we should've brought a chicken with us as a decoy.

June's head snaps my way. "Yeah. With a patient."

Mason makes a show of tearing the wrapper off the sucker in one loud, crinkly move, throwing it dramatically over his shoulder. "What've you been up to, June Bug?"

June melts a little his way when he starts smiling at her, not noticing me inching closer to the door that leads to the exam rooms. She practically dissolves into a puddle in her chair when he starts doing...*things* with his sucker. "Oh, just working."

"Yeah?" He eyes her up and down. "What time you get off?"

I risk another wince-gritted step.

"We stop seeing patients at 4:30, but I'm usually okay to leave around five..."

Another silent step forward, then I peek back at Mason, popping the sucker in his lips. His eyes flash my way in the signal for *go* before he melts it into an overly dramatic eye roll that's supposed to be cute. "Well..." he stretches out as I carefully push open the swinging door. It squeaks, and June's head starts to turn until Mason vaults up onto her desk, sitting on all her shit. "You ever gone mudding in a Ram Rebel?"

She makes a sound somewhere between a whimper and a sigh, and I slip through the door.

*Damn*, that was close. He isn't as good at that as he used to be.

I check around, and I don't see Adam, but I don't see anyone else, either. The sharp sting of antiseptic is nearly choking me, but it's nothing compared to the sour smell of dog puke, and it doesn't take long before my eyes start watering at the combination.

I limp down the hallway, past the empty exam rooms with open doors, and through another double set that says "STAFF ONLY" in red letters.

"Hey, Adam," I call out when I head inside, gagging on the even stronger stench. *Christ*, how does he do this every day? "You back here, man?"

"Billy? That you?" He pokes his head around a corner,

then the rest of him follows, wearing navy-blue scrubs and a stethoscope hanging from his neck. Eagle Scout smile is still the same, though. "Hey, man. I didn't know you were back in the States." He walks my way, holding his arm out. When I take a step to meet him there, his face falls as soon as he sees me limp. "Aw, buddy!" He jogs over but still shakes my hand before he claps me on the shoulder. "Whatcha do? Crash your bike again?"

I blow out a breath, shaking my head. "Nah. And better question: what's that smell?"

Adam laughs. "Yeah, I had a dog go exorcist on me earlier, poor guy. Why don't we, uh, head into one of the exam rooms. Little fresher."

"Actually..." I hate that I'm about to do this, but I've known Adam since high school football, and he's a real good guy. Even came home to open up his veterinary practice when he probably could've made more money setting up shop somewhere else. "You got an X-ray machine, right?"

He levels a look at me, glancing around even though it's just the two of us back here. "Yeah."

"Okay, well...you think I can maybe...borrow it?"

Adam scoffs. "No, you can't borrow it. It's an expensive machine, man. What's wrong with you?"

I stare at him pointedly. "I'm kinda hoping the X-ray will tell me that."

"Cheese and crackers, Billy," he says, and that's *bad* in Adam language. "Straight up, dude, I'd love to help you, but June's right. I'm a vet, not a people doctor."

"I know that, but I can't *go* to a people doctor."

He raises his pointy chin, all his Eagle Scout morality come to play. "How come?"

This time, I'm the one who glances around for eaves-droppers. "Look, it's complicated, and basically, I gotta keep this quiet."

"Mm-hmm." He shifts his weight, fidgeting with his stethoscope. "From Taryn?"

God, does everyone in this town have nothing better to do than worry about other people's business? "No, not from Taryn. She knows."

He tilts his head, examining me like I'm lying even though I'm not. Family reputations will do that for you. "And what's she say?"

"She says I need a damn X-ray, man." My patience is all about chewed up, even though I'm the loser asking for a favor. "You gonna help me out or not?"

Adam rolls his eyes, maybe because he's still the same shiny Eagle Scout, or maybe it's just pity. Either way. "All right, come on."

He claps me on the back and helps me toward the far corner where there's a bar-height table that reminds me of a prep station in a restaurant kitchen. Except there's also a pole sticking up the back, supporting a laptop off to the side, and something attached on top that looks like an orange lunch box. That's it?

Mason pokes his head past the door into the room. "Hey, I miss it?"

Adam looks over while I hop up onto the table. "Well, if it isn't the Muskrat himself."

Mason flips him off, still sore about his nickname from when he was getting hazed as a sophomore on the varsity football team. Which I promised to fully and completely forget so long as not a whiff of this gets back to Frank, Santos, or anyone else at the circuit.

Adam lifts my leg and sets my foot on the metal table.

I wince, gritting my teeth through my words. "How'd it go?"

"How do you think it went?" Mason grins. "Got me a hot date. But I think I'm coming down with something." He fakes a couple of coughs, then grins like it's funny while both Adam and I scowl his way.

"You aren't talking about June, are you?" Adam says.

I flare my eyes behind his back. If Mason blows me getting this X-ray, I swear...

"Ah, man, I was just joking." Mason bats his words away. "I've had a crush on that girl since I was in Sunday school. Can't wait to take her out. It's like a dream come true."

Christ. He's laying it on way too thick.

"Well, all right." Adam looks at me as I get started taking off my busted-up boot, the human lie detector clearly not falling for Mason's crap but letting it slide. "Just as long as you don't pull anything like you did at prom, ditching Sarah Summers in front of everybody just so you could make out with Laura Baker. Juniper's a nice woman."

Mason crosses his heart. "I'm taking her out to dinner at the Palais Madeleine"—he waves his hand and dramatically bows, Adam letting out a low whistle and my wallet already hurting—"then I'm taking her mudding. I'll have her home before my chariot turns back into a pumpkin, lickety-split."

Woman's probably not gonna cross her doorstep until after sunrise. She'll have a good time, though. Gotta give Mason that much—he may never date a woman twice, but he shows them a hell of a fun time.

Adam starts messing with the laptop, typing in a whole bunch of stuff that makes the orange lunch box start to whizz and hum. *Christ, please don't let there be anything there.*

"It's too cold to go mudding," I tell Mason, needing to distract myself.

"Shows what you know." Mason scoffs. "It is the *perfect* temperature to go mudding."

Adam chuckles, fixing the machine over my ankle. "Spring's better."

I point at Adam, looking at my brother. "See? You're not gonna get any good spray when the ground's frozen with frost."

Mason huffs. "Where the hell am I supposed to take her then? I'm already taking her to dinner." He thinks for a minute, then claps his hands like he's got it. "How about the bowling alley?"

"No," Adam and I say at the same time.

"Closed anyway," he adds.

My brow furrows. "For real?"

"Mm-hmm," he says to me. "Duke Bricker had a stroke three weeks ago and died. His family's selling it."

"Damn, I didn't know that," Mason says. "Hey, how much they want for it?"

Adam looks at him with all the cynicism I feel surrounding the matter. "Why? You gonna buy it?"

"Maybe," Mason spouts off. "I'm working on diversifying my portfolio."

That's the funniest damn thing I've heard since the first time his Ram Rebel pulled up the driveway. I crack up laughing, Adam along with me.

"Y'all don't got a three-inch dick between the two of you!" Mason storms off, his middle finger raised in the air. Whatever. He'll be back.

Adam steps away to put on a smock, still laughing when he comes back. "All right, man. You ready to find out what's behind door number three?"

I wave him on. "Rooting for the lifetime supply of Beefaroni."

"Aren't we all." Adam goes back and forth between the laptop and the X-ray machine, the lunch box clicking. After a second, he checks over his shoulder like he's making sure Mason isn't listening. Then he looks to my ankle, blowing out a breath and shaking his head. "Dang, man. Doesn't that hurt to walk on?"

I let out a tight laugh. "Yeah. It does."

He turns my leg a bit so he can get the side, then positions the thing over it, clearing his throat. "You know, Taryn was in here a couple of weeks ago." I look up, but he's looking at the orange lunch box. "Said she was looking for a buyer for Aston Magic."

My pulse takes off, and I instantly start sweating, though it isn't the first time I've heard about this. Especially since I'm the indirect cause of it all.

I tug at my hat a bit, suddenly itching to get out of here. "Yeah, I don't know if she's gonna go through with it."

"Well, I didn't have any names for her." He straightens, pushing the machine away. "You can put your boot on. I'm gonna go print these out."

"Thanks, man. I really appreciate you doing this."

"Sure thing, buddy." He pats me on the shoulder, and I wait until after he walks away to even start thinking about trying to put my boot on. It always feels like I'm gonna pass out whenever I do. I'm actually really looking forward to getting home so I can ice it and rewrap it like Taryn did. But that's gonna have to wait.

Lynn Hargrove texted me before Mason and I left the house, asking if I was gonna come by and ride Gidget today. Said he seemed kinda lonely. About broke my already shattered heart.

It's not fair that I've been neglecting riding him just because I haven't been doing so great, ever since Up-Chuck Buck's. I'm hardly sleeping, starving when I sit down to eat, then pushing my plate away after a couple of bites because I'm too nauseous to swallow.

I've been trying to accept that me and Taryn are really broken up this time—trying to reconcile my actions with my reasons and the never-ending windfall of consequences—except it doesn't even help that it feels real now. It just makes it worse. She's all I think about, our last conversation playing on repeat in my head as I wonder what she's doing, if she's out riding her bike or her horse. Wondering how long it's gonna be until she dances with someone new.

I hope he's nice.

I hope she hates him.

With a loud burp as his only warning, Mason comes strolling into the room, popping the top on a soda can like he ducked out for a smoke break instead of stomping off.

"You about done throwing your little fit?" I ask him, forcing myself to get my damn boot on, and *Christ*, that fucking hurt.

Maybe she's right, and I should get some new ones. These are comfortable, though.

"What are you talking about?" Mason slurps his soda. "I was thirsty."

I shake my head as Adam comes in, jerking his chin at Mason. "Sure you can handle seeing your brother's X-rays,

Muskrat? If memory serves, you got a fussy tummy, and I don't need you yacking on my stuff."

"Pardon me, Dr. Doolittle," Mason sneers, "but I'm the best damn bull rider in the state of Tennessee. I ain't afraid of nothing."

"Yeah?" Adam pulls his phone out of his chest pocket, unlocking the screen and messing with it for a second. Then he shows it to Mason. "What do you think of that, hot stuff?"

Mason turns green. "*Oh God…*" He turns and bolts the way he came, a second door blowing open in the distance before the faint sounds of the highway traffic drift in and out.

I turn to Adam. "The hell you got on your phone?" He shows it to me, and I nearly choke from laughing so hard. Figures a hog giving birth would make Mason toss his lunch. "Nice, man."

"Hey, not nearly as cool as what you got going on here." He tucks his phone into his pocket, then turns to what I thought was a whiteboard and clips up two big X-rays. He flicks a switch, and the whiteboard glows to life.

I blow out a breath. "What's the prognosis, Doc?"

Adam crosses his arms over his chest. "You're dying."

"*What?*"

He laughs, turning toward me. "Dang, dude. Lighten up." He walks over to the board and points. "Okay, you see all this?"

"Yeah."

"This is good. Healthy. All that milk your mama's been serving you at breakfast and supper has done your body real good."

"So…I'm fine? Why's it swelling, then? Hurts like a bitch."

"Well," he drawls, sucking his cheek until it clicks. "You see this skinny white line, kinda like a lightning bolt shooting down your ankle?"

Right where everything hurts the most. "Yup."

"That's where you broke it."

*Fuck.*

She was right.

---

I continue waiting next to Gidget, leaning against his shoulder as he stands under the grand old oak tree in the front yard. The crickets stopped chirping about a month ago, but if it weren't so cold, they'd be starting their nightly run right about now. Sunlight's been pulling back from the treetops for a good twenty minutes, the sky orange and red like it's burning. But the cold blue of night is coming in from the east, and it isn't slowing down for no one.

Gidget huffs, and I hand over another slice of the apple I've been whittling for us. "Sorry, bud. Shouldn't be much longer, then we can go."

I shrug my jacket a little tighter around my shoulders, cutting off another slice of apple and looking to savor the crisp burst of juice since I'm missing dinner. But the flavor's all muted. I check the fruit and it isn't rotten, but nothing's tasted right lately.

"That taste funny to you?" I hold out another slice to Gidget, who takes it happily and is already nudging my hand for more. Until the front door blows open.

"What are you—" The rock skids on the porch planks, her steps stopping short just outside the door.

I keep my hat and head down, but Gidget looks up and

swishes his tail so it whips me in the ass and the back of my legs. I keep staring at the grass, my heart pounding as I close my knife, then slip it into my pocket along with the rest of the apple.

As fast as I can, I turn and swing up into my saddle, trying not to spend any time on my ankle if I can help it. *Still hurt like hell, though.* I grit my jaw through the pain and remind myself not to set that foot in my stirrup, taking up Gidget's reins and trying with everything in me not to look.

I swore to myself I wouldn't say anything. But out of the corner of my eye, I can't help but watch as Taryn bends and picks up the piece of paper I had set under the rock. *Damn* if she isn't wearing my third-favorite set of pajamas: a faded Baylor sweatshirt that hangs off her shoulder because she cut off the neck and a green pair of my boxers she stole.

First favorite is one of my old baseball jerseys that's got my last name on the back and really isn't long enough for her to wear with nothing else, but she does anyway.

*Did.*

Something in me starts to hurt that definitely isn't the apple, and I give two clicks to Gidget and turn him away, starting the long walk back to Hargrove Ranch. It isn't the first time we've walked it. Usually, it's a lot darker. I don't really mind the sunset tonight, though. I could use the time to think and spend some time with my buddy. No questions about what I'm gonna do next, no judgments for the decisions I've made. To him, a little bit of quality time together is worth his weight in feed.

"Billy," Taryn calls behind me, and I almost don't stop.

*Almost.*

"Hold up, bud," I whisper to Gidget, half turning him toward Taryn, but we're definitely not walking back.

She's made it clear where she stands, and I'm gonna respect it. She said not to call her, and I haven't. But I thought she'd want to know, and since I'm not gonna text her like that's an acceptable exception, I brought it over. Probably could've left before she came outside since I anchored it with a rock, but I wanted to make sure she found it.

Taryn's got her hand over her mouth, her other holding the paper copy of my X-ray in front of her. When she looks up, her hand comes away and kinda pauses in midair like the list of things I've done wrong is so long, she can't figure out which one to get mad at first.

Finally, she exhales, shifting her weight and shaking her head, and I have no idea what she's gonna tell me to do now. Whatever it is, she's not happy about having to say it.

"When you get down off Gidget, don't swing your leg over backward like you normally do. Bring your other leg *forward.*"

My brow furrows; she doesn't sound mad, just worried.

"I know it's awkward, and it's gonna look funny, but this way you can kinda slide off the saddle and land softer on your good ankle without risking your knee. Okay?"

I nod, my heart aching in my chest. Touch my hat just in case, because it's getting darker by the minute. Then I turn Gidget and start heading for home.

Not that my horse's home is with me or that I really have one of my own—dreaming next to her was the closest I'd ever come.

# Chapter 8

*Taryn Ledell—Back Then*

WHEN YOUR LONG-DISTANCE BOYFRIEND IS UNBELIEV-
ably sweet, romantic, considerate, and has a body worthy
of a Michael Stokes photography shoot, there's only so
much phone sex you can have before you start to lose control. And any former ability of mine to be calm, patient,
polite, or gracious had disappeared long before I'd arrived
in Aragón, Spain, in mid-April.

Billy, however, was cool as a fucking cucumber. *Jackass.*

The SSP300 racers were burning up their practice
session behind me, cutting off Billy's every fourth word.
I pressed the phone closer to my ear, pacing in my pit box
and about to spontaneously combust from sexual frustration. "What? Say that last part again."

"One more week, honey," he repeated. "We're almost
there."

I flipped off the tool shelves taking up an entire wall
of my pit box, then scrubbed my hand through my hair,
everything in me pissed the hell off. What kind of relationship takes place entirely on the *phone*? I hadn't seen Billy
since the first time I met him, two freaking months before,
and I was desperate for human contact. The brush of his
hand, a hug, a kiss, the smell of his cologne, *anything.*

"I can't wait another week," I said, pathetic as it was,
but I didn't care. "This is killing me."

"Taryn, believe me, this isn't easy for me, either. But I

don't see us having any other choice. A couple more days, honey, and then you'll be home."

I was shaking my head before he was even done speaking, my impatience so ballooned that I heard the words fly from my lips despite my conscience already twisting over them. "*No.* We do have another choice, and it's very simple, and it's called you getting on a plane and coming to see me. You don't have anywhere to be, so come be with me."

"Honey." His voice was low, steady. It enraged me. Embarrassed me. That he could be so calm, and I couldn't get myself under control. But he was like a freaking expert at pushing all my buttons, one by one. "I just got home last night. And by the time I get there, you're gonna be done racing. So it doesn't make sense for me to spend eighteen hours getting to Spain only to turn around and spend another eighteen hours getting back to Memphis. It's not worth it, Taryn. I'm sorry."

I stopped dead still, no longer able to hear the chatter of my pit crew or redlining motorcycle engines from racers speeding down the track. All I could hear were his words ringing in my ears.

*Not worth it.*

"Oi! Taryn!" Sophie strolled into the edge of my garage, hooking a thumb over her shoulder, her box braids swishing backward with the force of the movement. "You see that shit? I was killing it out there! *Unh!*" She mimed a sexual thrust, and I waved her off. She flipped me off with her backward peace sign. "Tell your wanker boyfriend the faster the pussy, the better it tastes."

I whirled toward her. "Sophie!"

She shrugged, making another obscene gesture behind

a huge grin, then hollered down pit lane. "Miette! Yeah, I'm talking to you. Guess what my time was?"

I turned away, plugging my other ear with my finger, so far past seeing red I don't know what I was seeing. But it wasn't good. "Billy, you listen to me right now," I growled. "Don't you *ever* say to me that I am not worth your time. Ever."

"Taryn." The surprise was clear in his voice. "I didn't mean—"

"You've had two months to figure this out, and you haven't done it. So I'm gonna figure it out for you and make this real goddamn clear: get your ass on a plane, or I will find someone who *does* think I'm worth it. And believe me, *honey*, there are plenty of men a lot closer than *you*."

"Tar—"

I hung up. Turned off my phone.

My hands were shaking, my conscience scowling, and everything else in me screaming *fuck him*. Never had a man put up such a fight over being with me, and I'd had it.

*Who did he think he was?*

"T," Mike called over from where he'd been conspiring with my crew. "Five minutes."

I squeezed my dead phone in my hands, then stuffed it into my bag before I texted him something I'd inevitably regret. I tied off a low ponytail, then braided it and tied it with two rubber bands at the end just to be safe. I couldn't care about Billy King and his lazy drawl at home in Memphis. Not when he could've been sprawled out in my pit box, smiling from under his big black hat, his shitty old Ariat boots crossed at the ankles.

*Selfish jerk.*

Mike cleared his throat behind me. "Don't forget to watch the—"

"Downshift for turn nine. Yeah, I got it." I took my helmet from him and tugged it on, a different part of my soul coming alive under the fit of protective Styrofoam inserts and nylon chin straps. And when I flipped down my face shield, walking to my bike and swinging a leg over for my practice, I channeled it all.

How disappointed I'd been once I'd realized he wasn't showing up in Spain to surprise me. The needy ache in my chest from wanting to see his eyes and hear his voice in person and not through a phone screen, for *once*. The atomic rage burning in my heart from his utterly asinine "not worth it" comment.

I was fucking worth it. He'd just never have the satisfaction of finding out.

---

The next afternoon, I cruised down victory lane with my fist in the air, standing on my pegs and unable to hear myself cheering over the screams of the fans jumping up and down, dancing, and chanting my name. My heart was cracked in my chest from pride, from relief, from the pure fucking shock that always came with pulling out a win.

I swung into the spot for first place, the fans and press and crews and sponsors and camera people swarming everywhere. Familiar faces rushed me, securing my bike on its stand as I worked to unstrap my helmet.

Mike appeared, half crouched and his face exploding with excitement. "Taco Tuesday!"

I threw away my helmet, leaping onto him. "Every Sunday, bitches!"

He laughed and swung me around, the world perfect and mine, and everything I'd ever wanted securely in my hands. *Mine.*

Mike set me down, and my crew appeared, all of us taking turns as we screamed in one another's faces, then hugged and cheered and screamed and hugged again.

"Okay, okay." I pulled Mike aside, blowing out a breath while trying not to cry from pure freaking joy. And a really smart voice inside my happy racer heart told me I should shut up and not push it, but I just...I had to know. "Did Billy call?"

I'd been blowing up his phone nonstop. Leaving voicemail after voicemail apologizing for losing my temper and leveling that stupid ultimatum and going *way* too far and just everything I'd done wrong. But he wasn't answering, and he wasn't texting me back.

I didn't want to believe I'd lost him so fast, over one *fairly big* mistake. He was so sweet, so gentle. He had to be forgiving, too, right?

Mike's smile fell at my question, his hands settling heavy on my shoulders. I never should've asked. Why did I ask? "No, he didn't."

It hurt like fireworks, popping and popping and burning with colors too bright and leaving behind a thick smell of ash that stings your nose and you can't get out.

And it was hot. It was popping and burning, and it was all so damn *hot.*

Panic started to cinch my throat, prickling up my cheeks and toward my eyes, and I never should've followed Billy King at that rodeo. I never should've agreed to go out with him, dance with him, kiss him, or give him my number or let him see the real me or—

"He's here."

I rocked back, Mike's hands on my shoulders keeping me steady as I blinked and forgot how to breathe or think or exist. The relief, the shame, it was too much to sort out. Billy should've been pissed at me for this, not *agreed* to it.

The corner of Mike's smile turned up, something soft forming in his eyes as he looked over his shoulder. I followed his gaze, dumbstruck at the cowboy leaning against the wall in the corner. Battered boots crossed, blue duffel bag by his feet. And a big black hat with the rim pointed to the floor.

If there was any air left in the world, none of it was getting to my lungs.

The corner of his hat lifted a bit, his hand pulling from his pocket and giving me a small two-finger wave down by his belt. It took all my willpower not to run over there and jump him. But I did it; I resisted.

I looked up at Mike, who winked and said, "Thought he was gonna bust his voice box the way he was screaming, he was so damn excited for you. May wanna cut this one some slack."

I sniffled and lifted my chin, my manager giving me a small nod saying I was good to go. He squeezed my shoulders and turned away, and I walked slowly toward Billy, controlled and not shaking at all. Nope. Not my hands or my pulse fluttering or my stomach churning up a horde of butterflies or any of it. Especially when he'd flown all night across the world, then cheered himself hoarse over my win when he should've been furious with me.

He was taller than I remembered. Leaner.

Billy straightened as I got closer, his hand moving like he was flicking at his nose but keeping his hat low so I couldn't see his eyes.

"Hey" was my lame excuse of a greeting, mortification reducing me to a sliver of my former self. He probably couldn't even hear me over the fans and the impatient calls of the press corps. Clinging to my last traces of dignity, I cleared my throat, crossing my arms and shaking back my braid. Like my pulse wasn't raging in my chest. "What are you doing here, cowboy?"

"Ah, you know," he mumbled, shifting his weight. "Working on my Johnny-on-the-spot."

His voice was raspy and extra slow, and carefully, I reached out with a single finger and tipped up his hat. Billy's sweet blue eyes were shadowed and dark with exhaustion when they lifted up to mine.

"God, I'm so sorry," I rushed out, stretching up and hugging my arms around his neck. *Old Spice.* He felt even better than I remembered, and never in my life had I felt like such a jerk. "You didn't have to come here, Billy. You didn't. And I have no excuse for pulling that crap on you except to say that I really missed you, and I am so, so sorry."

"Aw, honey, no," he breathed, squeezing me tight and not even bothered by the bulky size of my leathers. "You were right: I should've come here straight to start with. I just didn't wanna bother you when you were at work. That isn't fair to do to you, just because I'm off."

My heart melted in my chest, and I couldn't believe him. Mostly because I *did*. Billy really would think that way, that he'd be a distraction, and it would be disrespectful to show up unannounced at the circuit. Even though it wasn't like he was a normal tourist—he knew how this job worked, the practices and the press and the back-and-forth all day long, because it was his job, too.

I swore to myself right then that if one thing was gonna come of this mess, it was that I wouldn't risk losing a man as wonderful as Billy King. He wasn't perfect, but he was fucking close enough, and it wasn't as if guys like him grew on trees or something. If they ever had, that forest had long been cut down.

I squeezed Billy tighter, then leaned back to see his face, cupping his scruffy jaw in my palms and still riddled with so much guilt, I was nearly sick with it. But there was also a very big part of me that was a little too excited at the prospect of making it all up to him. "I can't believe you came all the way here."

Billy chuckled. "I wasn't aware I'd been given a choice."

Shame soured my stomach all over again, and I dropped my forehead to his chest with a groan. "I'm so, *so* sorry."

His palm petted the back of my head, his lips dropping a kiss to my hair. "Hey," he breathed. "This is exactly where I want to be."

I dissolved fully against him, soaking in his forgiveness and finally letting it hit me that he was here, and I could feel him under my hands and against my body. My heart was nearly ready to burst from it all. *God*, I had missed him, more than I'd even realized.

I looked up at him, his eyes smiling despite him being so tired and always patient with me no matter what. "Kiss me, Billy. Before I lose any more of my mind."

His grin was so bright, I think it lit up the whole damn stadium. "Yes, ma'am."

He swooped down and captured my lips with his, nothing about him slow or simple this time. His hand on my neck and thumb on my jaw weren't playing around, calloused and strong as he nipped at my lips, then swept his tongue inside my mouth.

Hot and sharp, he kissed me breathless until my hands were desperately grasping his shirt just so I could stay standing. But Billy had me, his arm around my waist and his knee slipping between my thighs, my whole body ready to cave to his every command.

Until somewhere close by, a throat cleared, a German accent mumbling, "Excuse me."

*Werner. Shit!*

I pulled back from Billy, wiping a hand across my mouth and trying to get my raging hormones under control. *Real professional, Taryn.*

Werner, my manufacturer rep, didn't seem to mind, beaming as he held out both his hands for a double high five. I chuckled and met him, Werner linking his fingers through mine and shaking my arms joyously. We'd always been cool—he'd fought up and down to sign me, and it was actually his idea to recruit a publicist to protect my image in the first place. Though I wasn't sure how Sheldon had ended up being the one he hired.

"Congratulations!" Werner squealed, then he pulled me in for a quick hug and patted me between my shoulder blades. He was always so careful to be aboveboard with me. He leaned back, still beaming to the moon. "I cannot tell you how proud everyone is at MMW, Taryn."

I blushed from braid to boots. "Thanks, Werner. For giving me a chance and just everything."

He nodded, his eyes darting to Billy beside me.

"Oh! This is—"

"Billy," he said, extending his hand.

I waited and waited, but he never gave his last name.

"So nice to meet you, Mr. Billy." Werner shook his hand, but he didn't let go, pointing a finger at him. "I must say, you have a very familiar face to me. Have we met?"

Billy laughed, then winked at me, clapping Werner on the shoulder. "Sorry, no. Think I'd remember that."

I was dead; I had to be. But Werner just shrugged, letting go of Billy's hand. Then he turned to me, his mood and voice going right back to celebrating. "Well, our terrific Taryn! We have much to do, trophies to claim, photos to take. Will Mr. Billy be joining you? There is plenty of room in the friends and family area..."

I looked to Billy, who was already doing his best to politely wave off the offer while looking at me all panicked. "Oh no, I'm just visiting. I don't wanna—"

I took his hand, stilling his words when I clasped it in both of mine. "Come stand up there with me."

Something flooded Billy's eyes that looked like the three words I was feeling in every nerve in my body. And the more he calmed and steadied, the more I knew I was making the right choice.

Billy deserved to be first in someone's book, and he was going to be first in mine.

Even if I did have to figure out most of our story by myself.

---

With more determination than I'd had when I crossed the finish line, I slammed the bedroom door behind him, Billy falling back against it and tugging my body flush to his. He went right back to kissing me senseless as his hands hurried to unzip my leathers and peel them from my shoulders, my braid undone and all my responsibilities for the day finally freaking over with.

It took *hours* to deal with my win—interviews and extra photos and more interviews and Billy being a saint of patience the entire damn time. He made small talk with everyone important, and if anyone had recognized him, he must've not let them get carried away with it. I don't think he'd said his last name the whole night, always making sure to keep the spotlight trained on me. It only made me want him more.

He tugged my leathers down to my waist, my arms coming free as his lips trailed to my neck, his teeth nipping at the soft flesh.

"For the love of God, tell me you brought a condom with you," I whispered.

"In my bag, honey. Don't worry." Then he bit down, sending electricity surging through mc and short circuiting my brain.

"Good job."

Billy chuckled as I grabbed his shirt with both hands and ripped it open, thanking the sweet Lord for pearl-snap shirts and brilliant, effing *ripped* cowboys who wear them. I groaned, rubbing my hands down his chest and abs, his muscles flexing with the movement of his laughter and highlighting the delicious V of his hips that disappeared behind his belt buckle.

This wasn't just gym hot. This was *real* man, born and bred hardworking, could throw calves like they were feather pillows *h-o-t*.

I dropped to my knees, my mouth watering as I fumbled to undo his buckle and unable to make sense of the words engraved on it. Something about roping. Something about stars.

"Hey now, who says you get to go first?" he teased, his long fingers playing with my hair.

I scoffed, smirking up at him. "You realize you're talking to a motorcycle racer, right?"

Billy cracked up laughing, the sound dissolving into a moan when I got his pants undone and his cock delightfully free.

*Damn, dude.* Lucky me.

I took him all the way into my mouth, a sputtered gasp coming from somewhere above me and a moan tearing its way up my throat. I took Billy deeper, swirling my tongue around his head and learning the taste and feel of him. The thickness, the richness, the strength and tenderness, and all the ways he was sensitive and special and uniquely made to be mine. All the things I'd given up searching for and had accepted I'd never have for myself. Until he came along.

"Taryn, you're gonna… *Jesus*…"

I grasped Billy's hips and sucked and kissed, exactly as I'd fantasized about doing since I'd first met him and he'd totally swept me off my feet, right up to the moment he came down my throat, his hand light on my hair and his voice spitting curse words and moans until my name was godlike with the way he revered me. It still didn't come close to how I felt about him.

When he'd spilled all he had, I stood with the taste of him flooding my senses, pushing my leathers from my body but not having time to deal with the rest of my clothes. Billy launched from the door and swept me up in his arms, hugging me into him like I was salvation made existent. He pressed kisses to my shoulder over my T-shirt, against my neck, his hands shedding my panties as he stumbled us toward the bed.

I hit first, crashing backward as Billy tumbled down on top of me, both of us laughing as he struggled to squirm the rest of the way out of his boots and jeans. But he ditched them quick, luxuriously kissing his way up my legs.

I tore my hands through my hair, gasping with need and fucking *ruined* from the sight of his suntanned shoulders spreading my thighs wider apart. His thumb touched me first, just a press against me before his head dipped, and holy hell, *that* was his tongue.

*Fucking finally.*

I melted into my bed, my palm cupping the back of Billy's head as I rolled my hips and rode every tingle, every flame, every lick of pleasure until I was transported to the heaven that hurts *so good*, shaking and coming as he sank a long finger into me and sipped stronger at my clit, stealing a second orgasm I hadn't noticed he'd been crafting all along.

The power in it broke me, my back abandoning the grace of the bed as I cried out too loud for the busy paddock outside my RV, but it was too late to take it back. And Billy wasn't letting up, his palm on my belly entrapping me to take his endless gifts as he curled his finger deeper into me, moaning fire-hot kisses over my body and calling forth climax after climax until I was teary-eyed and pushing him away, pulling him hurriedly up to me.

I kissed him desperately as his body settled between my legs, and it was the purest weight, his bare skin soft against my thighs and his rough hands bunching in my shirt and palming my breasts over my bra. But he didn't rush to take off the rest of my clothes, and the significance behind it nearly wrecked me.

How much this was about being *together* and not about looks or ego or any of it. Just the simple need in his heart of hearts to be with me every way he physically could, as close as he ever could be, and me with him in return.

"Don't move," he whispered, his breath a silky slip of air across my lips before his tongue took another ravenous taste of me. "Please."

I nodded as he pulled back, and I missed him every moment, Billy moving quickly to get a condom from his bag. He tore it with care, then fitted it around himself with a practiced slip of his fist that made my mouth water for him all over again. But the rest of me was still jealous from before and eager to enjoy his body in all the ways I could convince him to give it to me.

Billy wasn't in a hurry, though. He grinned as he stalked his way back up my body, stopping to kiss me here and bite me there, teasing my legs with flicks of his tongue and tasting all the innocuous inches of me. It was the most magnificent torture, and I was trembling insatiably when he finally settled against me, drawing my leg around his hip.

I clawed at his lower back, tugging his hips forward and growling with impatience when I felt the first brush of him against me. Billy moaned darkly, his lips cascading from my cheek to my temple. "I really missed you," he said. Then inch by thick, delicious inch, he sank himself hopelessly into me.

I don't know if he'd realized: I'd sunk for him long before.

# Chapter 9

*Billy King—Present Day*

I TAKE ANOTHER BREATH AND ADJUST MY GRIP ON THE ax, sweating in the bitter December cold under cloudy, stormy skies and staring down the block of wood with my name on it. I grit my teeth, then *swing*, the force splitting the wood shocking its way up my arm, down my side, through my bad knee, and straight into my ankle.

*Goddamn, that hurt.*

"Hush now," Mason coos to the goat in his lap, not helping me stack up another block because he's too busy making kissy faces. He redips the purple and glittery hoof polish brush in the bottle, then goes back to painting the goat's hooves as I prepare myself for another swing. "So explain this to me again," he says. "I'm not braking right?"

He wanted to go out riding this afternoon, but I made up some extra chores that I said needed to get done. The truth is, I tried to ride my bike this morning, looking for the sweet release of open blacktop and a growling engine to clear my thoughts. But with the pain in my ankle being as bad as it is, I can't even shift gears at this point.

That's a bad way for a motorcycle racer to be.

I wipe the sweat off my brow, my shirt hanging open, but it's not really helping cool me down anymore. I take my stance. "Nope. You're going too early." Swing, crack, *ow*—this is killing me, but no way am I letting Mason know that. I do my best to keep the pain out of my voice, though he doesn't think a thing of me being breathless. "You do fine how you are, but if you wanna start making some moves, you're gonna have to get some Lorelai-sized balls."

"I got balls," he whines, looking to the goat snuggled in his arm. "Don't I? Of course I do, darling." He makes more kissy faces before he goes back to painting its hooves.

For the sake of our quiet afternoon, I let that go and grab another block of wood from the small pile I have left. "Not like Lorelai."

Mason scoffs. "That woman races like she's got a death wish."

"Yep. She wins, too." I grit my jaw and swing again, groaning out another breath when I'm done and resting on my ax, because I don't know if I could stay standing otherwise. "Probably gonna get moved up at the end of next year if there's any justice about it. So you better get ready to have her all over your ass, or she's gonna kick yours."

What's really probably gonna happen is my teammate, Francesco, will retire after putting it off for the last three years, and Yaalon will promote Lorelai as my "teammate slash mentee." But I'm not saying that to my brother.

Mason makes a face as I stack a block, then take another moment to rest and catch my breath. It's pretty much pointless with the way my arms are burning, my lungs on fire from the cold, and every time I swing this damn ax, it feels like I'm gonna break my ankle even worse.

*Can't fucking believe I can't shift gears. The hell am I gonna do?*

I use my shirt to wipe my face, eyeing the wood pile. Five more after this one, and I can do five. Though I haven't the first clue how I'm gonna explain it to my father once he realizes I've blown my career for good. At least his *favorite* son, Mason, will still have both of his.

I take my stance, adjusting my grip and preparing to swing.

"The *hell* are you doing?"

My head pops up at Taryn's voice, finding her inside the fence to my backyard and looking royally pissed the fuck off. She's wearing spandex pants and a workout jacket that isn't nearly warm enough for the wind. But her hair isn't up, which means she's on her way to the gym and not coming back from it.

My pulse spikes above the treetops, and when I look at Mason, he's very subtly closing the bottle of hoof polish.

We both look to Taryn. "Nothin'," we say together.

She starts storming toward us, and I straighten, swallowing, unsure what to do with the ax in my hand. *Damn*, she's pretty today. Since when does she wear makeup to go work out?

Mason mutters under his breath, "Told you that rock on the porch was a better idea than leaving the X-ray in the mailbox."

"Shut up," I growl back.

The goat bleats and jumps off his lap, but my brother's still sitting in the dirt, his eyes getting bigger the closer Taryn gets.

"Drunk already," she spits at him, and I mentally upgrade her mood to the one that comes with the warning label: *Words may be bitter, also highly regrettable. Take with a grain of salt. Flush with water if in pain. Do not operate heavy machinery.*

Mason's face explodes with indignation. "Am not!"

Taryn swipes the ax from my hand, her eyes furious

and yanking my stomach straight up into my throat. Then she *swings*.

"Oh *shit*!" I dive toward my brother, Mason screaming his head off as I tackle him into the ground.

"Jackass!" Taryn yells, wood clanking around the pile I'd stacked. "You're gonna hurt yourself even worse, screwing around like that!"

I uncover my head and peek over my shoulder, Mason shoving me off him. But I can't do more than roll away and lay on the ground beside my brother, starting to smile in shock as Taryn goes *berserk*: stacking up the rest of the wood pile, then starting to chop it all. And she isn't playing around, either.

Mason slips out his phone next to me, videoing the whole thing.

"In all my life"—swing, *crack*—"I have never seen"—swing, *crack*—"two brothers"—swing, *crack*—"who are so damn hot"—swing, *crack*—"and so goddamn reckless!"—swing, *crack!*

Neither Mason nor I move until long after Taryn's done: breathing hard and all our firewood split, the ax hanging lifeless in her hands. *God, she's amazing.* Guess she doesn't have to go to the gym now. Not that I'm saying it while she's hanging onto that ax and clearly is damn good at using it.

"That," Mason drawls, putting away his phone, "was *uh*-maz-ing. World Star, Taryn. World Star."

She glares at him, then points the ax in his direction: a harbinger of death with a big ol' score to settle, and his smart mouth just loves to play chicken with an ass whupping. "In case you somehow weren't aware of the mess you've caused, your brother now has a broken ankle. And

I don't know what the hell your problem is, letting him chop all this wood by himself when it's probably killing him to do it and it sure isn't helping him *get better*!" She's well into dog-whistle octaves by the time she's done, and she throws down the ax, disgust all over her face. "But who am I kidding, Mason. It's *you*."

"Hey," I pipe up before I think better of it. "Back off."

I get the full brunt of her attitude, her pointing finger drilling me deeper into the dirt until I'm probably due to pay my half of the worms' rent. "You? You're coming with me."

I swallow and look at my brother, who looks just as low as I feel. I reach out and lay a hand on Mason's arm, but he shakes me off. "It's all right. Go on." He jerks his chin toward Taryn, then gets up, dusting himself off.

Taryn crosses her arms, jutting out her hip so he can't walk away. He turns and offers me a hand, helping me up.

As soon as I get my feet under me, I pull him close, trying to keep my voice between us. "Hey, you know this isn't your fault, right?"

Taryn scoffs behind him, and I scowl at her over his shoulder. She grits her jaw and looks away, and I look back to Mason. He's nodding, but his eyes are still downcast.

"I make my own choices. And I'll pay for them."

"Okay," he mutters.

"Yeah, *okay*," Taryn mocks. "Except maybe if he didn't put you in the position to *make* those choices, we wouldn't have such a problem."

I look at her, something cold spreading through me where it's usually so warm. "Still was my choice. Mine."

She nods. "Damn straight. And that's why we're broken up. Let's go."

I clap Mason on the back, sending him off and making a mental note to think up something fun for us to do later. Once I'm done dealing with whatever the hell this is about.

"You, um, you need any help getting to the truck?" Taryn asks a lot more nicely after Mason is gone.

I stare her down. "Nope."

She sighs and shakes her head like she gets to be frustrated with me after she showed up here, yelled at us, and ruined Mason's whole day. When he wasn't even drinking, matter of fact.

Whatever.

I don't say anything else to her on our way out of the backyard, heading to her truck parked next to mine under the oak tree. Which is so completely unfair. I'm *mad* at her now, and the sight does something in me to turn down the volume on it. So I think hard over Mason's guilty face as I climb in the passenger side, shutting the door and propping my elbow on the window. Flick at my nose to get out the smell of her, but in her truck, I'm drowning in it.

Taryn doesn't start the engine right away, sitting in the driver's seat and staring out the windshield, her hands in her lap. "Did Adam take the X-ray?" she says quietly.

My brow furrows as I look at her, wondering what question she's really asking and how I'm supposed to answer. "Yeah. Me and Mason went over there."

"That's good," she says. "It's good that you did that." She looks over at me, guilt swimming in her eyes, but I'm not sure why. "Did he talk to you about it? What it means?"

Unfortunately. He said it should take me four to eight weeks to heal. If I stay off it. But it's been nearly four weeks already, and it isn't any closer to getting better. Probably because I *haven't* been staying off it. "Yeah."

"All right, then." Taryn doesn't say anything else as she starts her truck and backs out, taking care not to hit the covered flower beds while she turns around, then starts pulling out of my driveway.

I look into the back seat to see if I can get clued into what's going on, but all that's there is her hat, first aid kit, and her gym bag. "Where are we going anyway?"

"Work out." She glances at me, then to the road, checking her mirrors more than she needs and her hands at a perfect ten and two. Why's she nervous? "You left some stuff at my house, so I packed some clothes and shoes in my bag for you."

*Well, how about that.*

Packed "some" of my stuff, not "all" of my stuff. I haven't gotten a breakup box from her yet or a gimme-back list. It's been a week since I left that X-ray on her porch, and I was starting to worry I blew that apology, too. Never been so happy to be wrong, and I can't stop wondering if it's worth the risk to try teasing a smile out of her.

She's calmed down plenty, currently in the perfect middle ground of being irritated *just enough* to still be cute as hell as she's riding my ass. Which she loves to do, and I can't seem to get enough of. "You didn't burn enough calories chopping all that wood for me?"

She levels a look my way. "This isn't for me. It's for you. Because you're not gonna ask for help, your brother's too selfish to offer it, Frank and Yaalon can't know about any of this, and you need to stay in shape for the circuit. Furthermore—"

*Furthermore?* How long has she been practicing this little speech?

"—I am more than qualified to provide your physical

therapy and monitor your workouts so you don't hurt yourself even worse, so consider it part of my…uh, Hippocratic oath."

I face her a little more, incredibly touched by what she's doing when she hates me right now, insults to my brother aside. "You took an oath to be a hypocrite?"

She slams her palm on the steering wheel. "Hippocratic! And for the sake of our conversation, sure, why not."

I crack up laughing, loving that she's lying just to have an excuse to give me shit. She reaches over and swats at my arm, and it's so hard not to grab her hand and press a kiss to her palm like I would've done not that long ago. But I lost that privilege.

"Ridiculous," Taryn mutters, glaring out her windshield the rest of the drive to Hargrove Ranch.

I just chew on my thumbnail, trying not to stare at her and telling my rising hopes to sit their giddy asses right back down.

She's still angry and working through it. But she's been thinking about me, worrying about me, cared enough to come yell at me. And she still isn't talking to me like I'm a press agent or someone from her church. So I'm gonna do the only thing I can: hang onto this roller coaster and pray I make it to the end.

Once Taryn parks her truck at Hargrove Ranch, it's a short walk up to the small warehouse, converted into a home gym for Lorelai. But since Frank manages the three of us and Lorelai and Taryn are besties now, we all get to use it whenever we want.

I hike Taryn's gym bag farther up my shoulder, pulling open the door and letting her head in before me. "Thanks," she mumbles, either from habit or because she means it. I'm hoping it's the second one. "Hey, girl."

"Hey—oh *hell* no!" Lorelai stops her treadmill when she sees me, hopping down and striding in our direction, her finger pointed toward the door. "He can get right the hell out."

"Lor"—Taryn glances between me and her friend— "it's okay. He's with me."

My eyebrow arches at that but not before Lorelai's hit the roof. "You forgave him? After he—"

"I know what he did." Taryn holds up her hand, and I would've rather waited outside for this little spat. "And we're not back together."

Awesome.

Lorelai crosses her arms and stares me down, and I shift Taryn's bag on my shoulder, more uncomfortable than I'm strictly okay with. She knows enough information to fully tank my racing contract—and my whole career—if she wants. It would open up a big ol' spot on the Yaalon team for her taking, too. But Taryn swore that Lorelai wouldn't tell, and there isn't anything I can do about it now. I can't make her unknow what I did.

"You're lucky I still let you ride Gidget," she says, her voice only getting sharper with her threats. "And you can bet your ass I'm not gonna sell him to you now. Because in case you've forgotten, Billy, he isn't really my mom's horse. He's *mine*."

My eyes pop, shocked at how fast my heart can crash into my stomach.

"Lor!" Taryn says.

"Well?" Lorelai gestures my way. "I'm mad at him."

"I'm mad at him, too." Taryn peeks at me. "But he needs help working out. So I'm helping him. And don't…don't say things like that about Gidget when you don't mean them. I know you didn't, right?"

Lorelai throws a hand up. "Fine." She collects her water bottle and her towel, marching past us. "But don't be surprised when he pulls the same shit again in six months."

I cringe when the door slams behind her, the gym eerily quiet, stuffy and hot from the heater, and totally hers. The plantation house, the ranch, Gidget. One day, it's all gonna be Lorelai's. I, however, am primed to inherit a broken-down Ranger, a couple of chickens, some goats with purple glitter polish on their hooves, and not a damn speck of land to my name.

"Billy—"

"Thanks for that," I snap at Taryn. "Really. Can't tell you how much I was hoping to be reminded of what a piece of crap I am today and how everyone pretty much hates me now."

Her shoulders drop. "No one hates—"

"There are two sides to this story," I remind her. "And while you're running around town telling everyone your half, I can't say a word about mine. That isn't fair to do when I'm not allowed to defend myself."

"I'm sorry, okay! I didn't mean for that to happen. I didn't know she was gonna be here."

"You couldn't have called?" I yell at her.

I regret it instantly. Taryn spins away, her hands covering her face before she tosses her hair, and I start heading toward the bathroom to change, growling under my breath.

Maybe this was a mistake. Maybe people are right and some done things need to just stay done. But Taryn and I, we don't *feel* done.

I'm calming down by the time I'm finished changing into a T-shirt and workout shorts, trading my old boots for a pair of Nike running shoes. I don't remember leaving all this stuff at her house, but maybe I did.

My limp is a hell of a lot bigger out of my Ariats, and Taryn comes running as soon as she sees me, looping my arm around her neck and hers around my waist, and *God*, she smells good. How does she always smell like summer, even when it's freezing?

"Over here." She nods toward the wall where she's got a bunch of stuff laid out like she went back for her first aid kit while I was changing. "I'm gonna wrap your ankle before we start."

I nod, not risking talking when I might squeal from the pain. But I let her help me over to the wall, then wrap my ankle like she did outside Up-Chuck Buck's. The fact that she tied her hair up in a messy ponytail first and took off her jacket to reveal a strappy little workout top helps way more with the pain than it should. She's also never once balked at the scar from my knee surgery, but then again, she was always more interested in which techniques the doctor used and explaining how they've improved them since.

"You wanna do arms first?" she asks when she's done, standing and extending a hand to help me up.

I'm probably good after chopping all that wood, but no way am I telling her that. "Yeah, that's fine." We head over to the bench press station, Taryn giving me a hand as I lie down and position myself under the bar. She moves the weight anchor, and I scoff, moving it again.

"Stop trying to show off," she hassles me. "You're gonna hurt yourself worse, and it's not gonna earn you any points in my book."

I roll my eyes. "Honey, I'm not trying to show off. *That's* what I'm benching now."

She isn't buying it. "Since when?"

"A while."

She chews the inside of her lip as her eyes size me up, as though she's capable of determining how much force my muscles can exert just by looking at them. Except she also doesn't have the first clue how restrained I am when we're together. The first time I accidentally bruised her because I wasn't being careful with the strength in my hands, I thought I was gonna be sick. She just thought it was hot.

I flex just a little, and Taryn huffs. "Well, fine then. I guess."

*Sucker...*

She counts me off as I push through a circuit, my arms screaming from the extra weight, but it's totally worth it from the impressed hitch in the corner of her scowl. Probably wouldn't be so bad if I hadn't chopped all that wood, and maybe I do need to move up in weights a bit. Frank will hate it, but what else is new.

"All right, hero, knock it off," Taryn says when she decides I'm done.

And just like that, round and round we go from machine to machine, Taryn rigging them up in weird ways so I can use most of them and constantly bitching about the weight I use. So she started skipping numbers in counting my reps to try to make up for it.

"No, that was eighteen," she snaps from below me, flicking her ponytail over her shoulder and replanting her hands backward on her waist.

I hang from the pull-up bar, my ankles crossed and my sweaty fingers slipping. We've done arms, legs, back, core, legs, and now we're doing arms again because she's *evil*, and I'm starting to wonder if she's trying to kill me. It's taking everything in me to pull myself up again, halfway through our fourth circuit and gritting out, "Eighteen."

"Nineteen, jackass."

I lower myself with total control, trying to remain focused. I've gotta stay that way if my comeback is gonna last longer than a blip. But it's too much fun to rile her up. "Eighteen."

"Twenty!"

I kick at her a bit, then start pulling myself up again. "Ninete-*shit!*"

My overworked arms buckle, and my hands slip, all way-too-much of me crashing to the ground and directly on top of my goddamn ankle, an atomic blast of pain erupting into my foot and up my leg like I just shattered it.

"*Billy!*"

I roar with the full breadth of my throat under the agony, curling into myself on the ground and coughing through trying not to throw up. Taryn's hands settle on my body, pressing and searching in a dozen different places, like that's gonna do anything when I'm never gonna fucking walk again.

Hell, screw walking. I'm never gonna *ride* again—not my bike, not Gidget, because this isn't like when my knee blew and they said I was done. This is so much fucking *worse*.

"Oh God," she mutters, lying on top of me and hugging me. "I'm sorry. I'm so sorry I distracted you. *Shit...*"

I pant out a breath even though my whole future is gone, still trying to suck it up and not waste such a prime opportunity to roll over and kiss her when she's *on top of me apologizing*, but *God*, it hurts so fucking bad.

*This is it. My comeback's finished, and someone's gonna have to call Frank and tell him the bad news.*

Taryn sits up and starts stroking her fingers through my hair, running her palms down my back and my sides, and I stay there for I don't know how long. Letting her comfort me, soaking up the way she smells and feels and how she always makes me feel better, especially when I'm at my lowest.

After a while, she starts humming. Old songs from old movies that we used to watch when the hours in our bodies didn't match the ones on the clocks, our minds awake but our side of the world asleep, and just the two of us together on her old couch as we battled our familiar friend: jet lag.

She keeps humming, changing tunes, and as I try to imagine what kind of slow, simple future I'm going to have now, images swirl in my mind of western girls dancing with backwoods boys, of kids in costumes dancing on vaudeville stages. She changes to a new song again, and after a few minutes, I start to remember which song goes with what movie. But that isn't all I realize.

The simple awareness that I'm *fine*, that the pain's almost done bleeding out of me and I'm breathing okay long before I've even started thinking about moving away from her...

It hits me with the weight of an anvil dropping on my head, like in the cartoons I used to watch as a kid. But nothing's funny about it now. I've taken so much more from her than I've ever given. I didn't put her first like I should've. I dragged her back into a nightmare after she did everything in her power to put it behind her. And I've lied to her too many times about stuff no one should ever lie about. Way too many goddamn times.

It's all so suddenly obvious why she's leaving me, and I hate that I took that from her, too. So I sit up. Pull my feet in front of me. Keep my back to her and don't say a word.

"You okay?" she asks.

If I say yes, it's a lie. If I say no, she'll want to fix it. The first thing she ever said to me was "Can I help you?" and I've let her spend too much time doing just that. Too much effort when she's destined for so many greater things. But I can't say nothing.

I clear my throat, wiping at my nose. "You hear about Duke Bricker?"

"Yeah," she mumbles behind me. "I went to the funeral. You were gone. Valencia." She was supposed to be in Valencia *with me*, but considering she broke up with me days before, that didn't happen. "You know, Billy, I had forgotten how nice it is out there, how much space he had. It kind of reminded me of…" She trails off, but I already know what she was gonna say.

That it reminded her of the ranch we always talked about owning together: with more acres than you could see and a small house that didn't take away from the natural beauty of the land. Just enough space for us, the sky, and our horses, too.

I nod, clasping my hands in front of me. "Me and Mason, we spent a lot of time out there when we were in school. Duke had this, uh, this Arabian. Big, black, *beautiful* horse, and we used to sneak out there all the time, trying to ride it."

Taryn huffs, but it's not as judgmental as I expected. It's almost amused. "Sounds like something y'all would do."

I nod again, lost in the memory and nearly able to smell the wet grass after the afternoon rains. The mud that would cake my boots and dirty my lariat. "I'd rope him so we could get the tack on, let Mason go first. He'd *fly* on that horse, I tell you, that thing was so fast… But"—I start to quietly laugh, though something in me is shattering apart—"and I didn't find this out till years later, but apparently, Duke could see us screwing around with that horse from where he'd be smoking his pipe on his back porch. Which makes, just, perfect sense, ya know. Because it *never* failed that about five seconds after I'd cut Mason loose, our father would pull up, yelling and cussing up a storm..." I drop my head when my voice gives out, patting my hands over my hair like it can hold in all my feelings, all my regrets from spilling out, but it can't. "Never did get to ride that Arabian."

She rests her hand on my shoulder, light and gentle, and so much more forgiving than I deserve. "Hey, what's going on with you?"

I shake my head, my voice grainy and barely even making it all the way out. "Oh, you know, same old story." I lift my head and swallow, staring at the wall in front of me. "Some dumb cowboy with a broke-down truck lost his girl. Pitiful part is he can't even drink his way to getting over her, because he don't drink."

Her hand doesn't move. Not until I shake it off and stand up, starting to make my way to the bathroom to change. As if I'm even capable of such a thing.

"Billy—"

"It's fine." I half turn to look at her but keep my eyes low, trying not to see her. It hurts too much. "You can go. Thanks for the help."

Taryn sputters, shifting her weight. "I drove you. How are you gonna get home?"

*Home.* That word.

"I'm, uh, I'm gonna take Gidget for a ride. Before Lorelai changes her mind and puts a lock on his stall." I chuckle it off, though it's the furthest thing from funny in the whole damn world. "I'll catch a ride from a farmhand. Or call Mason."

Taryn bites her lip, still shifting in place. "Well, Bopper probably needs to be ridden, too. We can take them both out, and then I can—"

"Taryn, stop. You've done enough. I'm not your problem anymore."

A whole bunch of air rushes from her lips, and I'm sorry about making her feel bad, but she was right when she said it. No matter how much she wishes she weren't.

"It's not a problem to work out with you." Her voice is starting to melt a little, but then she pushes out more force and almost gets back to acting like she's fine. "I have to work out anyway, so it's not a big deal to do it together."

I stare at her, helpless to figure out why she's pushing this. "I'm fifteen miles in the opposite direction. And I can drive myself."

"Just let me do this for you!"

I step back, holding up my hands.

She looks just as pissed as she did when she caught me chopping wood, and I doubt *she* even knows why she's pushing this. But I've become painfully aware over the last few weeks that breaking up doesn't mean all the love you felt just gets canceled overnight. It lingers and lingers, no matter how mad anyone got.

Doesn't mean she wasn't right to do it, though.

Taryn's *always* right.

But I guess, for whatever reason, she's also made up her mind about hanging around me a bit more. Maybe trying to see if she can like me some again. And it's a lot easier to let her have her way than fight the rotation of the earth by trying to change it.

"I'm tired of arguing about petty shit." She tears the ponytail holder out of her hair, letting it fall like a shiny blond waterfall around her shoulders. "I'm picking you up tomorrow at three, so be ready to go."

"Yes, ma'am."

"And you really don't want a ride home?"

I shake my head. "I need to talk to Lynn. Try to convince her to let me cut her a check."

"Well…" Taryn crosses her arms, already back to thinking a million thoughts at a million miles an hour. "Where are you going to put Gidget if she says yes?"

She sounds just like Lynn. And I don't have an answer for either of them. Because Lynn already said Gidget can't stay at the ranch much longer, because she needs the space for a new horse she's about to buy.

Taryn doesn't wait long for my response. She shrugs, saying like it's nothing, "Well, let me know if she says yes. Gidget can stay at my house in the barn with Aston until you get it figured out."

I can barely speak, I'm so stunned by her offer. "What? Why?"

Taryn watches me. Everything about her getting softer. "Because I'm trying to forgive you, Billy," she says, and my throat chokes closed at how much she sounds like she means that. "Okay? I'm here, and I'm really trying. But sometimes, you really piss me off, and you don't make it easy. And before you ask, *no*, none of this is getting fixed overnight, so I'm still not comfortable with you calling me or coming over. I need more time."

"Okay." I can't argue with anything she said, not that

I want to if there really is hope. "So are you not…selling Aston anymore?"

She knows that's not all I'm asking. And there's a whole lot riding on that answer. "I don't know yet. I hope not. But that kind of depends on you."

God, just the fact that she said that… "Taryn, I swear to you I will *never* again—"

"I know. And I know you had your reasons, and you didn't mean to hurt me, and I know it could've been a hell of a lot worse, and I should be grateful for that, and I am. But I can't just wake up and pretend like it didn't happen, Billy. I can't just go back to before. I—" She stops herself, saying a lot more calmly, "I will see you tomorrow. That's the best I can do right now."

"It's enough," I promise. "It's more than enough."

She doesn't say anything else, and I don't push my luck any further. I just watch as she goes over and gathers up all her stuff, then heads toward the door. She stiff-arms it without another word of goodbye, stomping outside to her truck, and never once looks back.

But she's still fighting with me. Still chasing me and letting me chase her. And I guess between two motorcycle racers, that's all that really matters in the end.

"Guess we'll try again tomorrow."

# Chapter 10

IF THERE WAS ANYTHING ELSE IN THE WORLD I COULD have wanted, I couldn't think to name it, I was so damn happy. I smiled endlessly down at Billy, his hat on my head and his head in my lap, stretching out in a field somewhere in Hargrove Ranch as I combed my fingers through his hair. He'd been whittling that apple all afternoon, seemed like, peeling it in smooth chunks that came out looking like flattened silver dollars every single time.

"Tell me about our ranch again," I breathed down to him, soaking in the warmth of the mid-May sun shining down on us. "The land, the house. I want to hear about all of it."

His arm stretched up, extending another piece of apple to Gidget, who was standing directly next to us because they had some sort of separation anxiety, as best as I could tell. "Yeah? Well, it's gonna be a lot bigger and better than this one. And with way less people crawling all over it."

A chuckle tickled its way out of my chest, mostly from loving the way he shivered when I ran my nails across his scalp just so. "What do we need so much land for? It's not like you need to compensate for anything."

He snorted. "Awful kind of you to say. And yes, we do need all that land." He peeled another chunk of apple, acting like he was gonna give it to his horse, then eating it himself at the last minute. Gidget didn't seem amused, nipping at Billy's hand and stealing the rest of the apple. Billy just chuckled and scratched the underside of his horse's jaw, clicking closed his knife and hooking it onto his back pocket. "How are Gidget and Aston Magic supposed to stretch their legs on anything less than forty acres? Isn't that right, buddy? We need more space than that, don't we?"

"Oh, I get it. So Aston and Gidget get plenty of space, and we get stuffed into a teeny-tiny farmhouse?"

"Well," he said, peeking up at me. "We don't want to intrude on their privacy."

"Oh no, we definitely couldn't have that." I bent down and stole a kiss from his lips; he was always so sweet to Aston, bringing her different treats every time he came over. She hadn't even decided whether she fully liked him until he brought her a bunch of peppermint candy canes. After that, she started getting excited every time his diesel would pull up the driveway, and maybe she wasn't the only one.

I sat back up, fixing his hat on my head. I should've known better than to think I could make a clean getaway.

"Hey, where you going?" he drawled, reaching up to pull me back down with a crooked smile that was far too tempting.

I laughed—one kiss, one *anything*, was never enough, for either of us. "*No*, don't you look at me that way…"

My warnings didn't do me any good. Billy rolled over with a devilish smirk and tackled me into the ground. I burst into laughter as he growled at my neck and tickled my sides, wrapping my legs high around his waist. He captured my lips with his kiss, his arm looping under my neck and pulling me up against him, and there had never been a more enchanting freedom: rolling around and making out with him in spring-green pastures, horses grazing nearby, like we were still teenagers dreaming of *somedays* and *I'm gonnas*.

I may not have been a teenager anymore, but I was dreaming a little. Of the fields he'd started to speak of in the dark, of rooms in a house that would be ours and the stables where our horses would sleep. The *one day* when we'd be ready to slow down.

For now, he was too busy winding me up.

Billy pulled my legs tighter around him, his jaw secure between my palms and his hands adoring me everywhere, kissing me reckless and far past rational. Denim scraped against denim, Billy crawling closer as something hard settled deliciously firm between my legs.

"That your belt buckle?" I whispered against his lips. "Or you just happy to see me?"

He grinned and thrust against me, earning a gasped moan from my throat. "Both."

I laughed and fisted my hands in his shirt, tugging his lips back to mine and kissing him twice as hard. Until a great big shadow fell over us.

Billy pulled back with a frustrated groan and looked over his shoulder where Gidget's nose was waiting. "What?"

His horse huffed.

Billy looked at me, his brow incredulous. "You believe this animal? He's jeal—oh shit! We're late!"

"Huh?"

But Billy was already leaping up from the ground, taking my hand and pulling me up, then going back for his hat. "Dinner, honey." He stuck his hat on his head and spun me around, patting and brushing my shirt and picking grass out of my hair until he smacked me hard on the ass.

"*Seriously?*"

"Yep." Then he whistled sharp enough that I cringed, Gidget trotting over from where he'd started to graze a few feet away. "C'mere, buddy."

The stallion stopped next to Billy, and I audibly sighed *and* rolled my eyes. I hadn't ridden double since I was a kid, and we were definitely pushing Gidget's weight limit. But Billy just kept swearing that he knew his horse, and he was fine, and regardless, it was too late now.

Billy boosted me up, then vaulted up himself so I was sitting in front of him. I'd also firmly explained earlier how he was doing this backward, and I should be sitting behind so he could steer and there'd be less weight on Gidget's hindquarters. But he didn't want to listen to me about *that*, either.

"*Ugh.* Your horse is bony as hell," I groaned, adjusting my seat again and mentally apologizing to my vagina on repeat. Riding bareback was uncomfortable enough, but Gidget's high withers and overly muscled shoulders from years of dressage training made it even worse.

Billy hugged me into his chest. "I know, I know, I'm sorry," he said. He clicked twice and urged Gidget on, the rhythm of his horse's legs beneath us not nearly as intoxicating as Billy getting to work kissing on my shoulder. He nibbled his way up my neck, his hands roaming and teasing me despite the layers of denim between us. "Honey, you gonna drive?" he muttered into my skin after a minute. "His sense of direction is usually influenced primarily by his stomach."

I snorted, melting further into Billy's chest and moaning as he tilted my head deeper to the side, roughly kissing his way up my jaw. "You were the one who was starving," I reminded him. "And I have no idea where I'm going."

He groaned and made a last pass of quick kisses down my neck, my body warm and soft and eager to be naked and entangled with his again. But he pulled away with a sigh, locking his arm across my hips and taking up Gidget's reins with the other. "All right, let's get going."

It wasn't a long walk back to the barn, but I did my best to memorize every moment of the way he felt behind me. His cologne swirling on the wind and the sun starting to flirt with the idea of setting—time like this with Billy was nearly impossible to come by.

We'd gone home together after he'd flown to Spain, but the week in Memphis went by way too fast. Especially when he left with Mason for a two-day rodeo right in the damn middle of it.

I'd been *pissed* when he first told me he was leaving again. Billy wasn't exactly thrilled about it either, swearing up and down that he wouldn't be going if he had another choice. But Mason didn't ride a bull without someone from the family being there with him, Billy said. And their parents had to work but Billy didn't, so he needed to go. He had to make sure Mason would be okay. At the very least he needed to be there to bring the body home if he wasn't.

I was…not thrilled. But I understood. Kinda. Though no way in hell was I going with them to Georgia with no notice and still exhausted from being gone from my own race.

He left, and he came back, and everything was okay.

But when we looked at the calendar for our upcoming races, things just kept getting worse.

Most weeks, we had a matter of *hours* where we'd be in Memphis at the same time, one of us leaving while the other was coming back. But we had two whole days together this week before I had to leave for the UK, and we were taking every single second of it.

When we made it into the barn, a blush filled my cheeks thanks to the gawking and snickering farmhands. Billy didn't seem to care, just leading us toward Gidget's stall. Until a woman with curly brown hair led a great white horse around the corner, and he stiffened behind me, letting go of my hips as he reached to tip up his hat. "Lorelai."

*Ah, Lynn Hargrove's daughter.*

And according to Billy, the first of Frank's rodeo-racer experiments. But she was still held back in MotoA, even though Billy said it was bullshit, that it wouldn't be long before she was racing with him and Mason in MotoPro, where she should've been all along.

Lorelai stopped in place, planting a hand on her hip and scowling at him. "What are you doing? You know my mom doesn't like people riding double."

I swallowed, guilt choking me as she looked in my direction, arching an eyebrow.

"Yeah, I know," Billy drawled, stopping Gidget and dismounting more gracefully than I expected with me in the way. "But what she doesn't know won't hurt her, and I wouldn't do it with any other horse. Gidget's fine. Aren't ya, buddy?"

I swung my leg over, Billy's hands steadying me as I slid down and met solid ground. *Goddamn, that hurt.* Next time, I was insisting on a saddle like a rational human being.

When I turned around, Lorelai looked just as irritated with Billy as I'd been when he left for that rodeo. "That kind of attitude isn't going to earn you any points with her, and she's already pissed about you keeping him out all night the other week."

*Whoops.* My eyes darted to Billy.

He'd ridden Gidget over to my house at nearly midnight. Opened my window, tied his horse's lead to my desk just inside, and crawled into bed with me. Wasn't the first time, either, which was how he knew the window would be open and the desk was heavy enough to anchor Gidget.

My mama's getting more and more pissed about Gidget eating the roses that she planted for me when I was little. It'd be even worse if she knew he ate the plate of half-eaten dinner on my desk, because he stuck his big horse face right through the open window while Billy and I were making love, and I just...

Billy didn't even scold him! He just laughed and asked if we had any apples in the kitchen.

I *swear*, those two... I have no words for them.

Billy scrubbed the back of his neck at Lorelai's warning, avoiding my eyes. "Yeah, well, Lynn wasn't supposed to know about that, either."

"Mm-hmm." Lorelai sighed, looking over at me. "You gonna introduce me to your girlfriend?"

Billy nodded, still looking at the ground. "Yep. This is Taryn."

I scoffed at him, not sure why he was acting about as big as a bug, but I didn't want any part of it. "Taryn Ledell," I said, extending my hand to her.

This seemed to earn me some points—not that I was keeping score—and she took my hand. "The Superbike racer."

I blinked, genuinely surprised she recognized me by name. "Yeah."

She finally smiled. "Lorelai Hargrove. But Billy's about the only one who calls me that. Most people call me Lor or Lori."

Billy cleared his throat. "Unless you're Massimo."

"Shut it," Lorelai snapped.

Billy did—hands up, lips twisting to bury a grin, but he shut his mouth. Except to mutter, "I'm, uh, I'm gonna put Gidget away. Excuse me." He tipped his hat at us and took Gidget's lead, walking him toward his stall.

I squared my shoulders, turning to Lorelai and her great big mare. "Beautiful girl you've got here," I offered. Neutral ground.

"Gavenia Betis." She beamed up at her horse. "Thank you."

I cocked my head. "Betis? Like the river? In Spain?"

Lorelai's smile stayed just as bright as she nodded at me. "Yep. But I call her Betty White."

I chuckled at that, reaching out to pet her mare's brilliant snowy nose, something in me easing from the nudge of soft lips and teeth nibbling for treats.

"So woman racer to woman racer..." Something in Lorelai's eyes went a little sharper, but the rest of her expression was still as warm as the sun outside. "What the hell is up with your press photos?"

It felt like I had been slapped. I probably looked like it.

"Sorry, it's just..." She fidgeted with the lead rope in her hand. "There's not a lot of us out there, you know?

And I'm all for women owning their sexuality and every-thing, but…is that really the image you want to sell? With your leathers all but unzipped to your knees?" She shook her head. "And if you do, then…okay? I just, I had to ask."

I nearly scoffed. It sure as hell didn't sound like it was okay, and I damn sure didn't feel okay about it. But who the hell was she to shame me for my press kit? Like she was fucking perfect. I knew enough about her to know she had a temper, always fighting with the guys she raced. Even if she didn't take pictures like I did.

No one did, really.

My throat choked closed, my mind biting off insults my tongue wouldn't allow, and Lorelai's face fell.

"*Shit!* I'm sorry. Please don't be upset. Um, there's this guy at the circuit who makes my life a living hell, and everyone thinks I'm sleeping with him because I have the ovaries to flip him off. Billy included, apparently. And even though I have a boyfriend. Etienne. We just met at Le Mans." She shrugged, empathy pouring from her and piling up against my defensive walls, begging to be believed. "None of us are immune, I promise. It just…this *sucks*. But I get it, I swear I do."

"No, it's fine." I blew out a breath, checking over my shoulder, but I didn't see Billy. Probably brushing down Gidget. "It's just…it's mostly my publicist. *All* my publi-cist. He's always coming up with these poses and whisper-ing to the photographers, and I can't say anything."

Lorelai looked at me like I was as dense as I felt once I said it out loud. "Why the hell not? That's so freaking wrong!"

"Well…" My mind raced to come up with excuses. I didn't even know why, other than feeling attacked and like

I needed to defend myself. "Because my manufacturer rep hired him. And I don't, you know, wanna cause problems. You know what it's like. It's hard enough for us to get a chance in the first place."

She half nodded, giving me that. "Okay, well…how's your relationship with your rep?"

"He's…" Werner was… "It's good. He's cool."

Lorelai blinked at me and shook her head, but her voice was kind. "Then talk to him, Taryn. Tell him how you feel. And fire your fucking publicist. *Ugh.*" She pulled me in and hugged me with one arm—really squeezing me and *hugging* me. Then she leaned back, her hand super freaking strong on my shoulder for how petite she was. "You like clothes?"

Yeah, she was definitely a racer. Even *I* was having trouble keeping up with this girl. "I guess?"

"Well." Lorelai tossed her curly brown hair. "I don't know about you, but I have a major, major shopping problem after years of wearing leathers all the time. So anytime you want to borrow anything, *anything*, you come right over. Doesn't even matter if I'm not here. I'll tell my mom, and you raid my closet to your heart's desire. Okay? We're gonna stick together."

I tilted my head at her, more than a little intrigued. "What kind of clothes are we talking about exactly?"

Lorelai's eyes sparkled in a devilish way I knew all too well in my own soul. "Not counting the damage I just did in Paris this past weekend, let's just start with the entire Alice + Olivia collection from 2014 and on."

My jaw hit the dirt. They made the cutest, sexiest clothes *ever*. And they were way beyond the price of what I felt comfortable spending on myself. "Oh my God, I *like* you!"

Lorelai laughed, holding up her hand for a high five. "I like you, too. We'll hang out sometime. Go riding or shopping, whatever." She leaned a little closer. "By the way, Billy's a pretty okay guy. But make sure he's got his wallet before you go anywhere. He's always forgetting it someplace."

A nervous chuckle bubbled up from my throat. "Thanks."

The cowboy in question strolled up, his hat a little lower than normal and his posture kinda slouched, like he was worried he was gonna get kicked for approaching from behind. "How am I doing?" he called out warily. "It still safe for me over there?"

I grinned at Lorelai. She winked back, then looked at him, saying, "Depends. Got your wallet?"

"Yeah," he drawled, sounding offended. But he still patted his back pocket. Then his boots stuck in place like he'd been dried in cement, his face going as white as Lorelai's horse. "*Shit!*"

I burst out laughing, doubling over with the force of it.

Lorelai cracked up with me, but still managed to yell at him, "How do you *always* do this?"

"I don't know!" He looked over his shoulder at his butt like that was gonna make his wallet appear. Then his face whipped in my direction, eyes huge. "Honey, I swear this wasn't on purpose. I ran out the door because I was late coming to get you, and it's right there on my dresser. I can see it…" His eyes squinted, his hand reaching out toward his imaginary dresser and his fist closing as he gritted out a growl.

I could barely breathe for laughing. "We're not even at the restaurant yet, and you're already skipping the bill?"

"I'm not!" He was so damn panicked, it just made it so much funnier. "That's it. We're going to the house."

"Oh no, *no no no*!" But my yelling was no use as Billy stalked off toward his truck, panic seizing my throat and my voice going shrill. "I'll pay for dinner. *I'll pay for dinner!*"

Lorelai screeched, "I'm sorry, *what*?"

Billy spun around, shifting his weight, all indignant. Even though the subject had already been firmly and repeatedly settled. "She hasn't met my parents yet."

Lorelai glanced between me and him, dripping smugness as she drawled, "Really. Whatcha hiding, Billy?"

"Nothing," he bit off, gesturing toward me. "She won't go."

Lorelai snorted, swiveling all her amusement my way.

"I...have my reasons."

Damn straight I wouldn't go. Meeting his parents was serious, and Billy and I had only been dating for a matter of months. Most of which was happening thousands of miles apart on the phone. And yes, he'd met *my* parents, but that had been a disaster.

My mama hated him instantly, pegging him as a bull rider and swearing to his face that he looked like a silver-tongued liar. It didn't matter how many times we explained that his ropes were hung up. She had dried my tears too many times and knew how desperately I never wanted to go back to that life. She said she didn't trust that Billy was done riding bulls any farther than she could throw him. She barely spoke after that, just glaring at him the rest of the night.

My father, however, was more than happy to talk bulls and racing and ranching with Billy like he was the son he never had. They swapped rodeo stories, debated the last World Series and NFL draft, then went out back to look at a section of fence or something. I swear by the time we left, my father was ready to promise my hand in holy freaking matrimony and not even trying to hide it.

But either way, it didn't matter how serious any of it felt to me. Bringing Billy's parents into our…fling? Affair? Ridiculously strong crush? Whatever it was, it was too soon. My parents' reaction had proved that.

"Look, either way, we gotta go." Billy started walking toward me, and I looked to Lorelai, so grateful for her advice even if we'd just met and hoping we really would follow up on our offers to spend time together.

It was *hard* to make friends as an adult, especially when you were gone all the time. "Nice to meet you both," I said to her, reaching out to pet Betty White real quick.

"You too. Have Billy give you my number, and we'll hook up soon."

I threw her a little wave as Billy took my other hand, letting him hurry me along to his truck. We got in quick and shut the doors, Billy practically racing down the caliche driveway. I swatted at his arm, not that it really bothered me. "Slow down."

He chuckled, reaching over to squeeze my thigh. Because I wasn't sexually frustrated enough. "You know you're talking to a motorcycle racer, right?"

Oh *God*, he had to remind me. "Ha ha."

"Besides." He reached for the radio, turning on a country station but keeping the volume low. "We're gonna miss our reservation."

He was so ridiculous. "We don't need to eat anywhere that takes reservations. I told you: I am not that kind of girl. We can go to the Ryan's that just opened up. They have plenty of stuff I can eat."

Billy looked disgusted. "We're not going to *Ryan's*. We're going to the house, I'm getting my wallet, and then we're going to dinner. That's it."

*Oh, that's it?* I gritted my teeth, crossing my arms and legs even tighter. "I will pay for dinner, okay? Then we don't have to go to the house, and we'll still be able to make the reservation."

Billy glanced at me, clearly starting to get irritated, but his voice was still drenched with patience. "I'm driving without a license, honey."

"Shit," I muttered. "Fine. I'll drive."

Billy growled under his breath and kept driving, not saying another word the rest of the way. Not good.

He really wasn't as quiet as I'd suspected when we first met; he told me funny stories almost nonstop, and him giving me the silent treatment was not only the *worst*, it was incredibly effective considering how addicted I was to his voice. To the saccharine country things he said and how he always made me feel better, even if I was already feeling great.

Six different county roads with speed limits set way too low later, he pulled into a gravel driveway, and then a small house came into view: yellow and homey with flower beds blooming in front, a few chickens running around while some goats were going wild in the back. Two older trucks were parked under the attached garage; a third newer, jacked-up one was under a tree.

*Must be Mason's.*

Billy pulled up next to it, throwing his gearshift into Park and leaving the motor running as he got out. "Won't be five minutes." He didn't slam the door, but I still winced when he shut it, hating that I was hurting him.

I'd become painfully aware that he may be a king on the racetrack and in the rodeo arena, but when it came to the important things, Billy didn't believe in himself all that much. He always looked at me like I was nuts when I said I was crazy about him. But I wouldn't have introduced him to my parents if I honestly hadn't felt that way.

*Damn it.*

I turned off his truck and got out, Billy's steps halting halfway up the porch when I jogged up next to him. He blinked at me as I took his hand, lacing my fingers through his. Then I found a smile and stuck it on my lips like I wasn't scared shitless. "Let's meet your parents."

He let out a breath that dropped his shoulders back down to where they should've been. And after I stretched up, lifting a kiss from his lips, he led me up the porch steps and through the front door.

*Here goes nothing.*

"Hey, Mama," he called out, reaching behind us to catch the screen door at the last minute. The smell of berry candles and hot food washed over me, and maybe I was hungrier than I'd thought. But Billy was really good at distracting me from things like *eating*.

"Hey there, Billy Bear," a woman's voice called out. "Thought you were out for the night?"

"Forgot my wallet." Billy winked at me, taking my hands in his and pulling me along into the living room. A wood-paneled wall to my left bordered the kitchen I couldn't see but could hear his mama puttering around in. "Wanna show you something I found. It's *real* pretty."

I pulled one of my hands from his and lightly swatted at his arm for the comment. But a blush still took my cheeks as we rounded the corner. His hand settled on my lower back as I got my first sight of his mama standing at their stove.

She had the same blond hair as Billy but was a little shorter, like Mason. "Aww, cub." She banged a wooden spoon on the edge of her pot before laying it down, then wiped her hands on a dish towel. "You bring me flowers again?"

She turned toward us. Then she clamped her hands over her mouth, her eyes huge.

Billy jolted. "What's wrong? There a spider or something?" He looked at the ceiling, at the walls, at everything and everywhere but where *she* was looking: directly at me. "I don't see it."

She still hadn't moved. I swallowed uncomfortably, peeking up at him. "Billy, where's the bathroom?"

He was still looking toward his mama, but his other hand was sweet on my back, his thumb stroking soothingly over my spine. "Right down the hall, honey." He pointed. "Just around that corner."

"Excuse me," I muttered, shame crawling up my throat as I disappeared behind the safety of the wall, then let out a stifled gasp in the living room.

"The hell was that?" Billy whispered harshly.

"Oh my God," his mama whispered back. "I'm *so sorry*, but you took me by surprise bringing her here, and she's..."

I couldn't take hearing whatever she was going to say next, and I practically ran to the bathroom, shutting the door. There was no lock, though. How was there no lock?

I didn't have to pee so I scrubbed the hell out of my hands, especially after being outside and petting Gidget and Lorelai's horse. Looking up, I was almost scared to check my reflection. But nothing was wrong with my face, and I was dressed fine: jeans and boots, barrel-racing buckle, and a scoop-neck T-shirt. Not anything special but nothing horrific, either.

"Sir!" Billy's voice echoed angrily through the house, and I fell sideways against the door, my blood going cold like I was seconds away from fainting. "I need you in the kitchen, right now, please."

*What the hell have I caused now?*

A door opened and shut somewhere down the hall, and I seriously considered slipping out the front and waiting for Billy at his truck. I had the keys in my freaking hand.

Before I could decide, the bathroom door thrust open, launching me toward the bathtub. I caught my balance at the last second, then whipped around to find Mason sputtering at me. "*Shit*, I'm sorry, Taryn! I didn't know you were here. I, uh, I gotta piss."

*God, could this get any worse?*

"Right." I slid past him, left with no choice but to sneak into the living room. Where I could plainly hear Billy's parents bickering up a storm in the kitchen.

"Well, I'm sorry," his mama said. "But he hasn't brought a girl home since high school, and I take it seriously."

*Since high school? My ten-year reunion is coming up. Yeah, this is exactly why I told him I didn't want to do this…*

I hugged my arms over my chest, taking in all the pictures of the boys on the walls, little bitty things with baseball caps and standing in rodeo arenas holding prize saddles and belt buckles bigger than they were. They were so cute, it was absurd.

There were even more photos of them as older teens in the midst of riding bulls—hooves kicking in the air, black Stetsons and starched shirts with numbers on the back, a right arm bent into a perfect L. I could barely tell at first which were Billy and which were Mason, they looked so alike on a bull. But if I looked hard, I could see it. In the shoulders.

"What? He's brought home plenty of women since then," a deep voice said. Must've been his father. "What about...um...started with a P..."

"Nope, that was his prom date senior year. Mason's brought home women, but not Billy."

Gathering up my courage, I poked my head out far enough to see around the corner. Billy was leaning against the kitchen counter, his ankles crossed and both hands smashed to his face, his hat tipped low.

I restrained a snort. Bet he wasn't gonna forget his wallet after this ever again.

"Really? He hadn't brought home *one*?"

"No," his mama said again. "And your son isn't a boy anymore, he's a man. What do you think comes next, Bill?"

I rooted in place where I stood. *Oh geez, slow down, lady.*

"All right," his father grunted. "You got a point."

"*Ha!* Billy, you heard him say it. *I was right.*"

"I said you had a point, not that you were right."

Billy groaned and shifted his weight, crossing his arms. *Right there with ya, buddy.* The corner of his hat lifted a bit, two fingers waving at me from under his elbow, because he must've realized I was standing in the living room. Still safely out of sight of his parents, like the coward I was.

"All right, Billy, what's going on?" His father's voice was clear and to the point in that way fathers always did that said they wanted a straightforward answer to a straightly asked question. "You love this woman?"

I sucked in a breath, my eyes going wide and everything in the room stopping except for the slow click of the grandfather clock behind me. I wanted to run before he answered. I couldn't wait to hear what he said. *Fuck*, what was he gonna say?

I was kinda feeling it, but we hadn't said it yet, and he hadn't even come *close*… Not a heavy pause, a slip, or anything.

Billy chuckled softly at the floor, his arms crossed tight over the heart in question. When he lifted his head so I could see his face, there was some pink in his cheeks, but there was no hesitation in his eyes or his voice when he answered, "Yes, sir. I do."

My heart burst so bright, I'm pretty sure my smile lit up his whole damn living room.

*He loved me?*

"See?" his mama said. "I told you this was serious."

But Billy was already pushing off the counter and striding toward me, ignoring his father asking where he was going. I didn't have time to be embarrassed before Billy cradled my face in his hands and leaned his forehead to mine, his private smile for me deep and sweet and his thumbs sweeping gently over my cheeks.

It hit me with a boom like lightning as something locked into place, and I brushed a kiss to his palm, hoping he knew how much this wasn't one-sided and impatient to tell him.

There was no denying it any longer: I was hopelessly in love with Billy King. And the only future I wanted anymore was the one he had started dreaming for us—just him and me in a small house on an endless ranch, the Memphis sky, and our horses, too.

# Chapter 11

TARYN'S BEEN DONE WITH HER POSTWORKOUT stretch routine for a good ten minutes, equally the best and worst part of my day. Especially considering her exercise top is basically just a sports bra. But she's too busy giggling at my story to remember she wanted to leave five minutes ago to "beat the weather," whatever that means.

"That is so *ridiculous*!" She laughs across from me, sitting on the floor of the gym at Hargrove Ranch. One legging-clad leg is stretched all the way out to her side, the other tucked in with her knee lying flat, and it's *killing* me. Never wanted to be a shoe so much in my whole life.

"Uh, yeah," I drawl. "That's me trying to cook. Ridiculous."

"How…?"

I shrug. "Don't know. Mama said she'd never seen water boil down like that. I just thought that meant the noodles were done. Plus, I'd already added the powdered cheese stuff, but I don't think I stirred it right or something, because that just seemed to make it madder."

Taryn cracks up more, and *damn, I missed this.*

"Oh my God," she says. "I would have given anything to have been there. And what are you doing making your mama teach you to cook anyway? Aren't her days long enough? Oh *Jesus*, my cheeks hurt…" She presses her palms to her cheeks, making fish faces and looking so adorable, it's almost murder in the first degree.

"Um," I start, trying to avoid the echo of my father's voice in my head saying it was a waste of time, and *Hey, remember when Mason made that soufflé for French class? That was damn good!* But I can't find any good things to say to Taryn. Not when I'm really doing this for us and the future I'm still not sure we have. But I'm living on hope right now, so I settle on, "I have my reasons."

She gives me a look like that's a halfway acceptable answer, but it's clearly bugging her I'm not coming all the way clean. She's still smiling, though. "And you don't want to tell me what those reasons are?"

I bite my lip, squinting at her. "Not yet?"

"Fair enough." She starts chuckling again. "I still can't believe you almost set the kitchen on fire trying to boil water."

I chuckle along with her, mostly just loving how I already know I get to do all this again tomorrow. Because true to her word, Taryn's picked me up every day for the last three weeks at three o'clock, driving us over to Hargrove gym, helping me get through my workouts safely—the right amount of weights now included—and then taking me home. True to *my* word, I haven't lied to her about anything big or small, and I haven't asked for a thing from her.

I offer to drive us over here, but she always says no, claiming it isn't good for my ankle. And I never call her, even if to ask if she's on her way when she's running late. No texts, no flowers, no surprise visits at her window after midnight. I'm not even flirting with her all that much. Sometimes I do, but I think that's just the way I can't help being around her.

I *like* making her laugh. It's what I do best. And she's been laughing a lot lately.

Only time she doesn't is when we pass by Duke Bricker's old ranch on the way over here—can't really help it. Taryn's always wondering who's gonna buy it. If they'll keep the land in one piece or sell it off in bits. Really seems to bother her, and it's given me a couple of ideas. But I haven't found the right time to talk to her about them yet.

Mostly, I've been trying to focus on my recovery, doing everything Taryn says regarding icing and elevating my ankle and all the physical therapy exercises she walked me through how to do at home. Honestly, I have no idea what I would've done without her. And I'm not healed yet—end of January testing is getting closer every day, and I still can't shift gears—but I'm getting better.

Trying to anyway.

Taryn gives me a last beaming smile before she recrosses her legs and somehow uses that as a way to stand up, heading over to the pile of our stuff by the wall. I get myself up without much fuss, my limp a little more than halfway better thanks to the sock-like brace I ordered off the internet. Fits fine under my boot, too, and for a second, I thought Taryn was gonna kiss me again the first time she saw it. Didn't—just gave me a pleased little *hmpf*.

"Here you are." She reaches back to hand me my stuff. I take it from her and quietly set it back down, waiting as she threads her arms through the sleeves of her jacket, then untucks her ponytail. When she's done, she turns around to arch her eyebrow at me. "You're not gonna change? It's freezing outside."

I take a breath, just looking at her, and slowly, I start to smile.

Taryn's whole freaking face lights up, and she playfully pushes at me. "Stop it."

"No, wait, hold on," I rush out, ready to plead my case. Doesn't mean I'm not scared shitless about getting shot down, but I'm still going for it. "We've been doing...okay, right? I mean, I've been...pretty good. Being just friends."

Taryn rolls her eyes, but she still hasn't stopped smiling. She faces me all the way, crossing her arms. "I guess you've been okay."

"All right, well..." I remind myself not to swallow. No weakness, no fear. Wish my pulse understood that. "You think maybe I can get some kind of reward for good behavior? Maybe some time served?"

She bursts out laughing. "Absolutely not! You haven't been *that* good."

I let that one go and tell myself it's still okay to ask. That it's *important* to ask, because it's what I want, and she wants me to stand up for myself.

For her and for us.

And that's what I'm gonna start doing. Putting her first. No matter the consequences.

"One date," I offer, holding up a single finger. "Real thing. Let me call on you at your door, your mama can glare at me through the front window, and let me take you out. Show you off a bit. I won't..." This is the hard part. "I won't ask for another if you say no, and I won't pull nothing stupid. I mean...apart from the one *kinda* big, really important thing that I want to do—to give you—so I can show you that...that I'm ready to start over. And more than that, Taryn, I'm ready for us to take the next steps forward like you want. It's what *I* want. But for now, I'm just asking for one date. Please."

Taryn spends the longest time ever looking at me, that mind of hers going even faster than her bike does, and I'm praying for mercy every single second of it.

I didn't even call her honey *once*.

"What kind of big important thing?" she asks quietly.

I smile, unable to resist tempting her a bit more. "The kind you tell your grandkids about."

"Oh my God," she mutters, looking away like that'll keep me from noticing how red she just got. But she also doesn't look all that upset about the idea of us having grandkids one day, either. "Seriously?" she says, looking back at me. "You're doing this now?"

I shrug. "Well, yeah. What do you think? Want to give starting over a shot?" I hold up my fingers in a pinch motion. "Maybe just a little one?"

Taryn stares at my hand like there's something other than just space between my fingertips. Then she starts sputtering, her words struggling to keep up with her rapid-fire thoughts. "I think…I think I expected you to pull something like this for a while, but I guess it says something that it took you this long."

I bite the holy hell out of my tongue to keep from grinning.

"Though I don't know if that's actually a good thing or a bad one," Taryn rambles on, "because it still seems like you're putting Mason and everyone else ahead of you *and* me. But you still waited…and you're still asking. And you've been…clearly working on trying to be more honest with me, which I appreciate. So…" She swallows, shrugging a shoulder and giving me just a hint of a smile. "I guess. Yeah. We can go on a date."

I let my grin break free, though it doesn't begin to

compare to what's happening in my chest. This is like winning Valencia all over again. *Nah*, better. "Thank you."

Her smile ramps all the way up, fully blushing now. "Stop, okay? And when is this big important date happening?"

"Christmas Eve?"

She tilts her head at me, seeming more curious than ever. "That's, like, a week from now. You don't want to do this tomorrow? Or, like, Friday?"

"Well, Christmas is your favorite holiday, right?"

"Yeah…"

"Then it's definitely gotta be Christmas Eve."

Taryn bites her lip, looking just as nervous as she did while dancing with me on our first date. But in a really good way. "What are you up to, cowboy?"

I consider that. "Nothing I shouldn't have done a long time ago."

She seems to like that answer. "Okay, well, do I need to get dressed up or anything?"

"Yeah," I agree, "that would probably be good. You never know when pictures happen."

Taryn laughs, looking over her shoulder like she's embarrassed. "All right," she says, leaning over to grab her truck keys.

Still on my best behavior, I don't even try to steal a peek at her ass. Not a long one, anyway.

"Christmas Eve it is, then. But I doubt it's gonna earn you any points with my mama."

*We'll see about that.*

My heart's beating straight out of my chest the whole way up Duke Bricker's driveway, which I take as slow as my transmission will allow. My eyes catalog it all: the patched-up fence, the depth of the ditch lining it, the type of gravel, and the tree branches overhanging, sure to be heavy soon with the ice storms we're expecting.

It all looks so *different* now.

As the driveway turns, it opens up into rolling acres with a barn way back in the distance, the farmhouse dropped right in the middle of the clearing, and a grand old oak tree guarding it. I blow out a breath, giving my engine a little more gas and heading up to the house, telling myself I can do this. Plenty of people do. And I'm not even most people.

I'm a MotoPro World Champion. And I used to ride bulls for *fun*, damn it.

Still, it takes me more than a few minutes to get the guts to get out of my truck once I park. And I'm not even done closing the door before I have to go back for my hat.

I take the front porch steps easily, feeling pretty natural as I stroll up to the door.

So far, so good.

I knock politely, then clasp my hands in front of me and wait. The door opens a moment later, and a grin stretches across my face as I tip up my hat. "Hey, Annie."

"Hi, Billy." She steps back with a warm smile, opening the door for me. "It's good to see you. Come on in."

———

"So what do you think?" Annie says, standing by the kitchen table.

I blow out a breath for probably the fiftieth time in the last two hours, back in the main farmhouse after crawling every inch of the property with her and my head full with too much stuff to keep it all straight.

Eighty acres. Fenced mostly with high tensile wire. Ten acres of meadows and pasture, hot wire. Two wells. Stock pond with bass and catfish. Barn, stables, warehouse for farming equipment. Underground water and electric lines. Second farmhouse on the back forty—three bedrooms, one bathroom, tin roof, wood stove. Main house is four bedrooms, two bathrooms, two gas ovens, nine closets, ten minutes from the interstate, fifteen from the elementary school, and *oh my God, I can't breathe. I need Taryn.*

I turn toward the microwave and swallow a gasp that tastes like 2.5 million goddamn dollars, and I don't know what the hell I'm doing out here.

Duke Bricker's ranch. I must've lost my damned mind.

Too bad the devil on my shoulder keeps whispering how I'm making good money now, my winning bonus from Valencia and making the World Champion podium more than I'd planned to earn in a lifetime. And I've tried to be smart with it, and I've been saving. But there's no guarantee how long that career's gonna last me, especially when they've been talking about me retiring since the first time I hurt my knee, and I can't even ride my bike right now with my ankle the way it is and...

*Damn it.*

Worst part is...I want it. I want it *bad.*

Taryn was right. It's not just everything we talked about. It's *more.* It's fucking perfect. And with the way things have been going between me and her...I think it's a real possibility that she could still want this, too. Maybe not tomorrow, but someday. And I don't want to risk this place getting sold to someone else in the meantime.

She said she loved it out here, and she told me she wanted to feel safe. I *know* Taryn, and safe to her is feeling committed to, like she has a future she can count on. And this is the biggest way I can think of doing just that. A mortgage is gonna matter a hell of a lot more to her than any words I could ever say.

"Tell you what," Annie says, and I turn to find her gathering up her purse from the table and slinging it up her shoulder. God, I feel like such a piece of crap for wasting her time when this is all so clearly out of my league. "And I would never do this for anyone else, but seeing as I've known you since we were kids, and as long as you promise not to tell"—she winks at me—"I'm gonna go show some other houses to some other clients, and I'm gonna leave the keys with you. Stay as long as you like, look around, maybe have your dad come over and look at it with you— just a suggestion. And you just…drop the keys off tomorrow when you're done, okay?" She smiles like she isn't being way sweeter than she needs, considering the way she dumped me at the Freshman Winter Ball.

"Thank you," I tell her, meaning every letter of every word. "That's real kind, Annie."

She blushes, batting my words away. "You're too much, Billy King. But you always have been." She walks away with a wave over her shoulder, her wedding ring shining in the sunlight coming through the front windows. Because she ended up marrying Jack Henley about two seconds after we graduated high school, like we all reassured him she would.

The front door shuts behind her, and I lean against the

kitchen counter, smoothing my hands over the linoleum countertop and trying to take it all in.

The carpet's gross, but I'm not worried about it. The cabinets are in good shape, which I *was* concerned about, because replacing cabinetry is a bitch. Not too bothered about colors or paint, because it's all old and needs to be redone anyway. But the roof on the main house was reshingled five years ago, drywall's in good shape, and the plumbing is almost all brand new.

Six spacious horse stalls and a good-sized shed that could hold plenty of tools, farming equipment, trucks, four-wheelers, and *lots* of motorcycles.

Eighty raw, natural acres.

Two houses, seven bedrooms between them.

And all for the low, low price of 2.5 *million dollars*.

"Fuck me," I groan to the house, alone enough to use the worst of my words before I pull out my phone, doing what I always do when I'm about to do something stupid: I call my brother.

"Hey," he answers on the second ring, sounding all sorts of pissed off. Goats are bleating in the background like they're having some sort of bovid rave party. "I just cut the hell out of my thumb on the edge of the damn trash barrel because those damn stupid goats wouldn't stop kicking it as I was trying to move it over to where Daddy wanted—how you know when you need stitches?"

I sigh up at the ceiling, wondering how smart it is to bring his big mouth into my plans. "Wash it out, get a damn Band-Aid, then come meet me out here at Duke Bricker's ranch."

Mason snorts. "All right. I need to bring your lariat?"

I scrub a hand over my face. "Nah. Bring, uh…" I rack

my mind. Food? Music? Got plenty of fresh air… "Bring us some beer. And use the front door, not the back forty fence."

Mason waits a beat, then pointedly clears his throat. "I'm *sorry*," he drawls. "Did my sober-as-a-judge brother just ask me to bring him a six-pack? In the middle of a Wednesday? To Duke Bricker's ranch?"

I glance around at the counters, the double oven and the kitchen chairs, and the worn old furniture still in the living room. "Yep."

Mason's voice drops low, appropriately serious. "I'm on my way."

―――――

"So what do you think?"

Mason smiles sloppily from the second rocking chair next to me on the back porch, snuggled in his jacket against the cold night air and happily rocking back and forth. "I think I'm drunk."

I snort, taking another sip of my beer. I'm buzzing off the beer and a half I've had; Mason's already finished the rest of them, along with the flask he swore he stopped carrying more than a month ago, after the incident. "Yeah."

"Yeah," Mason says, sniffling and picking up speed. "I'm also thinking it's no fucking wonder we always got busted with that Arabian, because with any bit of moon-light, you can see that fence clear as day from where we're sitting. Billy…I think Duke told on us!"

I laugh, tipping my beer his direction. "You know, I think you're right."

"Man." Mason shakes his head, rocking in his chair. "That isn't right."

I can't believe him sometimes. "Mason. What. Do. You. Think?"

His head snaps my way, his eyes glassy and his tongue loose, which is exactly what I was hoping for. The honest truth from the person I trust second-most in the world. "Huh? Oh, right. Well…" He shrugs, looking out over the ranch. At the fields where that Arabian used to roam and the fence I know we busted at least once trying to climb over it. "Mama's gonna cry, but Mama always cries."

I take another sip, giving him that one. "Yeah."

Mason nods to himself, then his nose scrunches. "Daddy's gonna be *pissed*."

For some reason, this cracks me up something awful, Mason joining in until we're howling and crying with the force of it. I guess because it's the story of our whole laughable lives: Mama's gonna cry, and Daddy's gonna be pissed.

"Oh man, all right," I say after a minute, trying to catch my breath and get us reined in. Mason reaches over and swipes my beer, and I'm too tired to do anything but let him. I fold forward, patting my hands over my hair and groaning until I find the balls to get out the words I'd only ever say to him. And maybe Taryn. But she isn't here. For exactly this damn reason. "For real, though. What if… what if I can't do this?" I risk a glance up at my brother, who's already shaking his head and rolling his eyes as he stares out at the back forty. But he doesn't know what it's like to think you have it all and watch your time at the top fall away while someone else does it better. "What if this doesn't work? For people like…us?"

For *me*. I mean people like me.

Mason's eyes dart my way, then he slouches farther in his rocking chair. "I don't know, Billy. I mean…it's risky. Sure."

I cough out a scoff. "Ya fucking think?"

"Really fucking risky," he agrees, chugging the rest of my beer then looking around like he doesn't know what to do with the empty bottle. Gotta give him credit, at least he didn't chuck it.

I hold out my hand, and he passes it to me, collapsing back and shrugging his jacket closer around his shoulders, looking like he's close to passing out.

"Still, though," he slurs, his arm lazily rising to point at me. "Hell of a way to make a stand, Brother."

"Yeah, well…" I lean back in my chair, slowly rocking as Mason starts snoring.

After I double-check he isn't faking, I look out over the land, tickled green with the rays of moonlight filtering down. The meadows, the stalls, the fences, and the stock pond. The second house in the distance, barely visible from here.

I dare to risk the barest hint of a smile. "That's kind of the point."

# Chapter 12

"So, NO BULLSHIT, YOU'RE A REAL EFFING COWBOY?" Sophie's eyes were huge, her grin even wider, and she'd been so enraptured with meeting Billy that I think her British accent had somehow gotten thicker. Lunch was all but forgotten as she sat across from us on the paddock in sunny Monterey, California—home of the incomparable Laguna Seca raceway and its famous corkscrew I couldn't wait to tangle with.

Billy chuckled at his folded arms on the table, then squinted up at my friend from under his big black hat. "Yes, ma'am."

Sophie gave me a look that said there was no excuse not to be doing everything to him in bed I was already doing, *thank you very much*. "Girl, I know," I said with a laugh.

"Bet he's a whiskey drinker, though. Am I right?"

I smoothed my hand across Billy's back, hugging his side and so in love with him, I was nearly gooey with it.

"Actually," he drawled, "I don't drink."

Sophie scoffed, wiggling her finger his way. "Now *that* I don't believe."

"It's true," I confirmed, oddly proud as I breathed in Zest soap, clean sweat, Old Spice, and never a hint of alcohol.

My friend grinned wickedly, propping her chin in her hand and eyeing me. "Sounds like there's a story there."

I couldn't help but laugh a little, teasing Billy some more. "With this one? Always."

Billy groaned and tugged at his hat. *Bingo.* "All right, well, I was about…fifteen? Yeah, because Mason wasn't a freshman yet, so he must've been about thirteen…"

"*Brother,*" I mouthed to Sophie. She nodded.

"So yeah," Billy continued. "I was about fifteen the first time I got the guts to swipe one of my father's beers from the fridge. Snuck me and Mason out behind the chicken coop to drink it, and of course, about two seconds after I finally get the top off, we get busted."

I winced, but Billy shook his head.

"Damnedest thing, though: our father wasn't even the slightest bit mad. In fact, he said he was proud of us. That me stealing that beer was the first step I'd taken on the road to being a man."

I could not imagine the man I'd met saying these things. I looked at Sophie, her twisted brow confirming it wasn't just me that found this totally strange. "You're shitting me."

"Nope," Billy said. "He took us inside, sat us down, and gave us another beer each. When we were done, we were feeling…pretty good. And then he had a real good idea: since we were trying beer, why not try out all the alcohols and find out which ones we liked best?"

Sophie perked up. "Oh bloody hell, I think I know where this is going."

Billy pointed at her. "So being not just men now, but cowboy men"—Billy looked at me pointedly—"the most important thing for us to try next was—"

"Whiskey," we said at the same time.

Sophie chuckled. "Oh, go on then."

"So he poured us shots, and we knocked 'em back, and

damn that whiskey burned *good*. And hey, if you like the burn of whiskey, you know what else you'll probably like?" Billy glanced at me, and I covered my mouth with my hand, about to lose it. "Tequila."

Sophie lost it.

"Turns out gin's kinda okay too, once you get over the taste," Billy went on. "And vodka isn't that bad, either." He blinked a little, his nose starting to scrunch like he was smelling something bad. "Champagne wasn't my thing, though. And the red wine *really* did not sit well." Billy shuddered, then looked back to Sophie, smiling brightly. "And that's why I don't drink."

I finally gave up and burst into laughter, giggling into his arm and faintly registering a sweet, soft kiss to my hair. I felt so awful for the kid who got tricked so badly by his dad. And after having met Billy's father, I could absolutely see the eldest King pulling such a stunt on his unruly princes. "How in the world does Mason still drink?"

Billy scoffed. "Mason was stealing more beer the very next night and claiming hair of the dog. In eighth grade. And who do you think got blamed for him even knowing that term in the first place?"

"*Aww.*"

Billy nodded, then stole a quick kiss.

Sophie groaned like she was going to be sick. "You two are so cute, it's almost psychological warfare on those of us who are single."

I leveled a look at Sophie, even though my cousin April had said something similar when she'd met Billy. But that was just ridiculous considering she and her fiancé, Kenny, were way worse when it came to PDA. "Then go talk to Miette, and try not to call her a cunt this time."

Sophie sputtered. "I'd rather delete my entire Instagram of Natalie Dormer pics before I went anywhere *near* what's between the Ice Queen's legs."

I leaned forward, suspicions more than confirmed. "Sure you would."

She rolled her eyes, but her cheeks were tinting a little darker as she waved a hand in front of her face. "Whatever. I'm off. Cowboy Billy, it was lovely to have met you. Even if your girlfriend is a posh tosser."

I gasped playfully, but Billy was a perfect gentleman as always. "Very nice to meet you, Miss Sophie."

"*Ugh.*" Sophie got up from her seat. "They need to clone him. Twice. And make the second one a woman. Yeah, that ought to do it. Cheers!"

I snorted, watching her walk away and absently teasing my nails along the defined lines in Billy's back, my cheek resting on his sturdy arm. He felt as stable as home, like nothing bad could ever happen as long as he was around; he made me laugh too much for the monsters to be real.

"So that's Sophie." He peeked at me, his eyes full of the stories I'd told him about our years racing together.

I nodded. "That's Sophie. And thank you again for flying out here with me."

"There somewhere else you think I'd rather be?"

"I just… You don't get to be home much, not as much as I do anyway. And you're spending one of your weeks off to be here with me, and I…want you to know I appreciate it."

Billy's smile deepened, his voice lowering privately. "Taryn, I don't think I can take much more of your appreciation without an IV to keep me hydrated. Honey, it's *fine.*"

Heat flamed my neck, and I knew he'd said it was okay a dozen times already. But I still felt bad about being so selfish with him. I didn't want to share Billy with anyone. Least of all his ever-attention-demanding brother.

I was starting to get really attached to being alone together, especially for longer than a few hours at a time. Billy and I had been glued at the hip for *days* now—except when I was practicing or racing—but him traveling with me, staying together in my RV, and keeping me company in my pit box and on the paddock...it had all started making so much *sense*.

How easy it could be to love him. Not just infatuatedly but committedly after the newness and the goose bumps and the giggles wore off. The peace from knowing it would be his arms that would cradle me in my weak moments, strong enough to protect me and gentle enough to comfort me.

I trusted Billy implicitly. And it was getting to the point that no matter where we were or what we were doing, somewhere in the back of my heart, a part of me was already on a ranch in a *someday*. My palms teasing the tops of tall grass as I walked in forever fields, Billy mending wire fences in the distance, and our horses roaming together.

Billy took a sip from his water bottle, nudging me a bit and pulling me from my fantasy. A grin was teasing the corner of his lips as the California sun glistened off his arms, golden and rippling with untapped strength. "Something you wanna share?"

I sighed, shaking my head and not finding big enough words. Not when he was in every vision of my future and not when I couldn't wait to start it all. Full throttle, forget the brakes, and with the endless sky above promising us forever. "Fucking *crazy* about you."

Billy chuckled, picking a piece of chicken off my plate. "See, to me? That sounds crazy."

*Whatever.* He was always terrible at taking compliments, the ones that mattered anyway. I let him go so I could pick up the last of my garlic chicken lettuce wrap and take a bite. Which was just another item in the endless list of things I had to give Billy credit for: never *once* had he glutened me, accidentally or otherwise.

He glanced over, a satisfied smile teasing his lips and nearly glowing in the sunshine. "Good?"

I nodded as I shoveled the last of my lettuce wrap in my mouth, wiggling happily over my lunch and gorging on tangy chicken bursting with flavor, water chestnuts, and crunchy sprouts, and *God*, I loved him. I had no idea where he even found this. "Mm-hmm."

"Good," he repeated, taking another sip of his water.

Then the *worst* happened—one of the monsters found me.

"Tear-tear-*Taryn* it up," the voice I hated most in the world called out.

*Fuck, here we go.*

I hurried to finish chewing, wiping my mouth with a napkin. Billy's brow scrunched up, his eyes flicking behind us. But there was no time to explain. Not two seconds later, Colton was next to me, leaning onto the table with his face way too close to mine.

"Hey, sweetheart, whatcha eating? Aww, salad again?" He looked over my head in Billy's direction. "She's a vegetarian. Isn't she cute?"

"I'm not a vegetarian," I snapped at Colton, irritation taking over any and all rationality.

Confusion was plain in his big brainless eyes, that cheap

cologne he wore rolling off him in waves that threatened to upend my lunch. "Then what's with all the salads?"

What a dipshit. And it's not like I expected him to know the finer details of my life, but we'd been teammates for two years. I was fully and completely aware of his peanut allergy. "I can't eat gluten."

"Exactly." He gestured my way. "Vegetarian."

I thought my head was gonna explode. "Oh my God, that is not what that means."

"Oh excuse me, Miss 'I have a degree so I'm better than everyone else.'"

I gaped at him. "I do not think that!"

Billy clapped his hands behind me—once, loud and hard—and it startled me to freaking death. I'd actually forgotten he was sitting there for a second.

I whipped around to assess the damage, sure he was going to be furious about Colton calling me sweetheart and all the dick swinging going on. But Billy didn't look pissed. He looked *impressed* as he stood up, walking around behind me to poke Colton in the chest. "You're Colton Froggenbrains!"

Oh *holy hell*, he did not just—

"Freitag-Brahns," Colton bit out.

"Oh *man*, I've been a big fan of yours ever since you started racing! It's a real pleasure to meet you." Billy grinned and reached out to shake Colton's hand, the latter looking at me a little more smug than confused now, but I was firmly convinced I'd been transported to an alternate universe.

What the hell was Billy doing fawning all over his... competition?

"Pleasure's all mine, I'm sure." Colton winked at me, and I nearly threw up on him again.

"Man," Billy said with a chuckle, not releasing Colton's hand as he clapped him on the shoulder. "Your win last year in Portugal was a thing of beauty, especially considering the odds the bookies had stacked against you heading off the grid. And you know, you really did get the short end of the stick in Rimini. I felt for you, man. No one wants to go out that way."

Colton's face twitched, and I nearly choked with the realization of what was going on.

Billy knew.

He knew *everything*.

"So tell me, friend to fan…" Billy checked around and then lowered his voice like he was whispering a secret. "That slide you had in Argentina two years ago, when you came around turn eighteen in second gear and then you wiped out in turn nineteen—was it *really* a cold tire like you said? Because my little brother, he *swears* he saw the transmission on your OnBoard drop into first gear instead of popping up into third like it should've. But I told him that couldn't have been right, because *no way* you'd chicken out like that."

If someone had bumped me, I would've shattered.

Colton's neck and whole freaking face were turning red like he was *enraged*, but Billy was still grinning away like the dopiest devotee in Colton's fan club.

"You know," Colton growled, "I don't think I caught your name, friend."

Billy looked at me. "Oh my goodness, where are my manners?" Then he looked back to Colton, holding his hand out again. "Billy King, Yaalon Moto. Nice to meet you."

Colton didn't shake Billy's hand the second time. His

eyes flipped to me, screaming a thousand things I was sure I'd hear later during our photo shoot. Fine. Let him bring it on. This was worth every second of it. "The MotoPro racer," he gritted out.

"Yup," I popped, pride tingling down my spine and radiating through my whole body as I sat up straight and crossed my arms. "That's the one."

"Anyway, I'm sorry to have taken up so much of your time." Billy clapped Colton on the back hard enough to nudge him a bit. "I know y'all got a lot of prep work to do. Ma'am." Billy tipped his hat my way, then turned and walked off, whistling calmly toward pit lane.

I sputtered out a noise, sure I was gonna die from heart palpitations. He just *walked off*! He didn't kiss me or call me honey, imply he'd see me later, or say anything about us being together.

No claiming, no jealousy.

No fear.

Colton scoffed. "What an idiot," he sneered.

But I was worlds more aware than my teammate, and I shook my head slowly, beaming at Billy's back. "Nope. That's a man who knows *exactly* what he's doing."

If only I could've said the same for myself.

⁓⁓⁓

Little less than an hour later, Colton and I were still trading barbs. But this time, he had the pleasure of watching me squirm as he smeared his hands all over me in the press room.

"Back the fuck off," I hissed, leaning farther away from him as he palmed my lower back and I pushed harder at his chest. Even worse, I was being forced to fucking *smile* as that creep's hands crept closer to my ass, and all while knowing Billy was somewhere on the paddock.

"Not a chance," Colton breathed, tugging me even closer, and *oh my God, was he hard?*

"What is the problem now?" the photographer complained. "The girl looks constipated."

"Taryn," Sheldon whined through gum smacks. "Could you be a little less constipated, baby girl?"

My stomach roiled as my lower jaw started quivering, and a cold sweat of panic broke out across my skin—the telltale signs I was moments away from vomiting. Again. But this wasn't gluten wrecking my system; it was *them.*

"Actually, you know what? Let's, uh, try a new pose. Why don't you turn around and stand in front of Colton?" Sheldon knocked the photographer's chest. "Girl's got an ass that could sell satanism to a Baptist."

A thousand tiny comments he'd made in the past flashed through my head. And under the endless echo of *baby girl* spawned some kind of turbo rage that burned away the nausea swirling in my veins and replaced it with a bitter indignation that made me feel *invincible.* A Lorelai "Wreckless" Hargrove kind of invincible—she'd never put up with this shit. And she was right: I didn't have to, either.

No one should.

"That's *it!*" I shoved Colton off me for good, satisfaction blazing out of me as I watched him fall off the fake podium they had us standing on to land directly on his ass.

"Ow, you *bitch!*"

I flipped him off. With both hands. Shaking them in his face and roaring at him like a rabid fiend. I'd fucking had it.

I didn't care what Werner was going to do, gawking

at me from the corner with a sandwich in his hand and a bite half-chewed in his mouth. I couldn't care how disappointed Mike was going to be: standing dutifully on the sidelines, arms crossed over his Santa stomach, security badge tangled in his beard, and his jaw on the floor.

I stormed off the podium, straight up to Sheldon, and I punched him right in his goddamn gum-chewing face.

The crack of my fist against his jaw was louder than I'd expected, my hand exploding in pain as he stumbled. Fell. Then he started scrambling backward like the coward he was as I stalked forward.

"You're *fired*!" I spat at him, my voice starting to break from the tears threatening my eyes.

*Holy crap, my hand hurts!*

Sheldon gaped up at me, hands clasped over the bottom half of his face and his eyes wild. "Fuck you! You can't fire me!"

I didn't know if he was right. But it didn't matter anymore. I looked over at Werner, exhausted and exhilarated and completely heartbroken.

I'd given racing everything I had—years spent sacrificing my body, my pride to the curves of racetracks that only crave the taste of your leathers, to speed that tests the strength of your bones. Crashing my way through a calling until the fans were calling my name, a gorgeous mistress no one believed I could want. The surprise career after a lifetime of playing it safe and the bluff I called on destiny.

But no matter how much I loved it, it was still just a job, and I could find another. Another team, another sport if I had to. I had a degree, a supportive family, and I had Billy. I had options, and I didn't need...*this*!

I stared down Mike and Werner, the two men who had

always believed in me and dared to see me as fast when everyone else had only seen a face.

That time, my voice did break. "I quit."

The collective gasp seemed to suck the air from the room. Without another look at Mike or Colton or any of them, I turned for the door.

*God, how was I going to explain this? To Sophie and Billy and just...everyone?*

I didn't make it three steps before a hand landed on my arm.

"Taryn, please, let us talk this over!" Werner's eyes were panicked, rooting me in place as I choked back regret-filled tears. He looked over his shoulder, pointing toward Sheldon still lying on the floor and clutching at his face. "Someone, remove him," Werner barked. Then he turned back toward me, swallowing thickly. "Taryn," he said, a smile growing in the corner of his mouth and lighting up his eyes. "I am so proud and thankful you just did that!"

A rush of air swept from my lungs. There was no way I heard him right. "You are?"

"*Yes!*" he cried out, looking a lot more like the giddy executive who showed up in person to sign me. "We... MMW has always wanted you to be able to express your-self exactly as you wish. We believe in *you*. But we—*I*—hired Sheldon because I thought having an American publicist would help make you more comfortable while traveling abroad." He dropped his head into his hand, pinching at his eyes and muttering sharply at himself in German. When he looked up, he looked like he'd never felt so bad in his life. "I have made a horrible error in judg-ment, and I hope you can forgive me, Taryn. Had I known you were unhappy, I never would have allowed him to stay.

And I *should* have known. I should have realized." His jaw locked as he glanced back to where Sheldon had been only minutes before. "Please," Werner said, his voice strained as he looked at me, "do not quit now. Do not let him win. Let me try to fix my mistake."

I was too overwhelmed, too shocked by what I had done and all that had happened in the last few minutes… but *damn it*, he had a point. Fuck Sheldon.

I looked over at Mike, his eyes pleading with me not to make the hasty decision I wanted: to let Billy fly me home to Memphis and start a life together with a far less complicated schedule and forget that once upon a time, I'd been a motorcycle racer, too.

But as upset as I was, I knew Mike and Werner were right, and running wasn't the answer. No matter how good and simple and easy and wonderful it sounded. I couldn't let people like Sheldon or Colton win.

"Fine," I agreed. "I'll stay. But some things are going to change. Starting now."

---

Billy beamed up at me from my bed in my RV, naked as could be while I straddled his lap. His palms lazily caressed their way up my thighs as I danced my fingers down his chest, enjoying the exquisite view of perfect muscles and soft, tan skin. Everything in my body was still so wonderfully fuzzy from post-orgasmic bliss: a tribute to the attention he'd lavished on me after such a stressful day. "Show me again," he said, a devilish smirk to his lips.

"Seriously? Again?" We'd done this, like, four times already.

"Please?"

I sighed dramatically, but I was having a harder time than ever shutting down my smile. "I think *someone* has a secret masochistic fetish, and if need be, I'm open to discussing the implementation of handcuffs in our sex life."

Billy snorted, the movement doing something delicious between us. "I'm just proud, honey, and you should be, too."

"Fine," I muttered, but I still smirked and closed my fingers into a fist, playing like I was punching him in the chin. "Take that!"

"*Agh!*" Billy fluttered his eyes, falling against the headboard in a really terrible impression of being knocked out.

I couldn't help giggling as I captured his jaw in my palms and leaned down to kiss him again. Each squeeze of his hands on my hips and smoothing up my back threatened to reduce me to a puddle of limbs that was his to play with, and I couldn't be happier about it.

Billy always played *so* nicely. And totally in my favor.

"You are so corny."

"Yeah?" he mumbled, his voice thick as he brushed my hair from my face. My cheeks were cradled in his hands, my forehead leaned to his. "I may be corny. But you're fuckin' beautiful."

*Beautiful.*

It felt as though he'd dumped a bucket of ice water on my bare naked body. I sat up immediately, scoffing at him. After everything that had happened that day, that was what he chose to say? Not sweet or smart or a good racer or...

And the fact that he *knew* better than to be surprised, so he was making that *face* where he was dripping with stubbornness about it...

I got off his lap and left the bed.

Billy sighed, the sheets rustling behind me as he covered himself up. "Taryn—"

"No." I grabbed the nearest clothes off the floor, pulling up a pair of green boxer shorts that were clearly Billy's and not the pajamas shorts I thought I'd seen, but whatever. I tugged a shirt over my head, fighting to get my hair out of the collar. Then I turned toward him, hugging my arms over my chest because my nipples were still hard. *Stupid nipples.* "I already told you a million times: I *hate* it when you say that."

His arms were crossed over his chest, too, his jaw tight. "I'm sorry, honey," he muttered. "I just...I don't understand this. You *are* beautiful, Taryn. I've seen the tiaras and the banner from when you were crowned Miss Memphis. You being beautiful...it's a *fact.*"

"Stop!"

He threw up his hands, looking as frustrated as I was because I could not understand why he could *not* get this right. He understood everything else I needed, except for this one really important thing.

"Billy..." My voice was shaky with trying to keep my words slow, controlled. "Being 'beautiful' has been the worst curse of my life. It has brought me stalkers, assault, and men like Sheldon demeaning me in public *and* private. I need you to see me as more than a face, more than a body, and if that's what you like most about me, then we have a big fucking problem, because I am more than...*this.*"

Billy stared at me. Then he *laughed*, scrubbing his hands over his face.

*Jerk.*

He sat forward, clasping his hands around his bent

knees. "Honey, I need you to remind us how we met, please."

I stared at him, shocked he was relying on an example that served as proof to my argument but ready to drive home my point either way. "You hit on me at a rodeo, jackass."

Billy held up a finger. "That may be true, but do you remember what I said to you?"

My brow furrowed as I searched my mind, the burning hurt in my veins lowering to a slow simmer. "Something about Gidget wanting to meet Aston. Which was clearly a *lie*."

"Nope." Billy smiled bright and easy, and there was no hint of fabrication in his eyes. "And since you don't remember, I told you we saw y'all barrel racing. And that was why I was coming to talk to you."

*Shit, he did say that.*

"And if you recall, you were wearing a hat when you raced that morning because it was bright as hell out there at noon. I couldn't see your face, Taryn. I'd seen a woman who could fly on a horse and wasn't afraid to cut it really damn close to those barrels. And...well, I had to meet her. Didn't matter what you looked like. I just loved the way you *rode*."

My heart caught in my throat, Billy shrugging and leaning against my headboard, lacing his hands behind his head and staring at the door like he was lost in the memory.

"Imagine my delight when you turned out to be from Memphis, too. And *damn*, girl, you had my head spinning with how fast you busted me on Gidget being a Hargrove horse and him being built for dressage. But I guess I should've expected it with the way you raced." His eyes darted to me, then back to the door. "When you told me that night that you raced Superbike?" He shook his head, letting out a low whistle. "That was it for me. And I tell you, Taryn, I didn't know how it was gonna work out between us, with the distance and the opposite racing schedules and everything. But I was more than ready to start trying."

*God*, I did not deserve this guy.

I crept back to the bed, sitting on the edge and facing him, overflowing with love and regret and a million things I didn't know how to sort out. But I knew I wanted the time to do it; all the time in the world wouldn't be enough with him. "I'm sorry," I whispered.

"Well, you should be," he snapped like he was mad, but he winked immediately after.

I took that as my invitation to snuggle up on his chest, melting into the way his arms fell around me and tucked me closer to him. "I love you," I breathed, Billy holding me tighter and dropping a kiss to my hair.

"Well, of course you do." He brushed my hair from my face, tilting my chin up so I could see his eyes. "I'm damn hot!"

I found my smile and my laugh, reaching up to pull his lips down to mine, Billy kissing me sweetly and pouring into me all the depth of his devotion. And once again, I found myself wishing so much it could be like this always.

That we would be together every night, working through our lives' daily problems somewhere between eating dinner and getting ready for bed, whether on the road or at the ranch we dreamed of one day buying together. Laughing about anything and everything before sex, and after sex, and waking up in the morning to him snoring on his stomach, the covers totally mine and that tight ass of his completely exposed.

"Hey, Taryn?" Mike called, knocking softly on the door. "If you're still awake, I, uh, I gotta talk to you."

I groaned, lifting a last kiss from Billy's lips before I pulled away, getting out of bed. "Hold that thought," I whispered, Billy ghosting his fingertips over my arms and not even trying to hide the heat simmering in his eyes.

"I'm holding, honey."

I moaned again and turned away, blowing out a breath as I tried to get my hormones under control before I faced my manager. With a last peek at Billy in my bed, I slipped out of my room and shut the door behind me, finding Mike sitting at the mini kitchen table, bright red and wiggling like a kid about to open his birthday presents.

A slow smile crept across my face as I inched toward him. "What?"

He shook his head, practically bursting with glee as I slid into my place at the table. "Werner. Loves you. I just got off the phone with him, and MMW is...they're *thrilled* that piece of shit—I won't even say his name—is gone. They *hated* him, T. Almost more than you did, turns out. And Werner? He wants to make all this up to you, in a big way, and I think he's come up with a pretty good idea on how to do it."

My pulse was sky-high, goose bumps all over my skin. How could it possibly get better than firing Sheldon?

Mike reached over and took my hands, pride radiating from him. "He wants to move you to Germany. And I'll explain more about why in a second, but first, you should know he wants to set you up with your own place. Fully furnished however you want and completely paid for by

MMW. He's even going to hire a personal chef of *your* choosing to help stay ahead of your celiac, and he emailed me pictures of some of the condos he was looking at for you to choose from in Munich, and I...I didn't know those kinds of places existed in real life."

He shook his head, stars in his eyes.

"But the best part," Mike continued, his voice starting to shake, "and the reason he's doing all this is so that the very second you're settled in Germany, you and he can launch a new international image campaign under *your direction*. Interviews, magazines, radio, television, photo shoots...you'll call the shots every step of the way. You did it, Taryn!"

*Oh no...*

Feeling—awareness—bled from me, chased by the cold panic gripping my heart and rooting me in place.

I let go of his hands, sitting back in my seat.

Numb.

"I can't move to Germany."

Mike's face fell. "What?"

"I..." I glanced at my bedroom door, then at Mike, lowering my voice to a frantic whisper as lightning-fast images of all I'd lose sped through my mind. The ranch we'd never own together, the barn our horses would never share. The anniversaries and the birthdays and the Christmases and the breakfasts and the... "I can't move to Germany!"

"Taryn!" Mike's eyes were wild as he gestured toward my room, but he kept his voice low. "You cannot throw this away for him. This is the opportunity of a lifetime! You turn this down, I guarantee you won't get another offer like this in the future. What are you *doing*?"

I stared at my manager.

I pushed up from the table, taking a step toward my room.

Then I pivoted back, totally at a loss. "Maybe...maybe we can still do the campaign, but from the States. I know it's going to make it a million times harder for everyone, but I cannot just up and move to another freaking country, Mike. My family is in Memphis. I have a horse in Memphis. I have... My whole life is there. I *can't*."

Mike leaned back, crossing his arms and not giving me an existential inch. "You went away to college. To Texas. Four years."

"That was different!"

"You can do this too, Taryn," he gritted out. "You absolutely can, but it means letting some things *go* and recognizing that other things are more important. Your racing career *has* to be more important." He leaned closer, his eyes pleading with me. "Don't you want to go to your alma mater and talk to the kids? Give them hope? Well, this is your chance to rewrite your history until no one would ever remember the past. It's a chance for a clean start, one you can be proud of."

I shook my head, holding out my hand and unable to find the words for any of this. Other than no. Absolutely not. As much as I wanted a clean slate, I couldn't *do this*. Mike was wrong: this wasn't college, this was forever, and I couldn't leave home, couldn't leave the future Billy and I had been building. This wasn't our dream; this was absurd.

"You don't have to decide tonight," Mike grumbled. "But you will have to decide eventually. And I caution you, Taryn: don't throw away your whole life for a few moments of fun. It doesn't last, and your future is worth so much more than that."

I couldn't breathe under the weight of his words, the truth in them I knew better than I wanted to admit. But I didn't have a choice.

I had to breathe; I had to go back into my room. And I swore to myself ten times over it was absolutely the right decision not to tell Billy about the offer.

I wasn't lying if I wasn't going to take it, and it only would've caused problems. He'd probably *want* me to take it or at least argue I should, and it wasn't his call. It was mine. And I wasn't moving to Germany, no matter what Mike or anyone else said. Werner would come around, and we'd figure out how to do the image campaign another way.

I knew what I was doing.

I thought.

# Chapter 13

*Billy King—Present Day*

IT'S COLDER THAN ANYTHING AS I JOG MY WAY UP Taryn's porch on Christmas Eve, dressed to the nines in my new pair of boots, pressed jeans, the buckle I won the first time I met her, and a tie choking me over a freshly starched shirt. Was gonna wear a sports coat instead of my normal one, but it's too damn cold for that.

My fingers are already going numb around the bouquet of flowers in my hand, my nuts shriveling into peanuts every second it takes someone to answer the door after my shave-and-a-haircut knock. Lights are on, and I can hear them shuffling around and bickering in there, but I don't know what's taking so long.

*God*, it's fucking freezing.

Then I get fucking *wrecked*.

"Wow" is all I can breathlessly mumble when Taryn opens the door, my lungs collapsed from the red cocktail dress dripping down her body.

The neckline is high and straight across her collarbones, the bottom hem of her skirt halfway up her slender thighs. But it's not her legs that have me going absolutely gaga. It's the peek of her bare arms afforded by the red hoodless cape lightly flirting down her sides and drifting down her back to meet her skirt.

I look up at her, entranced by her soft, sexy makeup and blond hair all shiny and clean and just the littlest bit curly. I swallow, trying to find my voice. "You look…gross."

Taryn lights up brighter than the decorated tree in the living room behind her, one of those black high heels lifting to pet the back of her other calf. *God*, her legs look good. "You clean up pretty well yourself, cowboy." She eyes me up and down, but then her eyes stay down and she points. "Did you…did you get new boots?"

"Yeah," I rumble, trying not to let the hubris I'm feeling show on my face as Taryn's head pops up. "Was time, don't ya think?"

She doesn't look like she agrees. "Well…"

I scoff, reaching up to scrub at my forehead, because I can't *believe* her sometimes. "You've been telling me to get new boots for a year," I remind her.

She bites her red bottom lip. "Yeah, but…I *like* bitching about your boots. That's…our thing. And you just threw them away?"

I'm a hell of a lot warmer than I was a second ago. My voice, too. "Nah, honey. I still got 'em."

That perks her right back up. "Oh. Okay, then."

*Guess these are getting returned.* Weren't that comfortable anyway.

She reaches for the flowers, and I yank them back at the last minute. "*Uh-uh*, these aren't for you." She's not even done downshifting into offended when I lift my arm over her head, sliding past her into the house twanging with spicy cinnamon broomsticks.

"Hey, Billy," her father says from the kitchen, smiling as he leans against the counter and fusses with his bolo tie. "Merry Christmas."

I touch my hat in his direction. "Sir." He always did like me.

Time to offer myself up to the Beast.

Like the rest of us, she's all dressed up in her Sunday best, but she's glaring at me from her usual glaring spot—a statue of perpetual disappointment behind the sofa, her mouth pursed like she wishes her burgundy lips could whisper words that would burst me into flames on the spot, creamy Berber carpet be damned.

I slip off my hat and drop to my bad knee in front of her, holding up the flowers.

"Oh, good Lord." She looks around like she doesn't know what to make of me. But that's just weird, because she's had me pegged since the first time I walked through her front door and she called me a liar straight to my face.

"Mrs. Ledell," I start, staring at her pointy-toed shoes and trying to ignore the sound of Taryn's father snickering in the kitchen, along with the peripheral image of Taryn gawking at me from the front door. "I'm real sorry about what I did. I didn't just hurt Taryn with my actions, I hurt your whole family. And I'm really trying to make it right, so a big part of that means you hearing my apology from me. And I'm sorry."

No one says a word. Taryn's father even stops snickering. At least there's no chance of this ending up on ESPN later, unlike the rest of my most embarrassing moments.

After a beat, she snatches the flowers from my hand with the ferocity of a cobra strike, and I peek up. She's huffing and rolling her eyes, but she's got the bouquet cradled in her arm like the beauty queen Taryn says she was. "Get *up*."

"Yes, ma'am." I scramble to my feet and wince a bit because I do it too fast, a quick sting of pain echoing from my ankle. Taryn shifts from the door until I hold out a low hand to stop her, mouthing, "*I'm okay.*"

Taryn's mama takes another breath, her back straightening and chin lifting like her daughter's always does before she lays down the law. But only once I've already snuck my way into her forgiving me. "We are going to have a *long* talk about priorities come the new year, young man."

"Yes, ma'am," I say. "Happy to."

She grits out something else I can't understand and storms off around my side.

When I start breathing again, I put on my hat and push feeling through my limbs, walking back to Taryn. "Got your bible?"

She scrunches up her pretty face at me. "What? Why do I need my bible?"

I arch an eyebrow right back at her. "It's Christmas Eve. We're going to church."

Her scrunch goes from a solid six to a shrewd eleven. "*Church?* I thought we were going on a date."

"It's Christmas Eve," I repeat, then look to her parents. "Y'all are going, right?"

"Yeah," her father says, her mama looking slightly less wrathful now that she knows my nefarious plan to escort her daughter to a worship service. "It's Christmas Eve."

I look to Taryn, shrugging with the vindication of her father's agreement. She stomps off the way of her bedroom.

"Mama!" she yells a minute later. "You know where it is? I can't find it!"

"What?" Her mama whooshes past me on her way down the hallway.

I chuckle and check the time on my watch, then clasp my hands in front of me, waiting by the door.

"What do you mean you can't find it? How do you not know where your bible is?"

"Because I don't read it."

"Taryn Molly May!"

"Well?"

Since they're busy tearing apart Taryn's room, sounds like, her father takes the opportunity to sneak over my way, grinning and reaching his hand out. "How you been, Billy?"

"Good, sir." I shake his hand firmly, returning his smile with my own. "I'm hanging in there."

He lets out a quiet chuckle, clapping me on the shoulder. "Yeah, you are."

A breath blows from my lips as I glance toward Taryn's room and back at him.

He nods, getting it. "You just remember what I told you."

"I'm keeping it in mind, yes, sir."

"All right, then. You're a good man. Don't let 'em make you forget it." He gives me another smile, another pat. "And congratulations on Valencia, by the way." He heads back into the kitchen, pulling open the fridge.

"This is so stupid," Taryn says from her bedroom. "It's a church. They have bibles there."

I snap to attention as her high heels click fiercely down the hallway, and I pull open the front door so she never slows a bit as she storms around me and straight out onto the porch.

"I'll have her home early," I tell her mama, coming up the hallway behind her.

"You *better*."

With a last touch to my hat, I duck out and shut the door behind me, Taryn already getting in the passenger side of my truck. The overhead light shines on her like a halo, showing her fidgeting around all irritated and rubbing at her bare arms before she looks into the back seat, grabs the blue-jean patchwork quilt, pulls it into the front seat, then settles it over her lap.

The corner of my mouth turns up, and I head to my side, getting in and shutting the door. I'd left my truck running with the heater on, but her teeth are still chattering as she reaches to crank up the heat another notch.

"It's freezing like it's gonna snow." She pulls the quilt up to her chin, snuggling underneath it.

"Yeah, I know. I'm sorry."

She snorts. "Well, it's your fault."

I try to keep that in mind, her perfume already making my head fuzzy when I go to back out, then turn around to pull out of her driveway.

"So…" She's all devilish red lips and thick black eyelashes, with a naughty little sense of adventure that is way too damn tempting. "Where are we *really* going?"

My grin is so big it feels like my face is gonna break in half, and I tighten my hands on the steering wheel, growling over all my best-worst ideas. There's an entire world of possibilities before me with the open road ahead, and *damn*, I don't want to do the right thing. I want to do the fun one.

But that's not what this is about, second first date or not, and she deserves better from me than that. I promised her I wouldn't pull nothing stupid. No matter how much I may wanna.

"I told you, honey. It's Christmas Eve, and we're going to Christmas service. Just like your parents are doing, and my parents are doing, and practically the whole darn town, because that's what country people do."

Taryn grits out a frustrated huff and throws her hands up. "Fine. Take me to church!"

And yeah, I probably shouldn't have laughed at her for doing that. At least not that hard anyway. But that's what Taryn and I do—we bicker, and we dance, and we laugh and laugh.

It's how we *love*. It always has been, and I wouldn't want it any other way.

―〰―

"It's so good to see you, honey," my mama says for the dozenth time, hugging Taryn in the parking lot outside the chapel.

My father shifts his weight again, gnawing his toothpick into sawdust and looking at me like I'm next. His normal amount of patience has long since been chewed up, but he's finding some extra for me considering the situation. The hour service has been done for nearly fifteen minutes, but Mama and Taryn have been talking inside since we were dismissed with our last amen, and we've been freezing our nuts off outside waiting for them. Mason, too.

"I've missed you, too, Mrs. King." Taryn's already shivering from the cold, but when she pulls back, she looks like she really meant that.

My mama cups her cheeks between her hands. "We'll talk soon, okay?"

Taryn nods, and I reach out to lay a light hand on her lower back. "You ready?"

My mama lets her go and steps back, her hands tipped in prayer against her mouth. Why is she always acting like we're all dying?

Taryn peeks up at me, so much warmth in her eyes that now *I'm* dying to know what she and Mama talked about. But fat chance on her ever telling me. "Yeah. I'm ready."

"Sir," I say to my father, waiting until I get my nod to go before I start leading Taryn to my truck. We don't get far.

"Taryn, I'm…"

I pivot at my brother's timid voice, finding him staring at the gravel and holding his stomach like he doesn't feel good. Taryn's shoulders drop, and before I can ask what's going on, she slips away from me and walks straight toward him, stopping in front of Mason, who still isn't meeting her eyes.

She lays a hand on his arm. "Thank you for your letter."

My parents and I share surprised looks. Mason wrote a letter? To *Taryn*?

"What you wrote meant a lot to me, and I've been thinking a lot about what you said. And I…I do forgive you, Mason. I want you to know that." She squeezes his arm, ducking her head a little. "You're a really good writer, by the way."

His head drops a little lower before he looks up at her. Cracks just a touch of a smile, then touches his hat. "Merry Christmas, Taryn."

I'm still stunned as anything when he starts shuffling off, hands in the pockets of his jacket. My father looks my way—Mama, too—since they still don't know the details of what split me and Taryn up. Only that I screwed up the best thing that ever happened to me. They definitely don't know Mason's right smack-dab in the middle of it, and I'd much rather keep it that way.

I look quickly to Taryn, who's smiling like she's feeling ten pounds lighter as she takes my outstretched hand and lets me lead her to my truck before they start asking too many questions.

"Cold?" I ask her, gravel crunching under her high heels and the moonlight sparkling off her earrings. It's not far to my parked truck, but that dress isn't much, and I'm happy to hand over my jacket if need be.

"I'm okay." She beams up at me, her hand warm in mine. She spent the whole hour with my hand cradled in both of hers and keeping them on her lap as we listened and prayed and sang soft hymns that I don't know all the words to, but she does. "It was a beautiful service."

"Yeah, it was," I agree, taking out my keys.

"Lot about forgiveness."

I chuckle, nodding. "Yeah, that tends to happen around Christmas."

Taryn squints at me. "Thought that was normally Easter?"

I choke and cough through my laughter, opening up the passenger door for her. "I don't actually know, honey," I admit as she gets in. "I hardly make it up here save once a year, seems like."

She squeaks and points at me, and I wink as I playfully shut the door in her face.

*Sucker…*

I can still hear her laughing as I stroll around my tailgate, tossing my keys in my hand with all the vindication of winning a long, tough race. And when I open my door and get in, Taryn's already snuggled under the quilt my grandma sewed for me when I was little and got the chicken pox. It isn't the prettiest blanket, considering it's old and well used, but all the patches of my granddaddy's Wrangler and Levi blue jeans make it real heavy and warm, and it's my favorite on cold nights like this one.

I start my sputtering engine, praying the heater won't take all damn night to get warmed up. Should've just left it running during the hour service if I was being smart about it. Maybe Mason's right and heated seats are worth more than what you pay for them. But Taryn doesn't seem to mind my old truck, never really has.

When I pull out of the parking lot of the church, she's looking so damn content that I'm nearly melted with how much I've missed the simple sound of her breathing next to me as I drive. *Screw it.* I reach over and take her hand, something flooding her eyes that almost looks like the sparkle of tears but in a really, really good way.

It only spurs me on more, and I thread my fingers through hers and squeeze, bringing them up to press a kiss to the back of her hand because I can't keep it in—how much I love her and have missed her and how much I'm ready to start over. The right way. For all the right reasons.

She lets out a breath toward the windshield that's thick with everything I'm feeling and all we aren't saying. But at least I know she feels it, too.

———

It's not a long drive back to her house, but by the time I pull up, Taryn's whole side is pressed to mine on the bench seat, her head on my shoulder. I'm not ready for the night to end. Not by a long shot.

I put my truck into Park with heavy clicks of my gearshift, sitting back and turning down the Christmas music playing on the radio, though it wasn't playing that loud to start with. Taryn snuggles a little deeper into my side, and I tip my head against hers as she starts smoothing her palm against mine, kinda playing with my fingers and how they fit between hers. I can't resist a smile. I missed her hands, too. I missed everything about her.

"Do we have to go inside right away?" she whispers.

"Nah, honey. We don't have to go inside."

She holds onto me a little tighter, and I can barely think around the pull between us. She smells so damn good, all I want is to wrap her in my arms. It's been weeks since she's hugged me, and I can't survive that way. I *need* her hugs.

"I got you something," I whisper, my heart starting to race from all I'm about to set in motion. But there's no future I want that doesn't have her in it, front and center.

Taryn starts breathing a little harder, squeezing my hand before she looks up at me, her eyes searching mine. She's nervous, but she's brave, too, and I'm so damn lucky that the latter always wins with her. "Okay," she says. "I'm ready."

I unbuckle my seat belt and open my door, getting out and waving at her to follow. She gives me a curious smile and gets out a second later, leaving her door open so the light stays on and the radio is drifting out, but that's fine.

I lay down the tailgate, peeling back the tarp and unstrapping the cardboard box big enough for a giant beach ball, then slide it her way. Taryn's got a line twisting above her eyebrows, but there's a smile brewing in the corner of her mouth as she tucks her shiny hair behind her ear. "What's this?"

"Open it."

She's fully beaming now as she unfolds the top and stretches up to peek inside, then tilts her head at me. "Strips of paper?"

I nod slowly, like that will somehow explain how long that took me. "Lots of little strips of paper."

Taryn swoons my way like I gave her a box of puppies. "What do they say?"

I take a breath, looking deep into her beautiful blue eyes, and try to calm my nerves. This is my moment, and I gotta do this right. We're gonna remember this night forever.

"They're all my lies," I tell her, my voice soft and full of all the love I feel. "Every lie I ever told; all the ones I could remember. Big ones, small ones. Stupid ones, and important ones. They're all there. And I'm giving them to you. I don't need them anymore."

She looks to the box, reaching in and pulling out a handful. Pride starts warming me from hat to boots as she lifts them up, then lets them slip through her fingers like sand.

Slowly, I start to smile.

Until Taryn looks back at me, her eyes simmering with disappointment. "Is this your big important thing?" she asks quietly.

*Uh-oh.*

"I mean, after everything we've been through, this is what you're giving me tonight? Haven't I had enough lies from you?" Her voice breaks, nose getting red, and *shit*, she's not gonna cry, is she? She takes the first hasty swipe at her face, and Ground Control, we got a big problem.

"I don't know?" I don't even know how this happened. I thought this was the right thing—the thing we needed.

"Billy, I don't understand," she says, and *yeah*, that makes two of us. "You said we were gonna go on a date, and you take me to *church*? I'm not that kind of girl. I've never been that kind of girl, you *know that*... And now you give me this box of lies? *Damn it*, Billy. When you said you had a big important thing planned for us, a way to start over and take the next steps forward, I thought that meant you were gonna propose to me tonight."

I rock back like she just clocked me square across the jaw.

She thought *what*?

Taryn's hands fly to her mouth, so that was maybe not the right reaction.

"Well..." Is there still air in the world? I check to make sure my stiff new boots are on the ground. Yep. I look up at Taryn, dizzy. "Were you gonna say yes?"

She doesn't answer—other than to turn away and hide her face in her hands, her shoulders trembling like she's definitely crying now, and I don't know how this can get any worse. We're right up there with her birthday.

Kicker of the whole thing is she's completely right, again. I should've fucking proposed. My great-grandma's art deco ring in pocket or not, the second I saw her in that red dress, I should've dropped to my knee—*both* knees—and asked her to marry me.

*Christ*, I am a jackass.

"Taryn..." I slowly walk up behind her, scared to spook her, but I can't do nothing when she's this upset and it's my fault. She also isn't walking back into her house yet, which means I need to get my ass in gear before she does. "Honey, I'm...I didn't know you were there yet," I whisper as I stop behind her. "You're not even taking my calls right now."

She sniffles. "Like that even means anything. We still spend every single day together." Her voice is all raspy and choked, and I'm more confused than ever now, but that's pretty much par for the course.

I debate whether to rest a hand on her shoulder. "I'm sorry."

She whirls around and buries her face in my shirt, gripping my jacket with both her fists and trembling from top to bottom. I blink, still scared to touch her.

"I've missed you," she whimpers, and *oh goddamn it*, I'm never gonna unhear that. It's gonna haunt me for the rest of my life.

I try not to sigh out loud as my arms come around her, tucking her into me as tight as possible and doing my best to get her warm, and I feel like *such* a jerk. Especially with how much I'm loving having her against me again, even though she's just crying and crying away, holding onto me for dear life. But I've missed her, too, more than I knew it was ever possible to miss a person, even when you were still working out with them every day.

"I know, honey, I know." I take deep breaths in the hope she'll take some, too, and wait for the heat from my body to soak into hers. I rest my cheek against her shiny hair, breathing in summer peaches and soothing lavender, but I don't steal a kiss, even to her temple.

"I've been so mad at you," she whispers, and I nod, because I know she has been. "But I still love you, Billy."

I nearly crumble from how much I needed to hear that. "God, Taryn. I love *you*."

She snuggles a little closer under my chin, hugging her arms around me instead of clinging straight to my shirt, and I hope she isn't planning on letting go soon. I'll stand out here all night holding her if she'll let me.

"I don't know what to do," she says.

I consider that for a second, thinking over all the things I want to do, which ones she may be okay with and which ones she definitely won't be, and then I get it—I know what to do. It's so damn simple, I should've thought of it five minutes ago.

Reaching behind me, I find one of her hands on my lower back. I tuck my thumb into the middle of her palm, holding on, and then I start to move, just a little bit, from side to side, barely more than rocking her. But in time to the Christmas music playing on my radio and drifting out the open passenger door of my truck.

Taryn's chest moves kinda funny, almost like she's laughing to herself. But she slides her other hand up to cling to my shoulder, and she starts to move with me, letting me lead her.

I smile secretly with my cheek to her hair where she can't see. She's breathing normally now, swaying with me to old singers whose names I don't know, but I know the melodies to their songs. I risk a simple spin, letting her out under my arm so she twirls a bit and remembers how pretty I think she is, even if I'm not allowed to tell her, Taryn kinda smiling at me as she slowly spins back in.

"This wasn't what I meant," she says, still half smiling with her hand on my shoulder, mine on her lower back, and our other ones tangling together over my heart as I keep us dancing as long as I can. "I meant I don't know where we go from here."

I consider that, too, along with the snowflakes I think I saw drifting down and settling on the red fabric of her dress. "Well, how about inside?"

Taryn chuckles, stopping us and letting me go, reaching up to wipe at her face. "No."

"No?" I tease, helping wipe away some of the mascara from her cheek. I'm always ruining her best makeup. I don't know why she's always forgiving me for it, either. But I sure am thankful.

"No," she says again, firmer. "I'm still kind of mad at you."

"Great," I mutter under my breath, which based on Taryn's face was *definitely* the wrong thing to say. But since we're being honest… "Look, how long is all this gonna take?"

Her jaw lands somewhere on the ground starting to turn white with snow, a shocked little squeak popping from her throat right before she starts ripping me apart. "You want me to give you a date? Like on the calendar? Well, *sorry*, I don't have my planner with me, so I'll have to get back to you with the future time and place of our reunion! Why are you even asking me this? You in some kind of rush? Got a deadline?"

"Well," I barge in, because I know from experience she can keep going for a while, "considering we're leaving for work in a few weeks and I'm not gonna see you…yeah, kinda."

Taryn shakes her head at me, right back to being nothing but frustrated and acting like she wasn't literally crying over missing me two damn seconds ago. "Can't rush this, Billy."

"No, I know that. I just… *God*, Taryn, I miss you. And I'm trying, honey. I'm really trying to fix this. I'm doing everything I can think of, everything I know to do."

Her eyes drop to my new boots, her bare shoulders dusted with snowflakes. "I know you are."

"So what do I do next, huh? What's my next move here? I backed off, I gave you time, and I'll give you more, but I just… I don't understand when one minute, I can't call you, and the next, you wanna get married. So how do we get from here to there? Because every step I take seems to be the wrong one, and you're not exactly making it easy."

She takes a fast step toward me, her palms warm on my chest and her Aunt Sylvie's ruby ring sparkling under the moonlight. "Whoa, honey, slow down," she says, her perfume already working to calm my temper as she looks up into my eyes. "You're right, okay? I haven't been making it easy, but I swear I'm not doing it on purpose, and I'm sorry, Billy. I really am. And tonight getting messed up? That was *my* fault, okay? You didn't...*you* did everything right. I know I have a problem with putting..." She swallows before her next words like they're thick as honey. "Unreasonable expectations and demands on you."

*Huh.*

"But I'm going to work on it, I promise." Her hands on my chest get a little more desperate. "I know it's not fair to you, and I'm sorry. All this...this was my mistake."

*Aw hell.* "No, it's not," I mumble. Because if I had done this right, she'd be wearing my ring and a smile instead of her aunt's and a frown. "I mean, I appreciate you saying you're gonna work on that and all, but still. I did this all wrong, honey. I just wanted to show you... I don't know what I was thinking."

Her hands slide up to cup my jaw, soft and gentle and feeling so damn good, it nearly breaks me. "I do," she whispers. "Billy, I get it, okay? And I'm sorry I took all this too far. I just get excited sometimes and...well, you know how I get."

I risk a small grin. "Swept off your feet?"

Taryn snorts. "Shut up," she scolds immediately after, but I still got her to laugh a little. "And...well, yeah. I miss you."

"*Well…*" I nod toward the house, a dusting of snow coming off my hat with the movement. *Damn*, it's really starting to come down. "Let's go inside, then. Where it's warm."

*Really* warm.

She shakes her head, but her eyes are trying to be kind about it. "Billy, it's Christmas Eve."

I roll my eyes. "Yeah, thanks to my dumb idea."

Taryn smiles up at me, shifting a little closer and fidgeting with my tie. Like that isn't hurting me even worse. "Not dumb, and I can prove it to you. Why'd you pick it?"

"I don't know," I mutter. "Thought it would be romantic."

She melts a little more my way, in direct violation of the snow falling all over us. "It is romantic."

I look around at her front yard, the exhaust my truck is dumping, and the clear outline of her mama in the front window probably casting a spell on me. It isn't exactly Paris in September or Rome in the spring, but it's home. "Yeah, it kinda is, isn't it?"

Taryn softly laughs. "See? You always know what you're doing. You just act like you don't."

She turns and starts walking toward her front door, and I jog a little behind her to catch up, waiting as she turns the knob and cracks open the door, then spins to face me.

I rest my palm against the doorframe in my old leaning spot, unable to resist a grin. "Can I get a good-night kiss?"

She tilts her head. "I thought you said you weren't gonna ask for nothing?"

"I…said I wouldn't ask for another date. Not that I wouldn't ask for a kiss."

"Ah." Taryn starts to slip inside the door, her smile getting brighter and brighter. "Maybe next time, cowboy."

I groan from the depths of my soul, leaning closer toward her as she giggles and shuts the door a little more.

"Sweet dreams, Billy," she whispers, the cruelest two inches in the world separating my smile from hers.

With the look she's giving me? Sweet they will surely be. "Merry Christmas, honey."

---

"So that's it."

"That's it," Annie says.

The mortgage guy, Tom, looks at me from across his large desk: stocky and red-faced but sporting a huge grin with his hands clasped on top of a giant file that's got every debit card swipe, check deposit, balance transfer, tax filing, stock trade, and retirement investment I've made over the last two years. Reminds me of the day I signed with Yaalon: my whole future laid out perfectly ahead of me and bound in one big fat contract.

"So it's real straightforward from here, since you already gave us all the financial records the underwriters need." He knocks the file with his knuckle, then leans back in his enormous leather chair, rocking back and forth a little. "It'll take them some time to get it all squared away, probably a couple of weeks or so. Maybe a little quicker. But the most important thing is that no matter what, for the next few weeks, don't spend any money."

I laugh, then hurry to cover my mouth to hide it, feeling as jittery as I did the first time I drove my father's old truck. "That isn't hard for me."

Tom holds up a hand. "Well, I appreciate you saying that. But like I do for all my clients, I'll repeat the same to you: no new trucks, no diamond rings, no trips to Vegas with your buddies—hell, don't even go out to dinner that much. You do that, keep paying your bills, and keep those credit card balances low, I think we're gonna be just fine."

I blow out a breath, looking at Annie, so damn glad she's here because I need somebody else to know, and I'm not telling a soul until all this is in the bag—just in case. But she's known me since before I was stuttering my very first pickup lines, and if anyone in this room understands the gravity of what this means for my family, she does.

I shrug at her, about ready to burst. "I'm gonna own Duke Bricker's ranch."

She tilts her head, beaming at me and shaking her finger with that one-upper look she's had since we were kids. "Nope. You're gonna own the King Ranch."

"Oh *shit*, I like that." I laugh and stand up when she does, Annie slinging her purse up her shoulder as I reach over to shake Tom's hand, chuckling along with us like the jolly old Santa Claus he basically is to me. "All right, let's get it done."

# Chapter 14

*Taryn Ledell—Back Then*

THERE'S LIVING, AND THERE'S DANCING. AND THEN there's leading thousands of German Moto Grand Prix fans through how to do a country line dance while Garth Brooks blares through the Sachsenring stadium, Billy and Mason and Lorelai and me showing the kick-ass people of Chemnitz how we do it back in Memphis.

Mason said afterward it had only been fair to return the culture shock since Brazilians had all but taken over North American bull riding. But Mason drinks. Something he does a damn lot of when either of the King brothers pulls off a win. And Billy had won in Germany.

He'd won *big*.

"*Yeah!*" Mason roared again to the rest of the paddock. He leapt up from his chair within our circle, hoisting his brother's medal into the night air like a wrestler showing off their prize belt. Billy and Lorelai and I just laughed— Lor sober, me tipsy, Mason *wasted*, and Billy...Billy was actually catching a buzz.

"Sit down and shut up," he told his brother, chuckling while taking another sip of his winner's champagne. Then he melted my way: his leathers dirty but unzipped to show a bleach-spotted Baylor T-shirt he'd stolen from my closet and swore was good luck when he raced. "I love you."

The sweet mixture of his cologne tinged with racing exhaust washed over me, and proud wasn't a big enough word. After all the people always bugging him about retiring, after all his surgeries and the work he'd done in therapy to heal his knee and make it back to the circuit and reclaim his spot at the top... "I love *you*."

He leaned a little closer, his smile a little looser. "Especially that birthmark you got right at the top of—"

I clamped my hand over his mouth—*jackass*—then grasped his jaw and smacked a kiss on his lips. "Shut up."

"Okay." He smiled and swiveled his weight back into the middle of his chair, Mason falling backward into his own.

"Congratulations, Billy!" someone on the paddock called, and all of us—well, three of us—raised our drinks to the mystery congratulator.

I couldn't help it. I leaned over and pressed another kiss to Billy's cheek, smoothing my palm down the nape of his neck and loving how he shivered with goose bumps. "Congratulations again, honey."

"Why, thank you." He stole a soft kiss from my lips, one I was eager to follow into the bedroom of his RV.

Mason, however, had to go and point at his brother, ruining all my plans. "How much champagne you got left in that bottle?"

"Mason," I said to him, laughing but still meaning it. "You've had enough."

"Uh..." Billy swirled it around. "'Bout half?"

He'd drunk not even a quarter of it. Most had been sprayed on the podium earlier.

"What the fuck?" Mason cursed at him. "Drink that shit! Or I'm gonna."

Instead, Billy swiveled his face my way, making his best attempt at bedroom eyes. "Hey. You wanna get outta here? I know a great little place nearby."

*Fuck. Yeah.*

But I didn't get a chance to answer. Mason sprang from his chair, Billy bursting out laughing as he twisted away, trying to take a sip from the bottle while fending off his brother, who had tackled him in his seat and ended up kicking me in the shin in the process.

"*Ow*, Mason!"

The guys didn't hear me, still wrestling over the bottle until Mason ripped it away from Billy, spraying champagne over all of us.

"Seriously?" Lor stared at her champagne-speckled sweater, black leggings, and chunky ankle boots. "This is Marc Jacobs!"

Mason snorted. "He your boyfriend?"

Lor glared right back. "You know I'm dating Etienne. Have been since Le Mans."

"Where's he at then?" Mason glanced around. "Etienne! Olly olly oxen free!"

"It's not funny," Lor snapped, still clearly sore over her boyfriend's lack of communication skills. Last she told me, the voicemails had downgraded into texts, and even those were becoming fewer and fewer. But living in different countries didn't exactly bode well for a happily ever after.

Mason swigged from the bottle, collapsing into his chair again. "Yeah? 'Cause I think it's hilarious."

"Fucking idiot," Billy called him with a laugh. He glanced at me. "Sorry."

"It's fine, honey." I smoothed my hand across his shoulders, but I was getting more and more irritated as I watched Mason drink Billy's celebratory champagne. Not that Billy needed to drink, but that was *his*. He'd earned it, and Mason...*ugh*.

Billy twitched. "Uh-oh." He kicked at his brother's foot and jerked his chin at something behind Lor. Mason whipped around, then back to Billy with the same huge grin he always wore right before they ran off to do something dumb...and usually dangerous.

Lor looked between them, no longer concerned about her absent boyfriend or the champagne ruining her designer sweater. She sat up straighter. "What's going on?"

They didn't answer her. Mason just set down the bottle, both the guys singing, "Moss-*im*-oooooo!"

"*Shit!*" Her face went panicked, spiking my own anxiety as her eyes pleaded with me for help I didn't know how to give. She went for the next best thing: grabbing the champagne by Mason's feet and chugging it as my eyes went wide.

Lor hardly *ever* drank; she was a calorie counter and a fitness fiend, and she practically lived in her home gym when she was in Memphis.

Then my eyes went even *wider*.

"Ciao, the great American King brothers!" The infamous Massimo clapped slowly by his ear as he walked toward us, then pretended a sweeping bow and straightened.

He wasn't as tall as Billy, but he was taller than Mason. Darker, too—black hair shaved on the sides and thick on top, slicked back and just as menacing as the stubble shading his jaw. Dark steel dress shirt, olive skin, black eyes, and a tiny cross hanging from a chain around his neck.

Lor swallowed a last gulp of champagne before she locked eyes with me, sitting stark straight in her chair with the bottle dangling helpless in her hand.

He came up behind her, then knelt beside her legs. "Lorina."

I kept eyes with her for strength, for support. After everything with Colton, I got it. *God*, did I get it. But... she didn't *look* like I felt when Colton was around. She was breathing hard like he'd said a lot more than a weird version of her name, and there was an unmistakable excitement in her eyes.

Over our shopping trips and girls-only riding dates, she'd talked to me at length about her biggest rival on the circuit. The first time they met, the arguments, the emotional confusion, and the endless battle of wills. And as much as I wanted to tell her to maybe look a little more closely at what was really going on—playground antics and everything—she clearly wasn't ready to face it.

But we all had things we were having trouble facing in Germany.

No one said a word as Massimo kept kneeling next to Lorelai's chair, patiently waiting. And despite all the stories I'd heard about their epic showdowns—ones he started, according to her—nothing about the Italian moto racer's expression looked like he was trying to pick a fight. He looked...exactly like I expected someone to look after spending ten years chasing someone and never quite being able to catch her.

Billy took my hand, winking at me. He pulled it up and kissed the back of it, like watching them was just as romantic as an old movie or attending a friend's wedding. I glanced around to see if this was a common assessment, and sure enough, more than a few people were watching what was happening at our little circle. Even though most of the racers were having their own private parties on the paddock, like we were.

When I looked to Lor, I'd lost her in that small moment. Her eyes were down-tipped and meeting Massimo's. And then he started speaking to her. Very quietly, in Italian.

The words were so smooth, so freaking *sexy*, it felt intrusive to witness. I leaned toward Billy, swallowing over my thick tongue and whispering, "Do you know what he's saying?"

Billy barely shook his head. "Nope."

Mason snickered softly, propping his ankle on his opposite knee and seeming as boozily enraptured as the rest of us.

Massimo tilted his head, still gazing up at Lorelai in her chair like he was declaring himself before a queen on her throne. "Hmm? No, Tigrotta?"

She swallowed and ground her jaw, Massimo going right back to talking to her in hushed sentences that blurred together like the colors in a sunset.

I recrossed my legs, leaning toward Billy again. "Does *she* know what he's saying?"

A funny smile pulled at the corner of his mouth. "That's, uh, up for debate."

Massimo shifted where he was kneeling. It wasn't much, maybe an inch closer to her, but it was enough. Lorelai blasted to her feet, the chair shooting out behind her as she turned and stalked off, drinking deeply from Billy's bottle of champagne, her curly brown hair blowing wild in the wind.

Massimo rose to his feet. "Run away, Lorina," he called after her. "You always do."

She flipped him off over her shoulder, heading toward the area of the paddock where the RVs were parked. Massimo chuffed out a growl, a fierce smile on his face as he stood there for a minute, then started walking after her.

I sputtered out a squeak, waiting until they were definitely out of earshot before I spun to Billy. "Where are they going?"

He grinned at the ground, his racing boots crossed at the ankles and stretched out in front of him. "I don't know, honey. Where do you think they're going?"

I looked again toward the path they'd taken. It didn't look good, that was for sure. But I knew better than anyone how looks didn't mean shit, and Lor said she wasn't interested in Massimo. That he was cocky and rude, and they'd spent too many years fighting on and off the racetrack.

But then again, he was almost all she talked about whenever I brought up racing. And once, when the guys were out of town at a rodeo and she and I were slumber partying with a bottle of tequila, I totally got her to admit that not only did she think he was hot but that he was *damn hot*, and maybe she'd had a couple of dreams about him. But *"That doesn't mean anything, Taryn."*

Sure it didn't.

Just like it didn't mean anything that more and more, I'd catch myself daydreaming about my own press interviews. Ones where I would be asked about my background in sports medicine, and I'd talk about how even though I'd started late, I'd made it in the sport through hard work and determination. Not a word would be said about my looks, just the inspiration I was bringing to little girls with books in their backpacks and revving engines in their hearts.

But then I'd remember what it would cost to get me there: the move to Germany and the goodbyes, and every time, I would start to cry. Worse, keeping quiet about the reason behind my random breakdowns was getting harder and harder to do. I wasn't lying to Billy about it exactly, but

I hated the muddiness of secrets nonetheless. And I hated crying; it was exhausting.

The thing was, *sure*, I could've bullshitted my way through convincing myself that Billy and I could do long distance between different continents. But it was already hard enough to make it work when we lived in the same city. And yes, I could've run toward the offer with both hands and asked Billy to come along for the ride. But there was no way he was ever going to leave Memphis.

He did okay overseas, but it wasn't his home, and he always started to fade after a while, his smiles getting further and further apart until he'd start speaking in circles about needing to ride his horse or feeling like he was going to wake up with his body inside out.

I didn't know what that meant, but I knew it wasn't good. And Billy may have been a motorcycle racer, but he was a cowboy first. And you can't take a cowboy out of the country forever. You can't ask them to leave their pastures and their fields, their wide open skies and their hoofed soul mates for a two-bedroom high-rise condo in downtown Munich. Not even if it meant the chance to fix everything about my image I regretted.

If I was moving, Billy wasn't coming with me. And I didn't have the first clue how I was ever going to leave him. But I also knew no one, absolutely *no one*, would ever support me again or even try to understand if I gave up this offer for him.

The fear of making the wrong decision and what I suspected to be the right one...it was paralyzing.

"Hey..." Billy tapped my leg, and when I looked at him, his hand came up to cup my cheek, his thumb sweeping over my skin as he winked. "They'll figure it out, honey.

No need to worry about Lorelai. She knows what she's doing."

I nodded, sure he was right. Lor knew her mind, knew her worth, and she was her mother's daughter: she didn't let anyone give her shit without giving it back tenfold. I just wished like hell I could say the same for myself.

But the truth was, I couldn't, and I was running out of time to figure out what to do.

---

Stretched out on my couch in my parents' living room, I teased my fingernails through Billy's sunny blond hair. He was snoring into my stomach, oblivious to Mama Rose on the TV railing away at her daughter over a bathtub photo shoot. My own mama walked past us on the way to her bedroom, pissy and huffy as she scowled at Billy sleeping on me, but I didn't care.

I loved him as much as Mama Rose loved that cow act she'd been hauling around vaudeville all those years. I loved him with the moxy of Gypsy Rose Lee, confident and proud and finally on her own two feet. Even if her clothes were on the floor.

I shifted the throw pillow behind my head, checking on Billy again. Starting to drool on my shirt. I rolled my eyes, petting the back of his head. He'd flown in from Sepang two days before, and even though the digital display on my DVD player was reading four in the afternoon, his internal clock was ticking thirteen hours ahead and putting him right around five in the morning.

August and September had passed in a blur. Billy's schedule lightened up, and we scored days upon days at home that added up to weeks together. Riding horses, riding bikes, working out, and sleeping in. Hanging out with my cousin April and her fiancé, Kenny, as they bickered through wedding details. Dancing the night away at honky-tonks with Lor and Mason. Going to rodeos on the weekends and laughing and winning, making love anywhere and everywhere whenever we could finally get away from his damn brother.

They were a good two months. The *best*.

October had been a different story.

Billy was gone from 5:00 a.m. on the morning of the first until the end of the first week in November: bouncing from Thailand to Japan, off to Australia, and back to Malaysia before he finally crossed the Pacific into the States. I, however, had finished the Superbike circuit just before Halloween, then gone home alone, and I still hadn't given an answer to Werner.

He wasn't mad—it was worse. In an effort to entice me, he upgraded his offer to include a personal security service, trainer, housekeeper, car, another bike for fun at home...the sky was pretty much the limit. All while chomping at the bit to present a brand-new version of me to the world—the *right* version. But I couldn't tell Mike and Werner that I'd finally figured out what I wanted most when I needed to talk to Billy about it *first*.

Werner had actually given me the idea...or maybe it was all those late-night phone calls with Billy. Either way, I had started secretly looking at properties in the Memphis area. Houses, sometimes raw land, the few small ranches for sale. The pickings were slimmer than slim, but I'd found a couple that were...okay. One that would definitely work. It was barely enough space for one horse, let alone two, and it wasn't our dream, but it was a place to start.

Except I couldn't talk to Billy about something that big while he was gone for an entire month in Asia, then jet-lagged into oblivion the one week he was home to recover before he left again for Spain. Especially with all he had resting on that race, reputation and career-wise, with the calls to retire getting ever louder. But after that, after Valencia, he would be done for the year and we'd be able to sit down, and I could come clean about everything, and we could figure this out. Together.

We were so damn close.

I held him tighter against me, focused only on the rhythm of his breathing as Mama Rose belted out the chances she didn't take, the life she could've had, and the regrets that would haunt her forever and no fur coat would ever make up for.

Maybe watching *Gypsy* was a mistake.

When the movie ended a minute later, I had two choices: stay there and watch the credits and maybe the movie again, or wake Billy and put on something else.

Thankfully, my father walked in the front door, home early from work. I smiled up at him, throwing him a little wave. He snorted as he took off his hat and hung it on the hook by the door.

"Hey, sugar," he whispered, coming over to drop a kiss to my forehead. He headed straight to the TV afterward and the stack of movies I had on the console.

He turned and held up two cases, and I pointed to the left. He put it in and started it for me, walking around the couch and dropping another kiss to my hair on his way to the kitchen.

"Hey, Billy," he said a little louder than normal.

Billy's head snapped up. "Sir" popped from his lips before his eyes were fully open.

I smoothed my hands over his back, guiding his head down for him to go back to sleep. "It's okay, honey. He's just home."

Billy yawned into my stomach, and it killed me seeing him this tired. He handled the jet lag better than most of us, but this was the worst I'd ever seen him. "Did Mama Rose take over vaudeville?"

"Nope. Louise became a stripper, though."

"Dang, and I missed it?" He shifted and turned his head the other way, groaning when the new movie's opening credits started and the first swell of the overture came on. "Is this the one with the girl named Dumbass?"

"Dorcas," I corrected, combing my fingers through his hair the other way and messing it all up, just for fun. He needed a haircut, bad. "And yes."

"I hate this movie. Who needs twenty-five pounds of chewing tobacco?"

"Adam Pontipee," I answered lightly. "The Oregon backwoodsman with six scroungy brothers."

Billy looked up at me, his chin digging into my ribs. "Thought it was seven brothers?"

"Adam is the first, the six others make seven, and you should clearly go back to sleep."

"Ridiculous," he muttered, looking to the TV. "Put Mama Rose and the stripper girl back on."

I laughed, shifting my legs a little more comfortably around him. "You're grumpy."

"I am grumpy," he agreed, dropping a kiss to my stomach before he laid his head down. "I'm tired, and I missed you. And Gidget. And I haven't even got to see him yet."

I did my best to keep my chuckle out of my voice, but I sucked at it. "I know, honey. We'll go tonight, okay? Take him a whole big bag of apples."

"Okay," he mumbled, snuggling in for another nap. "Wake me up when it gets to the barn raising."

I shook my head with a smile and soaked him up, Billy getting comfortable enough to go back to sleep, which didn't take long. He was snoring before Adam and Milly were even married and long before she'd realized that she hadn't simply married Adam but was inheriting a whole mess of annoying backwoods brothers, too.

She'd just flipped the dinner table on their ungrateful selves when Mason busted through my front door.

"*Billy!*" He blew in like the whole goddamn world was on fire, tripping over the entry rug and landing face-first on the Berber carpet with a massive crash.

"The hell!" my father snapped from the kitchen.

"Mason!" I growled.

Billy just groaned.

Mason sprang up like a gopher, fixing his hat with his face an explosive red. "I'm sorry, I'm sorry!" he shouted to all of us, then hooked his hands onto the couch and started yelling down at his brother. "Billy! You'll never guess who just called me!"

Billy groaned again, and I hugged my arms and legs tighter around him.

Mason reached down to shake Billy's shoulder, but I smacked his hand away before he could lay a finger on his brother. "Damn it, Taryn!" he snarled.

Billy's head popped up. "Hey!" he warned his brother, always ready to defend me.

"Blake just called! Guess who's gonna be at the 30th Annual Cornucopia Exhibition? Just *guess*!"

Billy sniffed and looked at Mason's face. He sat up. Then he vaulted over the back of the goddamn couch, the guys clasping onto each other's arms and cheering like they do whenever one of them wins a moto race. *Seriously?* Billy pulled Mason in close, his forehead to his brother's and having some kind of bro moment that doesn't make sense to me as an only daughter. But Billy was also more overprotective of Mason than any big brother I'd ever seen, and the cute factor surrounding it had long worn off. Now, it was annoying as hell.

"Y'all wanna share the good news?" my father garbled from the kitchen table, his mouth full of something salty he probably wasn't supposed to be eating. Not with his blood pressure the way it was.

I gestured his way. "Right?"

The guys turned toward me, both stumbling to talk over each other so much, I barely caught what they were trying to say. But I definitely made out the words Smashbox, North Carolina, and rodeo.

*Goddamn it.*

Mason knocked Billy's chest. "You go. It's your girlfriend." He reached up to fix his hat, his face still red and breaths huffing from excitement.

Billy blew out a long string of air, his hands on his belt and his eyes already begging me for mercy. And I wasn't quite sure what he was gonna say, but I knew where it was gonna lead, and *damn* if I didn't already know what my answer was gonna be. And I hated it.

"Smashbox is Mason's unicorn," he said, and *yep*, that was the end of our week together. "Hardest bull he's ever tried to ride and the one that's bucked him the best. He isn't in rodeos much now because he's getting older, but that also means he's getting meaner, and...well, Mason wasn't gonna go to this one because our dad wasn't gonna be able to make it, but he hasn't withdrawn yet, and they just..." Billy took a breath and shifted his weight, his voice laced with guilt. "He's gonna draw him, honey. We know the guy who's making the matchups, and he knows this is Mason's bull. He's gonna draw Smashbox. And this is absolutely not a bull I can let him ride alone."

Motherfucker. Why couldn't Billy have been an only child?

"Come with us," Mason pleaded. "Please, Taryn? We always have more fun when you rodeo with us, and it'll be really cool for you to be there when I finally get eight seconds on that sombitch."

"Watch your mouth," my father rumbled.

Mason tipped his hat at him over his shoulder. "Sorry, sir."

"I can't," I told them, Billy's face falling further because he was probably just remembering... "My cousin's wedding is this weekend, and I have to go. It's Sylvie's daughter, Billy, and I have to be there for April."

His hand came up to pinch at his eyes. "No, I know you do," he said, his voice gritted. He shook his head again and then sighed and looked at his brother. "Mason, man, I..."

"*What?*" Mason screeched. "It's Smashbox! That's my bull!"

"I know he is. I know." Billy laid a hand on his brother's shoulder. "But this is a really important wedding in her family, man. And I promised weeks ago that I would go. What if...what if Cannonball goes with you?"

"Oh, so since Daddy can't take off work, you want me to ask if his *boss* will?"

"Look, I'm trying to solve this the best I can, all right? What about Frank? Or Adam?"

"Frank's in Nashville, and you know Adam doesn't like going to rodeos anymore. Says he always ends up working on his day off."

I let out a deep sigh. There wasn't anything else I could do. Didn't mean I had to be happy about it, though.

I waved my hand. "Go get your damn unicorn."

"*Yes!*" Mason launched in the air and slung himself over the couch, pecked my cheek, then bolted for the door. "Thank you, Taryn!"

Billy didn't move. He just watched me, remorse plain across his features. "Are you sure? I mean, it's April's wedding, honey. We RSVP'd and everything. Weeks ago."

"Mm-hmm."

Billy seemed unconvinced. "You know I really wanted to go to this, right? My suit's at the cleaner's getting pressed right now. And I like Kenny. A lot. He can't rope for crap, but he's a good guy, and April's really—"

"Billy," I said, trying not to laugh. "It's okay, honey. Just go."

He shook his head, drawling, "Okay." Then he leaned over the couch and grabbed his hat from the coffee table, setting it on his head before he cradled my cheeks in his wonderfully calloused hands. "I will be back as soon as I possibly can, and we will watch a dozen brides with a million brothers as many times as you want."

I snorted, already missing him. "Your math sucks."

"Billy! Let's go. We gotta go," Mason called from the door.

"Hold on!"

Billy's kiss across my lips was half-missed and thin, and

then he was gone, grabbing his battered old boots with a snatch of his hand, running out of my house, and never once looking back. I flinched when the door slammed behind them, something cold trickling through my veins.

"You're a good woman, sugar," my father said from the kitchen.

I sighed and turned toward the TV, just in time for the start of the barn-raising scene.

Two days. He'd be back in two days, three at the most, and I couldn't take it anymore: not the secrets or the distance or the waiting. When he got back, I was going to tell him about Werner, the nightmare offer to move to Germany, and my decision to turn it down—assuming Billy would agree to be around to make it worth it. Sleeping next to me in the teeny starter ranch I was also going to offer to cobuy as a proposal. Or at least a *pre*-proposal.

He was worth every penny, every stern look and disappointed whisper I'd have to face in the future from my parents and Mike and others. But nothing was going to change my mind about this.

Three days.

# Chapter 15

*Billy King—Present Day*

LIKE ALWAYS, JUST AS SOON AS TARYN AND I WERE getting somewhere good, I had to go and leave for work.

I look to the coming turn on the racetrack and downshift twice, leaning deep until my knee sliders are grazing the pavement, the world bent and a blur of frozen grass and brown dirt and white gravel curving past me. It's a sight so rare and pretty, I imagine it's close to watching a sunrise on Everest. Not just anyone gets to see this, and a lot will die trying.

Adrenaline is coursing thick through my veins as I come out of the turn and punch it, my pulse climbing higher with every tick of my speedometer. I duck low and eye the apex for the next turn. My ankle's been holding together so far, and the relief is almost too much to keep locked in my chest. I still have a chance of making it back, *again*.

I'm actually starting to look forward to Qatar—the way the lights sparkle on the track for the night race, and all of us battling our heads off, hopped up on the fans from the first showdown of the season. Almost as much as I can't wait to get home to Taryn.

My Christmas Eve date clothes were still wrinkled on my bedroom floor when Frank announced that Mason and Lorelai and I had screwed around long enough and we were starting practice. Unofficially, of course, which meant we had to load our bikes onto a horse trailer and sneak off to Frank's family's ranch just outside Nashville, where they have a quarter-mile racetrack on their land. A damn fun one, too. But all my excitement and eagerness—the kind that comes with the promise of tire-melting speed—was quickly spoiled by the announcement of a tagalong.

My father took the week off work to come with us and "supervise." He's been eyeing me a lot closer since Christmas Eve, and I'm not limping much at this point, but his gaze could catch a hummingbird hiccup, and I'm just barely flying under his radar. I *did* make sure to ask Mama to call Taryn and tell her, since I'm still operating under the phone embargo. Got a text from Taryn about an hour after we hit the road, wishing me safety and speed and saying she was looking forward to a second date when I got back.

Can't fucking *wait*. With how badly I bombed Christmas Eve, I'm praying it can only get better from there. But it's not my prayers that are getting answered lately.

Lorelai creeps up beside me, bent low over her bike and her brown braid whipping out behind her. She's been kicking mine and Mason's asses even harder since Dabria Corse called. Not only did they offer to move up Mason from his Blue Gator stock model to a full-on MotoPro prototype, but they offered the same for Lorelai, advancing her from the manufacturer-restricted MotoA.

She's finally gonna get to race with the big boys on the big toys, and they have no idea what's coming for them.

I, however, *do* know. And it isn't exactly boosting my confidence when I'm already struggling to get back in the saddle with the way my ankle has been aching. At least I can shift gears again, and I think—*I hope*—it's all gonna be okay come Qatar. But Frank's still riding my ass over why I'm slow every second he's not congratulating Mason. And I'm finally starting to keep up with Lorelai, but *damn*, that girl is fast.

As we head into the turn, I downshift once, then twice, my eyes noting the braking marker. But she's overshooting the apex from the inside, and it's a fucking dangerous thing to do. I hate playing chicken with her.

*Don't flinch.*

*Don't fucking flinch.*

I lean for the turn, trying to block the sight of her too damn close beside me and creeping closer as the track curves and momentum slings me toward her. Too close, way too goddamn close—

"*Fuck!*" I tap the brakes as her engine barks and she darts ahead, taking the apex and cutting me off, and I can't *believe* I just fell for that shit. If anyone from the circuit had seen that, the laughter would nearly drown out the people calling for Yaalon to replace me with someone younger, faster, and healthier.

When I come out of the turn and hit the straightaway, I check the side of the track. Frank is cheering on Lorelai from the dirt, but my father is screaming at me. Right before he starts waving his arm slow toward his head like he's out of energy and patience.

"Fuck," I repeat, chasing her through the next four turns but not really trying to catch her anymore. Mason's half the track back on his Blue Gator bike, and when I pull off to where Frank and my father are standing, Lorelai laps him.

"Go, go, go!" Frank yells, jogging a little down the track to keep cheering her on.

"The fuck are you doing out there?" my father snaps at me.

I rip off my helmet, wiping sweat from my head. The cold wind hits my face and helps a little, but I'm still soaked through my shirt underneath my leathers.

"You're late off the grid, you're braking early, and you just let her bully you out of the damn apex!"

I grit my teeth and try to keep my temper in check, everything in me still in fight mode after battling Lorelai on the track for the last damn week. *Christ*, I was a World Champion last season. I know what I'm fucking doing out there. But I guess he's the only one who's allowed to have a bad day.

My father gets in my face, the rim of his Stetson hitting my temple and his shoulders towering over where I'm sitting lower on the motorcycle. "Hey! You listening to me, boy? Or should I go ahead and pull your brother off the track and let him ride your damn bike since you don't seem capable of it?"

*That's fucking it.*

I shove myself off my bike, my pulse screaming and my teeth grinding together as I stride toward the pit box. I need water and a shower and a long phone call with Taryn where I tell her crappy jokes and listen to her laugh until I feel like I'm doing something important with my life. But I'm still not allowed to call her. I don't think.

"Where are you going?" he yells at my back. "You don't walk away from me!"

I whip around and storm back to him, so tired and pissed off that I get right in his face. "I'm going to take a fucking shower. That okay with you?"

"Watch it," he growls, pointing at me. "The shit's been

hitting the fan for you lately, so I'm gonna let you get away with that. But you better remember who you're talking to."

Oh, I know who I'm talking to. He just doesn't know how well I know him. "Why is it no matter what I do or how hard I try, it is *never* good enough for you?"

He looks around the track like he has no idea what's going on. "Have I done something to you I am not aware of here? Because as far as I can tell, I've kept a roof over your head, food in your belly, showed you how to do every damn thing you know how to do, and you're standing there yelling at me like I'm some kind of sombitch."

I size him up as Lorelai and Mason keep going in circles, wondering when I got as tall as him and confused as to why he still seems so much bigger than me. I sure don't feel as big as him when I tell him the secret I've known since I was five and my brother was three, and he got that new set of boots and I got my father's old hat. The one I'm still wearing to this damn day. "I may be your firstborn and your namesake, but Mason...Mason's your favorite."

"*What?*" he squawks. "Where'd you get that dumb idea?"

Nah, he isn't squirming out of this one. "Everything I've ever done, none of it was good enough. But when *Mason* does it, well, isn't he just king of your world."

My father looks at the sun like he's making sure the sky is still there. Checks his boots, and yep, they're still on the ground. Then he looks up at me with the same blue eyes that have been staring at me in the mirror every damn day of my life. "Billy, what are you talking about? You were the star pitcher of the baseball team, you were first in track, and in 4-H, you rode bulls like you were Lane Frost reincarnate...*hell*, you were the starting varsity quarterback!

Y'all went all the way to the state finals! I'd never been so proud in my life."

"Yeah, I'm sure you were. When Mason ran in the winning fucking touchdown!"

My father shakes his fists like he doesn't know what to do with me. "*Damn it*, Billy, he wasn't even supposed to be on the team in the first place! *You* were the one who insisted he was too good for JV even though he was a sophomore, and *you* were the one who started calling running plays in the fourth quarter after you'd thrown a three-touchdown lead!"

I stare at my father, breathing hard and rabidly pissed off and totally blank on how to counter his point. Because he's right: I was the one who wanted Mason on the team, because he wouldn't stop whining about the JV coach benching him for having a smart mouth. And yeah, I switched to running plays in the fourth quarter. But my wide receivers were done for, and I didn't trust the second string as much as I trusted Mason to muskrat his way into the end zone.

"Well, it's not like you ever said anything about it," I tell him. "You didn't complain about him being on the team *once*."

"Because it was done," he tells me. "You'd already gone to the coaches and the registrar to change his schedule, and I wasn't gonna be the asshole to stick Mason back in JV. He hated me enough as it was with me busting him drinking every damn weekend."

"See? That's exactly what I'm talking about! It's never mattered how many rules he breaks or how much he disrespects you. You still put him first."

"Me?" he says. "You are the one who's *always* laying over for him, if you ain't busy covering his ass, and I don't know what to do." He throws his hands out to his sides and shrugs, looking completely baffled. "I can't seem to stop you, no matter how mad I get. You're just bound and fucking determined to coddle him. And I tell you, Billy, he is never gonna learn how to pick himself up if you don't start letting him fall down."

*What?* I've been pushing my little brother's nose in the dirt since the day he could stand. "I don't coddle him."

"Sure you do," my father says. "Hell, he didn't even walk till he was a year and a half old because you insisted on carrying him everywhere. I had to get the pediatrician to yell at you just to make you stop."

I don't remember that. But then again, I would've been barely three, so I guess I wouldn't.

"And I guess it's a good thing he's got you looking out for him since you're the only one he halfway listens to. But, Son? *You* are the one who keeps putting Mason above yourself. And I think it's about damn time you stopped. Don't you?"

I blink at him. I don't even know what to say to that. I *really* don't like that it sounds a lot like what Taryn's been telling me for months.

"Well…" I'm starting to feel like a character in a "how to be a dipshit" after-school special, but *no way*. I've gotta be right about this. He's always been better than me. "How come he's allowed to ride bulls and I can't?"

My father shifts his weight and scrubs at his face. "Yeah," he drawls, sucking his cheeks and looking *weird* when he glances up. "We, um, we should probably talk about that." He squints at me, pain pulling at his eyes and the corners of his mouth. "I lied to you? There's nothing in your contract that says you can't ride bulls."

All the air in my chest locks in place, then squeaks out of my throat, and this must be what Taryn feels like when I finally come clean about shit.

This *sucks*.

"I'm sorry, you *what*?"

"Yeah." He nods, working his jaw. "Had Frank do it, too. Your mama knows, but she don't agree."

I stare at him, and for some reason, he doesn't look as tall as he did a minute ago. "Why?"

"Because it was worth it," he says, looking so much like Mason for a second that I almost do a double take. "You're a damn good bull rider, Son, but you had a really good shot at making a career of being a MotoPro racer, and I wasn't gonna let you risk that. So when you got moved up from MotoA I lied." He crosses his arms, and it's *guilt*. That weird look on his face I haven't ever seen before is *guilt*. "You're a good man, Billy, and I knew you wouldn't question me or disobey me, and it was an easy way for me to keep you safe. So...I lied. And I'm sorry."

I blink at him again, suddenly really pissed off I *didn't* question him or ever think to disobey. I didn't even read the damn contract. He said *Sign here*, and I did. "What about Mason?"

He throws his hands in the air. "*Mason* is a tornado of fucking chaos. I don't know what he's gonna do from one minute to the next, except the exact opposite of whatever I tell him. If he can make him some money riding bulls, then good. If he can make it racing, that's fine, too. But he needs more options because he is probably gonna fuck up most of them. *You* are different."

I don't even know how I'm still standing.

He just undid over twenty-five years of everything I

thought I knew. The reason behind every dumb decision I make and all the times I've let down the people who matter the most to me.

"So." He claps once, rubbing his hands together. "Now that we got that cleared up, let's go back to the part where you let Lorelai bully you out of the turn. The hell are you gonna do about that come Qatar?"

"I don't know," I mumble, unable to feel even the weight of my helmet in my hand anymore.

Because I thought I knew what I was doing when I deliberately said Taryn's name wrong the first time I met her. And I thought I knew what I was doing when I went with Mason to that rodeo in North Carolina. But I'm starting to realize I don't know a goddamn thing, because nothing about my life is what I thought it was.

All I know with any degree of certainty is that I miss Taryn, and I'm ready to go home.

---

The world is quiet in the minutes after midnight and freezing so bad, my legs are nearly numb. The little bit of heat I got flowing through me is purely from Gidget's flanks. That dusting of snow we got has long melted, but I still feel bad about bringing him out here. I couldn't risk my truck, though—too damn loud.

The last day of practice didn't go great, my ankle throbbing from being overworked and my mood turning more sour the more Lorelai talked about her new Dabria the whole way home, asking Frank a thousand times how soon she and Mason would get to test them and badgering him over whether they could push up the date.

I'm trying to be happy for her, because she deserves to move up. She should've moved up sooner. But it *also* means the gossips are probably gonna get their wish, and my reign at the top of the leaderboards is about to come crashing down.

Usually, it's Mason who dethrones me. Well, according to my liar father, I've been dethroning myself, which I'm still having trouble wrapping my head around. But Lorelai is a hardworking rancher's daughter, and like her mama, she doesn't know how to back down from anything once she sets her mind to it.

Either way, I'm a little tired of having my ass handed to me every time I look up. And after getting home to a hiccup with the mortgage company that took me forever to figure out, there's only one way I can think of to make myself feel better. The one thing no one else can do as well as me, and I'll be damned if anyone else ever tries.

When Gidget and I come out of the woods and up to the eastern crossing, light is pouring out the window to her room but muted and yellow like she's got the curtains drawn. She's awake, but she isn't expecting me, surprise visits included. The windows for her parents' room are dark, along with the rest of the house.

"What do you think?" I ask Gidget, his weight shifting under me and my pulse ticking up a notch. "Do we go for it?"

He huffs a little like my question was rhetorical, backing up a few steps and squaring off with the lowest part of the fence around her property: right where it dips a little because the tension is going slack and it hasn't been fixed yet. Gidget snorts and fluffs his mane when he's ready, setting his weight in his hindquarters because he isn't just a roping horse. He's primarily trained for dressage…and for show jumping.

"*Get it!*"

He charges, a smile in my heart and my heart in my horse as I hang on and let him do what he does best— barreling toward the fence before he launches and takes us over, landing a little rough and slipping a bit on the icy grass but trotting it off.

"Good *boy*!" I lean forward to hug and pat him, pulling some apple slices from my pocket and holding them down so he can eat them. I check back and the fence is fine, not even swinging. He cleared it, no problem. "Good boy," I tell him again, sitting back and taking up his reins, slowing him so the grass crunching under his hooves isn't as loud when we approach the house.

A good five feet back, I go ahead and get down from the saddle, leading him up to the window and carefully maneuvering around the rose bushes he's all but destroyed. I guess it's why her mama hasn't bothered to cover them. *Whoops.*

At least Taryn's awake, sitting on her bed and reading a piece of notebook paper folded like a letter. I wonder if it's the one Mason wrote. He still isn't spilling what it said, and it's *killing* me to know.

I hang just out of sight, clicking at Gidget. When he looks at me, I show him my teeth. He shows me his, and I hold up the flowers, my boy taking them and immediately starting to chew. "Those aren't yours," I whisper. He stops chewing, looking at me like I called him a bad name. I sigh and tap lightly on her window. Still out of sight.

It opens half a minute later, warmth and peaches and lavender flowing out. Then she softly giggles. "Hi, Gidget. Are those for me?"

I nod my head toward her, Gidget lowering his big horse face so Taryn can take the flowers from his mouth.

"Thank you." Her other hand comes out the window to pet up his nose, and he's just *loving* it. "Where's your cowboy?"

Gidget jerks his nose at me, giving away my position. Traitor.

"I see."

I peek around the corner, my mouth twisted with guilt because I'm not supposed to be doing this anymore, and I damn well know it. "Sorry?"

"Mm-hmm." She's fighting a hell of a smile behind her pursed lips, the flowers cradled in the crook of her arm. "Breaking all sorts of rules tonight, aren't we?"

I kneel in front of the window, tipping up my hat. "I know. But I needed to see you."

Something warms her expression that I haven't seen in so long, I can't quite remember what it is. But it's good, I know that much. "Something happen while you were gone?"

I shake my head, because I don't want to worry her or put more of my crap on her shoulders. But a disappointed sigh falls from my lips a second later, because I realize that's not telling her the truth, and I swore to be honest with her.

"Practice was...hard," I confess, shifting a bit in my crouch and laying my forearm on the windowsill, but it's hard to look up at her. "Lorelai kicked my ass all week. I'm not all the way back yet."

Warmth floods Taryn's eyes, and she half shrugs one shoulder. "You will be. You came back from your knee, and you'll recover from this, too. It just takes time, Billy."

I nod, letting her words settle over me like a prophecy,

because I need her to be right. And thank goodness for Taryn, because she's always right.

"It's freezing," she mutters, and *damn it*, that's my cue to go. "Why don't you, um, go put Gidget in the barn with Aston, and we can talk some more about it. For a bit."

I look up at her, hope bringing me back to life. "Aston's still here?"

"Yeah." Taryn smiles at her floor. "She's still here."

I swallow, letting that sink in. It takes me longer than it should, and when I speak again, my voice is weak with all I'm hoping she's telling me. "Won't be five minutes."

Taryn nods and tucks her hair behind her ear. I rise and lower the window, leaving it open a crack and collecting my horse, trying to keep my feet on the ground.

"Wanna go see your girlfriend?" I breathe to him, Gidget nodding up such a storm, he whips the reins out of my hand. I chuckle, getting them back. "Okay, buddy."

*Here goes nothing.*

# Chapter 16

*Taryn Ledell—Back Then*

"THANK YOU SO MUCH FOR COMING," MY COUSIN April said again, my hands in hers while she beamed at me in her mama's wedding dress.

"I wouldn't have missed it for anything," I swore to her. "It was so beautiful, and I know Billy was really sorry he couldn't be here. He sends you both his best."

Kenny laughed, leaning over to give me an awkward half hug. But it was only awkward because he hadn't been able to let go of April since my father gave her away. "Tell him to keep his best to himself and agree to a rematch the next time he's in town."

I chuckled as Kenny pulled back with the same bright smile I suspected he'd still be wearing long after his honeymoon was over. Because that was Kenny: always up for a laugh and constantly challenging Billy to friendly roping competitions. Though I have no idea why when Kenny sucked and Billy was amazing.

"I'll be sure to do that," I told him. "And congratulations again."

I stepped away before I took up any more time in the lineup, the people behind me already squealing their congratulations before I could finish letting go of April's hands. It really was a shame Billy missed the wedding. Not only did my cousin have a way with throwing the most elegant, understated parties—and her wedding was no exception—but the cocktail dress I borrowed from Lor was almost designed with Billy's personal catnip in mind.

The blue crepe fabric was just a shade darker than his motorcycle and stopped a little lower than halfway up my thigh. Not stretchy or sucked to me but fitted, and the back was zipped all the way up to my neck. But the darted front was shaped like a halter, and three little pearls attached the high-shoulder cap sleeves so just the *tiniest* sliver of skin arrowed toward my arms. *Just a peek.*

And he was missing it.

"Hey, Taryn," my father called from the door to the house, waving me toward him. April and Kenny had rented out the exquisite Casa Blanca for the reception, though most everything was set up in the gardens. "He's almost up."

A sick feeling rolled through my stomach; I hated watching Mason ride bulls. He was good at it, really good, but it was still so scary when it could all go so wrong, so fast. And under the draped lanterns casting a soft glow over the procession waiting to congratulate the bride and groom, it was too easy to imagine the wedding Bonnie Landry never had: reading a eulogy over Beau Blackwell's coffin instead, his body in the tux he was supposed to marry her in that very same day.

Shuddering off the memory of how her voice shook as she read the vows she'd never hear him say back to her, I hurried over to my father as best I could in my high heels, letting him lead me inside and past the other guests. Tables were overflowing with lilies and orchids and a million gifts, and the four-tiered wedding cake was being rolled out, which meant I was going to miss seeing April and Kenny get to cut it.

*Thanks a lot, Mason.*

"This way, sugar." He pushed open a door to a study rich with leather furniture, endless volumes of books on the walls, antique tables with ornate lamps, and a crowd of men in sport coats and cowboy hats gathered around a flat-screen. Where the 30th Annual Cornucopia Exhibition was playing. "Hey, he go yet?"

"Nah, not yet." My uncle Roy looked over his shoulder, lifting his beer bottle my way. "Hey, Turnip Pants."

"Rascal." I went to stand off to the side as he laughed, my father retaking his seat next to his brother and slapping his hands on the leather armrests like he was exhausted.

My uncle winked at me. "When are we gonna be having your wedding?"

I coughed out a scoff, though my heart was fluttering away. Mostly at the prospect that very soon, Billy and I would come home to the same place, no matter where we were coming from. "Don't even start with me. Aren't you on number four? I'll be sure to keep praying for you, by the way."

He harrumphed and waved off the king of Southern insults, and I turned to the screen, trying to listen over the cowboy chatter in the room to the things the announcers were saying about the bull being loaded into the chute. And looking super freaking pissed off about it, too. The silver-speckled animal rammed the gate with its shoulder again, kicking at the wall behind it.

"*Whoa!*" the announcer yelled. "Smashbox has gotta know what's going on, the way he's spoiling for a fight."

"Oh, no doubt about it, Jake," the second announcer said. "He could probably smell Mason King the second they unloaded him off the trailer. These two have a long history of swapping ends, and Smashbox just loves to let

Mason think he's got 'em before he takes him down at the whistle and just wrecks him. I tell you what, this is gonna be one of the biggest rides of the night."

Goose bumps struck out across my skin as the bull kept kicking and trying to buck in the chute, and I didn't know how the guys did this, brave as they were.

The cameras split so one stayed on Smashbox, the other panning to the wall where Mason was ready to go: bright blue shirt, black safety vest, full-face helmet, glove taped to his arm, and a rope in his hand. But my brow furrowed when Billy stepped in front of him, knocking his brother up the side of his helmet. *The hell was that?*

"What's taking your guy so long to get going?" my uncle quipped.

"It's his little brother," my father corrected. "Billy doesn't ride no more."

Damn right he didn't. *Thank God.* I'd like to actually enjoy my wedding night and have a marriage after. Complete with all the frustrating, hair-pulling, *wonderful* eternally-ever-after crap that comes with it.

"Not sure what the holdup is," the announcer said, the camera still on Billy leaning over Mason and pointing in his face like he was ripping his younger brother a new one. "Smashbox is going crazy in his chute the longer—hey, looks like we got something happening here…"

Billy waved toward some guy, jogging over to meet him. After a quick word and a clap to his shoulder, he jogged back to Mason. Then they ran off together down a hallway out of the arena, my uncle and father both looking at me. "What the hell's going on?"

I sputtered their way, as confused as they were. "How am I supposed to know?"

"Okay, folks, we just got the word, and it sounds like Mason's rope is fraying, so they gotta go grab another for him. They're gonna go ahead and pull Smashbox and let our next—whoa, you see that!"

"That bull is not happy about being delayed, either." The second announcer chuckled. "You know, I think Mason King may be in a lot bigger trouble than just a fraying rope!"

Everyone in the room laughed, but...I *knew* Mason. I'd gone with the guys to rodeos. And not only would Mason never walk into an arena with a fraying rope, but Billy wouldn't have let it make it out of the bag.

What the hell was going on?

The announcers turned their attention to the new bull and the new rider, and so did the rest of the men in the room. They cheered and winced and debated the guy's technique and the meanness of the bull. I checked around to see how long the guys had been gone, finding a large grandfather clock behind me.

It reminded me so much of the one in Billy's living room. He'd spent all afternoon with his hands in the guts of it once, using funny little tools he asked for by name like I was supposed to know which one was what. But I figured it out eventually, and he got it to keep time again.

I liked helping him work on stuff like that around the house. There wasn't anything he couldn't fix, seemed like, and it was just another reason in the long list of whys: why I'd felt safe in his capable hands since before our first slow dance and long before I knew just how clever his fingers truly were. The chance to build a home, a forever with him that was uniquely, messily, privately ours... I couldn't wait.

"Hey, here we go," the announcer said.

I turned to the TV, Mason jogging out of the tunnel: blue shirt, black safety vest, rope in his gloved hand, and the full-face helmet the rules now insisted on. But something wasn't right; Billy wasn't with him. "Looks like Mason's on his way out and—oh, man, Smashbox is not happy to see him at all, is he?"

"No, he is not."

The bull kept ramming and kicking at the gate, the fans roaring their excitement as the announcers recounted all Mason's biggest bull rides. Mason waved at the crowd as he approached the chute, and my eye twitched. *Not a wave at the wrist. A blink of his hand. Like he was Lane Frost reincarnate.*

My father looked over at me, smiled and winked, then turned to the screen like the world was still spinning. But it had stopped.

The bull rider climbed the gate and swung a leg over, waiting for a safe moment to mount the bull, and the camera was looking right down on his shoulders. Stretching the seams of the shirt, because it was too small for him. Not by a lot but a little.

"Daddy, I need your phone," I rushed out, my pulse through the roof and my hand shaking as I waited for the plastic to hit my palm.

"Huh? Taryn, Mason's about to—"

"Give me your phone!" My eyes darted to the TV as time ticked steadily away. When I looked back, my father flared his eyes like I was off my rocker. But he dug his phone out of his pocket, handing it to me.

"All right, he's mounting up," the announcer said. "Man, it's taking all of that gate crew to keep Mason steady so he can get that flank strap—"

"Whoa, whoa, whoa," the second announcer hollered. "He may not even make it out of the chute, the way Smash is tossing him in there. They need to get him loose!"

I dialed Mason's phone number from heart, my eyes glued to the TV and praying any second I'd hear the *Star Trek* theme song trickle through the speakers. The cowboy on the bull tugged and laid the flank strap over his palm as it rang on my end, other men's hands pressing on his shoulders and his chest, trying to keep him steady as Smashbox kept ramming.

"Hello?" Mason slurred.

The cowboy on the TV tugged harder on the flank strap.

The phone slipped from my stony hand, landing with a sharp crack on the wood floor and the screen shattering into a mountain of tiny pieces. Right along with my whole world, our future, our dreams...*everything*.

"Looks like he's ready," the announcer said. "Smashbox is ready to blow!"

The camera cut close to the chute. Time slowed as it focused on every heavy breath he was taking, pulling them in faster and faster. Head down, right hand on the gate and his left squeezing the flank strap for dear life.

Then Billy's voice boomed through the TV: "All right, boys! Let's do this!"

The gate swung open, and I spun around, my whole world in my heart and my heart on a bull. My eyes locked on the clock, the swinging pendulum counting the seconds I knew he was alive and still coming home to me.

Eight. I only had to make it to eight.

One.

"Damn, look at him spurring him!" my uncle yelled behind me.

Two.

"Elbow down, elbow down!" my father cheered.

Three.

"Hang on, hang on, he's got it! Don't let go!"

Four.

"Look at that bull bucking him! That boy is fearless!"

Five.

*"Don't have an act or a goal."*

Six.

*"I was just wondering if you'd let me hang around you a bit…"*

Seven.

*"…see if I can get you to like me some."*

Eight.

*"Good thing I'm not a bull rider no more…"*

An air horn blared, the longest breath I'd held in my life ready to barrel its way out of my chest. But it didn't get there.

"Hot damn!" the men in the room shouted. "He—*oh*!"

The room behind me gasped like they'd all taken a boot to the gut, and it shot a fire-hot rod straight through my spine, the ground disintegrating beneath my feet. Visions of a farmhouse in the middle of a clearing melted and washed away, blurring into flashes of the future being steadily erased, one after the other.

The clock kept ticking.

"*Hell!*" they swelled again. "Someone get him out of there!"

A sob ripped from my heart and crashed from my lips, all the best parts of me tearing jaggedly in two. I spun toward the screen but I couldn't see, too many tears in my eyes and too many men before me, tall and broad and wincing and yelling as they crowded closer to the screen. Why wasn't I up there with them? In front, where I should have been?

My father looked back at me, his face falling as he rushed to my side. "Sugar, hey, the bullfighters know what they're doing. Mason's gonna be all right."

I couldn't do more than shake my head, tears streaming down my cheeks and my voice lost to my broken heart. Too far away to save him and too goddamn late. "Daddy…"

"*Go-go-go-go-go!*" my uncle yelled. Then he laughed with relief along with the rest of the men, breaking their huddle around the television set. "Jesus Christ, that was close."

I nearly crumpled to the floor, my father tightening his grip on me to keep me upright.

*He was alive.*

My uncle looked over, then winked like that made all this better. "He's okay, Turnip Pants. The pickup riders got him out. Boyfriend's brother is gonna be A-OK."

"Damn bull tried to take a taste of him first though, didn't he?" someone else said.

They all snickered.

My father kept staring at me, his hands secure on my shoulders and not even noticing his phone, broken on the floor. I was too broken in front of him. "*What*, sugar? What is it?"

There was no way to lie, no way to hide from the truth. Even with as horrible as it was and all that it would mean. But there was no way to go back to before.

*I couldn't go back.* "Daddy, that wasn't Mason."

—◠◠◠—

My mama hadn't stopped petting my hair as I sat at our kitchen table, my face in my hands, horribly hungover, and everything good in me destroyed.

"You can do this, baby. Be strong," she said. "Don't forget what you deserve. And it isn't a man who risks your whole future to serve his ego."

I looked up at her, my heart already gathering the words I'd need to defend him. Which wasn't fair when I was so wrecked by what he'd done. I was still trying to figure out whether I might actually hate him. But it didn't *feel* like I hated him; it felt like I still loved him. But he'd also scared me to death, and I was furious about that, too.

My father squirmed from where he was leaning against the counter. "Now, come on, Valerie. Don't talk about the boy like that."

"He is not a boy," she snapped. "He is a grown man, and he lied to your daughter. For once and for all, whose side are you on?"

My father huffed but didn't say anything else. It was only another few minutes until Billy's diesel growled up my driveway, slowing and sputtering the way of the grand old oak tree and then cutting off.

My mama pressed another kiss to my head, and I swiped frantically at my eyes, looking up at her and wishing she could do this for me or tell me I didn't have to or anything that would make this better. She shook her head, cupping my cheeks. "There's nothing you can do about it now, baby. We won't be far." She pulled back and straightened, glaring at my father, who looked as heartbroken as I was. "Rob."

The porch steps creaked under Billy's weight, the quick *one-two-one-two* of his boots hitting the old wooden planks, but the *twos* didn't sound right. Like he'd barely landed.

"I like Billy, okay?" My father pushed off the counter, striding toward me and glancing at my mama on his way past. "Not that you ever gave him a fair chance." He leaned down and hugged me, the thud of Billy's steps crossing up to the door sending my pulse racing faster with every beat. "I love you, sugar. You do what's in your heart, and you'll make the right choice. You always have."

Fresh tears rushed into my eyes as he pressed a kiss to my temple, then let me go so he could get the door. My mama followed after him, looking back at me with a stern conviction I wished I had. But it all felt so wrong.

Billy had done some bad things, but he'd done so many good things, too. He *loved* me for who I was, in spite of my flaws, and he saw me. Really *saw me*. No one had ever made me laugh as much as he did. Had forgiven me for losing my temper and saying things I regretted. But for better or worse, I'd also drawn a line in the sand when we first met, and he'd absolutely crossed it.

My mama was right: if I didn't stand up for myself, my beliefs, and react firmly to him testing my boundaries, he'd never stop. He'd keep pushing past them until they were nothing but words I'd once said and he'd clearly forgotten.

I wouldn't risk forgetting how dangerous it was for him to ride those bulls, even if just for eight seconds. Beau Blackwell had only ridden for four when he'd snapped his neck. Those four seconds undid the rest of Bonnie's life, and I couldn't handle Billy risking my future that way. I wouldn't do it to him. And I deserved better.

"Hey, Billy," my father said, opening the door.

My mother's voice cut across the squeak in the hinges. "*Rob.*"

"Sir." Billy tipped up his hat, nodding toward my mama. "Ma'am."

Her arms were crossed over her chest, and she huffed at him so hard, he actually leaned back a little. Billy looked again to my father, the color fading from his face.

"We, um, we're just heading out. Taryn's inside. Waiting." He grabbed his hat from the hook by the door, glancing at me as he put it on.

I wiped at my face again, folding my hands on the table and sitting up straight.

I could do this.

It was the right thing, the only thing, to do.

My father put his arm around my mama, Billy stepping aside and holding open the door as they went out first. He looked at me, and I looked down, my eyes closing and unable to endure seeing him before me when I was trying to face the fact that he'd never be in my house again. Never climb through my window or smile the whole way though breakfast with his hand on my knee under the table, despite my mama scowling at him more with every bite.

I'd never cook for him again. We'd never sit at the table in the house we weren't gonna buy now. The one he didn't know about.

The hole that he had left gaping and raw in my future… I couldn't bear to look at him. But I still heard his steps cross inside and the door close gently behind him. I heard every small first step when he was probably surveying how bad the situation really was. I knew when he figured it out, because it wasn't long before his voice was beside me.

"Hi, honey." He brushed a soft kiss to my temple, his

cologne flooding my senses. The chair across from me nudged, and I opened my eyes to find his hat hooked on it, Billy wiping a hand over his hair as he stared at the table. "Taryn," he said quietly, "honey, you gotta understand—"

"No, I don't."

Billy met my gaze, and I held it as I stood up. I gathered the long, layered cardigan I had over my tank top and leggings, wrapping it more snugly around me. I was freezing, whether from being hungover from trying to drink away my broken heart the night before or maybe because half of me had been lost somewhere in North Carolina, and I wasn't getting it back. Ever.

I kept my voice steady, my eyes dry. "It's done. You need to leave."

"Taryn." His voice was low, controlled. I didn't let the tremor of fear in it affect me. He did this, not me. "I messed up, I know I did, but—"

"You crossed the line, Billy."

His eyes dropped to the floor, his breath coming hard and his neck getting red. "No. It isn't that simple."

"Oh yes, it is," I said, my temper snarling more with every word. "Because you told me you were going to that rodeo to keep him safe. And then you went and *switched places* with him. You wore his shirt, his number, his helmet. But it was you on that goddamn bull, and don't tell me it wasn't!"

"Taryn, I didn't want to do this!" he yelled back. "Mason was gonna lose his sponsors if they found out he'd been drinking—"

"I don't want to hear about Mason!" I screamed. "Mason is a grown-ass man who makes his own mistakes, and I'm tired of you paying for them. When are you ever going to start standing up for yourself? Standing up for *me*?"

"I do stand up for you," he sputtered. "All the time. I—"

"No. You knew how I felt about this. You know about Austin and Eric, and you know what happened to Beau"—my voice cracked, tears flooding into my eyes—"so you knew this was a line you could *not* cross with me. And you could've let Mason face the consequences of his actions, but you didn't. You saved his ass instead of caring about what was important to me, for *us*. So fine, Billy. You don't want Mason to deal with the consequences? Then you're gonna have to accept them. *All* of them."

He swallowed, his voice barely above a whisper. "What does that mean? That last part?"

I crossed my arms and shook back my hair, lifting my eyes so I wasn't meeting his. "Werner's asked me to move to Germany. He wants to launch a new image campaign under my direction. But to do that, he needs me closer. He offered to set me up with my own apartment, security service, personal chef, new bike, car, the whole thing. I've been telling him no, pushing back for months."

Billy stumbled back as if I'd punched him like I did Sheldon. But Billy didn't fall.

My whole body went cold, my sight narrowing on the wall ahead of me.

"I'm calling him today and telling him I'm accepting."

Billy looked like he was gonna be sick, his voice breathless and dismayed. "You can't...you can't move to Germany. What about... What about Aston? You can't just leave your horse. *Germany?*"

I forced myself to stay standing, looking hard at the old patterned plate on the wall behind him. I couldn't let my voice crack. "I'm selling her."

"Are you—! What is the matter with you?" he yelled.

I winced and hugged myself tighter, tears breaking past my barriers and flooding hot into my eyes.

The front door creaked, my father coming inside. "Billy, take a breath, son."

"No..." His voice broke as he stumbled farther back from me but gestured my way. "How are you gonna let her do this? Move to Germany?"

My father crossed in front of me, tears spilling down my cheeks when he gently rested his hands on Billy's shoulders. "I know."

"This isn't right! She's going too far, like she always does, and you know it."

My father pulled him close, breathing something in his ear that made Billy's eyes close and his head hang, his hand coming up to pinch at the bridge of his nose before he swiped at his eyes. My hands flew to my mouth, but my father just kept whispering, Billy nodding a bit before he huffed out a broken breath but still nodded again before my father released him. Then he handed him his hat.

Billy hooked it so low, I could barely see his chin. "I'm, um, I'm gonna be back in a week from Valencia." His voice was so choked, it didn't even sound like him. "I'm gonna call you before that, but I just...we're...we're gonna fix this when I get back."

I pulled my hands away, searching for any semblance of strength left in my body to force myself to say it. "No, Billy, we're not."

His hat dropped farther, my father hooking a palm on his shoulder and walking him toward the door, throwing me a pitying look on his way past. My mama rushed in from outside, blowing past them on their way out and heading straight toward me.

"Oh, baby," she whispered, catching me as I dissolved into a mess of tears. She gathered me into her arms and held me, walking us over to the couch and lowering us down.

I could hardly breathe for the pain radiating out from my chest, suffocating all the anger and hate because *why did he have to do this?*

I was ready to love him forever, no matter the cost.

"You did the right thing," Mama said, pulling a throw blanket over us and grabbing the box of tissues from the end table. "You're going to be so much happier without him, I promise you. And after we get you settled into that beautiful new apartment in Germany, all this will be behind you before you know it…"

Nothing about her words sounded right, even as true as I knew they were. One day, the pain would start to fade away—*right?* One day, it would all be just a memory. And I would be in Germany. A whole new life. A whole new me. A whole new image, just how I wanted.

Billy's diesel started up outside, then faded down the driveway. The front door shut as my father came back in the house, and I sobbed harder into my mama's arms.

All I could smell anymore was the sharp sting of my father's Brut cologne.

*Old Spice.*

# Chapter 17

*Billy King—Present Day*

I'M MORE SKITTISH THAN I WAS THE FIRST TIME I did this, but it still isn't stopping me. I lift up Taryn's window all the way, slipping off my hat so I'll fit and putting my first leg through. At least now I know not to hit the board that creaks as I come all the way in.

Silently, I straighten and close the window in one easy move my body still remembers too well, submerging myself fully into the land of peaches and lavender. I turn to find her smiling at me from her bed, sitting with one leg tucked under her while her other bare foot flirts with the floor.

She looks...*good*. Really good. Bright and sunny and warm, and my limbs are on fire from the feeling coming back after being in the cold for too damn long. I bite my lip, tentatively reaching out and hooking the corner of my hat onto her desk chair, letting it fall the rest of the way out of my hand and swing into place, like I used to do.

Taryn smiles, and I blow out a breath, my eyes floating over her walls, her desk, her chest of drawers and nightstand, all covered with pictures and racing medals, trophies and knickknacks, and a couple of tiaras from her beauty pageant days. Something new sparkles at me from one of her shelves, and *I'll be damned*.

My World Champion medal is all shiny and clean, no trace of the training pen she dug it out of, and hooked onto a pushpin so it dangles proudly off the corner.

Not a single other thing is out of place. Maybe the world's getting a little bit smaller again. I hope.

"So did you want to talk about your practice?" she says.

"Not really."

She blushes like this is funny, though I'm not sure why.

I pat down my hair, wishing I'd remembered to grab the breath mints from my truck before I left. "It's just, there isn't much else to say."

She nods a little. "Okay. Well, is there…anything else you wanna talk about? Maybe something I can do? To help?"

I really hope she means that.

"Yeah," I tell her, more than a little nervous about coming clean over why I dragged my horse out of his stall in the middle of the night and rode him to her house in thirty-degree weather when I'm specifically *not* supposed to be doing this for a whole bunch of reasons that only half include her. But she's right, and I'm never gonna get what I want if I don't start asking for it. "I, um, I was wondering if…if you'd let me kiss you good night. It'd make me feel a whole lot better."

Taryn crosses her arms, smiling at me from her bed. Then she *laughs*, the sound high and clear like tinkle bells. But something about it doesn't sound like a no. "I can't believe I let you steal my heart."

It's not really an answer, but it may be my favorite thing she's ever said to me.

I do my best to hold down my grin, but there's really not a damn thing I can do about it. "No, ma'am. Just borrowed it."

Taryn sits with that for a second. Then she gets up from her bed, slowly walking toward me with every inch of those legs of hers, pouring out of pink pajama shorts with little crowned goats all over them.

When she stops in front of me, I can't think outside the blue of her eyes and the way she always smells like summer, even in the snow. "Okay."

I flinch, my nose and eyebrows twitching like my face wants to smile, but I don't dare risk it. "Okay?"

"Mm-hmm." She plants her hands backward on her waist and tilts her chin up, that perfectly arched eyebrow challenging me to even *think* about disappointing her. "Kiss me, Billy. Before I change my mind."

My heart starts dancing in my chest, heavy as mud and moto fast, and *Christ*, please don't let me die of a heart attack right now, because it feels like I'm gonna.

I swallow, my mouth dry. Can't *believe* I forgot to grab my breath mints from my truck.

Hands on her waist or her hips?

Maybe I shouldn't touch her.

*Fuck*, I don't know what to do.

Taryn snorts a laugh, and I narrow my eyes at her, embarrassment burning away all my indecision. "Oh, *ha ha*. You ready or what?" For some reason, this just makes her laugh harder, her eyes pinched shut with the force of it. Awesome. "Enough, okay? *Hey*, I can do this."

"Okay, you're right. I'm sorry." She does her best to make her face serious, but it just looks like she's chewing on something. She waves at herself. "I'm ready."

I watch her, just waiting, and *yep*, she sputters another snort into her hands and bends over sideways laughing again a second later.

I turn for the window. "I'm going," I tell her.

"Hey, no! Wait, hold on." She grabs my hand and turns

me back, not laughing anymore but still smiling so bright, we probably don't need the light on. "I'm sorry, okay? I'm nervous, too."

That melts me faster than the ice my old boots are puddling on her wood floor. "I don't want you to be nervous." I squeeze her hand. "Not with me."

She shakes her head, laying her palm on my chest and speaking low but clear, like she wants to make sure I hear every word. "Billy, I have never been nervous to be alone with you. I'm nervous because it's been a long time, and it's us, and I've missed you." Her eyes drop to my lips, the corners of hers turning up before she looks up at me, no fear in any part of her I can see. And I can see a lot of Taryn, way down deep, where it matters. "Close your eyes."

A breath puffs from my chest, and I can't believe I'm gonna do this.

I close my eyes. My heart instantly starts beating so loud, I wonder if she can hear it. I focus on her palm, warm on my chest. Her other hand leaves mine, and I put my hands on my belt, feeling like a fool. Something touches my jaw, and then I feel her: the faintest brush of her lips against mine. Softer than our first kiss and infinitely more tender, and everything in me settles down and warms up. I know what to do now.

I go for the waist, just a tiny bit of pressure in my fingertips as they settle around the curves of her sides, bringing her closer. Her belly bumps mine, and my brilliant hands leave her waist to cup her cheeks, tilting her up to me. Taryn gives me all the time in the world as I sip from her lips all that I need in this life, finding my true north in the curve of her mouth and my purpose in the small crease between her lips, because every breath she takes is it. My *reason*.

I'm not ready to let go, but I still pull back from her slowly, savoring every last taste until we're apart but just barely.

*Damn,* that felt good.

Her eyes are hazy when they lift to mine, swimming with moans I'm desperate to hear and I know she's impatient to make.

I drop my hands from her face and turn away, walking fast toward the window. "Well, good night."

She sputters out a squeak behind me. "*Seriously?*"

"Nope! I'm just kidding." I whip around and jog back to her, Taryn already laughing as I swoop down to hug my arms around her waist and kiss her again, her hands soft on my shoulders until they slide up to my jaw, pulling me closer. And that little move right there is *exactly* what I've been waiting for.

I kiss her with all I've got now, relishing the taste of her tongue and the heat of her mouth, letting myself get a little lost in it because she feels so damn good, and she was right: it has been way too goddamn long.

Taryn ain't impressed. She rips my jacket off my shoulders and shucks it to the floor, then attacks my shirt and gets rid of that offensive article of clothing, too. It stings me with guilt all over again—that she's this wound up because I haven't had her in my care in months, and it's a dangerous way for her to be.

I may wake up hungry in the morning, just starving to damn death and feeling like I'm gonna cave in, but Taryn wakes up horny. And while I can keep a pretty tight lid on my carnal needs after years of staying in one-room motels with my brother and father and Frank, she *cannot.* It's part of the beautiful confusing cataclysm that comes with loving her, though. Because it hurts her to be called pretty, but she sure wants me to fuck her like she is, rough as I will allow, please and thank you, and *saddle up, cowboy, 'cause I want to ride again.*

I kiss her a little dirtier now that I'm half-undressed and she's got us barreling down the onramp, fisting my hand in her hair and tugging up so she gasps into my mouth. I pause to smile down at her, Taryn smiling back, and she knows I'm with her in all the ways that matter. I pull my hand from her hair and push at her hips, sending her stumbling back a step into her chest of drawers.

Taryn giggles and sways like she's tipsy, soft and compliant when I storm forward and grab her shoulders, kissing her wild and breathless until she's holding onto her dresser but sinking in her knees a little. Makes me hard as a fucking rock that she responds to me like that.

I rip my mouth from hers and practically toss her onto the chest of drawers, not being easy or slow or worrying about the strength in my hands as I grip her soft calves and toss them up around my waist. Taryn just laughs at me pretending to scowl at her, giggling harder through her moans when I tug her forward so my belt buckle lands flat between her legs. Her head lolls on her neck as I growl into her ear, "Something funny?"

More giggles lifting my soul somewhere above the clouds, more moans when I sneak my hand between her legs, petting her over her shorts and panties and listening to her whimper into my ear when she falls forward onto me, trusting me to keep her from falling any farther. And I will.

She hits her first one too fast, high and tight because she's too turned on, and *fuck*, I knew better than that. I flip my wrist and press the flat part of my fingers against her, holding them firm but absolutely still as I turn my head to kiss her, soft lips and a *lot* of tongue, slow and deep and doing everything I can to settle her down before she tops out early, still unsatisfied. It isn't easy, and she's still trembling, but she starts to rock against my hand again after a minute, and we're go for round two.

I'm always better on my second attempt. *Always.*

I lock my arm around her waist and lift her up enough so I can get her shorts and panties off, setting her down carefully and slipping them from her legs. Taryn welcomes me back with hungry arms and spread-apart thighs, our lips finding each other's with a simplicity that speaks of all the times we've done this, though it's never been as important as now.

I slip my hand up her thigh, creamy and silky as I guide her leg higher around my waist, but it's not as silky as when I brush my fingers against her. Still flat and still firm but smooth and unhurried, and *God*, she's so fucking *wet* and *soft* that I'm never going to be able to leave this damn bedroom again.

My dick swells uncomfortably thicker in my jeans, jealous and impatient and aching for a taste of her. But it damn well knows by now that it never goes first. I press a kiss to Taryn's cheek, looping her arms around my neck and taking my time following her hushed whimpers to what feels best for her, satisfying all the ways I need to touch her.

I make it last as long as I can, revving her up and backing her down so I can keep going as long as I need. It's still not enough, but when it's time, I drink the moans of her orgasm into my mouth, swallowing all the secrets of all the things we've done in the hours we weren't supposed to be doing them. But I can't stand to live in a world where I'm not allowed to give her what she needs, and she needs *me*.

I let her rest for a minute, my wrist, too, Taryn dopey and mumbling like she's drunk on my shoulder. But when I press my thumb to her again, she moans instead of jumps, and she's still just getting started. Damn two-month backlog is going to take me all night to work out of her, and I can't *wait*. Just hope we've got enough condoms in the stash, because that would be bad.

I straighten her up and take her beautiful face in my hands, then smack a kiss to her lips before I pull her forward and flip her over my shoulder. Taryn cracks up laughing as I carry her to the bed, and I slap her ass for good measure, which only makes her laugh harder.

"Oh, you're asking for it now." I carefully flip her onto the mattress, letting her fall the last foot so it feels a lot farther than it was.

She curls into herself with giggles, her shirt bunching up to reveal the bottom curve of her breasts—no bra—and the lower half of her body gorgeously naked, all for me. If there's a better sight in this world, I don't know what it is.

I point at her, my face serious. "Stay."

She nods, fake saluting me through her laughter. "Yes, sir."

I get the rest of the way naked and grab a condom from the…*cool*, half-full box in her nightstand so I won't have to stop again afterward. I haven't gone down on her since too long *before* we broke up, and I'm fucking dying with the need to taste her. Better, I know she needs it just as much as I want it.

I flick the condom onto the comforter, then grasp her ankles and yank her toward the edge of the bed.

"Door," she says, and my heart stops.

"You didn't lock it while I was putting Gidget in with Aston?"

She grins wickedly, devilish little thing that she is. "Nope."

I dash for the door and lock it as Taryn bursts out laughing. Then I run back to her, leaping onto the bed and lightly covering her mouth with my hand, trying not to smile as I snarl at her. "You are gonna get us in so much trouble."

She easily pushes my hand away, beaming up at me as her leg smooths up my side and wraps around my waist, pulling me closer. "Can't wait."

Yeah, me either.

---

I wake up slowly in Taryn's bed, my body so heavy and sunk into her pillow-top mattress that I'm not sure where I end and it begins. I'm also not sure where I end and *she* begins—Taryn's head on my arm and her back to my chest, peach-scented hair tickling my nose, and her icicle feet woven around mine. A smile sneaks onto my lips, and I inhale deeper the remedy of her, sloshing strength through my muscles so they flex against her soft body, telling me where her skin is against mine and where I need to move closer.

Taryn moans in her sleep and snuggles a little more against me, her foot petting my calf like she's scratching an itch. Once she's got it, she *hmpfs* and turns more onto her side, bumping her ass against my quickly hardening cock. I find my hand on her hip and absently begin strumming her skin even softer than I do my guitar, breathing her in again and nuzzling a kiss to her tangled hair. But it's not the warmth between her legs that has me moving closer.

It's the fire in my heart, simmering low but getting stronger with every lick of flame lapping up my lungs and singeing its way down my arms. It leaves a trail that sparkles like fresh snow under a sunrise, painting me new colors from the inside out.

Because it's her.

She's the one.

And it's not that I wasn't in love with her before. It's not that I hadn't thought about it or that we hadn't talked about it hypothetically or that I didn't know everyone was expecting it. But I never expected it would *actually* be a possibility, that in the real world outside of fantasies and dreams, of somedays and I'm gonnas, she might actually marry me.

That she'd want to or I wouldn't screw it up before then. That I'd ever settle down enough to face what it really means and takes to be someone's husband, the work and the sacrifices, the patience and the self-control, the honesty and humility required to be worthy of sharing a lifetime with someone. And as I listen to Taryn breathe in my arms, her body bare and warming from mine under the covers, there's one word I can't get out of my head: *cherish*.

I know why, too.

Not long after Annie and Jack Henley got married, Jack and I went fishing. He was still the same guy I'd known since he'd moved here at thirteen: scraggly and loud and telling bad jokes no one laughed at but me and Mason. But something about him was different, too. Like he was older than before.

When I asked him how married life was treating him, he said what I'd been thinking. Different than he'd expected. But better. Jack said he'd loved Annie before, more than he knew what to do with it, which was why he'd asked her to marry him at a green eighteen years old. But something had happened when he'd said those vows to her, he said. Like something had locked. And the way he saw her now, it was like she was the ground beneath his feet.

No matter where he was or what he was doing, that ground was gonna be there. And he wanted to be that for her, Jack said. He wanted Annie to have the same security she'd given him. He cherished her for it.

That was the word he used. Cherished.

I hadn't understood at the time, assuming his waxing poetic about commitment was gonna bite him in the ass when the whole thing probably fell apart faster than his Bundt cake in Home Economics.

It didn't, though. They got two little girls now that are the spitting image of Annie, and every time I see them around town, it's so customary to see them as a unit of four that it's hard to remember a time when they weren't.

With a featherlight touch, I brush Taryn's hair back from her shoulder, a long breath melting from my chest as I lightly trickle my fingertips down her arm and back up, so in love with her, I don't know what to do with it all. And for the first time in my life, I understand *exactly* why Jack Henley was puking in the locker room as we passed around the ring he'd bought. Because he needed Annie to say yes. He needed that ground beneath his feet, and he needed to be hers so much, he couldn't wait.

Goose bumps flutter across my skin, and I know it isn't fair, but it hurts too much to hold inside. I pull Taryn a little closer, closing my eyes and bowing my head to the back of hers, silently praying the vows I need to make, my voice in my mind asking questions and answering strongly, though my hands on her body are trembling with the weight of what's happening in my heart.

After the final one, I'm breathing fast and my pulse is racing, and I carefully lift my hand from her hip to pinch away the water at my eyes before I grasp her shoulder and kiss her tangled hair, settling comfortably into the new world before me and feeling as though I've grown up five years overnight.

Feels damn good, too, and I don't want to go back. I don't want to know another way to be other than this one, and I can't wait to tell her. About the ranch and how even though she may not be ready to get married yet, I am the moment she is.

She's the one.

I hold her as she sleeps for I don't know how long. I don't count the minutes or the seconds or her breaths or nothing. I just soak in the knowledge that she's going to be the woman I'll always wake up to. I think about the day when I won't be able to remember a time when we slept in separate beds, in different houses. And I wait impatiently for the rest of our lives to start.

We have some tough years ahead with the distance that stretches and pulls us during the circuit, but I'm not worried. For the first time ever, I'm totally at peace knowing my racing career won't last forever, and one day, we'll come home for good. I *know* we will, as much as I know there will always be ground beneath my feet.

When Taryn finally starts to leave the world of her dreams and come back to me, I'm no longer the same man she went to sleep with, and she must feel it. She hums and turns over, snuggling into me with a soft smile before she's even got her eyes open. "You're happy this morning," she whispers, brushing a kiss to my throat before her hands smooth over my hips, pulling them harder against her as she moans and nips at my collarbone.

I chuckle, tucking the covers tighter around her and lost somewhere beneath her fingernails teasing and tickling my side. *Yeah*, I'm happy. My mind's still echoing with the words we whispered to each other last night, starting with all the things I'd missed about her: big things, small things, stupid things, and important things. Things I'd taken for granted and won't again. Taryn said her own list, things I wasn't aware of and will make sure to keep doing because I hadn't known what they meant to her. We made apologies and a lot of promises, and it ended with Taryn saying that she was mine, and she wanted me to know that.

I'm still not sure how I feel about it, but I guess I understand what she meant. Because in a lot of ways, all the ones that matter, I'm hers, too. Have been for a while now.

I sweep some of the tangles back from her face, brushing a kiss to her forehead. "Morning, honey."

"I need coffee," she mumbles through a yawn. But then she winds her leg around mine so no one is getting out of this bed anytime soon. "I'll make us some eggs and biscuits for breakfast if you give me, like, five more minutes."

It floods me all over again, and I squeeze her tight. "I'm okay."

She shifts to squint up at me, all sleepy and pouty and more beautiful than I can ever remember her being. "What? You've literally woken me up twice before just from your stomach growling in the morning. You're *not* hungry? Are you sick?" She reaches up to feel my forehead, and I can't keep from laughing, turning my face into the pillow to try to keep quiet. Taryn starts tickling me, asking, "Huh? What's wrong, Billy? You don't like my cooking, is that it? What's the real story here?"

Her cooking's amazing and she knows it, and it just adds insult to injury that I'm gonna miss her perfect omelet with ham and cheese and onions and tomatoes and the biscuits she makes from scratch that are even fluffier than my mama's. I think because Taryn uses some kind of flour that isn't really flour.

But either way, I've stayed too long already. I gotta get Gidget back to his stall at Hargrove Ranch before Lynn notices he's gone and calls the damn sheriff on him missing. But I can push it five more minutes. Maybe ten.

I finally get enough air in my lungs to turn over and give Taryn some payback, stealing her wrists into my hand and locking her against me so she can't keep tickling me into oblivion.

"That's *it*," I growl, Taryn bursting out in giggles as I tackle her into the bed, my hands on either side of her propping me up as she laughs under me.

"Oh no, I'm gonna get it now..."

I pretend to scowl at her and slowly shake my head. "So much trouble."

Taryn cracks up even more, sliding her hands up my chest and settling them around my neck and looking so damn happy, it kills me that I'm gonna have to ruin it by telling her I gotta go.

I'm *always* telling her I gotta go, and it's not fair to either of us.

"Can't wait to hear what my punishment is gonna be,"

she says cheerfully, and I can't bring myself to do it—I lower down to kiss her instead. She's more important, and she needs me here. With her, right now, making up for the time we've lost.

Gidget's fine, and Lynn can get over it. Taryn comes first.

"Let me go make you some coffee," I whisper into her lips. "Won't be two minutes."

Taryn beams and lifts another hazy kiss from my lips, then pushes me off her. "Nope!" She tosses the covers over my head, leaving me fighting to get out from under them while she gets up from the bed. "I need you to live another day. You can get the wrath of my mama tomorrow."

I chuckle and prop my head in my hand, already missing her against me as I watch her get dressed in the same clothes I took off her last night.

"Two minutes," she says with a wink, slipping out of the room and shutting the door behind her.

I collapse into her bed, breathing in the trace of her shampoo on the pillow and the heady scent of sex still in the air, and not a single moving box anywhere in sight. I clap once, quietly, rethreading my hands behind my head and staring at her ceiling.

The ground steady beneath my feet.

I thought.

# Chapter 18

*Taryn Ledell—Present Day*

"Wow." Lor looks up, sitting across from me on her down comforter, her legs pretzeled and that great big horse painting above her bed scrutinizing everything that happens in here. The rest of her giant white room is silent apart from the blow of the heater swirling vanilla candles and rustling the notebook paper of Mason's letter in her hand. "He made…some really good points."

I nod so hard, her overly soft bed wiggles with the force of my agreement. "Mm-hmm."

She scrunches her face at me, leaning closer and her voice dropping like she's scared he's somehow going to hear her. "He's a really good writer."

I laugh, taking back the letter. "Right? Who would've thought?"

"Has Billy read it?"

"Nope," I tell her, folding it up and leaning over to put it back in my purse. Under the silk interior lining, where I unstitched the corner just enough to fit the folded letter inside, super secret and totally safe. "And he's not going to. Ever."

"So…" Lor shakes her head at me when I sit up and face her, but she's gotta already know what I'm gonna say based on how badly I've been beaming since I bounded up the stairs to her bedroom and threw open the door.

I keep it cool for a second. But not a very long one

before I throw my hands up excitedly and squeal, "We're back together!"

"*What?*" Lorelai grabs my shoulders, shaking me. "Are you serious? What did we talk about!"

I crack up laughing, still giddy and loose from undoubtedly the greatest three days of nonstop sex anyone could ever hope to have. "I don't care," I tell her, shaking my head and letting her shake me. "I don't even care."

"*Ugh!*" She throws me down sideways onto her bed, and I curl into myself, laughing so hard, my stomach hurts. I've missed being this happy, and it's so good to have it back. To have *all* of it back. Exactly how it's supposed to be. "You're hopeless."

"I know," I breathe, pushing myself into sitting up. "But hear me out, okay?"

"No." She crosses her arms, glaring at her trophy shelf. "I'm mad at you."

"Lor!" I chuckle. "Come on. You know I never wanted to break up with him. You were with me that night. It was... *bad.*"

She rolls her eyes, waving her hand over the words, "But you didn't have a choice because you backed yourself into a corner telling everyone you'd be out the door the second he even thought about riding a bull."

"Yeah." I lightly push at her shoulder. "Jerk."

She half shrugs. "Valid. But I still say you didn't have to take him back. He did ride the bull, in case you forgot."

I level a look at her. "*A,* he did it for a reason that was... okay, I don't agree with it, but I understand it. Billy doesn't know how to *not* protect his brother. And *B,* why would I *not* take him back when I'm still in love with him? I was really fucking pissed, sure. But mostly, I was just scared that night. And it didn't help that I'd been trying to figure out how to tell everyone that I was going to turn down the offer for him, and he went off and did the *one thing* that could jeopardize our future. Publicly. But the worst part is…none of this would've happened if I hadn't tried to tell him what to do in the first place."

Lor gapes at me. "What kind of freaking Kool-Aid does he have you drinking now?"

"Really." I blink at her. "You're gonna let a guy say what you're allowed to do?"

She wrinkles her nose, looking down at her comforter and mumbling, "Not if he wants to see me naked."

"Exactly," I tell her. "All those lines in the sand…they moved. And I'm not saying that what he did was right, but I am not willing to lose him forever over it. We both fucked up."

Lor shakes her head at me, seemingly at a loss. But with her own boyfriend distancing himself until their relationship concluded in a breakup voicemail, she hasn't exactly been feeling forgiving toward men in general.

"Well, I'm officially confused," she says. "Because if you were pissed when you broke up with him, and you were mad when we got home from Valencia, when exactly did you decide to take him back? Just…curious. For the rest of us trying to play catch-up over here."

I can't help but laugh. "I don't know. I mean, when he went and got that X-ray, that was a big deal. Billy would wrap himself in barbed wire before he'd complain, and he *hates* to ask for help. So the fact that he went over to Adam's, and he was taking the injury seriously… I knew he'd finally heard me outside Up-Chuck Buck's. That I wanted him to start standing up for himself and that I needed to feel safe about us having a future I could count on."

Lor flinches. "Hold on. When did y'all go to Up-Chuck Buck's?"

"Oh, get this," I tell her, because apparently in the mess of everything, I forgot. "Maggie and Jack invite me out there for Jack's birthday, and who do I run into? Billy. Because Mason had him out trying to get him laid the *first night* y'all got back from Valencia. His brother didn't waste a minute."

"Ugh." Lor reaches over to grab her beer from the nightstand. I've got a drink going warm somewhere over there, too, but mine's a hard sparkling water, peach flavored. "Guys always do try to screw their way over a broken heart, don't they?"

"Yep. And Billy is a really good guy. I'm never going to find someone else like him, and I don't even want to look. It *killed* me to tell him it was over, and he was so upset about it. But putting us back together just wasn't as simple as saying 'I forgive you' and acting like it never happened. There were so many things that needed to be fixed. Big things. And I needed time to calm down. We just needed…space. But not *too much* space."

Lor slowly pulls the bottle from her lips, her smile growing. "So *that* explains the workout sessions! You were keeping your tits in his face."

I sputter into a jumble of laughter. "No, I was not! I was keeping the door open."

Lor cracks up laughing. "Sure you were, Taryn. With the sports bras and leggings in thirty-degree weather."

"Oh my God!" I tell her, "I was fucking freezing the whole time!"

We both crack up harder, and I reach over for my can of hard sparkling water on her nightstand, taking a sip and trying to catch my breath. It's so weirdly relieving she just gets it, but she's always made me feel like I've got her in my corner. Because I do. And she's got me in hers, too, if she ever needs me.

"The thing is," I tell her once I'm settled enough to speak again, so much love in my heart and my whole body, it shouldn't fit inside me. "He just did his workouts and told me stories that made me laugh. Through this whole breakup, he did *everything* right. He respected my boundaries, he didn't push me, and he waited to ask for another chance. Three whole weeks he waited. And when I let him back in… He started being honest about everything, even the little stuff, and he apologized to my mama. Made an absolute fool of himself doing it, but he did. He said he was sorry, to her, and for hurting my whole family."

Lorelai's shoulders melt toward her plush comforter like she's swooning with me, a sappy smile on her face as we sit there for a second and bask in my words, in the wonderfulness that is Billy King. Then her smile falls. "Did you have to give an answer to Werner?"

"Oh," I remember, smiling. "Yeah, I did. Christmas Day, I called him and told him I couldn't do it."

The color bleeds from her face, Lor looking as shocked as I would've been had any friend of mine done the same. But this was different, and Billy was special.

"Are you *serious*? You really gave it all up? The condo, the trainer, the chef, the housekeeper, the car, the bikes…"

"Yeah," I admit, feeling more secure in my decision than ever. "I've had a lot of loves in my life, Lorelai. School, medicine, racing. I haven't loved any of it as much as I love laughing with Billy. And I'm gonna marry him. Maybe not tomorrow or this year, but that is the man I'm going to marry. Because I already know: when I'm old and I'm dying,

I'm not gonna regret the races I missed. I'm gonna regret the days I missed when I could've been laughing with him."

She shakes her head, blinking rapidly. Then she freaks. "Are you keeping your contract?"

"Of course." I set my water on her nightstand so I can take her hand.

To Lorelai, the idea of not being able to race is the absolute worst thing in the world. And it doesn't mean she's wrong or I am. We're just different, and I like that about our friendship. We balance each other. It helps keep our priorities in check. Not that anything could change my mind about this.

"Nothing else is changing on that front, and we're still going to figure out the image campaign. It won't be as big now, and it'll be a lot more complicated and will mean more travel probably, but I just…" I blow out a breath. "I haven't told Billy yet. How do I tell him this, Lor? The last time I said the word 'propose,' he looked like I clocked him across the jaw."

She snorts, shaking her head. "I don't know, Taryn. Maybe make him dinner first? You are a really good cook."

"Oh yeah, that'll work," I deadpan. "'Hey, honey, I'm not moving to Germany anymore because I gave up my offer for you, but please don't feel the need to get married anytime soon or anything. Pass the lasagna?'"

Her face goes sharp, her hand flying up between us. "Don't mention Italian food to me. Or anything related to Italy in general."

*Jackpot!*

"Why?" I drawl.

She gets up and heads toward her massive walk-in closet, flipping on the light. Then she disappears inside her safe space: racks of cocktail dresses, evening gowns, jeans and leather jackets, and tiny little designer tops that individually cost way more than my truck payment. I *love* shopping in her closet.

"What happened now?"

Hangers clink and clank, fabric swooshing and a zipper zipping. "So you know how both Luca and Piero retired, so Mason and I signed with Dabria Corse and we're getting moved up to MotoPro?"

I sit a little more comfortably on her bed, getting ready to receive whatever bomb she's gonna drop. "Yeah…."

A hanger clangs on the wood bar in the closet, then Lor sticks her head out, her voice black. "Francesco Lombardi is officially done, too. Massimo signed with Yaalon."

My jaw hits the bedding, dumbstruck that her biggest rival is now teammates with my boyfriend. "*No!* MotoPro?"

"Oh yes."

"Honey, I'm so *sorry!*"

She just can't seem to get away from that guy.

"Well…" She creeps out of the closet, her hands twisting in front of her, and I wonder if this is the moment she's going to admit her crush on him. "That's not the worst part."

I crack a smile, wishing I had popcorn for this. "What's the worst part?"

"*God*, you're gonna be pissed." She tears her hands through her hair, sending my stomach flipping before it knots and locks halfway up my throat.

"Lor," I say, my voice low.

"Okay, so, I swear to God I had nothing to do with this, and I thought you might not actually care that much because you and Billy were broken up, but now that I know what's really been going on…" She bites her lip, her shoulders up by her ears, and *did the heater kick up?* I just started sweating, bad. "My mom's really pissed at Billy. Like *really* pissed. He snuck Gidget out again the other night—"

"To come to my house! Gidget was in the barn with Aston the whole time!"

"Well, she's told Billy to stop doing that before, and the thing is, she bought Gidget to be mine, but he's not. He's just not! And as much as she loves Billy, she says she can't—*won't*—pay to feed and stable a horse for a farmhand who doesn't work for her anymore and who doesn't respect her rules."

I stare at Lorelai, praying she's not saying what I think she is.

It'll kill Billy. Like, drop him dead, on the spot.

She deflates, hugging her arms around her. "She's selling Gidget."

I leap off the bed, grabbing my purse and ripping out my phone. "When?"

"Like, today," Lorelai says. "The guy's supposed to be here in, like, an hour."

"Are you fucking serious?!" I scream at her. "How could you not tell me? Or him?"

She sputters, looking a lot smaller than she normally does and nothing like the reckless racer who can kick my boyfriend's ass if he's not 100 percent focused on the track. "I thought we were mad at him!"

I dial Billy's number, tearing my hand through my hair as it rings and rings.

"Hey, honey," he finally answers.

"Where are you!" I yell, freaking the fuck out that he's not already here and having no idea how I'm going to tell him this. How do you tell someone this? And over the *phone*?

"I'm…at the doctor?"

A whole new wave of horror strikes me straight in the center of my chest, my hand flying to my throat. "Why are you at the doctor? Are you hurt?"

"Nah. I, uh…" He clears his throat, then drops his voice. "I came clean to Frank about Smashbox. We're getting my ankle checked to make sure I'm okay to go back to work, since I'm still limping."

"Oh…"

The words cycle over themselves in my mind, settling on top of everything else I was supposed to say and now can't remember. He came clean? And got his manager to take him to a doctor instead of blowing it off like it'll probably be fine?

Pride melts through me, warm as each lap of hot air from the heater. He's changed so much. But thankfully not *too* much. "Really?"

"Yeah," he rumbles, a bit of a smile in his voice like he knows he did the right thing and knows I'm happy with him for it.

Lorelai swats at my arm.

*Shit!* She's right. "Honey, I'm sorry, and I know he's gonna be pissed, but you gotta leave and get to the ranch right now."

"Taryn, I can't—"

"Lynn's selling Gidget," I blurt out, my heart broken that I'm not next to him where I can hold his hand and promise we're gonna find a way to fix it, though I have no idea how in the hell we're gonna do that. "She's pissed, Billy. She's really pissed that you kept him out the other night, and the guy's gonna be here in an hour. You gotta get here *now*!"

There's no sound on the other end of the line.

I check the screen, and yeah, I've got full bars.

"Billy! Did you hear me? She's—"

"Stall her." His voice is so sharp, I almost wonder whether it's Frank speaking. Until I hear him yelling in the background.

"Hey! Where are you going?"

I look up at Lorelai, ice flooding my veins and no idea how I'm supposed to do what he's asking me. "Billy, I *can't*! This is Lynn Hargrove we're talking about!"

"Taryn, I don't have my wallet, and I gotta go to the house first. Fucking stall her!"

The phone clicks, and I stare at the useless piece of equipment in my hand.

*Christ!*

I dial the next number, grabbing Lorelai by the arm and running out the door to her room.

"Where are we going?" she says as we stumble down the stairs and around the banister, my boots slipping on the great big rug in her living room.

"We have to stall your mom! Billy has to go to the house first."

"Are you serious!" She rips open the front door to a blast of frigid January air, standing there as I blow past her and take off toward the barn, running for my life. "We can't go up against her!"

"Hey, baby," my mama answers, and if there is a God, my father will already be home from work. "What time do you think you'll be home for dinner? I'm gonna go ahead and assume I need to set a place for Billy, too. Though he eats enough for three people."

"Mama, I need a favor…"

# Chapter 19

*Billy King—Present Day*

I DON'T REMEMBER PULLING IN THROUGH THE GATE. I just know my tires are off the driveway and chewing through grass, and I'm flying way too fucking fast through the ranch in my beat-up old truck. It's not as fast as my heart's racing, my shaking hand laying on the horn as I slam the brakes and skid to a stop outside the barn.

"*Wait!*" I nearly fall out my door, slipping and stumbling on the icy grass before I start hauling ass for the barn, wind cutting my cheeks and blowing my hat from my head. "Wait!" Straight past Taryn's father, waving me on like a third-base coach next to his truck with the horse trailer hooked up.

"*Go*, Billy! Go, go, *go*!"

Thank fucking God for her.

"Are you out of your fucking mind?" Lynn screams when I run into the barn, pointing the way I came. "You don't drive that way on my ranch, and you don't approach a barn like that! Get off my property!"

"That is my horse!" I roar right back at her.

Some guy I've never seen before has Gidget's lead rope in his hand. It tears me apart almost worse than those pictures of Colton's hands all over Taryn's body. Lorelai's standing in front of him, showing him something on her phone that he isn't interested in but she's just going on and on and on. Taryn's standing between him and Gidget, hugging my horse's neck and petting him, trying to keep him calm because I can already see him shivering and shaking like he's scared, and I know he is. We all are.

My eyes flick back to Taryn. She isn't wearing a jacket. It's freezing.

"Gidget, it's okay," I tell him, calming my voice and trying to find a smile for him. He swishes his tail, looking between Lynn and the guy and me, and he doesn't know what the hell is going on, but he knows it isn't good. "You're coming home with me, buddy."

"Oh *no*, he is not!"

I ignore Lynn and go over to the guy, getting in his face. He isn't that big, and he's older, and I could take him if I had to. My right arm can throw a glove-cracking fastball that only my brother can catch, and my left can hold all solid muscle of me to a bucking bull for eight long goddamn seconds. "Give me the lead."

He blanches, the color fading from the brim of his hat and down to his pressed jeans. The smell of fear and body odor and cheap beer starts pouring off him, because I've got him sweating where he's standing, and his eyes flick toward Lynn over my shoulder.

"Give me the goddamn lead!"

He spooks and tosses the lead rope at my chest, and I give it to Taryn, looking her in the eyes and wishing I could say how thankful I am for her. She's trembling to damn death, her eyes huge and afraid, and I brush a kiss to her forehead, breathing in summer peaches as I shrug off my jacket, putting it around her shoulders. "It's gonna be okay. Don't let go of him. No matter what."

"Okay," she whispers, threading one arm through a sleeve, then another. Then she tightens her hands around the lead rope, locking down on the second love of my life and getting ready for battle. She isn't gonna let Gidget go.

I turn to face Lynn, who is glaring me into the dirt. "How much?"

She shakes her head, but it's barely more than a twitch, her temper's got her wound up so tight. "Nope. You are not getting him."

"That is *my* horse. Everything he knows how to do, I taught him. Now you sell him to me right now!"

She leans forward, her voice dark with stubbornness and her eyes whipping me like the wind slashing through the barn, riling up the other horses in their stalls and a bunch of farmhands having a hell of a time settling them down while acting like they aren't staring at us. "*No.*"

"Goddamn it," I curse her. "Why not?"

"Because you're not gonna take care of him, Billy!"

"Mom!" Lorelai screeches.

"Well, he's not," Lynn says to her, the resemblance between them uncanny when they're spatting in identical blue jeans and Outback Trading Company jackets, their curly brown hair blowing wild around their faces, and two stubborn attitudes too big for this one damn barn. "Y'all are gone all the time racing. And Morningside's Golden Chariot—"

"Gidget," I cut her off.

"Gidget"—she glowers at me with those strict brown eyes of hers—"deserves better. He is a prize Akhal-Teke stallion with some damn fine bloodlines, and he should be on a ranch where he's gonna be rode and shown and studded. And I'm sorry, Billy, I know you care about him, but you can't give him what he needs. You don't…you don't even have any land to put him on."

There it is. The curse of my whole borrower life.

Before I can feel the weighted punch of all my worst fears coming true, Taryn pipes up. "Yes, he does," she says.

My head snaps her way, and her chin is high as hell, staring down Lynn Hargrove with my horse standing at attention next to her.

"With me. I have plenty of space, and Gidget is used to my stables already. Since that's where he was the other night. With Aston."

She's breathing hard, but her voice didn't shake once, and I'm so damn proud of her, I can't even speak, not that I'd even know what to say. I look at Lynn to see if that did it, because Taryn is always right, and she always saves my ass when I fall short. And I know that isn't fair, but I just can't live without her. I wouldn't make it.

"Taryn, honey." Lynn glances at me and then lowers her voice. "You're moving to Germany. Adam called me, and I know you're selling Aston Magic. I was even gonna offer to buy her from you, but I hadn't gotten the chance to talk to you about it yet. And I appreciate that you're trying to help him by lying to me—"

"I'm not going." Taryn's voice is clear and firm, arching that mighty eyebrow of hers down at Lynn, even though Lynn's taller.

I do my best not to react on the outside, but the rest of me is going apeshit on the inside.

I look to Lorelai. She's got her arms crossed, her weight shifting, but she's nodding along like she knows what Taryn said is the truth. And I had my suspicions, but it's a hell of a lot better hearing it out loud, even though I'm sure we would've figured it out either way.

"And I'm not selling my horse," Taryn bites off. "Now sell Billy his!"

Lynn's head jerks back. Mine, too, and I think Lynn might have forgotten about me, she looks so upset with Taryn. "You gave up your offer for him? Honey, what are you doing with your life?" She covers her mouth with her hand, so much disappointment rippling off her that I'm just about to shut this down when Taryn does it for me, again.

"At least I'm not so afraid of looking like a fool that I'll look past what's right. I stand up for it. Especially when it's hard, and most of all when it doesn't make sense to anyone else. And what I did doesn't have to make sense to you, and I damn well don't need your permission. I know what's right in my heart, and I *followed* it. And you know in your heart this is wrong. I expected more of you, Mrs. Hargrove."

We all stand there, none of us breathing. Except for Gidget. The farmhands aren't even pretending they're not watching now. The whole barn has stopped still at Taryn's words.

*No one* talks to Lynn Hargrove like that and gets away with it, and I still can't believe it was Taryn that did it. Miss "Kill 'em with kindness" just chewed out the toughest rancher in Memphis, and she isn't even shaking.

Lynn looks at me, and not even from Valerie Ledell have I ever received such a scowl of disgust. "I've had enough of this," Lynn says. "Lorelai, go to the house and call the sheriff."

"What? No way!"

"Lorelai! Do as I say!"

"Mom, just sell him the horse!"

"I won't!" Lynn snaps, then she looks to the guy next to Taryn, her voice at half the level of before. "Harry, I'm really sorry about this."

The son-of-a-bitch has the nerve to chuckle. "It's okay, Lynn. I got farmhands, too."

"I am not a farmhand anymore," I growl at him.

Taryn nods at me, and I take the strength pouring from her eyes and drink it into myself as best I can. Then I turn back to Lynn. Ready.

I'm always better on my second attempt. *Always.*

"Lynn, I understand what you're saying about him being a show horse. And I understand I got a job that gets me gone a lot. But I *swear* to you with everything in me that I will take care of him, because the *only* thing in this world more important to me than that horse is the woman holding his lead, and I'm not leaving here without either. He *wants* to be with me, and you can't deny that. And once again, you may not understand it, and you don't have to like it, but you know selling him to anyone else isn't right. Now, I'll pay you whatever you want. I'll give you double, even triple what this guy was gonna offer you. But I'm not leaving here without my horse. So *how much*?"

Lynn looks at me for a long time. She looks at Taryn, too, the wind still raging and the temperature dropping by the second. Then she hangs her head and shakes it, sighing and shifting her weight. I check on Taryn, warm in my jacket, and Lorelai snuggled in hers. When I look back to Lynn, she looks up, glaring at all three of us again before she grits out a curse under her breath. Then she looks at the guy behind me. "Harry, I'm sorry."

"Wha—" he sputters. "You're gonna—"

"Yep." Lynn's eyes dial in on me, brown and pissed off but kind of weirdly pleased, too. "Billy, I swear to God… *ugh*, I hope you got your damn checkbook."

She storms off around my side, gravel crunching angrily under her boots, and I stand there, unable to move.

Not stunned from relief. And not frozen from joy.

I'm locked in place from pure fucking horror.

*My checkbook. That I can't use.*

Farmhands start moving again in the background, horses whinnying as they get led out and put back in, fed and patted and saddled and washed. Gidget snorts and whinnies as the Harry guy walks out of the barn after Lynn, their voices blurring together like the parents in the Charlie Brown cartoons.

"Billy?" Taryn says. "Honey, are you okay? Do you need me to start getting him loaded for you?"

She means into her father's trailer. Hooked onto his truck and ready to go because she was goddamn *brilliant* enough to think that far ahead when all I could think about was getting here.

I didn't *think.*

"Billy!" Lynn yells, standing outside the barn with her arms crossed. That Harry guy keeps walking toward a second truck and horse trailer I hadn't noticed until now, and my eyes start prickling as the realization sets in of what I'm gonna have to do. "Get your fat-check-writing ass over here!"

I turn away, stumbling toward the opposite side of the barn.

"Hey, where are you going?" Lynn calls after me.

The sting of the wind bites bitterly against my skin, my throat and lungs burning as my breath puffs hot in front of my face. I double over when my boots hit the grass, wiping at my face and my stomach rolling like I'm gonna be sick.

"Billy, what's wrong!" Taryn yells.

Gidget whinnies like he's just as worried as she is, and I can't believe this is happening. I was so close to having it all. Now...

*I have no idea how I'm ever going to get over him.*

"Lorelai, take Gidget's lead," I hear behind me. Next thing I know, Taryn is in front of me, her hands on my jaw guiding me to straighten and her eyes finding mine. "What's going on?"

I shake my head. "I can't...I can't buy him."

She doesn't blink or flinch, her voice strong. "Why?"

"Because," I breathe, my hands settling on her hips because I don't know if I can stay standing if I don't hold onto her. "Honey, I have to tell you something."

# Chapter 20

PANIC ROOTS DEEP IN MY CHEST. BILLY'S BARELY GET-ting words out, his grip on me so desperate it almost hurts, and I don't know how many more surprises I can take today. Not after everything. I'm so tired.

"I…" He swallows, but his voice is still shredded over the words. "I was supposed to tell you this a different way, with my great-grandma's ring and…"

My eyes go huge, my heart slamming in my chest. What is he—

"Honey, I bought our ranch."

*He…*

"What?" I gasp.

"Duke Bricker's ranch," he says. "I bought it."

My hands slip from his jaw to his shoulders, and the words are starting to sound weird in my mind. Like they're losing their meaning. There's a word for when that happens, but I don't remember what that is, either.

"Is that okay?" he says, and I can't make sense of what he's asking. Is it okay that he bought Duke Bricker's ranch? "I mean, you liked it, right?"

I blink at him. Do I like it? I was just there for the funeral. *Think, Taryn, think…* The house is…okay, my mind already repainting stuff and getting rid of the gross carpet and worse furniture, and yeah…that's good. That's totally doable. That's *way* more than doable, that's…*wow*.

And he…he's got land. A fucking *ton* of it. Stables…I think he's even got a second house on the back forty.

Just like that, all the pieces of the puzzle finally start clicking into place, my heart quickly catching up. "Oh my God," I mutter, because I can't find any other words for this.

Our dream.

The someday, when we were gonna be free and together. Us and our horses, too.

He did it. *He fucking did it!*

"You bought Duke Bricker's ranch!" I scream at him, my face feeling like it's gonna break in half from pure fucking joy.

"Yeah." He still looks so heartbroken.

I don't get it. *I don't get it!* "Why aren't we celebrating?"

"Because," he says, taking my hands in his and holding on tight. His voice is wrecked, so damn wrecked. "I haven't closed yet."

"What is the holdup?" Lynn yells from across the barn, but Billy doesn't even acknowledge her.

I shake my head, at a loss. "Billy, I don't know what that means."

"It means…" He stares at the ground between our boots like he's praying God will strike him dead before he has to say it. He waits a long time, but when nothing happens, he looks back at me, resigned. "It isn't ours until I do. And the last *fucking* thing the guy said to me was to not spend any money till after I closed."

I still don't get it. Billy never spends money, so that shouldn't be a problem for him.

Then Gidget whimpers from where Lorelai is holding his lead, and my eyes snap to Billy, growing horrified.

He shakes his head, his voice cracking but his grip on my hands only getting stronger. "It's our ranch, honey, and I can't do both. You come first."

I look to Gidget, swishing his tail happily next to Lorelai, and tears slip down my cheeks. This can't be happening. I feel like I'm going to be sick.

Billy pulls me into him and hugs his arms tight around me, and it breaks my heart in half with how much he must be hurting right now. It's *wrong* for him to lose his horse.

"It's okay. It's gonna be okay," he says on repeat, but I don't think he's saying it for me, and *fuck this*.

"Wait a minute—" I lean back, staring up at him: tall and lean in hard-worked Ariat boots and Wrangler jeans, a champion belt buckle, and a pearl-snap shirt because he knows I like them best. The setting sun is shining on his blond hair, but his face looks like he's dying, and I can't have that. Not when I can do something about it. "I'll buy him."

As soon as I say it, I know it's the right call, and I can't *believe* I didn't think of it sooner. I was going to offer to cobuy our house anyway. And Gidget may end up costing me more than any down payment I had planned on, but Werner pays me well, and I do have the money in savings...

I can totally do this. And Gidget's more than worth every penny. *Billy's* worth it.

Billy gapes at me. "Taryn, he's gonna cost—"

*Is he serious right now?* "And how much is Duke Bricker's ranch?" I ask.

Billy swallows. Goes a little pale. "Two point five," he mutters.

A noise squeaks from my throat. *Two point five million goddamn dollars?*

"Yeah," I say with a dazed laugh. "Honey, I'm buying your horse for you. Don't you worry, I got this. Lynn!" I yell.

Billy's still staring at me. A gorgeous statue of a dazed cowboy, silhouetted against wide open land and tall trees in the background. I press a hasty kiss to his lips, then run off after Lynn.

Did he say something about a ring earlier? We're gonna have to circle back to that. *Two point five.* That's it. He's getting a new truck and trailer from me, too. I don't care what he says; he deserves it, he'll need it to haul Gidget, and I'm tired of freezing.

"What's going on?" Lorelai says on my way past her, Gidget watching me and then looking back to Billy, the stallion huffing a bit. "Are we loading him up or what?"

"Yeah, go and get him started. We'll be right behind you."

"Whatever. Come on, Gidget." She clicks twice and starts to lead Gidget toward my father's truck, and it only takes me a second to sort everything out with Lynn before I'm running back across the barn to Billy. Who is still standing in the exact same spot.

That's okay. I can fix that, too.

"Okay," I start when I stop in front of him, kinda breathless in the cold and my brain still going a million miles an hour. "So she doesn't really care which one of us writes her a check as long as it clears, and she's fine with waiting until I can bring her one tomorrow. So Lorelai's gonna start getting Gidget loaded up so we can get him back to the house and start getting him settled. See? We got this. Everything's fine."

It takes him a second, but then Billy nods, his jaw so

tight, he can't even speak. I smooth my palm down his arm, giving him a moment to let it all settle in. I totally get it—I can't wait to go crawl into my bed and sleep for, like, a week after this. Except I still gotta get to the bank. Poor Billy's probably gonna be sick after standing around in the cold in just his shirt and no jacket all afternoon. *Damn it*, he's been running on his ankle again, too.

Yeah, I need to get him home. Showered. Leg up. Then I'm going to sleep. I'll go to the bank in the morning. It's probably closed for the night by now anyway.

"Taryn," he grits out, "I'm so…"

"I know," I tell him. "Me too." The storm in his blue eyes is already resolving as I step close enough to slide my hands up his chest, then lock my arms around his neck, because he always feels safer with me against him. A little more fearless.

His hands settle on my hips, gentle and strong and rough with calluses that scrape *so good*. And when he drops his forehead to mine, his breaths tight with all he's feeling, it's impossible for me not to get swept up in it, too. How much this is going to be my always and forever and how ready I am to start it all with him.

But first, I gotta get us home.

"One thing at a time, cowboy," I whisper. "Let's go get Gidget settled in, okay? Then you can tell me all about our new ranch, because I cannot *wait* for us to move in."

Billy finally smiles, calming down enough to lift a soft kiss from my lips and his voice almost back to normal. "Who says you're invited?"

I can't help laughing, relief flowing through me when he takes my hands, pulling me along as he starts walking backward. Toward his truck and his horse loaded onto my trailer and our future farmhouse twelve miles down the road.

"Maybe you can come visit," he adds with a wink. And this time, he sounds exactly like he's supposed to.

"Oh, thanks."

He turns so we can walk side by side through the barn, his arm around my shoulders and mine hugged around his waist, the comforting scent of his cologne filling my lungs. He squeezes my shoulder and drops a kiss to my hair, sounding a little dismayed when he mutters, "I can't believe Gidget is mine."

I smile into his shirt, wondering how long he's gonna be saying that. "Yep. Not borrowed, honey. Yours."

Billy squeezes me again. "Which stall are we putting him in?"

"Um, the last one, I think? Mama's cleaning it out for you as we speak." That's what my father said when he got here, anyway: that my mama was already in our barn getting the stall ready, probably shoveling straw in her cotton nightgown, and I have no idea how to thank her enough. Both of them. They didn't blink an eye at the prospect of taking on another horse when I called, and all I can think is they must know. That it's Billy for me. And it's okay.

It's all going to be okay.

Billy's steps slow down, a guilty sigh falling from his lips as he shakes his head. "Thank you, honey," he whispers. "For always saving my ass."

"Oh, honey, no," I breathe, stepping around him to look up into his eyes. "Saving each other…that's what we're supposed to do. And you don't have to thank me for that. You don't have to say anything at all."

He halfway laughs, gesturing behind me. "Taryn, I can't *not* say something when you just bought my horse."

"Well, you bought our ranch," I counter. "And

besides"—I give him a wink just to soothe the last of his nerves—"don't you know there are only three words I ever wanna hear you say?"

He crosses his arms, but his grin is purely teasing. "Oh yeah? What's that?" he says. "I love you? You were right? Or I'm already naked?"

I snort a laugh, a little mesmerized by his grin alone. The rest of the barn has returned to normal life, horses happily bedding down and farmhands hanging up their tack for the night. And with Gidget sure to be safely loaded in my trailer, I know we need to get going. But there's no sight I've ever loved more than my cowboy in the sunset.

"Those are pretty good," I tell him, trying to think outside the blue of his eyes and the muscles I know are waiting to warm me underneath his clothes. "But I got something better."

He playfully groans and waves me on with one hand. "I'm not promising I'll say it, but let's hear it."

I can't help but smile, stretching up on my toes to lift a soft kiss from his lips. And when I pull back to look at him, his smile calm and infinitely steady, I gift him the three words I know he's been waiting all his life to say, and I'm gonna make damn sure he only ever says to me:

"Honey, I'm home."

# Epilogue

*Billy King—A Little While Later*

"WHAT ABOUT A BOTANICAL GARDEN OR SOMETHING like that?" I turn the thought over in my mind, the sway of Gidget beneath me rocking the idea into place until it feels like a decision. "That would be kinda cool. The pictures would be nice."

Taryn looks over at me from her saddle on Aston Magic, walking beside me and Gidget through the pasture back toward our house. "Billy, I love you, but let's be real here: you are not the kind of guy who proposes in a botanical garden. It's gotta feel like *us*, honey. And that's…that's someone else."

"Yeah, I guess you're right."

I sigh as I look out over our ranch, the sun setting on all eighty of our acres and shining down on our back porch. Taryn's got a pot roast going in the Crock-Pot in the kitchen, my new truck is parked beside hers out front, and her bike is up on a jack around back because I'm changing out her clutch *again*. When I check, the lights are glowing through the windows in the second house on the back forty—the farmhands we hired, Dax and Bryan, are probably finishing up dinner after working all day, busy dealing with the ant beds that infested Aston's favorite meadow.

The wind kicks up a little, stirring the tops of wildflowers as our horses take their time strolling toward our barn, and *this* feels like us. But I don't want to propose to her at home, and I just can't seem to figure this out.

Mason's ideas are all terrible, my father's even worse, and the internet has offered me nothing but different ways to spend money. I even asked Dax and Bryan for ideas on how to propose to Taryn. They had some good ones, and I kinda liked how Bryan proposed to Dax—putting it in the previews at a local movie theater they were at—but that's *their* thing.

"Honey, you don't have to figure this out right now," Taryn says gently, letting Aston Magic stop to graze. I don't even have to halt Gidget. He's already eating beside her, happy to follow her lead. "We agreed we weren't going to talk about planning a wedding for at least a year. It's just... it's too much money after the ranch and everything, Billy."

I roll my eyes. "Planning a wedding and getting engaged are not the same thing," I tell her. "We can do one without the other. Ever heard of a long engagement?"

Taryn laughs. "I appreciate you giving me that much credit. Really, I do. But there is no way in hell that I'm gonna be able to wait to marry you once you propose to me, cowboy. I don't have that kind of patience." She gestures in front of her like she's declaring a path. "Once we go, we go."

"Fine," I agree, because she's right: she doesn't have that much patience. Taryn is all about instant gratification. "We will wait."

"Don't be mad," she says, reaching down to pet her mare's neck.

"I'm not mad, I just..." I wanna get married to her. Tomorrow, if she'd let us. But she wants a nice wedding, and I want one, too, and we did just spend a bunch of money. And I was the one who freaked out and said we need to take it easy for a minute, but... "Hey, what about at a race?" I ask her. "That's us."

She makes a face. "Not anything public, please. Definitely no jumbotrons or anything like that. I want this to be about us, you know? Not something for people to tweet about and hashtag into oblivion."

*So much for my rodeo idea.* I groan, clicking at Gidget to stop eating before I encourage him to walk on. "This is impossible."

"Hey, Billy, hold on," Taryn says, clicking at Aston until she's catching up, back to walking beside us. "However you want to propose is going to be more than perfect. I promise, I'm gonna love whatever you do."

I shrug. "It's okay."

"Okay," she mutters. "And besides..." She winks at me, her smile already halfway back to normal. "You know you still have to talk to my dad first, right?"

I nod like I'm realizing that. Then I peek at her. "And what makes you think I haven't?"

Taryn's cheeks start blazing, her smile growing wider. "Really? When?"

"You really wanna know?"

She thinks for a second, biting her bottom lip as the wind swirls the long ends of her hair flowing down her back. Then she whispers, "I don't know?"

That means yes. And I can't believe I'm gonna tell her this, but Taryn and I don't keep secrets from each other. Not anymore. And she was right: it is so much better this way. "The day you broke up with me."

Taryn flinches in her saddle, her voice going flat with surprise. "What?"

I can't help but chuckle, letting the sway of my horse beneath me comfort any pain that comes along with the memory. "When I started getting upset and he got between us and he was talking to me."

"Oh," Taryn says, but she's still got that crinkle above her eyebrows like she doesn't understand.

"He said"—I can still hear his voice in my head, the calm way he whispered it with absolute conviction—"'When y'all get through this, and you're gonna get through this, I want you to come talk to me before you ask her to marry you. And I'm gonna tell you yes.'"

*But for now, you gotta go.*

It still hurts a little to remember but not as much when I look over to find Taryn watching me. Her horse is walking slowly next to mine, everything else the same as before, but Taryn's got the same look in her eyes that she gets when we watch romantic movies and the couple gets back together in the end. She always cries at that part.

I sidle Gidget closer to Aston, enough to lean over and lift a kiss from Taryn's lips, lingering longer than I should, but I can't help it. I don't know if she'll ever understand how much I love her, how thankful I am that she gave me a chance in the first place, and that she let us start over after we crashed and burned.

But I think, maybe, in her own way, she gets it. Because she sniffles when I lean back but in a really, really good way.

"Your mama was harder to convince," I add, getting back to steering Gidget and trying not to notice when Taryn discreetly wipes at her eyes. But she laughs quietly, too.

"Yeah, I bet she was." She adjusts her seat in her saddle, then her eyes dart my way, clear and blue and my entire world inside them. "Would've loved to have been a fly on the wall for that conversation."

"Well, she videotaped it, so I'm sure you can watch it if you want to."

Taryn bursts out laughing. "No, she did not."

"Oh yes, she did," I tell her. "Said she wanted me swearing on video that I'd never hurt you. That way, she could use it in court if it came down to it."

Taryn's jaw hits the dirt.

"Yep," I tell her. "Pretty sure she taped over your ballet recital to do it, too."

"Seriously?" Taryn says.

Aston turns her head and huffs at me like I'm the one who's done something wrong. I'll give her some extra peppermints tonight, though, and she'll forget all about it.

"The one where I was a butterfly? Or the balloon ballet?"

"Butterfly."

"That bitch!"

It's my turn to crack up laughing. "I know, honey. I tried to tell her…"

"No, I'm sure you did, but…" Taryn looks back at me, the fire in her eyes already calming down and the rest of her kinda melting. "I can't believe you did that. Swore on video you'd never hurt me."

Me either. Her father thought it was hilarious. I couldn't decide whether to call my lawyer. "Whatever it takes, honey."

"Well, it shouldn't take that."

*No kidding.*

I peek over at Taryn, tall and lean and swaying lazily in

her saddle, and she's so damn pretty that I need to hear it again. "You're gonna say yes, right?"

She instantly downshifts into her nervous laugh. "You really think I'm gonna say no?"

Gidget snorts and shakes his mane beneath me, like he agrees with Taryn that my question was ridiculous. "Hey, I have been wrong about this kind of stuff before," I tease her. "I'm not taking anything for granted here."

Taryn just smiles and smiles at me, her hands light on her reins and the setting sun sneaking past her hat and lighting up her face. "No jumbotrons."

*There's my yes.* "No jumbotrons."

Taryn softly laughs to herself, shaking her head and glancing away, and maybe she's right. Maybe proposing at home would be best: one night when everything is normal and she's not expecting it, sitting at our kitchen table eating whatever *damn-good* dinner she made us. Or when we're snuggled up on our overstuffed couch afterward, watching a movie we've seen a dozen times already. And in that simple moment, everything around us slow and steady, Taryn undeniably safe, and the ground solid beneath my feet, I'll ask her. For that perfect night to be our *every* night, for the rest of our lives.

Taryn glances over at me, and with the way she smiles when I wink at her, I know for sure she's right about me waiting to propose. There's no way I'll be able to resist getting married to her, either.

Once we go, we go.

"Race you back to the house?" she says far too innocently. "Last one there does the dishes."

I laugh, shifting in my saddle and shaking my head. "Fine." I always do them anyway, since she does the cooking, but I bet that's part of her plan. "How about the last one there does the laun—*hey!* Come back here!"

But Taryn's already got Aston Magic bolting across the pasture, her hat slinging down to her back as her hair flashes out behind her and the clear sound of her laugh echoing back to me on the wind. "You said fine!"

"Damn it," I mutter. She's totally gonna beat me home now. I whistle at Gidget to launch after Aston, the mare kicking up all sorts of mud on her race to beat us back. I duck a little lower over my stallion, unable to resist a grin as pure power pushes through Gidget's legs and trees blur past in the distance. "Cheaters forfeit," I call up toward Taryn.

She peeks over her shoulder at me with a smile that never fails to get me going. "Guess I'm gonna get it now!" Then she looks forward and gets her horse into a higher gear, letting me chase her back to the house until she lets me catch her, and *damn*, it is good to be home.

# Acknowledgments

There's no way I could have turned my dreams into a reality without the support of a lot of incredible people, and I have to start by giving a million thanks to my rock star agent, Kelly Peterson. Signing with you continues to be one of my favorite birthday presents ever.

To Mary Altman, who took a chance on this series and saw a side to it that I didn't even know existed until we created it together—I'm so glad it was you. The entire team at Sourcebooks has brought this story to life in a way I never could've imagined, and I'm eternally grateful.

Michelle Hazen...you're my pillar. The Bob Ross to my doubts, the voice in my head and the one making llama jokes in my comment boxes—there would be no books without you. And I don't want to write them alongside anyone else. P.S. Your tea is in the microwave.

All the awards (and tacos) should be given to Maxym Martineau, Lindsay Hess, Shanna Alderstein, and Tara Gilbert, who also provided their invaluable feedback on the first draft of this book. I am so sorry. And don't worry, I cut that thing ;)

Everyone else who had a hand in this through years of querying and writing contests and teaching me pretty much everything I know (though they may not know it): Shira Hoffman, Shannon Powers, Kat Kerr, Lisa Rodgers, Michelle Hauck, Amy Trueblood, Sun vs Snow, Query Kombat, Brenda Drake, Pitch Wars and PitMad, Sandra Lombardo, Hoku Clements, and The Fellowship. Y'all really know your stuff. (And I probably forgot a lot of people. My bad.)

I am incredibly lucky to have the support of an adoring father and doting stepmother, who made sure I had every opportunity available growing up and did their best to be patient when I squandered most of it. Y'all are the definition of kick-ass parents, I hope you know.

To my mother in heaven: I think you'll like Billy, Mom. I wrote him with you in mind.

Morgan Lancaster, my sister and twin flame, who sat and organized notebooks of handwritten poetry with me as a child and knew I was destined for words when all I saw was everything but... How are you not sick of me yet?

My wonderful son: you continue to inspire me daily through your kindness, selflessness, and generosity of spirit, and I have no idea where you get it from. Probably your dad.

And finally, to my darling husband: I still need five more minutes. Though I doubt forever will be enough time with you.

# About the Author

Katie Golding is a racing fan with a writing problem. The recovering cheerleader lives in a small town outside of Austin, Texas, mom to a future philanthropist, and wife to a superman. Her writing playlists range from '80s love songs to '90s grunge to '00s punk to new age underground in less time than it takes her to burn dinner, and she is currently at work on her next romance novel, unless she's tweeting about it. Represented by Kelly Peterson of Rees Literary Agency. Visit her website at katiegoldingbooks.com.

# RELENTLESS IN TEXAS

Bestselling author Kari Lynn Dell puts
you right in the middle of the action with
her thrilling Texas Rodeo series!

Gil Sanchez was once rodeo's biggest and baddest hotshot. Now he's
thirteen years sober and finally free of the pain that ended his skyrocketing career. Given one last shot to claw his way back to rodeo glory,
he can't let fantasies of happily-ever-after dull his razor edge...but
Carmelita White Fox is every dream he's never let himself have.

Carma may come from a Blackfeet family noted for its healing abil-
ities, but even she knows better than to try to fix this scarred, cynical
cowboy. Yet she's the only one who can reach past Gil's jaded armor.
Gil needs Carma just as much as she needs him, but as the pressure
builds and the spotlight intensifies, they'll have to fight like hell to save
the one thing neither can live without.

**"Look out, world! There's a new cowboy in town."**

—Carolyn Brown, *New York Times* bestselling author, for
*Tangled in Texas*

For more info about Sourcebooks's
books and authors, visit:
**sourcebooks.com**

# WRECKLESS

Can this hometown girl beat her biggest competitor when she finally sees him as something more than her best/worst rival?

When Lorelai Hargrove traded in her cowgirl hat for a racing helmet, she vowed to sacrifice anything to earn her place in the male-dominated sport of professional motorcycle racing—her love life included. But winning a MotoGP World Championship is easier said than done when her Italian rival keeps cutting her off on the turns and sending her mixed signals off the track.

When Massimo Vitolo follows Lorelai all the way to her Memphis ranch after a confidence-shattering accident, the former foes start to see each other as more than competition. But when Lorelai's sponsors threaten to drop her if she doesn't bring home a MotoGP World Championship, they'll have to decide whether a win will cost them the relationship they'd risk everything to keep.

### "Vivid and fearless."

—Kari Lynn Dell, bestselling author, for *Fearless*

For more info about Sourcebooks's books and authors, visit:
**sourcebooks.com**